Fearless

May 23, 2019

To Reynolds —

Stay Fearless

Fearless

A NOVEL BY
Raima Larter

Raima Larter

COPYRIGHT © 2019 by Raima Larter
COVER AND BOOK DESIGN by Alexandru Oprescu

All rights reserved. Published by New Meridian, part of the non-profit organization New Meridian Arts, 2019.

No part of this publication may be reproduced, or stored in a retrieval system, or transmitted in any form or by any means, electronic, mechanical, photocopying, or otherwise, without written permission of the publisher, except in the case of brief quotations in reviews. For information regarding permission, write to newmeridianarts1@gmail.com

LIBRARY OF CONGRESS CATALOGING-IN-PUBLICATION DATA

Fearless
Authored by Raima Larter

ISBN: 9780999461761
LCCN: 2018968035

Disclaimer:
This is a work of fiction. Names, characters, businesses, places, events, and incidents are either the products of the author's imagination or used in a fictitious manner. Any resemblance to actual persons, living or dead, is purely coincidental.

Contents

PART ONE

    CHAPTER 1 3
    CHAPTER 2 19
    CHAPTER 3 39
    CHAPTER 4 55
    CHAPTER 5 73
    CHAPTER 6 85

PART TWO

    CHAPTER 7 105
    CHAPTER 8 125
    CHAPTER 9 137
    CHAPTER 10 149
    CHAPTER 11 157
    CHAPTER 12 169

PART THREE

    CHAPTER 13 185
    CHAPTER 14 201
    CHAPTER 15 225
    CHAPTER 16 251
    CHAPTER 17 259
    CHAPTER 18 271

PART FOUR

    CHAPTER 19 279
    CHAPTER 20 285
    CHAPTER 21 297
    CHAPTER 22 303
    CHAPTER 23 309
    CHAPTER 24 333

Part One

1

THERE'S BEEN ANOTHER BOMBING. Father Mike has spent the entire week counseling frightened parishioners, some panicked, some despairing, others angry or wanting to flee, despite the fact that no one in his parish was hurt. It's the old fight or flight response he learned about back in his pre-med days, before he became a priest, and it's the only way he's found to understand the grip of fear on his people. Some of them won't be comforted, though, no matter how many prayers or platitudes or statistics he quotes to them.

He's on his way back to St. Rita's after a quick cold supper at the nearby deli. Night fell while he ate his sandwich, and the temperature fell with it. A blustery wind howls down the canyon-like boulevard, and he pulls his scarf tightly around his neck to block the wind but also to hide his collar. The white band encasing his throat announces more facts (and myths) about him to the world than he cares to broadcast tonight. He hurries toward the front steps of the church, dry leaves swirling about his ankles, his heels clicking on the pitted sidewalk, when something—he doesn't know what—urges him to look up.

There, in the dimly lit rose window above the massive front doors of the church, is a dark silhouette—large, human-shaped, and with something resembling wings arching away from the shoulders.

At least, they look like wings. Father Mike stands trembling on the empty city street with no one but God—if there is a god—as his witness. Great buildings rise into the night along either side of the wide boulevard. He tries to ignore the shaking in his gut, rationalizing it as the body's natural reaction to the cold.

Why is he being tortured like this? *Another* angel? What the hell?

Of course, to be fair, there was no proof that what he'd seen in the chapel last week was an angel either. He doesn't believe in such things, despite what his collar proclaims to the world. Also, last week's "angel" looked nothing like the apparition he sees in the round window above. Whoever is up there playing tricks on him is an adult, not a curly-haired youngster like the one he'd seen in the sanctuary last Monday.

He glances up and down the street, searching in vain for another human soul he can ask, "Do you see something up there?" But when he looks back toward the window—he knows this will be true before he even looks—the shape is gone.

It's always like that, isn't it? You catch a glimpse of the divine, of something extraordinary, and there's never anyone to compare notes with. We're all in the sea of unknowing together and there's never a way to know the truth—the real truth.

THE NEXT MORNING, Jenna takes the elevator to the top floor of the Columbia Health building, the floor used only by the maintenance staff. The short hallway smells of oil and grease and is lit by a bare yellow bulb. She steps out of the heavy metal door and into the bright blustery day.

The wind tries to yank the door from her hands. She lets go, and it clangs against the wall. The floor she's reached isn't a real floor—it's actually the roof. She looks up at a sky as blue and devoid of clouds as her mind is of thoughts, then leans into the strong wind, head down, and strides toward the low wall that runs around the edge of the roof, the wind whipping her long auburn hair around her face.

She's determined to do this. Nothing else has worked. She reaches the edge of the roof and kicks off her shoes. The concrete beneath her feet is freezing, but it will be easier to climb onto the wall without shoes. She's practiced this in her mind and, in the end, it's easy and requires only one step. Swift and purposeful, and in less than a second, she's standing on the low wall, fourteen stories above the boulevard below.

The wind buffets her, causing her to sway off balance. She waits, hoping that this time, her experiment will work. But, no. Nothing.

She feels absolutely nothing. Even though she can see the street far below, a sight that would make any normal person dizzy, Jenna feels as safe as if she were standing on the curb at street level. She flings her hands in the air and leans back to face the sky. "I can't believe this," she shouts. "How can I not be scared?"

It has been like this for a while. Nothing scares her any more. Nothing. She feels no fear—of anything. This isn't normal, she knows that, but she doesn't remember life being any other way. Not that she remembers much of her life. It's as if there's a hole inside her, a gaping emptiness where the Jenna she used to be would live, if only that self still existed.

FATHER MIKE WALKS DOWN THE BOULEVARD, holding a paper cup of coffee, a rich dark roast scent escaping the tiny hole in the cap. Near the church a dozen or more people stand on the sidewalk, looking up. Surely the apparition he'd seen last night isn't there again?

But they aren't looking toward the rose window. Their gazes are all fixed on the tall building next to the church, the one that houses a large insurance company. A man in a brown coat and cap pulls a cellphone from his pocket and punches at it, his gaze fixed upward. Two women stand shoulder to shoulder, their heads leaned together, whispering furiously. One of them points at the top of the insurance building. Other people murmur or shuffle their feet or hold their faces in their hands.

The front of St. Rita's is blocking Father Mike's view, so he takes two steps down the street and that's when he sees what they're all looking at: a woman, standing on the edge of the roof. The wind whips her long dark hair around her face. She's got her hands raised to the sky, but wobbles when a gust hits her. A gasp rises from the crowd around Father Mike. Something cold and hard and painful grips his belly.

"Oh my God," says one of the women.

"Is she going to jump?" asks another.

The man with the cellphone still clutched in his hand steps closer. "What should we do?" he asks, with the same pleading tone Father Mike's been hearing all week in his confessional. The bombings have everyone on edge and his booth has been over-flowing with frightened people. "I called 911," the man says, "but is there something else we can do?"

Mike shakes his head. The man is terrified, he can see that. He has no words to share, no relief to offer from the unrelenting terror that surrounds them—and he wonders, again, as has become so common these days, if maybe he chose the wrong path. Maybe the rejected path would have been a better one for coping with the fear-filled world that afflicts the people around him.

"Yes." The man searches Mike's face. "We can pray. We *should* pray."

Mike wants to rip the collar from his throat. *Father* Mike, it proclaims, and he understands, intellectually, all that the collar and the title imply—wearing it, after all, is a sign that Mike represents the real Father, God Himself. He understands that his face, though human, is the one faithful people look to when they are searching for comfort and meaning in their broken world. He gets that, he does, and he *wants* to help them, but it all seems futile lately.

If only he had as much confidence that his prayers—anyone's prayers—were being heard. After all, the bombings have continued, unabated. The authorities keep ruling out foreign terrorists, hinting that these are home-grown terrorists, but are no closer to finding the culprits. And then there are all those school shootings, dozens of them, all perpetrated by kids. *Kids.*

Where is God in all this? When the man's imploring gaze turns to anger, Mike looks away. He's failed another one. He wishes he could rise to the level this man expects of him, the level they all expect. He wants to keep his thoughts on the situation unfolding on the roof above him. He wishes he could stop thinking about himself, stop thinking about the little visitor to his sanctuary, stop thinking about the silhouette he glimpsed in the rose window last night.

"Look!" It's one of the women and she's pointing upward again. Mike's head swivels, along with everyone else's, and they watch the dark-haired woman step back from the edge. And then she's gone, as if no one had ever been there at all.

AFTER TEETERING ON THE ROOFTOP for a few moments, Jenna realizes her latest experiment has failed as miserably as all those before it, so she's stepped away from the edge. She's tried everything she can think of to scare herself, to recover the lost emotion of fear she seems entirely incapable of feeling. She was sure this time her experiment would work—but it hasn't.

She slides her feet back into her shoes and runs toward the metal door, pulling it shut behind her with a clang. She hurries back through the oily-smelling hallway and punches the down button for the elevator. She gets on, but it stops again, immediately, on the fourteenth floor—the real top floor of the building, the one with offices, not just a flat roof.

The elevator doors slide open and there stands Pete. He starts to get in, but stops between the doors, holding them open with his hand. "Hey, Jenna." She nods but averts her eyes. "Aren't you getting off?" he asks, frowning.

She shakes her head. "Going down."

"How can you be going down? This is the top floor." Pete's pasty white skin is sprinkled with freckles and it looks like he's gotten a new haircut. Two strips of even whiter skin outline the tops of his ears beneath his closely trimmed carrot-red hair. Jenna shrugs and looks at the floor. Pete finally lets the door go and steps all the way in, punching the button for the lobby. "Suit yourself," he mumbles.

Pete, who works for IT, had been present for her very first experiment several months earlier, the first failed experiment, that is, the one that led to all the others: walks down darkened alleys, trips to sketchy parts of town and, finally, today's rooftop experiment. She knew she'd alarmed Pete in that first failed attempt to induce fear, and she was sorry for the distress she caused him—but it had been necessary. A failure, in the end, but she had to try.

Everyone was on edge since the bombing at the market by the harbor, which had followed soon after three school shootings in a row. Everyone, that is, except Jenna. She'd noticed that her coworkers would sometimes literally tremble as they talked about the events that might or might not be terrorist attacks. Jenna, though, felt nothing but a mild curiosity, about as interested in it as she would be in a crossword puzzle. She wouldn't admit this to anyone, though. How could anyone be so cold-hearted? That's what the lack of fear felt like to her: totally cold-hearted, as if she simply could not take in the terrors that so obviously surrounded them all.

They'd been on their way to lunch—Jenna, Pete and Monica—and were not far from the building when Jenna came up with her first idea. They'd passed that old church next door, Saint somebody's (she can't remember the name) and were headed for the deli. Garlic and salami smells wafted out the open deli door toward them. Pete's red hair bobbed up and down as he walked. It was a little longer then, and he moved in his usual bouncing way, springing up onto his toes, each step sending his red hair flopping. He was a few steps ahead of her and Monica, ranting about some guy in his division he apparently didn't get along with, shouting things back over his shoulder as the three of them made their way down the street.

And that's when she saw the white car. It was speeding down the street, weaving in and out of traffic, and was about a half block ahead when she spotted it—actually on the other side of the street, across two full lanes, a fact that only made her quickly evolving plan that much more compelling.

She turned to Monica and said, "Sorry—I have to take care of something," then dashed into the street. The white car was about a hundred yards away by then, still moving fast. The lanes on their side were empty and she sprinted across.

A horn blared, and then another as she stepped into the opposite lane. Monica screamed from somewhere. Jenna heard brakes squeal but kept her eyes fixed on the oncoming vehicle and stood directly in front of it. If this didn't scare her, nothing would.

Something heavy knocked into her side. It was Pete, grabbing her around the shoulders, hauling her up onto the curb on the opposite side of the street, yelling. "What the hell are you doing?" he shouted, his face twisted in anger.

She couldn't get any words out but watched as Monica waited at the crosswalk for the light, then sprinted across the street. She ran up and grabbed Jenna in a hug. "Thank God you're okay," she breathed, and then held Jenna back at arms' length. "Didn't you see that car?"

"She saw it," Pete said, disgust washing over his face. He turned to Jenna, furious. "Why did you *do* that?"

She couldn't blame him for being angry. And she was sure both he and Monica thought she was crazy. And maybe she was, but she wasn't suicidal. She hadn't wanted the car to hit her, any more than she'd wanted to jump off the building. All she wanted was to hear the tires squeal, the horn blast, the driver shout at her—she'd wanted all these things to happen so that maybe, just maybe, she'd be afraid.

But she'd felt nothing at all as that car barreled toward her—merely a mild curiosity about what might happen if it slammed into her body. She'd watched the car approach with anticipation, sure, but no pounding heart, no twisted stomach, no hairs standing up on her neck—none of the things normal people would feel if they were in danger.

What is wrong with her? What in the *hell* is wrong with her?

MIKE IS IN HIS CHURCH. His empty church, which is the way he likes it best—not teeming with people, the old or the young. No shuffling feet of the elderly and infirm as they make their way up the aisle to the communion rail. No fidgeting children playing on the floor beneath the pews with toy trucks or forbidden video games. No little Sunday shoes whacking into the undersides of the pews, the sudden clunks unleashing a torrent of hissed warnings from the parents. No young couples, holding hands, trying to listen to Father Mike's sermon, the one he—no doubt—had finished late the previous evening.

This week would likely be the same, as here it was Thursday and he still didn't have his sermon finished for the coming weekend. He'd started it on Monday but got interrupted by a flood of parishioners who'd poured into the church after that bomb went off in the market down by the harbor. They were all frightened and he thinks, as he so often does, if maybe his original career trajectory would have been more useful in helping people cope with all the fear in the world these days.

No one had been killed in that attack, but that made it the exception more than the rule. The authorities, of course, could not say if it was terrorism or not. It didn't matter, though, not really—the people were terrorized, regardless of the intent of the one who'd set the bomb.

Today, it's blessedly empty in the sanctuary and he just wants to sit here and rest in the quiet, breathe the scent of old incense and wax mixed with the ever-present smell of rusty plumbing. No time for that, though. He's just finished trying, without success, to repair the broken lock on the door that leads to the bell tower. The fire marshal had condemned the steps that led to the tower and ordered them to keep the door closed. The padlock he'd used was too rusty and wouldn't stay shut, so he needs to make a trip to the hardware store to get another.

Something, who knows what, reminds him that he needs to check the ledger, see if they can afford to call a repairman for that radiator in the side chapel. He's just finished coaxing the nearly dead thing back to life once again, performing what has become a near-weekly little resurrection miracle of his own. He's by the bare altar, stripped of its usual linens, lying fresh and open, ready to receive its savior who refuses, as usual, to make Himself known.

Thou knowest, Lord, the secrets of our hearts. Shut not thy merciful ears to our prayer.

Mike walks across the nave, his shoes clicking on the stone slabs of the century-old floor. Their rhythmic tapping is the only sound in the empty church besides the discordant squawks of some crows outside in the garden. He can't see them now but knows that were he to peek out through the one clear pane of the side chapel stained-glass window, they'd be there, a long row of ratty crows perched in a nodding, bobbing line along the wall above the tombs.

Earth to earth, ashes to ashes, dust to dust.

The stone slabs on the patio beneath the row of black birds hold the remains of parishioners, laid there by their families and the priests who'd come before him: Father Ted, his immediate predecessor, Father Robert before him—a long unbroken line of priests stretching back a hundred years. Here is the final resting place of a few dozen souls who put their trust in the church—and the nation, establishing the parish he is now responsible for. America was to be the land of their salvation and many had risked life and limb to cross the ocean, only to find the squalor and poverty of America equal to, if not greater than, the squalor and poverty they'd fled in Ireland.

And yet, the existence of the little parish, St. Rita's, was for them a reminder of the home they'd never see again. It was their new spiritual home, and Mike was always aware how much trust had been placed in him by those who called him to his post—priest to St. Rita's Parish.

He'd once thought the difference in ethnic background would be a problem for them, but they'd accepted "Father Mike," as Italian-American as you can get, as one of their own when he'd arrived a couple years back. They were good people and they'd been the ones who chose to call him by his first name. It was really the older members who'd taken him into their hearts as if he was their own son. Despite the fact they called him Father, he knew many of the older members saw him that way—as an adopted child.

They cried out to you and were delivered. They trusted in you and were not put to shame.

Mike reaches the door of the nave and turns back to look at the altar, shrouded in a dim light. That was where he'd seen the boy—or angel, if that's indeed what it was. Just steps from the altar, in the side chapel. He wasn't exactly sure it was a boy. It might have been a girl. It was a child, though, that much was clear—a child with tight yellow curls covering a small head, in which were set intense blue eyes, dressed only in what for all the world appeared to be a tattered loincloth.

World without end, Amen.

IT HAD HAPPENED THE PREVIOUS MONDAY. Since Monday always follows a heavy Sunday service schedule, the radiator in the side chapel had, as usual, stopped working, worn out from its weekend efforts to heat the massive stone-clad space. Mike had just retrieved a pipe wrench from the supply closet and was down on the cold floor, kneeling—but not in prayer!—in front of the ancient radiator. A chronically stuck valve regularly plunged this side of the church to near-freezing temperatures.

A weak, yellowish light spilled through the smudged window, bathing the little side chapel with its tiny altar and handful of kneelers in a slight golden glow. The rusty plumbing smell was strong in this particular corner of the sanctuary, given that its source was the finicky radiator that was currently demanding Mike's attention. He carefully adjusted the pipe wrench, not sure he'd chosen the right size. Dad always said ninety-nine percent of the battle was choosing the right tool for the job, so he may have already lost the battle, if not the war. He placed the wrench over the stuck valve and leaned in, using his body weight as leverage. Something slipped, and he smacked his knuckles into the radiator. Hard.

"God damn it!" His shout was nearly drowned out by the clatter of the wrench as it hit the stone floor. As he sat back on his heels, sucking at the blood welling from his scraped knuckle, he glanced up at the crucifix. There He hung, the same stony face that looked back at Mike every day. "And you? What do you think I should do? Should I just resign?"

What was he doing talking to a statue? There was no choice anymore. He was going to have to speak to Ted—or, better yet, the bishop. The flood of doubts had grown deeper and wider, sweeping away what little shred of faith he might once have had. The people of St. Rita's, his charges, deserved better. They were good, trusting people, and they certainly didn't need an atheist for a priest.

He did once have it. Faith, that is. He'd freely chosen seminary, after all, over med school—despite Mom and Dad's disappointment. He'd embarked on this path completely of his own will, not coerced by anyone—unless it was God who had done the coercion. He thought of that Presence, the one he'd first encountered in the cathedrals of Europe, the one that seemed to offer him a way out of the ethical dilemma he'd found himself in as a pre-med student—and realized that he'd felt *seen* and had equated the Presence he sensed with God Himself. It seemed a logical conclusion at the time.

Mike laughed, a bitter laugh. As if there's a god that pays any attention to an individual life. As if there's a great cosmic presence that plays any role in determining one's life path or choices. As if there's anyone out there, *up* there, watching over us. Mike used to believe there was. He remembers believing it—it's all past tense now, though.

He pushed the unplanned and unsettling thoughts away and returned his attention to the radiator, placing the wrench on the frozen valve and leaning in again. Nothing. It was stuck fast.

He looked up, then, at the stony face of Jesus, trying to think how long it had been since he felt that Presence, the one that had driven him all the way to seminary and beyond to find out what—or Who—it was. The Presence (it was the only name he ever had for it) had once seemed so real, but now seemed less than a distant memory—more like something that had happened to another person altogether.

And that's when the sudden thought hit him: Maybe it wasn't the Presence that disappeared but Mike Albertino himself who had gone astray. Maybe it wasn't that the Presence had left him—perhaps he was the negligent one. After all, when was the last time he'd actually prayed? *Really* prayed, that is, in the privacy of his own heart and mind. He'd given voice to words, after all, that probably *sounded* like prayer to his parishioners, but Mike knew he'd just been going through the motions.

He honestly could not remember when he'd last truly prayed, but it was just one more dishonest thing his parishioners could add to the list of ways Father Mike was a fraud—if they ever found out who he really was.

What could it hurt to try? He was already on his knees after all, still down there on that cold stone of the side chapel floor. He crawled up onto the nearest kneeler. If he were going to pray, he ought to at least do it properly.

He clasped his hands together and, giving one last glance toward the silent figure of Christ hanging above his head, closed his eyes. *Please*, he thought. *Are you there? I just need to know this one thing. Are you still there?*

And that was when he heard a voice, a child's voice, answering: "He's going to kill another one."

Mike's eyes flew open and there stood a little waif with tight yellow curls, thin arms and chest, wearing nothing but a graying loincloth. The child, almost naked and bathed in golden light streaming through the chapel window peered at him from around the corner of the small altar.

Mike unclasped his hands and leaned toward him—or was it a girl? "What did you say?"

The child drew back, staring, saying nothing.

Mike tried to stand, reaching toward the kid's arm. "How did you get in here?" It seemed unlikely the child, dressed in such a grubby cloth, would be one of the students at St. Rita's School, but how else could the kid have gotten into the locked church?

The child, who appeared to be about six or seven and looked more like a boy than a girl now that Mike was closer, shrank away from him. His skinny arms and wan face were smeared with mud. Mike peered more closely. Or maybe blood? He reached again for the kid, thinking he'd best just lead him back to the school section, see if one of the sisters could help, but the boy's eyes grew wide and he pressed himself into the space behind the altar.

Grunting, Mike hoisted himself to his feet and stepped around the altar to grab the child. But no one was there. The boy had, somehow, disappeared. Mike turned quickly, peering into the dark corners of the large sanctuary. The place was always shrouded in semi-darkness, due to the need to keep the electric bill down. No sign of anyone, unless the kid was hiding under one of the pews.

Or, maybe, he'd scampered down the hall and was heading back to school where he ought to be. Mike tried to shake off the sudden, heavy sense of foreboding—what had the child said, something about a killing?

He had no time to deal with it, though. He had a sermon to write, and really needed to decide if they could afford a repairman. Someone who knew how to fix things, someone who knew what he was doing.

He headed for his living quarters, a tiny apartment tucked up behind the organ pipes. As he came around a corner in the darkened hallway, he nearly collided with Sister Mary Katherine, one of the teachers at St. Rita's School, her head down, hurrying toward him. She was either lost in thought or looking for a lost child—a possibility that brought with it a great deal of comfort.

He pulled up short. "Sister."

He must have shouted, because she flinched. "Father!" A frail hand flew to her heart and she stumbled back. "I didn't see you—it's so dark in here."

He patted her shoulder. "I'm sorry, Sister. I didn't mean to frighten you."

She laughed, a nervous warble, and looked out at him with a wide-eyed stare from behind her glasses. "I was just looking for—" She pointed down the hallway toward the sanctuary, just as the bell in the school section rang. "Oh, never mind," she said and hurried away.

JENNA EXITS THE ELEVATOR at her own floor, lifting a hand in a brief wave to Pete as she gets off. She winds down the darkened hallway toward her cubicle, pulls a stack of claim forms next to her computer and resumes inputting data. She'd been at it for only twenty minutes when Monica sticks her head in.

"Up for yoga tonight?" Monica asks. Her long, black hair is gathered into its usual messy topknot above eyes outlined with thick dark liner. Jenna thinks the eyeliner makes Monica look slutty—though she'd never say such a thing to her. Right now, Monica's the only friend she has.

"I don't know. Maybe." Jenna keeps her gaze on the screen. "What time is the class?"

"Five-thirty, just like last week. So, do you want to go or not?"

Jenna shrugs. "I guess. Stop by on your way and I'll let you know for sure." She looks over a shoulder and sees that Monica has stepped into her cramped cubicle. Her arms are crossed and she's frowning. Jenna swivels her chair around to face her. "What?"

"You tell me. What the hell is going on with you lately?"

Jenna glares. No problem with her ability to feel anger, apparently. She lifts her chin. "I don't know what you're talking about."

"First of all, you were the one who suggested we sign up for yoga, but you never want to go. And second of all, Pete just said he found you in the elevator coming down from the roof."

"So?"

"So, you were on the roof, weren't you?"

"I repeat: so?"

Monica grabs a stack of folders teetering on the spare chair in Jenna's office and moves them to the floor. She plops into the chair and scoots it closer. "Jenna, I'm worried about you. What's going on?"

Tears sting her eyes. No problem with her sadness-feeling ability, either.

Monica grabs both her hands. "Tell me."

But Jenna just shakes her head. Something's wrong, she knows that. And she'd tell Monica if she had any idea how to do it.

Monica finally leaves after extracting a weak promise from Jenna to go to yoga after work. She finishes a few more folders, then grabs her lunch sack and makes her way out of the building, heading for the park down the street, bundled in a scarf and coat. The day, still as brilliant and blustery as when she'd teetered on the roof, had started off chilly, but the bright sun has warmed things up. She loosens her scarf and unbuttons her coat as she crosses the street. Car exhaust and diesel fumes on the boulevard give way to more pleasant smells as she steps into the park: musty, drying leaves and an earthy scent wafting up from the no-longer-green lawn.

Leaves turned to red and gold rustle on a dozen or more trees scattered around the park. A flash of color—blue and green and purple—from the wooded area across the way catches her eye as she looks for a place to sit. She's not sure what the purple and blue and a most unnatural-looking neon green in those trees is due to, but it's a stark contrast to the grass, which has turned a dull brown as October has progressed. That hasn't stopped a few folks from spreading out blankets on it, though. One man sprawls on a dark plaid blanket with a little boy, maybe six or seven years old. The boy is on his hands and knees playing with tiny metal cars. Most of the benches are full of people, some reading newspapers or books, others munching on food. The sight of so many people enjoying what is probably one of the last warm days of the year lifts her spirits a little.

She finally locates a seat at the end of a bench occupied by only one man—a priest, judging from the collar. He scribbles with a pen in a notebook and doesn't seem to notice her as she walks up, but when she sits down, he smiles briefly, then goes back to writing.

He's cute, handsome even, looks to be about Jenna's age, late thirties or early forties, perhaps. She gazes at his wavy dark hair and coal-black eyes, wondering if he's working on a sermon. She wonders if priests always write their sermons by hand, not on computers—scribbling in notebooks in the park. She wonders if he's married—but, then, priests can't be married, right? Not Catholic ones, anyway.

Jenna tries to push the thoughts away. Just because her dating life is nonexistent is no reason to go looking at such a totally inappropriate person. Her thirty-eighth birthday is right around the corner and she's still single, with no hope of ever getting married, much less having the child she longs for. She has no reason to go off the deep end, resorting to what is clearly fantasy.

The guy's a priest. Even if he isn't gay, which he probably is, he's obviously not available.

She peers into her rumpled brown sack, pulls out the soggy tuna salad sandwich and plastic bag of cut-up carrots and celery. It doesn't look at all appealing, but she should eat something. She looks out over the crowd as she takes a bite of the tasteless sandwich. She used to like tuna salad, she's sure of it, but nothing tastes good anymore. A man on a nearby bench has given up on his book and clutched it across his chest, his face tipped back toward the weak rays of the late-autumn sun, eyes closed and dozing. She watches him, wondering what it must be like to be able to relax so fully in a public place.

She takes another bite. The man and little boy have gotten up from their blanket and the man is now tossing a Frisbee to the boy. The sight gives her a start, as if it should mean something. There's a surge inside her, something she can't identify. She stares at the Frisbee as it sails from the man to the boy, outlined against the flawless blue sky.

That Frisbee—it means something, but what? The boy runs, stretches out his arms, jumps. He reaches both arms toward the flying disc. The strange sense, almost like déjà vu, but not quite, deepens. It all seems so familiar. The boy misses and the Frisbee tumbles to the ground. The boy lands next to it, in the grass, laughing on hands and knees. The man runs to help him up and leans to pluck the Frisbee from the ground.

The tiny surge of feeling, whatever it is, intensifies as the man throws the Frisbee again. She watches the boy leap, mesmerized by this otherwise ordinary scene. A hundred feet or so beyond the man and his son, a woman pushes a stroller over the lumpy grass. A little girl skips along next to her, holding her hand. The tiny surge of feeling becomes an exhilaration. The girl, maybe four or five years old, is dressed in a blue buttoned-up coat. The sight of that blue makes Jenna's stomach flutter, but is it excitement or fear she's feeling? How can it be fear? She hasn't felt fear in—well, she's not sure how long.

A gust of wind sweeps across the park, swirling leaves around the blue-coated girl, rattling the pages of the priest's notebook and whipping Jenna's hair around her face. She brushes the strands from her eyes just as the blast reaches the stand of trees across the way, dislodging a flurry of leaves.

A whirlwind of gold and red swirls downward, unveiling the flash of color she'd seen before. Tangled around the bare branches are long ribbon-like strands of purple, blue and neon green. The colorful sight brings a wave of dread and doom. She doesn't understand it. Her hands shake and the sandwich she's holding flops open, spilling bits of tuna salad onto the dry grass at her feet.

She's afraid. She's actually afraid! Jenna is thrilled.

The priest leans toward her. "Are you okay?" he asks.

His eyes are kind and, as he leans closer, she catches a whiff of incense on his clothes. The scent brings with it a memory she can't quite place: a dark room, somewhere that feels solemn and maybe a little sad. She tries not to look at those colorful ribbons, but there's something about them—she can't say what it is. Just a feeling, a sense of recognition.

He's frowning at her now. "I'm sorry. I don't mean to intrude, but you cried out and—"

"I cried out? Are you sure?"

He sucks his lips in. "I don't see anybody else on this bench, do you?" And then he smiles. It's one of those kinds of smiles that crinkle the skin around the eyes. It looks nice on him, like he's lived a life that might've left a mark on his face. "Are you okay?" he repeats.

She dissolves in tears. For no apparent reason. Why is she crying? The fear, so exciting and yet unexpected, so desperately longed for, has disappeared and been replaced by the more familiar emotion of despair. She can't bear it. She'd almost grasped it, the fear she most wants to feel, but it's slipped away again.

The priest closes his notebook and shifts sideways on the bench toward her. "It's okay if you don't want to tell me. But if you do, I'm happy to listen."

Tell him what? That she was afraid and now she's not and she's disappointed because the fear is gone? He'd think she was nuts—and she is, of course. "I'm sorry." She glances at him, then looks away again. "I didn't mean to disturb you. It's just that I had this weird feeling—"

The wind whips across the park again, swirling bits of trash, sparkly candy wrappers and paper into tiny dust devils. The earthy smell she'd noticed before grows stronger as the dusty whirlwind spins past, fluttering the bright ribbons in the branches across the lawn. She looks away. She doesn't know why, but she just doesn't want to see those colorful streamers anymore.

Jenna stands up. "I didn't mean to bother you." She stuffs the remains of her sandwich back into the paper sack. "Plus, I'd better get back to work."

He jumps up and holds out a business card. "My name's Mike. If you want to talk, I'm at St. Rita's, right up the street."

She nods, accepting the card, and looks at it. *Father Mike Albertino*, it reads. He does seem like a nice guy, but that collar—he's probably just trying to convert her. And she can't explain this, anyway. To him, to anyone really. "Thanks— maybe I'll see you around." She tucks the card into her pocket. "I work in the building next to your church."

He smiles again. "Yes—I know the place. It's an insurance company, right?" He opens his notebook and pulls a pen from his pocket.

She nods. "Columbia Health." He's letting her off the hook. She can see that and is grateful she doesn't have to continue forcing small talk. "Enjoy the weather—it's a beautiful day."

"That it is." He lifts a hand in a small wave as she turns and hurries away.

MIKE GETS PART-WAY THROUGH A DRAFT of his sermon before getting stuck again. He closes the notebook and heads back toward St. Rita's, still thinking about the young woman on the park bench. He doubts very much she'll come talk to him, but he had to invite her. After all, he's pretty sure she's the one who was on the roof earlier—same long dark hair, for one thing. He'd not been able to see her face from the sidewalk, but it could have been her—she worked in the same building.

And she seemed disturbed by something. If she was suicidal, he had to at least try to help, even though he thinks it's probably pointless. Suicidal people are unlikely to accept help from a stranger, even a priest. He knows that, knows he's rationalizing his interest in her, knows that what he should do is just stop this right now before it gets out of hand. He has enough problems as it is.

He trudges up the stairs behind the organ toward his apartment, opens the door into his tiny living space and throws the notebook on his messy desk. He should spend a little more time with his sermon, try to coax his mind back to the topic, but he just can't seem to get the right tone, much less keep his thoughts on it.

The lesson for that week is the prodigal son, a parable he usually has no trouble with. This time, though, he wonders how convincing he can be. He can't shake the thought that it's all a case of wishful thinking. The idea that God would welcome back a wayward soul the way the prodigal's father welcomed him home after years of absence—well, Mike could see why people would *want* to believe this. But where is the evidence?

He leans back in his chair, sighing, and looks around at his cramped office—the toppling towers of books and papers on his battered desk, the frayed sofa pushed up against a wall, the grimy window. He likes this room in his apartment best because of the window, such as it is. Dark curtains partially cover the tall, narrow slit of glass, and the view isn't much—just a corner of the yellow brick wall of the school. The place always smells a bit musty, since the window is a mere plate of glass that doesn't open. At least it lets in a little light, but it also forces him to see the brick façade of the school building, which has started to crumble, as has most everything in the church-school complex that's become Mike's domain—including the heating system and its ailing radiator.

Which reminds him—he should go to the hardware store and get a new padlock for the bell tower stairs. Another chore among endless chores he should pay attention to but can't stomach right now.

Next to the window hangs a small crucifix. Out of habit, or perhaps nostalgia, he crosses himself when his eyes light upon it, then turns to the disheveled stack of papers on his desk. Somewhere in this mess is the contact information for the radiator repair company. *Lord, you are in the midst of us, and we are called by your Name...* He sighs and begins to sort through the pile, one piece of paper at a time.

MIKE IS ON HOLD with the radiator repair company, trying not to listen to the scratchy music coming through his phone. He really has to finish that sermon, but he can't even think about it clearly. It surprises him, suddenly, just how rare moments of inactivity have become in his life. When he'd entered seminary some sixteen years earlier, he'd somehow had the idea that all priests did all day was meditate and pray. Of course, he'd been all of twenty-two then, and what does a kid that age know anyway?

Sister Mary Katherine pokes her head into his open door. "Father? The budget committee is here for your meeting."

He sighs and plunks the phone back to its cradle. Not going to get this chore done today, apparently. "Thank you, Sister." He stands, grabs his suit jacket from the back of the chair, and follows her out the door. They clomp down the darkened stairs. "Is the meeting in the small front room?"

"Yes, Father," she says, her hands jammed inside the sleeves of her habit.

"This hallway is cold again, isn't it?" He wishes he could skip the upcoming meeting and get back to the phone call he should be making.

"A bit, Father." She hugs herself as she turns away from him at the bottom of the stairs. "I need to get back—the children are coming in from recess soon."

He nods at her and turns toward the hallway, ready to sit down for what promises to be another unpleasant budget meeting. He passes the kitchen, which is giving off a delicious scent of fresh-baked bread and some kind of soup—the beginnings of today's lunch, ready to be served to the street people who will gather soon outside the kitchen door.

He continues to the small front room, sighing, wishing he didn't have to sit through this meeting. The committee members are nice enough, but the news is always bad. Plate offerings are coming in low again, as they have been for the entire year. Attendance is shrinking, but not enough to account for this. The plate offerings are only ten percent lower than in previous years, but the parish has no wiggle-room in the operating budget. The committee thinks people are tightening their belts, unable—or unwilling—to give.

Mike reaches the door of the small room and steps in. Three smiling faces turn to him, all three somewhat elderly men who have been in the congregation for decades. "Good morning, Father," Mr. McPherson, the committee chair, says. He waves Mike to the one empty chair. As Mike takes his seat, Mr. McPherson clasps his hands together and leans toward him. "I'm afraid I'm going to have to ask you to make another plea in your sermon, Father."

Mike knew it was coming. Mr. McPherson has said the same thing in all of the last three budget meetings. Here it is again, and Mike is suddenly distracted, thinking of that damn broken radiator. If he doesn't get it fixed, the pipes will freeze, and then they'll have real problems.

McPherson is looking at him, silent. Mike just smiles and nods and the meeting begins. Papers are handed around showing columns of figures, numbers that paint a depressing picture. The meeting drones on. Mike tries to pay attention but has soon checked out—mentally.

Mike's thoughts wander from the small conference room into the hallway and across to the chilly sanctuary with its dying radiator. So much for the life of solitude he once thought he'd have. He's more like the church handyman than its priest lately, but there's no one else to take care of this stuff. And now he needs to be chief fundraiser as well.

He tries, he really does, to keep up with the maintenance needs of the aging structures that house St. Rita's Catholic Church and School, but the bishop has become exceedingly tight. No funds for repairs, not to mention basic maintenance.

Mike knows what this means. It isn't the sort of thing they teach you in seminary, but the implication has been clear for months: The bishop intends to close his parish and is going to do it by squeezing the financial life out of them.

It's the parishioners he worries about more than himself. Many of their families have been members for three or four generations. They can't seem to fathom St. Rita's not existing. It's been here since their ancestors settled this part of Philly in the late 1800s and they believe it always will be here.

They deserve better. None of them, though, seem to have an inkling that their priest has no business consecrating the Host—or pretending to—or hearing confessions. He has no business carrying out any of these priestly duties. How has he let things get so bad? One day he's graduating from college and taking the summer off to ride trains through Europe—and the next he's a priest who no longer believes.

"I think that about does it," Mr. McPherson says, bringing Mike's attention back to the meeting. All three committee members are on their feet, pulling jackets from the row of wooden pegs by the door. Mike stands and opens the door.

One of the men turns to McPherson. "Any news about your granddaughter?"

McPherson shakes his head and turns away. Mike notices a glint of tears in the man's eyes as McPherson pulls on his somewhat-shabby suit jacket. Mike moves closer and wraps an arm around McPherson's shoulders. The older man smells of Ivory soap mixed with a faint hint of mothballs. "Anytime you need to talk about it," Mike says, "I'm always here."

"Thank you, Father." McPherson blinks rapidly. "My wife and I—we've made our peace with it, but my son and daughter-in-law? Not so much. How can you ever feel peace when it's your own child missing?"

Sophie McPherson, a first-grader at St. Rita's, had been missing for nearly a year. No one expected her to be found alive, but her name had been on the prayer list every week since the day her mother reported her disappearance. Mike squeezes the old man's shoulders again, hoping it's reassuring, but knowing he's powerless to do anything about the sad situation. He longs for the days when he would simply say a quick prayer. He can't, in good conscience, do even that.

That summer in Europe, he'd done nothing *but* pray, or so it seemed. It was easy. All he had to do was walk into one of those soaring cathedrals. If he was lucky enough to catch a service, he'd sit in the back pew, breathing in the thick clouds of incense that poured from the thurible as it was swung on a chain by a priest walking slowly up the aisle. The scent had been one draw, but there were others. He'd traveled from one cathedral to the next, never able to satisfy his hunger for some sort of Presence that he'd found in those spaces. A Presence he'd never expected to find—there or anywhere.

It had caught him completely off guard, the Presence. The ineffable Something—he still doesn't know what it was, not then or even now—showed up in all the sacred places he visited that summer. He'd walk into the cool interior of one great stone-clad sanctuary after another, slide into a pew at the back and be enveloped by something that felt like a blanket of energy wrapping itself around him. And there was a sense of someone there, with him. *It's you,* he'd think, gazing at one pane of stained-glass after another. *You're here.*

And the Presence would acknowledge: *I'm here. I'm always here.* Mike thought it would be with him forever. He can taste the bitterness in his throat. That's what he gets for trusting in an illusion. Here he is alone, doing the best he can for a decaying old church in a decaying American city, ministering to a decaying congregation that's shrinking in numbers as fast as it's increasing in average age. If he was called to something, he no longer knows what it was.

Back then, he was convinced that his choice to go to seminary meant the Presence was guiding him. Now, he can barely remember how that felt. He was sure, at the time, it was God who was leading him. This God didn't seem to be the one he'd learned about as a kid. It was definitely an "it," not a "He," which confused him at first, but left him with a sense of awe that something so mysterious it was beyond personhood had taken notice of him. There he was, an ordinary guy from Newark—known as Mikey to his high school buds, middle son of Frank and Polly Albertino's eight children—far from special, yet he felt he'd been seen, sought out even, by something fundamentally unknowable, a loving entity whose existence he would never understand but also could not deny.

Until now. He *could* deny it now. His certainty that he was being watched over, pursued even, has faded with time and he wonders now if maybe he imagined the entire thing. It had been a long time since he'd sensed that Presence—or anyone, really—watching him, anyone other than his aging and increasingly frail congregants, of course, who still insist on calling him "Father," even though they have no business thinking he can parent anyone.

Mr. McPherson and the other men on the budget committee have gathered up their things. Mike walks them to the front door, then heads back to his office, returning to his never-ending tasks. He is soon, yet again, on hold with the repair company. The scratchy Muzak continues to play. Mike yawns. He should probably hang up and go do something else, but he's invested a good twenty minutes already in waiting for them to schedule the radiator repair. Can't give up now.

PETE IS ABOUT TO LEVEL UP when Monica steps into his cube. "Lunch?"

He clicks out of the video game and over to his emergency screensaver, a fake spreadsheet he pulls up whenever the boss comes by unexpectedly. Although Monica's definitely not his boss, better safe than sorry. He still can't quite believe that a good-looking girl like her seems more than willing to spend time with him. He swivels in his chair to face her. Although she stands on the opposite side of his cubicle, he can smell her perfume from where he sits. It's something sharp and tangy, a scent that fits her. "Sure—is Jenna downstairs waiting for us?"

"She said she already ate, although not much. Not hungry again, apparently."

He frowns. "I wonder what's up with her? I told you I found her coming down from the roof earlier—and now she doesn't want to eat?"

Monica shrugs. "I am worried, I'll admit that, but she doesn't seem to want to talk about it. Maybe there's a reason—something she's not telling me."

"Why wouldn't she tell you?"

She shrugs again. "I only met her a few months ago. We really aren't all that close, but I may need to just ask her again."

Pete slaps his hands on his thighs and stands up. "Okay, I guess it's just you and me then. Where do you want to go?" Time alone with Monica sounds good to him. He reaches for his jacket and pulls it on.

"I'm thinking just a salad. Want to go to the pizza place? I can get a salad there—and I know you like your pizza." She peers at his computer monitor. "Playing games again, I see."

His face grows warm, as he leans to click the computer off. "If you're nice, I'll show you something I found this morning."

They head down the hall. "Hacking again, Pete? I'm shocked." She smiles as they reach the elevator and punches at the down button.

"No, not hacking—not exactly. It's that damn sealed-function, you know the one they use to lock certain records? Figured out how to get around it." He beams, pleased with himself, and he figures he should be. The coders who'd built their database system probably figured that "sealed" meant really, actually *sealed*—but Pete, Hacker Extraordinaire, has figured out how to get past their so-called "lock."

Monica grins and he can almost believe she's impressed. She steps into the elevator, which has just arrived. "Sounds like hacking to me. But, sure. I'd love to see what you found."

JENNA IS TAPPING AWAY at her computer when Monica pokes her head into Jenna's cubicle. "You ready?" A lime-green yoga mat is tucked under Monica's arm.

Jenna glances at her phone—five o'clock already. Somehow. Just the thought of getting up, much less moving around, makes her tired. She's missed this class several times already—what a waste of money. She never should have signed up. "Okay, hang on," she finally says. "I'll be ready in a minute." She shuts down her computer and begins stashing things into her tote bag.

"Come *on*." Monica reaches behind the file cabinet and pulls out Jenna's rolled-up mat. "We're gonna be late."

They hurry to the yoga studio, past the looming church with its once impressive stone front, now streaked with black stains, past the garlic-scented deli, past the bar that appears to be offering happy hour again. *Mid-Week Happy Hour! Today! Free food!*

Monica points at the sign as they dash past. "We should go. After class."

"I don't know—"

"Well, *I'm* going. You can be a stick in the mud if you want to." She storms in through the studio door, letting it slam closed behind her.

Jenna flinches and stares at the door for a moment, then grabs the handle and follows Monica into the studio dressing room. She kicks off her shoes, changes into yoga pants and a top, then pads in sock feet into the cool studio. It smells of burning wax. Monica has placed her mat near the front of the room and is already warming up. A squat candle glows from a low altar. Behind the candle a dancing Shiva statue stands guard. One of Shiva's feet is lifted at a graceful angle and he stretches multiple arms resembling wings toward the circle surrounding him. Candlelight flickers on his stony face.

Jenna looks at it for a moment, wondering how many times she's been in this room and never noticed that statue. She looks around, wishing she could leave, but unrolls her mat on the polished floor, lies down on her back and immediately yawns. She rubs the heels of her hands into her eyelids, listening to the yoga teacher speak softly to someone across the room.

The teacher's voice is soothing, but Jenna can't make out the words. She stops trying to listen and sees, in her mind's eye, the little girl, the one in the park. She's got that blue coat on, buttoned up in front. The girl had been walking next to a woman pushing a stroller, but now Jenna envisions her running across the grass.

But the grass is no longer brown. It's green. Bright green, like new grass in the spring. The little girl is laughing, her dark hair bobbing. She's pointing up. Above her, long ribbons of blue, purple and bright green flutter against a cloudless sky. The blue-coated child laughs and jumps up, trying to reach the fluttering streamers.

Something hard slams into Jenna's forehead and she groans, rolling to her side, rolling into herself. The pain in her head is intense and she claps a hand across her eyes.

"Are you okay?"

Jenna opens her eyes a little. The teacher is there, crouched next to her. She looks concerned. "What?" Jenna whispers.

"You cried out."

The same thing the priest had said, but she doesn't remember making any sound—not then, and not now.

The candle at the front of the room flickers. She can see its dim glow through the teacher's hair, creating a sort of halo around her head. Dark shapes flicker behind her—a shadowy image of Shiva projected on the wall above the altar. "Is something wrong?" the teacher whispers, reaching a hand to Jenna's arm.

Jenna shakes her head and looks away. "I'm okay. I'm sorry."

"There's nothing to be sorry about, Jenna. Just take care of yourself, okay? If class becomes too much, let me know, and we'll set you up with some restorative poses."

A few minutes later, the teacher begins calling poses: mountain, *tadasana*; forward fold, *uttanasana*; chair, *utkatasana*. Jenna follows along with the familiar sequence, but always a second or two behind the others. The teacher continues with the pose names in the expected order: down dog, *adho mukha svanasana*; plank, *chaturanga*; cobra, *bhujangasana*; child's pose, *balasana*.

Jenna sinks back into child's pose, her feet tucked beneath her folded legs. Her forehead rests on the mat, sweat pouring from her brow. She's breathing hard, which is ridiculous so early in class. Less than ten minutes of yoga and she's already exhausted. Jenna forces herself to the next pose, but the class has already moved on. She skips a few poses in the sequence to catch up but is soon falling behind again.

The class drags on forever, one down dog after another, sun salutations until she thinks she'll drop dead. When the instructor finally announces after more than an hour that it's time for final relaxation, *savasana*, corpse pose, Jenna lies down on her mat and stretches out on her back, exhausted but relieved. Finally—a pose she can actually do.

The lights go down. The teacher's soothing voice floats across the darkened room. "Focus on your breath. When thoughts arise, as they inevitably will, return your awareness to the breath." She says the same thing each class. "Let those thoughts go," or "Empty your mind," or any number of other puzzling instructions Jenna can never accomplish. How does a person empty their mind anyway?

MIKE MAKES HIS WAY to the kitchen, following the delicious smells of the soup being prepared for the daily meal, something with onion and vegetables. Volunteers will arrive soon to ladle it into bowls for the street people who are probably already lining up in the alleyway next to the kitchen door. He's standing there by the large kettle, dishing up a bowl of vegetable-tomato for himself, when he spots the boy.

The first thing he sees is the tangle of yellow curls, then that dirty face, eyes wide, looking up at him. The child has wedged himself into the narrow space between the deep metal sink and the large industrial-sized refrigerator and is, as before, nearly naked, clad only in that same graying loincloth.

The boy steps out into the kitchen. "It's going to happen again," he says in a high-pitched voice, holding his grubby hands out toward Mike. "Maybe tomorrow."

"Why are you here?" Mike asks. The boy must be freezing, wearing almost nothing. Although it's only late October, the weather has gotten downright nippy in the last week.

Mike reaches for him, but the child grabs his sleeve, causing soup to slop to the floor. Red splotches splash across the linoleum and onto the boy's dirty feet. "He's going to kill again," the boy says. "And he's in the line right outside—come on." He tugs on Mike's sleeve, pulling him toward the side door of the kitchen, pushing it open with his grimy hand.

Snow flurries swirl in through the door as it creaks open, bringing a blast of cold wind into the steamy kitchen and, with it, the smell of rotting garbage from the dumpster that sits in the alley near the side street. A line of a dozen or so men stretches away from the door. They're all dressed in the uniform of the city's homeless—tattered dark coats, unshaven chins, eyes sunk deep into faces painted with pain. Some lean against the brick wall, as if exhausted.

The nearly naked waif steps out into the cold winter-like day. Several sets of deep-set eyes swivel toward the door, but their gazes sweep over the boy and settle on Mike, who stands with one hand holding the heavy metal door open. None of the men appear to notice the child, who stands barefoot in the freezing alleyway.

"Wait right there," Mike says to the child. "It's too cold out—" He goes back in, places his soup on the counter top and returns to the door. He pushes it open, but the boy is gone. Again.

Mike lets the door swing closed behind him as he steps out into the narrow space between buildings. His eyes scan up and down the alleyway, searching for the child who had, moments before, been tugging on his sleeve. He walks down the line of men, looking around their legs, peering behind their heavy coats, searching the dark corners of the alleyway for any sign of the child.

"Something wrong?" one of the men asks in a gravelly voice. He's got a knit cap pulled over his hair and regards Mike suspiciously.

Mike stops and steps closer to the man, who averts his gaze. He smells of old sweat and alcohol. Spikes of white-blond hair poke out from under the guy's cap. His nose is a bit crooked, as if it had healed wrong after being broken. "Did you see a young boy?" Mike asks.

The man glances over his shoulder. "A—a what?"

He's going to kill again. He's in the line outside.

Mike stumbles backward. Snow swirls in a sudden gust down the alley, picking up trash and whirling it along with dust into their faces. There's something there, in the man's gaze. The man knows something. Mike is sure of it.

Mike looks, once more, for the child he knows is no longer there—if he ever was. The men stare at him for several long moments until Mike looks away, shaken and wondering about his own sanity. He steps back into the kitchen, letting the heavy door clang shut behind him.

3

JENNA LEAVES WORK LATE and hurries back to her apartment building. She's almost made it inside when old Mrs. Freund steps out her front door. She has her cat, an enormous black and white one, at the end of a leash. It's the biggest cat Jenna's ever seen—its head reaches above Mrs. Freund's knee.

"Jenna." The old woman nods at her. Curls of bluish-gray hair frame her doughy face. Deep black circles stretch down from beneath her eyes. She gives Jenna that look again, the one she always gives her—a look of pity—and pulls her cloth coat tight to her throat. Jenna can smell Mrs. Freund's perfume: something floral, maybe lilac.

The cat looks at Jenna and lays its ears back on its head, then ducks behind Mrs. Freund's legs. Every night Mrs. Freund walks this cat on its leash, as if it were a dog. As if this were normal.

And maybe it is. Jenna can't remember ever seeing anyone walk a cat on a leash, but she can't seem to remember much these days. She wonders, briefly, if she's starting to develop dementia. Is thirty-eight too young for something like that?

The cat squints its eyes at Jenna. She shudders and stands up straight. "Have a good evening, Mrs. Freund," she says, then heads around the side wall of the apartment building. Her door opens onto the alley in the back. She takes the two stairs up to it, lets herself in, and flops onto the couch, yawning. Maybe she should've gone to yoga again—Monica had stopped by with her mat, just like yesterday, but Jenna was too tired, maybe still exhausted from yesterday's class, so passed on the offer.

She should eat. She's not hungry, though. As usual. Could this be another sign of dementia? She has no idea, but rummages in the cupboard and comes up with a can of clam chowder. She heats a cup of it in the microwave, then curls up in the chair by the window. She stares into the darkness outside and sips at the steaming soup, wind rattling the pane.

Her cell phone rings from somewhere inside her bag and she fishes it out. "Hi, Sam." She hasn't talked to her brother in—well, she's not sure how long. Another thing she can't remember. "Where are you?"

"At JFK, waiting for a shuttle." A confusion of noise comes at Jenna through the phone—brakes squeaking, horns honking, shouts. "We're heading to Kazakhstan tomorrow."

"Really? What are you doing there?" As soon as she asks, she wonders if this trip of his is yet another thing she's forgotten.

"My business partner and I are getting a bunch of volunteers ready to distribute cellphones to villagers."

"Business partner?" Is this someone she should know?

"You met him last year at Mom's. On Thanksgiving." There's a long pause from Sam's end. More traffic noise. "It's been a year, so maybe you forgot—well, over a year, I guess, since we formed our non-profit. Summer before this last one."

"Has it been that long?" She still has no idea who Sam's business partner is and hopes this will make her sound only slightly forgetful. She stares out at the darkening night. The wind picks up, rattling the window again. She doesn't remember Sam's partner, but even worse, she doesn't remember last year's Thanksgiving.

They'd spent it at Mom's, that much was clear. But, then, they always had Thanksgiving at her mother's. She remembers Sam arguing with Dad that day, a curly lock of dark hair falling across Sam's forehead as their voices rose—but that could have happened any year. Sam and Dad argued every Thanksgiving. She shakes her head, trying to dislodge the discomfort of not knowing even these basic facts of her own life. "How long will you be in Kazakhstan?" she asks.

"Six weeks, at least—maybe longer. Just as well. It'll give me an excuse to skip Thanksgiving. Not sure I can take it again this year."

"I can understand that. I—I'm not sure I'm going either."

There's a long pause. "I can see that," he finally says. "Why do something like that to yourself, after all? Mom will just drink herself into a stupor, as usual, and Dad will lecture you about abandoning your law career. You don't need anymore stress." His voice is nearly drowned out by a sudden roar, like the sound of a jet engine.

Law career? How could she have forgotten an *entire career*? She shakes his words away, trying to focus. "Oh, I don't know how much stress I have—"

"Sorry, I probably shouldn't have mentioned it." He's raised his voice, but it's hard to make out his words through the noise. "It's just that you have your own problems, right? No reason to torment yourself with *their* problems." He's shouting into the phone now. There's a loud commotion on his end, more brakes squealing, people yelling. "Jenna, I have to go—looks like my shuttle is here."

He'd be hanging up soon, so she blurts, "When will I see you?"

"I don't know. Christmas maybe?"

"That would be nice."

"Hey, I gotta go, but I'll try to call when we get to Europe, okay?"

"Have a safe trip," she says. "I love you."

After hanging up, Jenna washes the few dirty dishes that have accumulated that day. The wind whistles through a crack in her kitchen window as she puts away cups and plates and sweeps the floor. By the time she crawls into bed, it's bending the large trees outside, swaying them from side to side, rattling the windows even more and invading her dreams. She drifts in and out of sleep. She dreams of a kite in a violent wind, a large kite, with long ribbons for a tail, blue, purple and green. She dreams of a little girl in a blue coat, running in the wind, laughing, trying to catch the kite tail in her outstretched hand. She dreams the little girl becomes a tiny plastic doll, battered and damaged. One arm of the doll is completely broken off and half its hair is missing. She wakes after that and blinks into the dark, listening to the wind outside, wondering about the dream. She's sure she's had that same dream before—but when?

The next day, bleary-eyed from lack of sleep, Jenna struggles to get through her work. She loses her place repeatedly, makes one mistake after another. She can't stop yawning. Break time finally arrives.

She hurries from the building, intent on coffee, hoping for a short line at the deli so she can make it back to her cubicle before break time is over. As she strides past the stone-clad church, its massive front door swings open and out steps the priest she met at the park.

His face lights up as he takes the steps down toward her. "Hello!"

"Hi." She nods. "Father Mike, right?"

"Nice to see you again." That crinkly eyed smile. He doesn't act like a priest, at least not like any priest she's ever known. But would she remember knowing any priests? She's forgotten a great deal—even her own career, apparently.

She knows the fact she's forgotten so much about her life should be scaring the wits out of her, but all she really feels is confused. Puzzled. She should be frightened, but that, alas, is a feeling only other people have.

"I'm sorry," Father Mike says, interrupting her thoughts. "I didn't catch your name when we met before."

"Jenna." She tries to smile and extends her hand.

He shakes it and gestures down the block. "I was just heading over for a cup of coffee. Want to join me?"

"Oh, gosh, I wish I could, but I have only a fifteen-minute break and—"

"How about lunch, then?"

Was he asking her out? Can a priest do that? "I'm sorry." Her face grows hot. Now *why* is she blushing? Well, the answer to that is obvious. He's definitely an attractive man. "I'm sorry—but *lunch*?"

His cheeks turn a little pink. "I just thought you might want to talk. You know—since we didn't get to do that yesterday."

What is it with this guy? "Are you asking me out?"

He smiles broadly, eyes crinkling again. "I guess it might seem that way—but, no, I'm just doing what priests do. I see somebody in need and I try to help."

Maybe it's a creative pick-up line. She doesn't have much experience with priests (not that she'd remember)—but what did he mean by "somebody in need"? She walks toward the deli and he falls in beside her. She glances sideways at him. "You sound like my brother." He's a good eight inches or more taller than her, broad shoulders and chest, somewhat athletic in appearance.

"Your brother is a priest?"

She's glad to be the one rattling him this time, instead of the other way around. "No—not a priest, although maybe he should have been. Dad always called him a do-gooder."

"Nothing wrong with doing good," Father Mike says as they reach the deli. He pulls the door open and delicious smells waft out—strong coffee, something sweet and scented with cinnamon. He waits for her to enter, then follows her in. When they've both ordered and stepped back outside, holding steaming paper cups in their gloved hands, he turns to her. "So, lunch?"

She shrugs. "Well, I brought my lunch, so—"

"Great. So did I." He smiles again, clearly not willing to let her off the hook. "How about we meet at the park? I heard it's supposed to warm up by noon."

She isn't going to be able to say no to him, she can see that. He'll seek her out and make her talk—and, oh hell, why not? "Okay." She sighs. "Around noon?"

"Sounds good." He takes the steps up to the church door. "See you then."

She finds him on the same park bench where they'd met a couple days before. It had, as he predicted, gotten warmer. The crowd around them may or may not be the same people—no man and boy with a Frisbee this time, although there are plenty of office workers again, reading newspapers and books, eating out of paper sacks and small pizza boxes.

They nibble at their sandwiches. Jenna chats nervously about the weather, unsure how to talk to a priest. It's not like chatting up some guy in a bar, is it? Maybe it is—who would know? The real problem is that she has no idea how to explain what's happening to her. If she says, *I can't feel fear*, what would he think? How could anyone understand such a thing? Besides, that's not accurate. She's also missing a lot of memories. And she did feel fear, one time anyway—but not when she expected it. She glances at the shiny ribbons fluttering in the trees across the park, then looks away, rubbing at her forehead, unwilling to let the fear in again.

Mike turns to her, brushing crumbs from his lap to the ground at their feet. "Is there anything on your heart and mind today, Jenna?"

So odd, and strangely formal. But she's grateful he's given her an opening. "I don't know, maybe." She shrugs. "I didn't sleep well last night. Strange dreams, you know?" She stares at the dry grass, thinking about her dream—the little girl in the blue coat, the doll with the broken arm. She shakes her head, trying to sort it out. "And then Monica wanted to go to happy hour the other night," she says. "It wasn't unexpected. We've been going for the last few weeks, but this time I just didn't want to. I went home and straight to bed. Very unlike me…" Her voice trails off and she glances at him. She shrugs. "Strange dreams, as I said."

Mike's eyebrows go up. "Monica is your friend?"

Jenna shrugs again. "Not really a *friend*. We work at the same place." She gestures toward the boulevard. "Columbia Health. I've only known her for a little while. She joined the company just this past summer." Tears fill her eyes. Unexpected. Unexplained. She blinks furiously.

Mike sits silently, watching her for a long moment. "So, Monica is not your friend." His voice has become soft.

She can't meet his gaze. If she looks at him, she'll cry, and he'll want an explanation. But she has no explanation.

"Actually, I don't think I have any friends." She blinks again, trying to get the tears to go back in, wishing she hadn't started talking to him. "I feel so foolish. How can a person not have friends? I used to have friends—I mean, I *must* have." She shakes her head and finally looks up at him. He seems very kind. And not at all impatient. He waits, as if he might wait all day for her to get the words out. "It's so weird. I look back over the last five years or so and I cannot remember what happened to all those friends I must have had."

There. She's said it, told somebody finally. It feels like a weight lifts off her back and shoulders. She gazes at his large hands, clasped together in his lap. They're big hands, like her father's. It gives her a great deal of comfort to simply sit there with him, in silence—she didn't know how much she'd needed someone to share this with. He stares at his thumbs for another long moment, then looks up.

"So, you're saying you don't remember how you lost those friendships?"

She shakes her head. "It's not that. I don't even remember who those people were." She searches his face now, as if the answers she's seeking to the questions she can't even formulate might be hidden there.

He folds his arms across his barrel of a chest and cradles one cheek in his palm. "What happened five years ago?"

"I have no idea." She shakes her head. "No, that's not right. I *do* know one thing. I met Howard around that time. More like six years ago, I guess, but five years ago we—we broke it off." She's confused now, trying to calculate dates, not sure when she and Howard had broken up. The memories, such as they are, make her stomach twist painfully.

"Howard was your boyfriend?"

Of course he'd think that, after what she'd just said. "Boyfriend's not quite the right word. We weren't supposed to be together at all, you see." Heat rises into her cheeks. She really shouldn't be talking to him, a priest for God's sake, about this.

"So, you and Howard, whatever he was, broke up five years ago?" She nods, and he goes on. "Why? If you don't mind my asking, what caused the breakup?"

He seems honestly interested, but all she can do is stare. "I don't want to say."

He lets his breath out heavily and unfolds his arms. "Jenna, look. I'm a priest. I've heard it all, believe me, but if you don't want to tell me, you don't have to." He pauses. "It's just that I get the distinct impression you need to talk."

"He was married."

He leans back on the bench. "Aha."

Now that she's spilled out the worst of it, the words roll quickly from her mouth. "As I said, we were not even supposed to be together. I was not supposed to exist—at least not in his world. So, he broke it off." She shakes her head, confused again. "At least I think that's what happened." How odd—she can remember being with Howard, then not being with him, but how did it end? Did she break it off or did he? She should know but realizes she has absolutely no idea how it ended with Howard. How could someone forget something like that?

She stands up quickly, folding the now-empty brown paper bag and sliding it into her pocket, agitated and angry. The slow simmer that resides in her belly expands whenever she thinks of Howard and has erupted yet again. "Thanks for lunch," she says, nodding. "I need to get back to work."

Mike stands up and shakes her hand. Stiffly. Formally. As if he's carrying out a duty he knows he should carry out but doesn't want to. "If you'd ever like to talk more, don't hesitate to drop by." He points toward the boulevard. "I'm at—"

"I remember. St. Rita's." She forces a smile. Father Mike's nice, thoughtful, and she feels like an ingrate running off this way. It's not the Father's fault Howard is such a jerk. "Thank you for listening. I'm sorry if I wasn't very articulate, but I'm having a few problems these days and—" Her voice trails off.

"It's okay," he says, softly. "Anytime you want to talk, I'll be ready." He smiles and his eyes crinkle. Again. Something inside Jenna softens and unwinds, releasing a tension she didn't realize was there.

She watches him walk away, headed for his church, and even as the distance between them increases, she feels a tether, some sort of invisible thread, linking them together. It remains in place, binding them invisibly, even as he crosses the boulevard and gets lost in the crowd. She knows then, in some inexplicable way, that this is a man she's going to see a lot more of. And the thought of that makes her glad.

PETE PULLS THE NEWSPAPER in front of his face as Jenna walks by, apparently on her way back to the office. He hadn't really meant to spy on them, but when he caught sight of her in the park, talking to a priest, of all things, he grabbed a seat on a nearby bench.

It was a good sign, really it was, that she was talking to someone—all that crazy stuff about standing on the roof, jumping in front of cars. A priest seems a good choice for a counselor. Clearly the girl is suicidal, but why? It's not really his business, or Monica's either. Monica, though, keeps chattering on and on about Jenna, day in and day out. Worse, she seems to want to make it Pete's business, too.

Pete had become increasingly curious about Jenna after that day he ran into her and her family at what was, apparently, a funeral at that church where the priest he's just seen her with works. He'd noticed, when he was doing his maintenance rounds, upgrading all the computer stations on her floor, that there'd been a two-week period when Jenna was away. He checked her HR records at the time, never mind how he did it, and found out she was on medical leave.

It was the oddest thing. She was a different person when she came back from leave. The coworker he'd known before had been sad, depressed and so quiet people hardly noticed her. The one who came back was totally different—still quiet, but friendlier. When Monica joined the company, it was Jenna, of all people, who'd been the first one to befriend her. For his part, Pete couldn't figure out what to say to this new girl, Monica, although he very much wanted to talk to her. She was gorgeous—dark hair, dark eyes, a quirky smile—and she always wore this intoxicating citrus-scented perfume. He couldn't take his eyes off her.

And then the two women started inviting Pete to lunch. He thought he'd died and gone to heaven. No one, certainly none of the women at the office, had *ever* included him in their lunch invitations. Pete didn't know what to think about this development, but he kept his musings to himself, since he'd somehow, thanks to Jenna, got what he wanted. Even after he and Monica became friends, he never told her about the strange shift in Jenna's personality that he'd noticed—didn't want to jinx his good fortune.

THE WEATHER TAKES A NOSEDIVE after that and October becomes November, bringing squalls of dry snow and unexpected ice slicks on the sidewalk around the church. One day, Mike takes the bus to another part of town. The street where he gets off is busy, filled with buses and taxis and the smell of diesel. He's dressed in a dark overcoat, his hands encased in heavy gloves and has tied his scarf around his neck again, supposedly to keep the cold out. Apparently, though, it's gone askew, judging from the double takes and stares he's getting as he picks his way down the icy sidewalk toward the restaurant where he's meeting Ted for a cup of tea.

It's always the same, like with that young woman from the insurance company. What was her name? Jenna? He still kicks himself, thinking he could play the part of the understanding priest, when all he apparently did was make her uncomfortable and embarrassed. She'd never come back to see him, and he didn't blame her. It's like that with all of them. He'll see a young woman, walking toward him, say—she'll glance up and her eyes will light, first, on his face. This might bring on a smile or, at the very least, a look that indicates some interest or perhaps just friendliness.

Inevitably, her gaze will travel downward, making it as far as his collar before the pleasant look fades, replaced by something else. He's never quite sure what their alarmed expressions mean. Guilt? Fear? Disgust? Sometimes, but rarely, one of these otherwise polite young women will nod and greet him with a formal and brief, "Father," while hurrying past, but usually they just avoid further eye contact.

It's to be expected, of course. He's a priest after all, no longer "just some guy," as he'd once been. It's been a decade since he was ordained, since he and the other seminarians were warned to get used to people treating them as if they were the Father Himself. Some people do seem to treat him this way, of course, especially his older parishioners. But thanks to all the news stories about pedophile priests for the last several years, he feels more like a suspect most of the time than a divine emissary. He's not sure which is worse.

He reaches the restaurant and pulls the door open. Snow flurries in behind him as he steps inside. The place is about half full, the lunchtime crowd partly dissipated. Waiters and waitresses move from table to table, gathering plates and bringing bills. Mike inhales a mixture of luscious scents—garlic, fresh bread, some sort of roasted meat, and spots Ted, seated at a table by the fogged-over window. He lifts a hand in greeting when he sees Mike.

Mike walks over and when he reaches the table, Ted nods at the steaming mug at his elbow. "I hope you don't mind—I got here a little early."

Mike shrugs out of his coat. "No, no. It's fine—I'm grateful you could find the time to talk to me." He sits down, and a waitress appears. After she scribbles his drink order and hurries away to fetch another cup of tea, he unfolds the starched white napkin and spreads it across his knee. "So, are you enjoying retirement?"

Ted chuckles. "I wouldn't call it *that*." He smiles, and the smile takes in his whole face, including his light blue eyes. Ted looks just like what he is: a kindly priest, the sort of person you could go to with your problems. Mike's pretty sure he looks nothing like this and doesn't think he ever will. Ted takes a sip of tea then says, "The bishop has asked me to serve as interim. Two different parishes unexpectedly lost their priests and he's deciding which one to send me to."

"What happened to the priests?"

"One was that fellow from Oklahoma. He could never get used to the big east-coast-city thing, so asked for a transfer."

Ted offers a weak smile and sips at his mug again. "The other—well that was one you could probably guess if you knew him. He was advised to resign before any more complaints were filed." He shakes his head, sighing. "I don't condone his actions, obviously, but can't help worrying about the future of the church when young priests go astray."

Mike ignores his twisting stomach and nods a thank-you at the waitress as she slides a second steaming mug onto the table. "What was he accused of? If you don't mind my asking."

"The usual. Some sort of sexual indiscretion. I actually don't know the details. Thank God no children were involved." A small muscle in Ted's jaw clenches and unclenches a few times. He looks up at Mike. "So, what can I do for you, Father?"

It gives him a start to hear Ted use his title. He should be used to it by now, but it's started to feel radioactive lately. He wraps his hands around the hot mug and breathes out heavily before the bitter laugh that has risen into his throat can escape. "See, that's just it, Ted," he says. "I can't, in good conscience, go by that title anymore."

Ted regards him calmly. He's silent for a long moment then says, "We all have doubts from time to time, Mike."

He shakes his head. "No, no—it's not that."

"What then? A girl?"

The laughs finally escape, and he sits back in the chair. "I wish. If only it were that simple." He hesitates, thinking of the young woman from the insurance company, Jenna. "No, maybe I don't wish for that. I have enough problems as it is."

"Like what?"

All the words he'd wanted to say seem to lodge in his throat. So much for the speech he'd practiced as he lay awake unable to sleep and, again, all the way over in the bus. He'd wanted to complain to Ted about the bishop's financial maneuverings, the disintegrating building, the empty repair and maintenance fund. Even more, though, he'd wanted to tell him he no longer believed in God, nor in any of the things he was supposed to believe in.

He wants—needs—to tell Ted all this, but instead he blurts, "You know, *problems*. Like the nearly naked child I keep seeing in the church."

Ted frowns at him. The silence between them grows louder, as if magnified by the clinking of forks on plates and the murmurs of the other people in the restaurant. "Mike." Ted clears his throat. "Are you saying—?"

Mike furiously shakes his head. "That's *not* what I mean. It was this child, and he just showed up, wearing virtually nothing. *Twice*."

Ted closes his eyes briefly. When he opens them, he asks, "Where did you see the child?"

Mike breathes out, relieved, although he's not sure why. He needs to talk about this. He needs to tell someone. "In the side chapel, the first time. Then the kitchen. But, Ted, it was what he said that really got to me."

"And what was that?"

He can't tell him. Ted would never believe it. "It was a warning, I guess you'd say," he finally mumbles. He stares at the tablecloth, suddenly embarrassed.

Ted lets out a soft sigh. Mike looks up, surprised to see Ted's eyes closed again, his face serene. He nods, as if agreeing with something only he can hear. When he opens his eyes, he levels his gaze at Mike. "Maybe it was an angel."

Mike flinches. "A—a what?"

A slow smile spreads across Ted's face. "I know you are not unfamiliar with the concept of angels, Father Mike," he teases. "You know—a messenger. From God."

Mike forces a smile. Ted is trying to be understanding, he knows that. But Ted's suggestion that the child is an angel is something he'd already considered—considered *and* rejected. It can't be the explanation. Angels are not real, after all.

Ted was clearly the wrong person to discuss this with. What Mike needs is help. Real help.

4

JENNA IS HEADED FOR WORK and when she passes the park, she sees her: the little girl in the blue coat. She's skipping along behind that same woman, probably her mother, who's pushing a stroller containing an infant wrapped tight in blankets.

Jenna sprints and catches up with them at the curb where the woman stands, waiting for the crosswalk light to change, her gloved hands resting lightly on the stroller handles. "Excuse me," Jenna says. The little dark-haired girl, who appears to be about four or five, turns and looks up at her, eyes wide. She bites her lower lip and leans into her mother's side. "I'm sorry to intrude," Jenna says. The woman stares straight ahead. "Have we met? I keep thinking I know you."

The woman looks at her then and when she catches sight of Jenna's face, she flinches back. "No," she says, her voice shaky. "I don't believe we've actually *met*."

Jenna frowns. "I'm sorry—I just keep thinking I recognize you." She looks down at the blue-coated girl. "Both of you."

The woman reaches for the little girl's hand and squeezes it. "Well, we do remember you from the park. Isn't that right, Annie?" The little girl tips her head back and nods at her mother.

"Maybe that's it. When I saw you the other day, it was in the park, after all." The crosswalk light blinks from orange to white and the woman hurriedly pushes the stroller into the street. The little girl trots along beside her and Jenna follows, a step or two behind, until they reach the other side.

The woman turns her stroller away from the Columbia Health building. She glances at Jenna and gives her a weak smile—and, then, that same look Mrs. Freund always turns on her: pity. "I don't think I ever said how sorry I was about what happened," the woman says.

"Sorry?" Jenna has started to shake. Is it fear again? She's not sure—it's either fear or excitement. How does one tell the difference?

"I'm sure you don't want to talk about it," the woman says. Something glints in the corner of one eye.

The little girl tugs at the woman's hand. "Mommy, I'm cold."

"Okay, sweetie." The woman blinks back tears. She looks again at Jenna. "She's due for a nap, so I need to run." The woman turns and hurries away, the little girl jogging along behind her.

Jenna watches them leave and just as she's about to turn and head back to the office, her phone buzzes in her pocket. She pulls it out, stares at the display for a long moment, then punches the button. "Hi, Howard. What's up?"

"I have a couple questions," he says. She can hear a commotion in the background, voices, doors slamming. He must be at court.

"About what?"

"First one's simple: Your mother called and asked if I was coming for Thanksgiving. I guess I'm invited, but I'm assuming you don't want me there."

"I don't know. I'm not even sure I'm going. Sam is out of the country and—"

"Where is he?"

"Kazak—something? What's that place called?"

"Oh, right—he said last year they were moving into that region. Right?"

Even Howard remembers more about her life than she does. "You said you had a couple questions?" She's reached the front door of the Columbia building, so stops and leans against the stone wall, her head bowed forward, staring at a crack in the sidewalk.

"Yes. Well." He clears his throat before saying, "This isn't actually a question, I guess. I just wanted to let you know that the restraining order against that Josh Reynolds character has been renewed. The judge immediately agreed he was still a danger."

The name rings a bell. Is this someone she knows? Maybe it's just one of Howard's clients. "I—okay. Thanks for letting me know."

"Sure thing. I figured you would want to be informed." He pauses and the commotion she can hear on his end gets louder. "Gotta run, sweetheart. Judge is calling us back."

She stares at the dead phone for a long moment, wishing she had some clue what Howard was talking about. So many things she doesn't remember.

Later that afternoon, as Jenna struggles with a complicated claim form, looking through a thick manual of treatment codes, trying to decipher some unintelligible scribbles, Monica comes by with her yoga mat.

Jenna lowers the manual. "Yoga again?"

"We've both missed a bunch of classes. We need to make them up soon, you know. Especially you."

"You're right. I've really wasted my money on this class. I doubt I've been to half of them so far." She waves at the teetering stack of folders on her desk. "But I can't leave. I have to finish this group by tomorrow and I'm totally stuck on this one. I can't seem to find the treatment code." She flips through a few more pages of the manual, her eyes scanning for the elusive combination of letters.

Monica pulls the spare chair closer and sits down. "What's the treatment?"

Jenna picks up the claim form and peers at it again. "Something about PTSD. I know that part, of course. Post traumatic stress disorder. But after that there's a couple words I can't make out—why can't people write clearly? It looks like it says 'squid.' What the hell does that mean?"

Monica takes the form and inspects it closely. "Yes, it does say squid, but look: It's all caps. An acronym." She pauses, thinking. "I've seen this somewhere." She grabs Jenna's keyboard and pulls up Google, tapping a few keys. "Yes, see? SQUID: Superconducting Quantum Interference Device."

Jenna shrugs. "Is that supposed to clarify anything? What does that mean?"

Monica turns the monitor toward Jenna. "Here's something that might help." She points at a box on the screen. "It's in Wikipedia. Look: *An array of SQUIDs can be used to make measurements of neural activity.*"

Jenna nods. "Anything that monitors neural activity is consistent with PTSD. But what does this SQUID thing do?"

"Got me there. I always put stuff like that under 'experimental treatment,' and it goes through. If it's not in the manual, Columbia will deny payment anyway, so it doesn't really matter what you put."

Jenna flings the treatment manual onto her desk. "I suppose you're right." She types in the code for experimental treatment and punches the submit button. "Okay, that's one hard one finished. Now I have only ten more before I can leave." She smiles weakly at Monica. "Say hi to everyone for me—I gotta stay late and finish these."

It's nearly seven p.m. by the time Jenna finishes. She's starving, so pulls on her coat and takes the long way home, past the take-out Chinese food place.

When she enters the shop, a blast of moist, warm air smelling of deep-fried spring rolls hits her. The large plate-glass window is steamed nearly to its top and several people sit waiting at a handful of Formica-covered tables arrayed beneath it. Jenna studies a menu, then steps up to the counter.

An older man with round glasses, round cheeks and a thin wisp of dark hair stands behind the register and looks up. "Oh," he stammers. "I mean—nice to see you tonight."

As if he knows her. And maybe he does. The place is only a few blocks from her apartment, after all. Yet another part of her memory lost. She smiles, not wanting to be rude. "I'd like an order of moo shu pork. To go, please."

"Fried rice?" He scribbles on the pad as Jenna nods. "About ten minutes." He rips the top sheet from the pad and gestures toward the tables. "Please wait." He shouts something in Chinese toward the kitchen in the back and smacks the paper onto a spike on the counter behind him.

Jenna takes a chair near the door and loosens her scarf. She looks absently at the other folks, every one of them staring at a phone. She yawns a few times as the minutes tick by, five minutes, then ten. She finally pulls out her own phone and there's a text from Sam:

> we're in Amsterdam!!! will write more
> once we're on the train to kazakh xoxo

She smiles. Sam was always a huge train fan, even as a kid. He'd drag all of them to train stations wherever the family went, just so he could watch the engines pull in or out. He'd bounce up and down on the platform, his dark wavy hair that always needed to be cut dangling in his eyes, so excited by the noise and enormity of the trains that he could barely stay still. It drove Dad crazy.

"Mrs. Wright!" The round-cheeked man is by the register, holding a brown paper bag. He nods her way. "Your order is ready."

She pays for the order and is reaching for the bag when a short Asian woman with red cheeks and damp hair, a stained white apron wrapped around her middle, comes out from the back. She gives Jenna a sad smile, then leans close to the man, whispering. He answers, in Chinese, then reaches beneath the counter and pulls out a large cookie, possibly oatmeal, wrapped in plastic.

He opens Jenna's brown paper sack and puts the cookie inside. "My wife and I wish you to take this—to honor the dead."

She flinches and pulls back. "To—what?"

The woman with the red cheeks leans forward. "Those who leave this world too soon sometimes wander, you know."

The man nods. "Yes—they not know how to get next world."

The hairs on Jenna's arms stand erect. Wow—a little glimmer of fear. If only she knew why the man and woman were talking to her about dead people.

The man rolls the top of the bag shut tight and pushes it toward her. "My wife say take the cookie home, place in front of candle." He nods and then both of them bow to her.

Jenna reaches for the bag. Her hand shakes, rattling the paper.

"Sorry." The man bows again. "Sorry to disturb."

Another man steps around Jenna and pushes close to the counter. "Can I place my order?" He gives the man and woman an annoyed look.

"Certainly." The Asian man fumbles with his order pad. "What you have?"

Jenna hurries out and heads toward her apartment. What in the world was that all about? Candles? And dead people who wander? And why did the man call her *Mrs.* Wright? She walks quickly, the cold wind whipping her scarf around and rustling the dried leaves on the spindly trees that line the block. When she rounds the corner and catches sight of her building, something darts from under the bushes.

It's a cat. A large one—black and white. The giant feline looks at Jenna, hissing, then burrows beneath the shrubs. Mrs. Freund's door swings open and the old lady sticks her head out. There's a light on behind her, casting her features in shadow. Jenna can't make out her face, but she knows it's her neighbor. "Kitty, kitty!" Mrs. Freund calls. She steps onto the porch, clutching the neckline of her robe close to her throat, peering into the dark.

She doesn't seem to see Jenna standing right there, although Jenna is close enough to catch a whiff of her lilac-scented perfume. The cat leaps from the bushes and darts in through the open door. "There you are," Mrs. Freund says. "What were you doing out here anyway—chasing ghosts?" She follows the cat inside, chuckling. "Beauregard, you are a silly cat—we're weeks past Halloween. No ghosts out here."

After Jenna gets to her own apartment, she places the food containers on the table, then rummages in the closet for a few minutes before she finds what she's looking for: a small spiral notebook. She tears out the few used pages, mainly to-do and shopping lists, crumples them into the trash, and sits at the table.

Between bites of moo shu pork, she scribbles notations in the notebook. At the top of the page she writes CLUES and makes the start of a bulleted list:

- *Little girl in blue coat*
- *Kite in the park*
- *"Mrs." Wright*

―

THE RADIATOR REPAIRMAN has come and gone and they're finally getting some heat in the side chapel. The newly repaired radiator clicks, exuding heat that retains the radiator's ever-present scent of rusty water. Mike had just shown the fellow out and is sitting in the front pew in the sanctuary, reading through the invoice.

Sister Mary Katherine pops into the sanctuary and hurries across the front of the nave. "Oh!" she says when he stands up, her hand fluttering toward her heart. "I didn't see you here, Father."

"No, no—I'm the one who should be sorry. I didn't mean to frighten you."

She waves a hand at him and turns toward the hall. "No problem—I need to keep looking for—oh, never mind." And then she's gone.

Maybe he should just send the bill directly to the bishop. Plead for help, since the balance in the maintenance fund will barely cover this. If anything else breaks, they'll be up a creek without the proverbial paddle.

He sinks into the front pew, slumping, wondering how it is that he's ended up with such a sorry excuse for a life. Papers are scattered across the floor at his feet. He looks down at them—bits of last Sunday's bulletin, which must've escaped the notice of the cleaning committee.

Better pick them up while he's here or the place will turn into a sty. He gets down on hands and knees and reaches beneath the pew to scoop the wayward pages into a pile. When he looks up, the child is there. Standing at the end of the row.

Mike trembles. He can barely make out the kid's face since it's cast into shadow. Golden light from the side chapel shines through his yellow hair, creating something that looks very much like a halo around the small head.

Maybe it's an angel. He scoffs, remembering Ted's words. The possibility this child is not really a child, but some sort of divine messenger is too much to accept.

He's had just about enough of this nonsense. "Who are you?" he demands, his voice a little louder than he'd intended. He remembers that this is a kid, from all appearances, and is momentarily surprised at the harsh tone in his own voice. He softens his face and tries again. "Are you a student from the school?"

He starts to turn, thinking he'll call for the sister, tell her he's found the child she was obviously looking for, when a thought occurs to him: *Don't turn away. Every time you turn away, the child disappears.*

He keeps his gaze fixed on the boy, even though the sun has gotten suddenly a lot brighter outside. He shields his eyes, trying to see.

The light streaming through the side chapel window ramps up even higher in intensity and the boy's hair glows a brilliant gold. He steps toward Mike. "You must listen," he says, his voice louder than Mike remembers it being. "You must listen to the word or it will happen again. He will kill, and the body will be there—beneath the black waters, under the flag of many colors."

Mike, shaking, scrambles to his feet. "What are you talking about?" He steps backward from the boy—if it *is* a boy. The voice is so different now. Almost like a bell ringing. And what in the world does the boy mean, anyway—black waters? Flag of many colors?

The light is growing brighter by the second and is now so intense he needs to raise his arm to shield his eyes. Can it really be the sun? It's so bright. He tries to keep his gaze fixed on the boy, whose entire body seems now to be glowing, but the pain from the light is excruciating and he finally turns away.

When it grows dim and he turns back, he knows what he will see even before he looks. Nothing. The boy is gone.

THE WEEK HAS COMPLETELY WORN JENNA DOWN. Her boss brings in an unexpectedly large stack of claim forms on Friday afternoon and she has to work late again. All this on top of not sleeping well all week.

It's the wind, which howls all night through the windows of her apartment. And her dreams—they're incessant, all about kites and little girls in blue coats. Inevitably a doll appears by the end of each dream. A doll with a broken-off arm and half its hair missing.

Saturday morning she drags herself to the grocery store, half-heartedly filling her basket with food she doesn't really want. She wanders through the produce section, picking up oranges and sniffing at their tangy scent before putting them back. The bakery is equally unappetizing. Nothing much tastes good anymore. She finally gives up, buys a few things, plunks the bags into her car trunk and drives home. It's a gray sort of day—overcast, chilly. And windy, too, the sort of day you just want to stay inside, have some tea and read a book.

She's just finished putting the food away and is placing the kettle on the stove when the kitchen door snaps open. A blast of wind swirls in carrying dry leaves into the kitchen. The breeze dislodges some brown paper bags she's tucked in front of the broom between the cabinet and the recycling bin. The bags tumble to the floor. A half dozen or so fan across the linoleum. Jenna starts to push the door shut against the wind but Mrs. Freund's cat dashes inside, in hot pursuit of what appears to be a tiny mouse.

Jenna jumps back as the mouse scurries by, disappearing into the space beside the recycling bin, somewhere behind the stack of brown bags. The cat, even larger than Jenna'd remembered it, crouches low on her kitchen floor, its tail twitching side to side. "Shoo!" She waves her hand at the cat. "You need to go home." The cat lays its ears back on its head and emits a low rumbling growl that soon becomes more of a screeching yowl.

Jenna looks at the large cat's long teeth and jerks her hand away. She reaches for the broom, hoping she can use it to push the cat out the door and avoid getting bitten. The cat lunges and lands on one of the brown sacks, skidding across the floor and colliding with the remaining sacks. They tumble away from the cabinet and onto the floor. The cat turns and gazes at her for a long moment, the fur on the back of its neck standing straight up. The little mouse darts out from behind the bags and out the door, Mrs. Freund's cat loping after it.

Jenna stares at the tumbled-over bags. There on the linoleum, lying among a pile of dry leaves and brown sacks, is a little plastic doll. Half its hair is missing and one arm is completely broken off.

MIKE GRABS HIS ALARM CLOCK. He's overslept but is awake now. Barely. He's somehow managed to switch off the alarm—or maybe he forgot to set it? He tossed and turned all night, fending off disturbing dreams about angels and devils, lost children, even one especially odd nightmare about a nun struggling with a broken radiator that belched steam into the church as the walls crumbled around her. If he doesn't hurry, he'll be late for Saturday morning confessions. He hops out of bed, dresses quickly, and is still fastening his collar around his neck as he sprints down the steps from his apartment. He hurries through the darkened hallway behind the organ and into the cavernous nave.

Several people have already arrived and are sitting in the pews, avoiding each other's eyes. He tries not to look at them as he passes, but a sloppily dressed man in a dark overcoat catches his eye. A lock of white-blond hair pokes out from under his knit cap.

It's him. The man from the soup line.

Mike looks away. He really should remind the man that no hats are allowed in church, but it seems a trivial concern compared to everything else that's going on. Trembling, he hurries to the wooden booth and slides into his seat. The curtain between his side and the other is drawn nearly shut across the opening. He lets his breath out, only then noticing that he'd been holding it, and breathes in the scent of old wood and incense. He closes his eyes and leans his head against the wall. *Give me strength that I may do your will.*

The words seem to pop into his mind of their own accord. He needs strength, this much is true, but what he doesn't need is the torrent of questioning thoughts that come after his silent prayer, the ones that torment him day after blessed day. *Who* is he talking to, for Christ's sake? He laughs at his own private joke.

Not only is he being stalked by an angel-child (perhaps) but now these prayers are popping, unbidden, into his mind.

Why am I being stalked? Why?

I know, I know—yes, Jacob, wrestling all night with his own angel.

Yes, I know—I saw him, the disheveled man sitting out there on the pew.

Could he be the one the angel-child spoke about, the killer?

Is the man out there a murderer and the boy a messenger sent to warn me?

And, if all this unlikely stuff is true, why am I being warned?

What in God's name do You want from me?

He laughs again, knowing this is *not* the way to pray. It seems the joke's on Mike. He can't imagine a God who could listen to such a torrent of drivel from one who ought to know better. Tears sting his eyes and he draws a deep breath, trying to quiet his frantic thoughts and compose himself. There are people out there counting on him, looking to him for guidance and comfort. He needs to get a grip. Now.

The door of the outer booth opens and someone steps in and slides onto the bench, along with a strong scent of old cigarette smoke. "Father, bless me for I have sinned." The voice, disembodied as always, sounds young, like a teenage boy.

He knows his part. Knows his lines. All he has to do is play along and soon morning confession will be over and then he can walk out and go call someone, maybe the bishop. He should have done it weeks ago.

He takes another breath, swallows hard and says, "And how have you sinned, my son?"

Silence from the other side. It always takes them a long time to spit it out, he's noticed, as if giving voice to the behaviors that torment them is the hardest part. And, of course, they're right—it is the hardest part.

Finally, the boy speaks. "Me and my girlfriend—well, we, you know."

He sighs. "No, I don't know. Why don't you just tell me?"

The words rush out. They sound harsh and uncaring, not at all the way he'd intended. But there they are, hanging in the air between him and the other side of the booth, and he can't take them back.

The boy snorts, as if suppressing a laugh. His next words, spoken so quietly Mike can barely hear them, are clearly not meant for Mike. "Of course you wouldn't know." And then, a bit louder: "Me and my girlfriend—we had sex." A pause. "Twice."

He should be used to this by now. They all think he's a virgin (which he isn't) or gay (which he isn't) or inexperienced and easily flustered when it comes to the ways of men and women. That part is true, but he'd been just as much a dork when he was a pre-med student as he is now. Ordination did not change that particular aspect of Mike Albertino's life— once a gawky, awkward nerd, always a gawky, awkward nerd.

He clears his throat. "Twice you say?" His voice squeaks, and he hates himself.

"Yes, Father," the boy says, snickering.

"Are you using protection?"

"Father?"

He imagines the boy drawing back, shocked, no doubt, at Mike's words. But he can't go there. It is forbidden to discuss such things with them, despite the fact the boy really ought to be using condoms and Mike should tell him so—but, instead, he says what he's supposed to say, tells him to stop doing what he's doing with his girlfriend, gives him a prayer prescription as if it's a drug that can remove all his perfectly natural youthful urges, and sends him on his way.

After that, it's a continual stream of people. They enter the booth, one by one: first, an older woman, torn by guilt, whose elderly husband is suffering from severe dementia. The woman wishes he would die, she says. Mike can see this, tells her it's an understandable desire but prescribes a round of Hail Marys. She seems grateful—as if the prayers will take away her remorse.

Then there's a young boy, even younger than the first. He's been shoplifting—little things, like pens and lighters. "It gives me a thrill," the boy says. Mike tells him to stop, tells him he knows it's wrong to steal or he wouldn't have come to confession. He dispenses another prayer prescription and waits for the next person to enter the booth. They continue streaming through with their tales of sins, large and small—but mostly small.

He's heard about a dozen or so confessions when someone shuffles in. Then, nothing but silence from the booth on the other side. He'd heard the shuffling of feet, felt the door slam shut, smelled the scent that wafted in—sweat and a faint tinge of alcohol—but then nothing. He pulls the curtain back, just a fraction of an inch.

A man in a frayed dark overcoat and a knit cap sits staring at his hands, mumbling words Mike cannot make out.

Mike clears his throat. "Do you wish to make a confession?"

The man's gaze jumps toward the opening where Mike sits holding the curtain back. His black eyes widen. "Yes. That I do."

Mike drops the curtain and it swings shut. The guy had on a knit cap, so Mike couldn't see whether his hair was white-blond and spiky, like the guy in the soup line. It might be him, though. It very well might.

A trembling in Mike's belly shakes his body from torso to head, but he tries to ignore it. "Please. Go ahead," he whispers.

"All right, then," the man says, clearing his throat. "I din't mean to do it. She was making a commotion and I had to git her to stop."

"Who?"

"Dunno. I never know their names." The man sighs and there's a long pause. "Just a kid I got to talkin' to. I—I just wanted to talk to her, I swear. I shouldn'ta done it. She got upset when I touched her, and I tried to get her to stop yellin.'" Another long pause. "Well, she's good and stopped now."

"What do you mean?"

"She's gone now. Like the others."

"Gone?"

"You know—dead."

The words slam into him, as if the guy had actually slugged him. Mike's thoughts whirl toward frenzy. He should go to the police. Like *right now*. But how can he do that? There's the sanctity of the confessional to consider. He can't repeat what he hears in here—it requires the utmost in confidentiality.

As if that matters. Why oh why does he care about confidentiality and *sanctity*? After all these months when he's said he doesn't care about any of that—why now, when it matters, is he hesitating?

The man has stopped talking and for one horrifying instant Mike is sure the man has fled while he dithered. He yanks back the curtain, but the man is still there, still staring at his hands, but wringing them together now.

"When did this happen?" Mike asks.

"Dunno. I keep thinkin' about that, tryin' to figure the dates. It seems like a year but maybe a few days? Dunno. Could be a couple years." The man's voice grows louder. "Aren't you gonna tell me I'm forgiven? Ain't that how it works? I come in, confess, and you make it go away?"

The man is right. It's his job—they confess, he absolves them of their sin, and that's that. He has to do it—but how can he keep going through with this charade?

"I'm sorry," Mike says. "I can't—" As soon as the words pop out of his mouth, he starts to tremble. He knows what he's done: denied the sacrament to a penitent.

But before Mike can say another word, the man jumps up and flings the door open with a bang. "Well, fuck you then." His shout echoes through the stone church.

Mike scrambles to his feet and bolts from the booth, just in time to see the man flee through the front door of the church, out to the boulevard. A half dozen people sit in the back pews, eyes wide, mouths open, as Mike dashes out onto the sidewalk.

He looks left, then right. Nothing. No sign of the guy whatsoever.

5

MIKE TRIES, FOR HOURS, to find a moment to do something about that guy's confession, but it's just one thing after another. As soon as he comes back in from chasing after the guy who'd confessed in his booth, one of the volunteers grabs him. There's a flood in the kitchen coming from somewhere under the sink, she says, and he has to deal with it immediately before it causes even more damage. As he has his head under the sink, one of the sisters runs in with news about a broken window in the back wing of the school. Cold air is blowing in, she says. The heating bill is already sky high, so, after he's fixed the leak, Mike runs to the hardware store for a board to nail over the window. By the time he finishes all that, it's almost four p.m. Confession ended hours ago, and the guy is probably long gone, but he heads to the police station anyway.

It's only two blocks from the church to the precinct station, a gray stone building with bars on the windows, right across the street from the park. He enters through the heavy glass and metal doors and steps into a cacophony of voices and ringing phones. The place smells like toilet bowl disinfectant mixed with stale cigarette smoke. Somewhere a door slams and then another. Blue uniformed officers swarm the narrow hallway. Waiting room chairs filled with all sorts of scruffy-looking characters line the walls. For a moment, Mike thinks he sees the guy among them, but the truth is, and he's ashamed to think this, all these street people look alike to him.

A young black woman with short hair, wearing a police uniform, stands behind the counter, tapping at a computer and chewing gum. She looks at him as he walks over and leans on the countertop. "Excuse me," he says. "I need to speak to someone about a murder."

She turns slowly. He can smell mint on her breath. "Okay, you got my attention." She snaps her gum and smiles as her gaze slides from his face downward. When her eyes reach his collar, her smile fades.

Mike's stomach clenches. Even the police find him suspicious.

The woman reaches beneath the counter, pulls out a clipboard with a form on top and shoves it toward him. "Fill this out," she says brusquely, snapping her gum again, "and take a seat. We'll be with you as soon as possible."

He looks at the form, with lines for name, address, phone number, and so forth. "I'm sorry," he says. "But how long do you think it will be before I can talk to someone?"

"You're talkin' to me," she says, her eyes glued to the screen, fingers tapping on the keyboard.

"What I mean is, I have to get back to the church—Mass is at five, you know, and I only have a few minutes."

She sighs and steps back from her computer. "Just a sec—let me see if the detective is free."

Detective Sloan—a wiry man smelling strongly of aftershave and wearing a slouchy gray suit a couple sizes too big for him—is equally brusque, but listens to his statement, taking notes on a large yellow pad while Mike talks. He can't be sure the confessor had really admitted to a murder, he says, as Sloan nods, but he has reason to believe the guy was telling the truth.

"What reason?" Sloan asks, his pen hovering over the paper.

Mike hesitates. He can't tell him about the boy—or angel, if that's really what he is. He mumbles, "I just have a feeling."

The detective puts his pen down and lowers his gaze to look at him. "You just *have a feeling*," he repeats.

Mike's face goes hot and even though he thinks that the more left unsaid the better, he blurts, "I just have a sense that he was telling the truth."

Sloan is silent for a long moment then asks, "Do you have any 'sense' about who he killed? Or where the body might be?"

He has to say what he knows, even if there's no earthly reason why he should know. "It might be a child," he says. "A girl. And she might be in that pond in the park—you know, right across the street."

"So, this guy who confessed to you said he'd killed a child, possibly female, and the body is in the pond?"

Mike stares at the clipboard in his hands. "No. No, he didn't say it exactly. He was actually kind of vague, didn't even really say he had killed anyone." He hesitates. "It—well, I know that one of our young students, Sophie McPherson, went missing some months ago and has not been found. It—it could be her, I suppose."

"Did he say something that made you think it might be that particular child? Her name perhaps?"

"No, no—it's just—her grandparents are my parishioners, you see, and I was hoping maybe this might help—" He shrugs. "Maybe what this fellow said is not related, but could you check?"

Sloan stands up. "We'll do our best," he says, smiling perfunctorily. "Thank you, Father." He's perfectly polite, shaking Mike's hand as he backs out. Sloan reminds him to fill out the form and leave it at the desk outside. After Mike fills it with his name and contact information, he hurries back to the church with barely enough time to robe for five p.m. Mass. He's striding into the sanctuary just as folks start streaming in. As he lifts the Host and looks out over the congregation, he sees her: Jenna, sliding into the back pew.

JENNA KNOWS SHE MUST BE PRETTY DESPERATE to be doing what she's doing, but where else can she turn? She squeezes into a corner of the backmost pew at St. Rita's, trying to look inconspicuous. The dim interior, lit by only a handful of candles, is so dark she can barely see. Even the stained-glass is dark and streaked with the rain that started to fall just as she stepped into the church.

The sign outside said Mass was at five p.m., so it's been going on for a while. He's up there, wearing a robe, holding a gilded cup aloft and intoning words she can't make out. They echo around the stone interior, filling her with sorrow. She can't tell what he's saying, but the sound is familiar, like something she should probably remember, but doesn't.

She hasn't been to church in years. Not that she can remember, but then what does that show? She doesn't know who she is, who she was. Strange images flash through her mind, vivid and striking:

Rows of people, heads bowed, sitting in darkened pews.

A priest with a bald head lifting a golden goblet and intoning some words.

A baby in a lacy white dress, a splash of water, laughter and shouts echoing from the stone walls.

Jenna wonders if she should have called a doctor instead of coming here. She reaches into her bag and pulls out the small spiral notebook. She's added an item to her bulleted list: *Small doll, arm broken off.* She adds two more: *Baldheaded priest; baby in white dress.* It seems like it should add up to something, but what?

Maybe she should have gone to the ER instead, but what would she tell them? *I can't feel fear.* If she said *that*, they'd put her in the psych ward, although maybe that's where she should be. A doctor would probably be more help—but a priest is the only one who can answer the question she has today.

Jenna is hit with a sudden longing—for what, she doesn't know, but as she looks around at the people, their heads bowed, listens to the quiet voices murmuring prayers, smells the faint scent of incense that seems to have permeated all the surfaces and books in this place—she wonders if it's God she's longing for. She doesn't remember being much of a churchgoer, doesn't recall participating in any sort of religious events, but what does that prove? She thinks, then, of the small object she's tucked into her purse, the item that's brought her here, and wonders if it's a sign. Some sort of divine sign, perhaps, a message from who-knows-where.

The people sitting in the pew in front of her stand up. Something is happening near the altar. Father Mike and the woman with him, a nun in a light blue habit, have moved toward the rail below the altar. He holds a silver dish and she clutches the gilded cup to her chest. People begin filing out of the pews and heading toward the front of the church.

It must be communion. She watches the backs of the people as they move slowly toward the front. The crowd is a strange combination of shuffling old folks and young couples.

The older people are bundled in heavy coats and scarves. The young couples are dressed up.

Communion seems to be taking forever. She hugs herself, impatient, wanting to ask him her question. Maybe he won't have time—maybe he'll be too tired after the service to talk to her. Besides, what will he think? That she's crazy, that's what.

And she probably is.

The people begin returning to their seats and Father Mike intones a few more words and then he and the nun place the goblet and other items into a wooden cabinet. Jenna sits stiffly, averting her eyes from the crowd as the people stream past, heading for the large doors behind her.

She searches the crowd, looking for him, wondering if he will even come to the back of the church. Maybe she should go up front, in case he leaves that way. As she heads up the aisle, against the flux of people, she comes face to face with Mrs. Freund, heavily scented with lilac and dressed in her usual cloth coat, the one she wears when she walks her cat.

"Jenna!" she warbles. "I had no idea you were a member of this parish."

Jenna searches the dark area around the old woman. "Where's your cat?"

Mrs. Freund snorts. "Who would bring a cat to church?" Mrs. Freund regards her with that usual look—pity.

Jenna's face grows hot. What a stupid thing to stay. "Of course," she stammers. "How silly of me. What I meant to say is that I saw your cat earlier today. I—I hope she came home." She peers again around Mrs. Freund, this time looking for Father Mike. Is he still there? Maybe she missed him.

"He."

Jenna frowns. "I'm sorry. What?"

Mrs. Freund clasps her hands in front of her buttoned-up coat. "The cat is a he." She lifts her chin. "His name is Beauregard. My husband, Harvey—rest his soul—adored that cat. And, yes, Beauregard came home. He'd dashed out earlier and was gone for a while but returned just before I left for church." Mrs. Freund narrows her eyes at Jenna. "You saw Beauregard?"

Jenna nods. "He ran into my kitchen. I tried to catch him, but he growled, and I was afraid he might bite. Or scratch."

Mrs. Freund nods, smiling. "Thank you for trying to catch him, but he's a finicky creature. Best not to touch him." Mrs. Freund folds her arms over her chest. "But, Jenna, as I said: I didn't know you were a member of this parish."

"I'm not." Jenna averts her gaze. "Just here to meet someone."

"Who?" Mrs. Freund looks around at the crowd and suddenly there he is, smiling and striding down the aisle toward them, his robes billowing out behind as he walks briskly toward her.

The tension drains from her shoulders. She hadn't even noticed she was tense until the sight of him coming toward her washes it away.

"Who are you meeting?" Mrs. Freund repeats.

"A friend." Jenna wishes she would just *leave*.

Mrs. Freund looks at Father Mike then back at Jenna, her eyebrows hiked high. "I see. Well, have a good evening, dear." She reaches in her pocket and pulls out a pair of slim leather gloves. As she puts them on, she moves toward the exit, glancing over her shoulder twice, her brow furrowed.

Jenna turns her back on Mrs. Freund and slides into the last pew. Mike steps in from the aisle and sits beside her. "What a surprise to see you at Mass."

"I really didn't come for Mass, Father Mike."

He draws back and holds up his hands. "Please—call me Mike." Jenna glances at his robes and he laughs, leaning back in the pew. His cheeks turn distinctly pink. "I guess I should expect that, wearing an outfit like this."

She smiles. "I'm glad you're dressed like that, actually. Like a priest, I mean. I need to ask you a question about God."

He flinches a little, or maybe she imagines it, since he just smiles. "I've been known to have a few opinions on that topic." His smile crinkles the skin around his eyes, as usual, but now there's something sad there as well. Curious.

She opens her purse and pulls out the little broken doll. "I found this in my kitchen today. I don't know how long it's been there, but I think it may be a message."

He shudders. "What do you mean by message?"

"You know—a message from God."

He visibly flinches this time and looks away for a long moment. He sighs, heavily, then turns back to her, reaching for the doll. "May I?" She hands it to him and he turns it over in his hands, inspecting it. "Tell me. Why do you think this is a message?"

"Because, before I found it today, I'd seen it in my dreams. Multiple times." She takes a deep breath. "I've been having nightmares all week. This doll was in every one of them and now here it is."

He shakes his head. "I don't understand. Is this yours? From childhood I mean."

"That could be it. I really don't know." She stares at the wooden pew in front of her. She thinks she should be able to feel something, but all that's there is an aching emptiness. It swells inside her, creating an unbearable pressure that doesn't let up until she says, "I don't remember *anything*. It's like I've lost who I was, even though I have no idea when this happened, no idea who I might have been." Now that she's started talking, she can't seem to stop. The words gush out, welling up from what she thought had been a deep hole of nothingness. "All I know for certain is I'm working at a mind-numbing job, getting older by the minute, living in a dingy apartment all alone. I think I should know more about why my life is like this, but I don't." She shrugs, staring at him, certain she's making zero sense.

"But why do you think this doll is a message?"

She notices he doesn't say "message from God," and wonders if that's significant, but can't imagine why. Could he mean message from someone else? She takes the doll from him and strokes the rough tangled hair. She places a fingertip in the hole where the arm should be. It all looks and seems so familiar. She's seen it a thousand times, a million times, and not just in her dreams—but where? "It was in my dream, which I had before that cat knocked it out from behind some stuff in my kitchen. And there's this little girl in the dream as well. She's always chasing a kite. A kite with a tail—long colored streamers." He stares at her, his eyes grown wide, so she goes on. "I've had that dream so many times." A wave of exhaustion washes over her. "Ever since I saw that damn kite I've been plagued with these dreams. I just don't get it—"

He lifts a hand. "Hold it."

"Oh, I'm sorry. I didn't even think of what I was saying. I didn't mean to swear, here in church, in front of you. It just popped out."

He shakes his head. "No, no. It's not that. Jenna, where did you see a kite?"

"What?"

"You just said you had these dreams after you saw a kite—where?"

"It was that day we met—in the park, remember? It wasn't a kite, exactly. More the remains of one, tangled up in the branches of a tree. When the wind blew the leaves away, I saw it." Her palms have grown moist and her heart is beating harder, as if just thinking about that sight has brought on a hint of fear.

He sits stock-still and looks at her. "It's in a tree at the park?"

"Yes, the wind blew the leaves off and that's when I saw these colorful streamers. Like ribbons, blue, purple and green."

"The flag of many colors."

"What?"

He shakes his head. "The wind blows where it wishes," he says. "You hear its sound but don't know where it comes from or where it goes."

"I don't understand—"

"I have all these bits of scripture floating in my head, you know. They just pop out at odd moments. That last one is a passage from the book of John." He averts his eyes for a brief moment, then looks back. "The wind is often a way of talking about spirit—in this case, the spirit of God."

"So, you *do* think it's a message from God."

He suddenly sits upright and slaps his hands on his thighs. "I'm starving—want to get some pizza?"

She stares at him. He's grinning. Those crinkly eyes again. It's like he's secretly delighted about something, as if there's a joy inside him that escapes through his eyes when he looks at her. Her gaze wanders from his face to his shoulders and chest and down to his robe-clad body. He's a large man and she's not sure the robe really suits him. "Sure." She smiles at him. "Pizza sounds good."

MIKE EXCUSES HIMSELF to change out of his robe. What in the hell made him ask this young woman out? *If* he's actually "asked her out." He really doesn't know if going for pizza would qualify, but she's come to him this time, after all, clearly in need of a chance to talk. He shouldn't take time for pizza, although he *is* hungry. He never did get any lunch.

He saw her come in as he was consecrating the Host. She'd slid into the back pew, probably hoping no one would notice her there. He'd noticed, though, and now he can't stop thinking about what she'd said about the remains of a kite at the park, colorful ribbons tangled among the tree branches.

Beneath the black waters. Under the flag of many colors.

This young woman—Jenna—seems seriously disturbed, maybe suffering from some sort of mental illness, but is he any better himself? He's talking to angels, for Christ's sake. Where does he get off thinking he can help someone like her, someone who has serious problems?

After he's in street clothes, he hurries down the darkened stairs toward the sanctuary where Jenna will be waiting for him. He needs an excuse to get out of this ill-thought-out "date." He'll have to apologize for suggesting pizza, tell her "something has come up," maybe a parishioner needs him. It's only a white lie—some parishioner *always* needs him.

As he enters the dim stony interior of the church, still smelling of burning wax although the altar candles have been extinguished, he sees her in the back pew, shoulders slumped forward, looking at a small notebook. Waiting patiently. She turns when he steps in. Even in the dim light he can see how sad she is.

He sighs, deflated. Here is someone in need, someone who has come to him for help. How can he turn his back? He may have made a mockery of his vows once today, but he doesn't have to destroy another soul doing it again. He plasters a smile on his face and strides confidently toward her.

6

THEY WALK TO THE PIZZA PLACE at the corner. After ordering a large pepperoni with extra cheese at the counter, Mike suggests a booth at the back. People stare as they pass, some of them smiling shyly. At first Jenna thinks they're looking at her, but quickly realizes it's his collar that has drawn their attention. Perhaps they recognize him from church.

They reach their booth and he stops, unbuttoning his coat. He seems curiously quiet. Jenna asks, "Does it bother you? When people stare at you like that?"

"It does." He hangs both their coats on a hook by the booth. "I miss the days when I could walk into a place like this and be invisible."

She slides into the booth. The restaurant is warm and steamy and smells of toasted cheese and garlic. "It must be difficult to be on display all the time."

He sits across from her. "It comes with the territory. And I knew what I was getting into when I went to seminary."

He looks so tired. A surge of affection for him rushes into her chest. What must it be like to be so conspicuously different from everyone around you? "I can't even imagine doing something like that," she says. "Going to seminary, I mean. What made you decide to go into the ministry?"

"I ask myself that a lot."

She pauses for a moment, trying, but failing, to read his expression. "Surely you don't regret it."

He clasps his hands together on the table, staring at his thumbs. "A little." He looks up at her, searching her face. "You give up a lot of normal stuff, things everyone else takes for granted, you know? So, yes, I'd say I do regret it. Sometimes."

He stares out at the room, the people hurrying in through the door, unwrapping their scarves, hanging up their coats. Dishes clank and muffled shouts come from the kitchen. Waitstaff rush up and down the aisle, carrying steaming pans. Two young boys a few booths down are both tugging at the same slice of pizza. Dangling strings of cheese cause them to giggle as they pull at it with their chubby fingers.

Jenna smiles. "I never come here. It always seems too crowded, but it's actually nice."

Mike sits back in the booth. "I come here too often, probably. I think it reminds me of home. With five boys and three girls underfoot, my parents' home was a lot like this."

"Where did you grow up?"

"Jersey."

"Really! Me too—in the Cherry Hill area. Where in Jersey are you from?"

"Trenton suburbs. The Albertinos have been there for three generations." He pauses, smiling, lost in thought.

He seems to want to talk about himself, which is just as well. Jenna asks, "You said five boys and three girls?"

He nods. "I'm the fifth of eight."

"I can't imagine being in such a large family. I have only one brother."

"The one who should have been a priest?"

She grins. "I'm surprised you remember that."

"I remember what people say when it seems significant. And this did."

"Why?"

He shrugs. "Maybe because he sounds a little bit like me. Like—you know, like you'd understand me a little better because of him." Red creeps into his cheeks.

He really does want to talk about himself. She wonders, again, about the broken doll in her purse but pushes the thoughts away. Hopefully there will be time to talk about it later. She's so tired of dwelling on her own life, tired of trying to figure things out, to find ways to scare herself, to be normal again.

"I'd like to understand you better," she says. "Tell me how it is you decided to go to seminary."

"I'd thought of it for years, actually, but never told a soul. Not my parents. Certainly not my brothers and sisters. My parents are good Catholics and they raised us in the church, but not a one of my siblings has turned out to be religious." He laughs, tugging at his collar. "Obviously I was the anomaly, but when I went to college, I chose pre-med as a major, not wanting to face what I was feeling. I wanted to help people, I guess, and it seemed a way to do that. My parents were thrilled, too, at the prospect of a doctor in the family."

She can see him as a doctor. He has a way of listening to you that's very doctor-like. "Did you go to med school before seminary?"

"No—never got far with the med school idea. I was already thinking about the priesthood." A darkness flits across his face and he looks away, distracted. When he looks back at her, he says, "When I should have been taking the MCATs and filing my applications, I dropped out of school. Went to Europe for a year."

"I wanted to do that," she says, remembering that she once did want it, but not sure if she ever took a trip. Yet another thing she's forgotten. She shakes herself back to attention. He's looking at her with a quizzical expression, so she asks, "What did you do in Europe?"

He smiles. "Absolutely nothing. Rode a lot of trains. Went from one country to another, stayed in youth hostels, visited every museum and church known to man, probably. After a while I realized I was just running—away from my call. You know."

She shakes her head. "No, actually I don't know. What does that mean?"

"You know, my message from God."

She thinks of her notebook with its list of scribbled clues. "I wish I could be as sure as you that God sends messages."

He smiles. "I didn't say I was sure."

A waiter approaches their booth with a bubbling pan of pizza. "Here you go," the waiter says, sliding the pizza onto the table between them. A luscious scent floats up to Jenna and she realizes it actually smells good—maybe the first time food has been appealing in months. After the waiter leaves, Mike puts a slice on a cheap paper plate for her.

"Thanks," she says, taking the plate from him. "So, why did you go to seminary then? I mean, if you were 'running away,' as you said."

"I asked myself the same question after the first year when my class had dwindled to just two guys. We started with two dozen, you know, but within twelve months it was down to just Dave and myself. It seems the others knew something we didn't."

She blows on the steaming slice and gingerly takes a bite, then wipes her mouth with a napkin. "That must've been discouraging. Did you think of quitting too?"

"You know, I really didn't. I didn't allow any doubts to surface until well after I was ordained. I'd felt something during those travels in Europe, something compelling—something I was chasing, I guess you'd say." He takes a bite of pizza and chews thoughtfully for a moment. "It was only after I got to St. Rita's that I started to wonder if I'd made the right decision."

"Why then? What happened?"

"Oh, nothing actually *happened*—the bishop just always makes it clear that the very existence of the parish is in question." He stops for a moment, coloring slightly. "I don't know why I'm telling you this. I shouldn't be talking about it." She starts to answer, but he says, "What the hell. I've already spilled most of it out. The problem is actually money. Not such a huge thing, I suppose, but it's been an uphill battle the whole time I've been there."

"Well, I'm glad you didn't drop out. They're lucky to have you at that church."

"Well, thanks," he says, brightly. "I think I needed to hear that." He takes another large bite then scrubs at his lips with a napkin. "All I've done is talk about myself. I'm seriously failing at being a priest tonight."

She waves her hand. "It's okay. Really. I'm pretty tired of my own problems, anyway, to tell you the truth."

He nods. "I can understand—but maybe we should talk about it more anyway." He pushes his soggy paper plate to the side and folds his hands together on the table. "Tell me more about this doll."

"I'm not sure there's anything to tell. I just feel like it showed up in my dream for a reason—like a message. You know?"

"You say you don't remember the doll, that the first place you saw it was in a dream, right? But isn't it possible you've had it for some time and just forgot?"

"So, you don't think it's a message then?"

He shakes his head. "I didn't say that. And I don't know, actually, but you said yourself you can't remember much of anything for the last five years." He shrugs. "Maybe this is just one more thing you've forgotten."

She stares at her clasped hands, propped on the table in front of her. He's trying to be kind, she can see that, but anger flares in her chest. She'd hoped he could help her, but he isn't behaving like a priest. Why is he so quickly dismissing the idea that the doll is a message from God?

"Jenna, listen to me." He reaches across the table and grabs her hand. His hand is warm. And soft. She's immediately comforted by the gesture, but why is he holding her hand? "I'm concerned that you seem to have some sort of amnesia. Maybe just partial, but it's still concerning to me. Have you seen a doctor?"

"No." She pauses, watching a man with white-blond hair dressed in jeans and a slouchy sweatshirt walk past staring at them. "Or maybe I should say I don't *remember* seeing a doctor. I suppose it's possible I did see one and then forgot."

The blond man stops and comes back to their booth. His spiky hair is covered with a lot of hair gel. He's unshaven and has a crooked nose, like it was broken once and didn't heal right. "Jennifer!" he says, looking at her. Now that he's closer, she can smell beer on his breath.

"No, sorry," she says. "You must've mistaken me for—"

He snaps his fingers. "That's not it. *Jenna*. Right?"

He looks vaguely familiar to her. Maybe someone who works at Columbia? Or someone else she's forgotten?

"It's Josh. Remember? We met at—uh, at McGinty's a few months ago? I think that was it. At Happy Hour? I think you and your friend came in after yoga class."

"Oh, yes." She forces a smile. She doesn't remember him at all, but that means nothing. Howard mentioned somebody named Josh, but it's probably a coincidence. Josh is a common name. Mike is staring at her, his eyes wide. "Oh, I'm sorry. Josh, this is Father Mike."

The two men shake hands and Josh backs away. "Didn't mean to interrupt."

"It's okay," Mike says. "We're about done here anyway."

"Say, Jenna," Josh says, jamming both his hands into his front jean pockets. "Steve is having a few people over to watch the game tonight. Mona is coming." He rocks back on his heels. "If you'd like to join us, I mean—"

She shakes her head. "Mona? I don't think I know a Mona. Or Steve either."

He snaps his fingers again. "Not Mona. *Monica.*" He grins. "Sorry. Having a bit of trouble with names tonight. Monica and Steve—you met him that night at McGinty's, too. Remember? Anyway, they seem to be hitting it off—if you know what I mean." He shoots a chagrined look at Mike. "Oops—sorry, Father. I didn't mean—"

Mike waves his hand as if it doesn't matter, but Jenna sees a flash of anger in his eyes. "No problem," Mike says, then looks at her, raising his eyebrows.

"Do you mind?" Jenna says. "Maybe I should go with Josh. Might do me good to spend some time relaxing with friends." Why is she "out" with a priest, a totally unavailable guy, when a perfectly acceptable man, albeit one she really doesn't remember meeting, is inviting her out? She wonders, briefly, if this is one of those times she should be afraid, but her still-unmarried status at an age verging on forty looms in front of her like a wall she'll never surmount. What's there to be afraid of?

Josh stands patiently, his hands hidden in his pockets. Mike looks at her, saying nothing. Josh is a bit young, but what does that matter? "Why not," she says, laughing. "When's the game?"

A broad smile spreads across his face. "Starts in about an hour." He points to the back of the restaurant. "I'll just duck in the restroom. The pizza I'm picking up should be ready soon. We can walk to Steve's place from here."

"Okay, then. I'll meet you up front in a little bit."

After Josh disappears into the back hallway, Mike explodes. "Jenna, what are you doing?"

"Uh—sorry?"

"Are you sure about this guy?"

"What do you mean?"

"You don't seem to know him. You're going to just go to his apartment?"

He's right, of course. She doesn't know the guy at all. Any sane person would be more cautious. Maybe this *is* that lack of fear again. She can never really tell, so she asks, "Is there something about Josh I didn't notice?"

Patches of red spread up Mike's neck and into his face. He looks away, then back at her. "I may be too suspicious, but it just seems odd to me that you would agree to go somewhere with a guy who can't even remember your name."

She stares at the table for a while. "I see what you mean. This is the other thing I'm concerned about." She looks up, searching his face. "I—I don't seem to feel fear anymore."

"You don't?" He looks shaken. "Is that even possible?"

She shakes her head. "You would think this is something a person would want. I mean, who wouldn't wish to be free of fear? Wouldn't it be *wonderful* to be fearless?" she asks, sarcasm dripping from her words. She's shaking now, overcome more with anger at her inability to function normally. "It's far from wonderful, though, Mike. It's awful. I feel like a freak. I step in front of cars, stand on top of buildings, go into darkened alleyways—in any situation that would lead a normal person to be afraid, I feel nothing."

He stares. "You stand on top of buildings?"

"Yes—I tried that one a few weeks ago. Out of sheer desperation."

"It was the Columbia Health building."

She frowns. "How—?"

He shakes his head, sighing. "Okay—here's the thing. I saw you up there that day. I—I thought you were going to jump."

"Wait." She stares at him. "You *saw* me?"

"Yes—I and a couple dozen other people. We saw you and watched for several long agonizing minutes as you teetered on that wall. We were sure you were going to jump but were so relieved when you didn't." He lets out a big breath. She thinks she sees a tiny glint of tears in his eyes. "It was really scary."

"Well, at least someone was scared."

He stares at her, aghast. "Of course we were scared. Who wouldn't be?"

Who wouldn't be? Jenna Wright, that's who.

Josh appears by their table, hands jammed into his front jeans pockets. "I'll go pick up the pizza at the front counter and we can go to Steve's from there—okay?"

She can feel Mike's gaze on her as she looks up at Josh. "I'm really sorry, but I just remembered that I have some work to do tonight."

Josh's face grows dark and he looks quickly at Mike, then back at her. There's a forced fake-looking smile on Josh's face and he seems angry. "Uh—okay. Maybe another time?"

She nods. "Sure. Sure thing."

After Josh leaves, Mike reaches across the table and grabs her hand again. "Promise me you'll see a doctor. I really don't think I can help you, but you need to talk to somebody about this lack of fear. Not to mention the memory problems."

She nods, trying to stuff the tears that are now stinging her eyes. "So, you thought I was going to jump?" He thinks she's suicidal. That's why he's spending so much time with her.

"Jenna, listen. It's not that I'm saying I won't talk to you again—in fact, I've really enjoyed our conversation tonight." The tears finally spill over her lashes and she wipes them away, refusing to meet his eyes. "Promise me," he says. "Just call a doctor and get this checked out. Okay?"

"I'll call somebody Monday. I promise. But can I see you again?"

"Of course." He smiles. "Anytime, just come on by."

PETE IS STANDING at the take-out counter, waiting for his pizza order when Jenna walks by, her eyes rimmed with red, in the company of that priest again. What's going on with her? Is she having an affair with a *priest*?

He ducks behind a guy with big shoulders, hoping she hasn't spotted him. Jenna and the priest keep on walking, apparently unaware Pete is there watching them. They step outside as Pete waits impatiently for his order. When it finally arrives, he pays, grabs the pizza box and hurries outside, heading for the church. It's on his way home, after all, but he knows he's spying on them. So be it. She should be more discreet if she doesn't want people to know.

The church is dark and, apparently, locked up for the night. No sign of Jenna or the priest, either, but there's a fellow lurking by the heavy front doors. He's got shockingly white hair, formed with some sort of gel into spikes that stick straight up from his head, in the style popular with those neo-Nazi groups lately.

The heavy front door of the church opens a crack, pushed open from the inside by someone Pete can't make out in the dark. The guy with spiky white hair slips inside, and the door clicks shut behind him.

Pete stands there for a moment, trying to think what to do. After several long, indecisive seconds, he hurries up to the door and pulls at the handle. Locked tight. He steps down to the sidewalk and leans back to look at the round stained-glass window, centered above the massive front doors. A faint light has come on inside from somewhere up high in the top of the church. He waits another few minutes, buffeted by the cold wind, which is surely going to make his pizza inedible if he stays here much longer. Monica has been going on and on about her worries about Jenna, none of which he really understands. There's something going on here, though, something involving this priest—and now involving creepy guys with white hair who seem to be lurking around the priest's church. Pete needs to keep an eye on this. Maybe he can find out something useful for Monica.

The light in the round window has been on for at least ten minutes. Pete's hands are getting cold, as is his pizza, so when the light above finally goes out, he lets his breath out heavily and hurries away, back to his apartment.

MIKE WALKS DOWN THE BOULEVARD, lined with tall buildings that form a sort of urban canyon. He's a block or so from St. Rita's and it's dark, early evening. Drizzle coats the walkway in front of him. Lights from passing cars glint from its rain-slicked surface. Shoppers bundled against the chill hurry past with shopping bags, their coats pulled tightly around their necks.

An explosion rips the night apart, shattering the silence and tossing people outward in a blossom-like pattern. Mike watches as those who have not been toppled turn and stare at the source of the blast: the twisted remnants of a metal garbage container, identical to many that dot this boulevard and streets like it all over the city. Mike looks at the people's faces. Their mouths are open but there's no sound coming out, as if they're trying to scream, but can't. They are no longer looking at the blasted-apart trash can but up, toward the tops of the buildings.

He turns to look. There, on the roof of one of the tallest buildings, is a dark figure with something resembling wings stretching out from its demonic body. It's the angel of death, looking down upon them. "I saw that before," Mike thinks, "but it wasn't like this—it was in the rose window of the church."

His hand wanders to his throat, as if to check for his priest's collar. It's still there of course, but he's yanking at it, tearing at his throat, trying to wrench the collar away and as he gets it free, the scream he's been suppressing finally erupts. Only it's not a scream, it's a guttural explosion of rage—at whoever has done this act of terror, but also rage at the universe and the God who would allow such things to happen.

He hears a small whimper from nearby. "Please." He turns and there's a woman, fallen to the sidewalk, her face splashed with blood. There's more blood on her legs and around her is an ever-widening pool of it. She's wearing a khaki trench coat that's been ripped at the shoulder. A red and blue scarf dangles at her neck, also drenched in blood. "Please help me," the woman says, reaching toward him, and that's when Mike sees her leg—a bloody mass that's more wound than leg.

He reaches for her, but he's too far away, so he tries to take the few steps needed to get to her, but he can't move his legs. He looks down and sees that they are bloodied, too, but his feet are, somehow, stuck to the sidewalk. His legs feel like they're made of stone and no matter how much effort he exerts, he can't walk. He cannot get to the bloodied woman whose cries are becoming increasingly frantic, although fading away.

Mike wakes, drenched in sweat, his heart racing. He shivers violently and sits up, the tangled covers tumbling from his cramped bed onto the floor of his tiny apartment. No sign of any explosion, but there's a flashing red light in the room and when he turns to look out the window, sees the familiar blinking neon sign that says "Bar," directly across the street from the back of the church.

The dream is fading, turning to fuzzy images of shops, a dark shape up above, and then it's gone completely and he's thinking about the bar. There'd been a sign in the window when he walked by earlier, something about happy hour. He wonders if she's there, in the bar. Maybe with her friend. Was her friend's name Monica? He thinks that was it, and he remembers Jenna talking about happy hour. Are the two of them there? Is Jenna in there, drinking and laughing and letting herself get picked up by men who frequent such places? He thinks again of the guy at the pizza place the other night who tried to pick her up. Mike had thought at the time the guy looked familiar—but why?

There's something he's forgetting. Something about an explosion. Blood. A dark-winged creature atop a tall building. What is he remembering? Maybe it's a dream he's remembering. Or something he saw on the news? So many things like that have been on the news lately—well, no dark-winged creatures atop buildings. That's only for Mike, apparently, but everyone is plagued by the rest: plenty of explosions, terrorist attacks, gunmen in schools. And those neo-Nazi groups, white supremacists who have become emboldened, meeting openly and threatening violence on all who don't share their vision of what society should be.

It's like they live in a war zone. It's like they're all soldiers in an unseen war, expected to weather the horror of battle, but without help.

Jenna had claimed she couldn't feel fear. He'd read of a few cases like that, back in his pre-med days, during his senior project—and they were all traceable to some sort of brain damage, usually to the amygdala. Yet again, he wonders if he might have made a mistake in abandoning that project, veering away from medicine and going to seminary.

He flops back to his damp pillow and rubs his eyes. He's sure she's there, in the bar. He could put on some clothes—no collar, though—and just walk over and find her, let her know he's been thinking of her. It would be so easy, and yet it's impossible.

He can't do it. He knows this. He can't just walk into a bar and find the girl he can't stop thinking about, buy her a drink, tell her he can't get her out of his mind. He can't do that.

He's a priest.

THE NEXT DAY, Mike heads out of the church to the boulevard. It's Sunday afternoon and he's finished with his duties for the day. Tomorrow is, supposedly, his "day off," although he's got that broken radiator to deal with again. The repair held for a week and then it stopped working again. More money down the drain.

The Christmas shopping season has started despite the fact it's not even Thanksgiving yet. It's earlier every year. People duck into shops along the boulevard, hurrying down the sidewalk with shopping bags, dodging one another as they make their way around each other. He walks past a shop whose door sports a large green wreath smelling of pine. The bell ringer with his red kettle is already there, set up in his usual place outside the convenience shop near the corner.

Dry snow swirls down the sidewalk and Mike pulls his scarf more tightly around his neck. Green wreaths with red berries hang from the light poles along the curb and a few of the storefronts have installed blinking lights around their plate-glass windows. It's just past four in the afternoon and, at this time of the year, beginning to get dark already. He passes in front of the department store window, inside which is a display with a small decorated tree and a tiny train. As he watches the train go round and round on a track, he catches a glimpse of a priest inside.

It takes him a moment to realize he's seeing his own reflection in the glass. It was the collar that caught his eye and the thought, "a priest—I wonder if it's someone I know," has nearly completed itself in his mind before he realizes his mistake. He stops and turns to the window, looking at himself looking back as the tiny train zips round and round its little track inside the window display.

A man with spiky blond hair passes behind him. Mike can see the man's reflection in the glass and he catches a strong scent of phosphorus, like a large supply of matches. He turns to watch as the white-haired man walks down the sidewalk.

He has a bulky backpack hooked over both his shoulders that looks unnaturally large. He looks a bit like the guy who stopped and said something to Jenna at the pizza place. Mike isn't sure it's him, but the guy's hair has a distinctive blond spike to it. Rather neo-Nazi like, Mike thinks, although that's the style lately, apparently, judging from the young people who frequent his Saturday five p.m. Mass these days. He's sure he's seen the guy somewhere.

He remembers, then, the man in his confessional—the knit cap, the spikes of whitish hair poking out, the odd confession. Is it him? Is it the same man?

The blond guy stops next to a large metal trash container and turns to look around. It's as if he realizes Mike is looking at him.

Mike edges closer to a nearby building and watches. The guy seems agitated, looking first up the street, then down, his gloved-hand yanking repeatedly at the backpack strap looped over his shoulder.

A woman, laden with shopping bags and wearing a khaki trench coat and high-heeled boots, passes the blond guy, heading his way. Mike stares at her blue and red scarf. Time slows, as if the hands of the celestial clock that governs the universe have gotten stuck in molasses.

It's her. The woman in his dream. The one whose leg was blown off.

She walks toward him, unaware of the danger that Mike can feel crackling in the air around him. Her head is down. Her heels click on the cement walk. Mike stares, watching the guy with the spiky hair shrug the backpack off his shoulders. He drops it in the large metal trash can and turns, walking rapidly away from Mike.

It all comes together in Mike's mind faster than he can follow the sequence of thoughts, and before he knows what he's doing, before he's decided to do anything, he's moving, lunging for the woman, wrapping his arms around her. He can smell her perfume, something expensive, as he wrestles her toward the building, twisting her away from where he knows the blast will be coming any second now.

The woman screams, "What are you doing?" She lands hard on her knee. Blood pours through her torn stocking. "Why did you do that?" She stares at his collar, confusion mixed with anger on her face. Her eyes turn slightly and she's looking over his shoulder and the anger on her face turns to fear—

Mike puts his hand on the back of her head, pushing her down to the walkway. He curls his body over hers as the explosion rips through the twilight. The scent of something acrid blasts him, burning his nostrils, as shards, hard and sharp, pummel his back. And it's happening, just like in his dream, except the woman isn't hurt, not the way he'd feared. Her leg is intact, although she's scraped her knee, and she's screaming and crying and, now, clinging to him. "Oh my God, oh my God, oh my God," she says, over and over.

And he's shushing her and holding her head to his chest even as the pain spreads across his shoulder blades and he can feel the hot wetness of his own blood seeping through his coat where something (shrapnel from the metal can?) has pierced his back. He knows he's done the right thing, but how did he know?

It was just a dream he'd had. Not a premonition, right? But how else can he explain this? He knew what the blond man was going to do—

He lifts his head and looks around behind him. Twisted scraps of metal are scattered around a burning object, probably the remains of the backpack. The man with the spiky white hair is nowhere in sight. Another man in a food-stained white apron with rolled up sleeves rushes out of his shop, the pizza place where Mike and Jenna had eaten just the other night. It's the owner—he remembers now. He comes to Mass sometimes. The owner reaches into his pants pocket and pulls out a cellphone, punching numbers, and when he looks up, spotting Mike, he shouts, "Father, you okay?"

Mike nods, although he knows he's not okay. He's far from okay.

Part Two

7

THE EXPLOSION HAS CRACKED THE GLASS of the pizzeria's front window and blown out one pane from the door of the shop next to it. The woman's knee is bleeding. She doesn't seem to be seriously hurt, but is shaking and clinging to Mike's arm, crying. Over and over she says, "Thank God you were here. Thank God."

When the police show up, red and blue lights twirling in the twilight, the first person out of the police car is the same detective Mike spoke to at the station. He stops short as Mike stands to greet him. "Don't tell me," Detective Sloan says. "You just had a *feeling* there was going to be trouble tonight, right?"

Mike averts his eyes, struggling to quell the flash of anger that balloons up inside him. "I was heading back to the church," he says between clenched teeth. "I saw this guy drop a large backpack in the garbage can." He shrugs, deflated, unable to tell the full truth. *I saw it happen in a dream. I knew it was happening again.* "Something clicked," he finally says. "I—I can't fully explain how I knew what was about to happen."

Sloan sighs and pulls out a notepad. As the paramedics arrive and begin to tend to the injured, Mike gives his description of the bomber: spiky blond hair, light-colored jacket and sneakers, jeans. The medics check Mike out as well but find only superficial wounds. They urge him to wash when he gets home and give him sharply scented antibiotic ointment to smear on his back. The woman he'd pushed to the sidewalk has only minor injuries, just a skinned knee, but she's panicked, and the paramedics put her on a stretcher anyway. As Mike watches them leave, the detective thanks him for his help and moves on to interview another witness.

Mike worries all week that Sloan will show up at St. Rita's, bearing a warrant for his arrest, but it never happens. He can barely keep his mind on his work. Images from the bloody afternoon repeatedly invade his thoughts: the phosphorus scent he'd smelled as the bomber walked past; the flash of light followed by the loud bang; the woman's bloody knee, her pleading face; Sloan's skeptical gaze as he scribbled notes while taking Mike's statement.

Mike spends an inordinate amount of time on the internet searching for information about, first, the bombing and, later, the other thing he can't stop thinking about. He has an idea about what's going on with Jenna, a vague sense, but it's only when he finally stumbles on a string of articles in the local newspaper from some eighteen months before that he begins to sort it out. He prints the pages from the archived articles, knowing what he should do, but not wanting to do it.

And then, before Mike can truly process any of it, it's Sunday and he's celebrating three Masses in a row, and people are mobbing him after each service, wanting to introduce their visiting relatives, wanting to shake his hand, wanting to talk to him about getting their child into St. Rita's preschool, wanting to tell him how wonderful the sermon was, and on and on.

Mike does not believe the comments about his sermon at all—he'd cobbled it together in fifteen minutes, stringing together a bunch of platitudes like *God is with us* and *Be not afraid*. All the while he was preaching, he knew he was a total hypocrite: He *was* afraid. As afraid as he'd ever been. He thinks often of Jenna and her lack of ability to feel fear. How nice that would be—for himself, but also for all the panicky people around him.

When he finally breaks free of the grasping horde that is his parish, he heads to his tiny apartment. Despite his congregation's shrinking numbers, they are simply too much for him. He falls into bed, exhausted, and sleeps for almost ten hours. It's a dreamless sleep for which he is grateful after he awakes, although he can't seem to get up to face the day. He lies in bed staring at the ceiling for almost an hour, trying not to think what he's thinking. Angels, premonitions, bombings right outside his church—what is going on? If there's a deeper message in all of this, if there truly is a God that's trying to get a message to him, Mike wishes He were more articulate.

He needs someone to talk to, someone who communicates in English, not signs. He finally gets out of bed, has a quick breakfast and heads to his old rusted-out Toyota, parked in its usual spot behind St. Rita's school. A half-hour later, he pulls into the hospital parking lot, switches off the engine and fishes in the glove compartment for his pass. When he finds it, emblazoned with the words "Hospital Chaplain," he clips it to his front pocket and heads inside. The place smells like it always does: an antiseptic scent mixed with floor cleaner. It's not his day for chaplain duty, but he hopes Ted is on the schedule. He heads for the tiny chapel that is just off the lobby.

As Mike comes around the corner, he notices Ted near the chapel, talking quietly to an older man and woman. The couple's shoulders are hunched forward—in worry or, possibly, grief. Mike holds back, waiting for Ted to finish with them, trying to look inconspicuous—although he has that damn collar on again and people passing in the hallway keep giving him the inevitable double take. Ted has his collar on as well, of course, but it looks absolutely normal on him—as if the white band has become a permanent part of his body.

Ted glances up and sees him then. He says something to the couple, pats the woman on the shoulder and shakes the man's hand. As they shuffle away, Ted smiles and walks toward him.

"Fancy meeting you here." Ted grins, but his smile fades as he takes in Mike's expression. "Is one of your parishioners in the hospital?"

Mike shakes his head. "No, nothing like that. I was hoping to find you, actually. Do you have a minute?"

"Yes, I just finished the prayer service. Maybe we can talk inside the chapel?"

They enter the darkened space, filled with a sweet floral scent. A half-dozen rows of chairs are set in front of a modest lectern. Behind it is an altar with two unlit candles and a large bouquet of flowers. One of the walls is covered with stained-glass in an abstract pattern. The entire place exudes quiet and calm and a vague hint of religiosity, but with absolutely no overt signs of religion—no cross or crucifix in sight anywhere.

Ted takes a chair and Mike pulls another around to face him. "I'm glad you have a moment. I really don't know where else to turn."

Ted leans forward, frowning slightly. "What is it?"

Mike shrugs and heaves a heavy sigh. "It's that thing I talked to you about before—you know, the angel?" Just saying the word, angel, as if it's something people talk about regularly in casual conversation, makes him flinch.

Ted nods. "Has something happened?"

"Well, I did see that boy again. Or perhaps he's an angel, as you suggested—I don't really know. And then, as if that wasn't enough, there was an explosion right outside the church."

"I saw that on the news. Were you there?"

Mike nods. "The police are investigating, but it seemed like one of those terrorist bombings to me. I saw a guy put a large backpack in a garbage bin—"

Ted's eyes widen. "You saw the bomber?"

Mike nods. "Not only that, but I knew it was going to happen. I—I saw it before—before—"

Ted reaches out and grabs Mike's forearm. "Slow down, Mike. Breathe."

It feels like the blood is draining out of his head, making it difficult to think. He takes a deep breath and looks in Ted's eyes. "I saw it in a dream, Ted. The night before. And then it was happening, just like my dream, and—"

"A premonition."

Mike lets his breath out and sags forward. "It would seem like it." He pauses, watching a variety of expressions roll across Ted's face—curiosity, horror, worry. "The big thing, though, Ted, is that I heard a disturbing confession the other day." Ted watches him silently, waiting for him to go on. He's just going to have to spit it out. "This guy. He came in to the confessional—a street person, I think—and I'd have to say he's mentally ill from the way he talked, but—but—" He looks again at Ted, overcome with a sense of utter helplessness. He takes a deep breath, and plunges in. "He claimed to have killed someone."

Ted draws his breath in and sits back. "Oh my. That *is* a hard one."

Mike nods. "I might have thought the guy was delusional, but like I said before, there was this boy who'd said—I'm still not convinced it was an angel. Of course, I'm not convinced it *wasn't*."

"But wait—what *did* he say? The boy, I mean."

Mike's face grows hot. "I should've told you that before, when I saw you last, but I really didn't believe it myself."

"Mike, tell me what he said, so we can figure out what to do."

A wave of comfort washes through him. *We.* Just knowing that Ted is with him, will *be* with him, is comforting. He hadn't realized until that moment how alone he'd felt in all of this. He clears his throat and goes on. "He warned me, as I said before. It was vague, but the boy said 'he,' whoever that is, was going to kill again. He even pointed to a line of men waiting outside St. Rita's kitchen for lunch, said he was out there—I think one of them was the guy I saw at confession."

Ted is silent for a long moment, thinking. "So, what do you suggest we do?"

"I actually already did something. I went to the police. On Saturday. They took my statement about what I'd heard, but I worry I may have been too late." He pauses, trying to calm himself, but not particularly succeeding. "And then, last night, when the bomb went off—well, that same detective came to investigate."

"It's breaking the sanctity of the confessional, of course," Ted says.

"I know—"

"Father, you know you can't repeat what you hear in there." He glares. "You went to the police."

Mike lets out a big sigh. Of course, but does that matter? He's already violated his vows as it is—big time. "Ted. It's worse. I didn't give him absolution either."

"Why not?"

"I just couldn't—he demanded it, of course, but I couldn't do that."

"How did he 'demand' it?"

"You know—he swore at me, said it was my job to rid him of his sin with a wave of my hand. I heard no remorse, Ted. He barely admitted to any guilt at all."

Ted presses his lips together for a long moment and looks away. When he looks back, he says, "But he was at confession. Surely that should've been enough."

"I know. I'm just saying I'd already gone against my vows by refusing him absolution—so breaking the sanctity of the confessional really doesn't matter anymore, right?"

Ted shakes his head. "I don't know if I agree with that logic." He turns a piercing gaze on Mike's face. "Will your statement to the police help? I mean, if this man *did* kill somebody, do you know any details? Like where the body is?"

"Yes. I know where it is."

Ted's eyebrows arch high. "How do you know *that*?"

Mike stares at his hands clasped together on his knees. "The angel, if that's what that boy is, told me." He looks up, searching Ted's face. "He said the body is in the pond at the park. There's a tattered kite right above the spot."

"Wait. You told the police an *angel* told you?"

"No, no. I'm telling you—and, honestly Ted, I still don't know if that's what that boy is. Was." He pauses, clenching and unclenching his fists, not sure what he's feeling now. Anger? Frustration? The printed pages from his latest computer search are tucked in his pocket, and it feels like they're burning a hole into his chest, straight into his heart. "It's like this, Ted. I think there's a body in that pond. Probably a child. Probably a girl."

"Which girl?"

"It might be Sophie McPherson—you know, the St. Rita's student who went missing months ago."

Ted narrows his eyes. "And the only way you know all this is because an angel told you." He crosses his arms and brings a finger to his lips, tapping at them several times. "The problem is there's no *earthly* reason why you should know where that body is."

"Right." Mike lets his breath out with a heavy sigh. "Now you see my problem." He presses a hand to his chest pocket, aware that the pages he printed earlier are still in there—he should tell Ted this too, but he just can't seem to do it. Not now. Not yet.

IT'S MONDAY AGAIN and Jenna's at work. She'd updated her bulleted list and added two items: "white spiky hair" and "Josh." She still doesn't remember him but searched her phone contacts while still at home. No Josh. She did, though, find a name she doesn't know: a Dr. Peter Andrews. *A doctor.*

There's a stack of claim forms waiting for her attention, but instead of starting on them, she opens the browser and goes straight to Google. Her search returns a long list of links, but the one near the top is purple—as if she's clicked on it before. She goes to the page and there it is in inch-high letters: "Dr. Peter Andrews, Neurology," and below that, "Andrews Neurological Associates," with a photo of an otherwise bland brick building.

She recognizes it immediately. She's been to that building. She's sure of it. This Peter Andrews must be her doctor but, as usual, she has no recollection of him. She pulls out her notebook and copies the address into it. She could just go there on her lunch hour, but maybe there's a quicker way to get the information she needs.

Fingers trembling, she pulls up the company database application. She knows she's not supposed to do this, knows she could be fired for looking up personal records. It's strictly forbidden, as is using company resources for something that has nothing to do with her job. She types it anyway: "Peter Andrews" and clicks the box labeled "Lookup."

The search returns thousands of records. Gynecology, orthopedics, radiology, endless lab tests—all probably irrelevant. She carries out a more complex search, this time cross-linking "Neurology" with Andrews's name. Her second attempt returns a smaller number of records, but still numbering in the thousands.

She tries again, this time including her own name as a third search term. Only forty-eight records this time. And all of them are for Andrews Neurological Associates.

A wave of satisfaction passes through her but promptly turns to something else. She'd say "fear," but what would that feel like? It does worry her, though. Could she really have been to see this doctor forty-eight times and not know it? It seems impossible that she wouldn't remember, but she doesn't. Not a single visit. She clicks on the first record that turns out to be an order for blood work, a complete panel. Nothing unusual to it, although she doesn't remember the test. Two more records have the same uninteresting content: simple blood tests.

The fourth record brings up a screen she's seen only a few times. A bright red banner stretches across the top of the page: SEALED, it says.

"Wow!" Jenna says to her otherwise empty cubicle. She sits back in the chair, stunned. She's only seen this red banner a handful of times before, and always for sensitive procedures—abortions, usually.

Her palm comes to her belly and she looks away from the screen. How could she forget an abortion? For that matter, how could she forget being pregnant? She looks at her hand and notices that she's trembling. She can actually imagine what it feels like to rest her hand on a belly swollen with child—she's seen pregnant women sit that way. She can feel it in her arm and shoulder—the way the elbow bends to lift the hand to the height of a baby bump, the way the shoulder relaxes as the hand rests on the woman's built-in shelf. It's as if her body remembers the sensation of holding a child inside, even though she's never been pregnant.

She refuses to believe such an elaborate fantasy, turns back to the screen and clicks on the red banner. This brings a beep out of the computer and a second box, this one blue. Inside it are the words, SEALED BY ORDER OF DEPARTMENT OF DEFENSE.

Hairs spike to attention on the back of her neck. Is this a glimmer of fear again? She should be excited by the hair standing on end, but this bright blue banner has her worried. Why would the military seal her records? Sam's words float back to her, the ones he'd said as he boarded the plane to Kazakhstan: *You don't need any more stress,* he'd said. *You have your own problems now.*

She punches a few buttons on the computer, takes a screenshot of the red and blue image, prints it while she's pulling on her coat, then folds it into her pocket.

Later that morning as she's on her way to lunch, she walks past the pitted and crumbling front steps of St. Rita's. The door is partly open.

She takes the steps and enters the darkened church with its faint smell of incense and melted wax. The scent brings her immediately back to the evening when she'd sat there, in the back pew, waiting for Mike to finish celebrating Mass. It's a comforting scent, a familiar one, and she wonders again if this is who she was—someone who believed in God. She seems to have no opinion about that one way or another these days, except for this: What's happening to her seems infused with meaning, as if something bigger than her own life is at work here. She wants to believe there's more to Jenna than a job and an achingly empty apartment.

A handful of mostly older women are scattered among the pews, straightening hymnals and dusting. Two women work in a little side chapel polishing silver goblets as soft colored light spills over them through the stained-glass. Three others are at the altar, folding linens. A blue-veiled nun, perhaps the same one who'd been helping Mike with Mass the other night, sits in a chair by the door, a Bible opened up in her lap.

Jenna walks to the seated nun. "Excuse me. I'm looking for Father Mike."

The woman looks up and frowns, her eyes traveling up and down the front of Jenna's body. "Is he expecting you?"

"No, I'm sorry, he isn't. But something's come up. Is he in?"

The nun sighs, closes the Bible and stands up. "I believe someone saw him go out, but I can check."

She walks softly down the hall, leaving Jenna to stand alone in the dim stone-clad interior, idly watching the women work. The place exudes peace, quiet and comfort. A few minutes later, the blue-veiled nun returns. "I'm sorry. The Father is out doing an errand. Perhaps you can try again later? Or I can give him a message."

Jenna reaches into her pocket, idly fingering the printout. She'd wanted to show it to Mike, but it will have to wait. She shakes her head. "No message—I was just dropping by to say hello. I'll try later." She thanks the nun again and heads out the door.

She's got her lunch in her tote bag. Even though it's a bit cold out, the bright noontime sun makes it tolerable, and the sky is a brilliant blue. She heads for the park, and as she approaches it, she sees them: lights. Red and blue lights, all whirling and flashing atop a half-dozen police cars. Brightly colored streamers dangle from the trees, tangled in the branches.

She stops, unable to move. She stares at the scene.

Something snaps in her brain, and Jenna falls to her knees on the dry grass.

The tote bag she'd been clutching tumbles to the ground as she grabs for the side of her head where a searing pain has erupted. It feels like someone has stabbed her in the temple with a knife. A sudden wave of dizziness brings her palms to the grass. She can feel the spiky blades press into her flesh, smell the damp earth, feel the breeze toss her hair around her head. Time slows.

The cold November sun is still shining upon her, but it's as if she's transported from that day to a different one. The dry grass underneath her hands turns soft, the brown color fading to green. The chill in the air disappears, replaced by balmy warmth and a soft breeze. The smells around her shift from dried leaves to sweet spring flowers, reminiscent of daffodils or tulips. She knows this cannot be real, and if her head wasn't hurting so much, she'd find it fascinating.

Jenna, barely able to breathe, watches carefully, with her mind's eye, as something that feels like dozens of tiny spiders inside her head hurry in multiple directions, spinning invisible silky threads of thought, their tiny feet galloping across her brain.

The threads coalesce. An image leaps to mind.

A little girl in a blue coat.

Something hard hits Jenna's forehead and she cries out. Another image.

A little boy holding a string that stretches toward the sky.

Jenna sobs, the pain in her head growing stronger as the spiders increase their activity, weaving, weaving, weaving. A web of images grows inside her head and begins to move, like a video or movie.

The boy's string is attached to a kite from which dangle long ribbons, purple, blue and green.

The little blue-coated girl reaches for Jenna's hand.

Jenna can feel a child's soft tiny hand in hers. She's held this child's hand before. She's sure of it.

A large yellow dog rams into Jenna's legs.

The girl in the little blue coat runs. She's chasing the boy with the kite, laughing.

Jenna is on the ground, on her hands and knees, frozen in place. She must stop the girl, but Jenna can't seem to move.

The little girl is in danger. Great danger.

"You okay, miss?"

A man runs past Jenna, heading for a flying Frisbee. He jumps, trying to catch it, but it hits Jenna in the head. The dog barks, lunging at the Frisbee, its yellow fur flying.

JENNA, ON HER BACK on the spiky dry grass, looks up into a pair of concerned eyes. An older man smelling vaguely of cinnamon and dressed in a faded red sweatshirt, his long gray hair pulled back in a curly ponytail, leans close, worried. "Miss, you all right?"

"I—I—" Jenna tries to speak but can't make words. What has happened? She remembers something about strokes, wonders if she's had one.

"Let me help ya up." The man reaches for her elbow. She notices a gap where one of the man's front teeth is missing. She stumbles to her feet, and he brushes bits of dried grass and twigs from her sleeves. "Are ya all right?" he asks. "Didja fall?"

"Uh—I'm not sure," Jenna says, grateful that her attempt to speak produces words this time. She looks toward the trees across the park where the colorful streamers, blue, purple, neon green, tangled among the arching bare branches, blow about in the breeze. Those ribbons—they mean something, but what?

No police cars, though. No whirling red and blue lights. No crime scene tape. Nothing. How can that be? They were just there. *She'd seen it.*

"Such a shame," the man says. "Reminds me of that day when they found that little girl's body."

"Excuse me?" Jenna realizes she's trembling.

"A'course, the weather was quite different that day." The man gazes at the trees and the fluttering ribbons. "Don't know what made me think of it."

She cannot stop shaking. The images are still there, like a memory now, although she doesn't know what she's remembering. *A little girl, in a blue coat, running after a boy with a kite. A kite with blue, purple and green ribbons streaming after it.*

"So sad." He shakes his head and makes tsking sounds. "But enough of that. How are ya feelin'?"

"Uh—okay, I guess. Yes. I'm fine." She pauses, watching him hover by her elbow. "Thank you."

He narrows his eyes at her. "Well, since yer okay, I think I'll be on my way."

"Yes, yes—thank you, I'm fine."

He nods at her and then walks away.

JENNA IS HEADING IN THROUGH the front doors of the Columbia Health building when Monica runs up. "Jenna. I've been looking all over for you."

"Why?"

"Eleanor came by saying you weren't at your desk, hadn't been there for hours. We were worried. Where were you?"

"I—I just went to lunch." She points down the street toward the park. "Why are you so worried?"

Monica shrugs. "You know—I just thought you might be on the roof again."

Anger flares inside her chest. "Well, I'm not. I've got some things going on, and I just wish you would quit hovering." She pushes past and heads into the lobby.

Monica follows her to the elevator and steps around in front of her. "What kind of things?" she asks, stabbing at the up button.

"I don't know how to explain it. Memory problems, I guess you'd say."

The elevator arrives and Monica steps inside. She holds the door open with one hand and stands there waiting. Jenna steps onto the elevator as the door slides closed behind her, averting her eyes from Monica's probing gaze. The silence hangs in the air, stabbing and full of pain. Jenna tries, without success, to push it away.

When they reach Jenna's floor, she gets off, Monica right behind her. They walk into Jenna's cubicle and Monica says, "Okay. Maybe you should tell me what's *really* going on." She flops into the spare chair. "I assume it has something to do with a priest. A *cute* priest."

Jenna stares. "How do you know about him?"

Monica puts both hands over her eyes and shakes her head. When she pulls her hands away, she says, "It doesn't really matter how I know, but Pete saw you the other night. The two of you were having pizza. Who is he?"

"Just a friend."

Monica folds her arms over her chest and leans back in the chair. "A friend who's a priest. Right."

"He is! He works next door to us—you know, at that old grimy church."

"St. Rita's." Monica chews at her lip. "So what were you out with a priest for?"

Jenna clenches her fists. "I wasn't *out* with him. I came by to ask him a question and he suggested pizza—that's it."

Monica lets a blast of air out through her nose. "*What* question?"

She can see she'll never get rid of Monica until she tells her at least some of this, so she wakes up her computer and pulls up the record she'd found that morning. The red banner reading "SEALED" glows at her from the screen. She turns it a few degrees to the side so Monica can see. "Look at this."

Monica scoots her chair closer and peers at the screen. "What is it?"

"It's one of my own claims."

Monica sucks in air between her teeth, whistling. "Oh my." She shakes her head and turns a sad face toward Jenna. "Did you have an abortion?"

Jenna shakes her head. "I'm not sure, but I don't think so. I think it's something much worse."

"What could be worse? Wait. How can you *not know* if you had an abortion?"

Tears sting Jenna's eyes. "That's just it. I *can't* remember. Not that. Not much of anything, actually."

Monica frowns. "I don't understand what you mean. You don't remember—?"

"Just watch." Jenna clicks on the red banner, revealing the second blue box: "SEALED BY ORDER OF DEPARTMENT OF DEFENSE."

Jenna stares at her hands in her lap for a long moment. Finally, she looks up. "I'm not sure what's going on, but the entire last five years seem extremely vague to me." She nods toward the screen. "Something tells me this medical procedure, whatever it is, has something to do with why that is. Of course, I have no idea *what* it is, since it has this seal on it."

Monica stares at her. "What in the world does the Defense Department have to do with you?" She thinks for a long moment, staring at the blinking blue box on the screen. "Let me try something." She grabs Jenna's keyboard and taps the keys. She clicks the mouse a few times, then peers closely at the screen. "Voila," she says, beaming. "I got past the seal."

Jenna's mouth falls open. "How did you do that?"

Monica grins. "It helps to have friends in IT. Pete showed me how to circumvent the security code." She turns the monitor to the side so Jenna can see. "Look at this," she says pointing at the dense block of text on the screen.

Bits of words and fragments of sentences leap at her from the dense paragraph: *amygdala… partial resection… PTSD*. And then, about halfway down the screen, she sees it, in big block letters nestled in the thick medical jargon: SQUID.

"Look. There's that squid thing again."

"I know—that's what I was showing you. But *why* is it in *your record*?"

Jenna shrugs. "Let's see. 'Partial resection' means they've removed part of the brain, right?" She realizes she's started to shake. "And didn't you look up that squid acronym and find out it has something to do with brain cells?" She rubs at her scalp.

Monica stares at her, eyes wide. "Well, maybe this explains why you can't remember some things." She leans forward, peering intently at Jenna. "What are we going to do?"

Jenna pulls back. "We?"

"Yes. *We*. You don't think you're going to tackle this on your own, do you?" She shakes her head and looks away, out through the cubicle opening into the darkened hallway. "Maybe Pete can help us find out more—"

"No, Monica." Jenna stands up. "I—I don't know what's going on anymore than you do, but let's just keep this to ourselves now, okay?"

"But why? Why shouldn't we get whoever we can to help?"

"I don't know, but there must be a reason why my records were sealed. And by the government, no less."

"Maybe so." Monica leans to Jenna's keyboard and clicks a few keys. "Here—let's print this out so we can read it, at least try to figure out what they did."

As the paper curls out of Jenna's printer, two pages covered with dense text she knows she won't be able to understand, the first glimmer of an idea forms. *Why shouldn't we get whoever we can to help?*

Why indeed—and Jenna realizes she knows just the person to ask.

8

WHEN JENNA GETS HOME THAT NIGHT, she goes into the bathroom, turns on all the lights, and combs through her hair with her fingers, searching her reflection in the mirror for anything out of the ordinary on her scalp. Nothing's there—no scar, no sign her brain might have been operated on. Nothing consistent with a "partial resection of the amygdala" she'd found in her claim form.

Maybe the claim is fraudulent. It's happened, people have submitted bogus claims before, but it would be the first time it had been done using her own name. She goes to the sofa and reaches for her bag, pulling out the sheets of paper they'd printed earlier, after Monica had broken the seal on her records. She settles back into the sofa cushions and reads:

> *Patient presented with severe post-traumatic stress (PTS) symptoms and was identified as a good candidate for treatment with the extinction training protocol developed at Hopkins. Administration of a drug regimen designed to shut down specific glutamate A1 receptors in the amygdala was carried out over several days. A unique drug-delivery system utilizing magnetic beads moved to the target zone via a superconducting quantum interference device (SQUID) was used. Monitoring of progress in severing the associated neural circuitry was also accomplished using SQUID-facilitated imaging. Successful suppression of the*

> PTSD *response was ascertained both from* SQUID *data and interviews with the patient using a battery of triggering questions. Further confirmation of successful treatment was achieved by measuring the amounts of calcium-permeable* AMPA *receptor protein in the associated brain region. Functional magnetic resonance (fMRI) scans are included in the appendices attached to this claim. The results of all follow-up tests were consistent with successful chemical resection of the amygdala. We conclude that this procedure, although still classified as experimental by the* FDA, *is equivalent to surgical removal and should be classified, for insurance purposes, as an allowed alternative to clinically established fear amelioration treatments.*

The claim details are written in the usual medical jargon, filled with words she really doesn't understand. The phrase in that last sentence, "equivalent to surgical removal," causes the hairs on the back of her neck to stand at attention. She rubs at them, marveling at yet another glimmer of fear, not wanting to hope that it's back. What does it all mean? It sounds like they've done something they call "chemical resection" and are claiming it's the same as taking out part of the brain.

If all of this really happened, of course.

Of course, if it really happened like this, there would be no scar. There might, though, be other signs.

Signs like memory loss.

In her job, Jenna never needs to truly understand the medical detail that peppers the innumerable claim forms that cross her desk every day. Her job is merely to convert handwritten information to digital form and to assign codes. She's never before had to fully understand the procedures themselves—but this time she does. The best she can tell, she's been treated with some sort of drug—a drug that, apparently, did to her brain what a surgeon would do with a knife. She needs someone who can read this and interpret the jargon. The idea she'd been formulating earlier begins to gel. She needs to consult an expert and she knows just the guy: Mike Albertino.

Sleep eludes her that night. The wind buffets her bedroom window repeatedly, howling through a crack between the glass and the sill. She tosses in bed, drifting in and out of sleep then wakes with a start, grabbing the clock. She's slept through her alarm and is going to be late for work.

She gets up and pulls back the curtain. Another surprise—snow. A couple inches at least. A thick layer of white coats everything outside her apartment—tree branches, cars, garbage cans—all of it covered in a sparkly frozen blanket. The wind that had kept her awake must've brought the first true blast of winter with it.

No time for breakfast. She dresses quickly, pulling her snow boots from the back of the closet, and stops by the deli on her way to work. She stamps her feet to dislodge snow from her boots before she swings in through the door and heads for the back of the line. The door opens again behind her and there's Mike.

His face lights up as he steps inside. "Good morning. How are you?"

She tries to be polite but is so tired. "Not great, to tell you the truth." She smiles weakly, stifling a yawn. "A good night's sleep one of these days would definitely help."

"Yes, that storm kept me up all night, too." The line they are standing in inches forward to the counter. The bustling deli is filled with warm scents: coffee, cinnamon and fresh-baked bread. Most of the tables are occupied, but there's an empty one near the window. "Can you sit and have coffee for a few minutes?" he asks, gesturing toward it. "I found something I want to show you."

"Perfect," she says. "I'm glad I ran into you. I found something, too."

After they order and carry their cups to a table near the window, she sits and removes the plastic lid, watching steam twirl up and away as he sheds his coat and sits down across from her. She rummages through her bag for the printout of her claim file and is pulling a stack of sheets out just as Monica walks by their table. She's wrapped in a coat and scarf, toting a large brown grocery bag with something obviously heavy inside. In her other hand she clutches a paper cup of coffee. She doesn't seem to see them until she's right next to their table.

"Jenna!" she says, and glances at Mike, smiling broadly.

"This is my friend, Mike Albertino," Jenna says. "Mike, this is Monica."

He's blushing a little, but nods. "I understand you and Jenna work together?"

Monica grimaces and plunks her cup onto their table, shaking her hand. "Wow, that coffee is hot. Mind if I join you?"

Before either of them can answer, Monica has dragged a chair from another table toward theirs. Mike grins at Jenna. She covers her mouth with a hand, hoping to hide her smile as Monica sinks into the chair, plops the grocery bag to the floor at her feet, and leans back. She loosens her scarf. "Whew." She fans her face with one hand. "Kinda warm in this place, don't you think?"

Jenna smiles and sips at her steaming cup. "I was about to show Mike the claim info you helped me find yesterday." She turns to Mike and adds, "It's okay—I've told Monica what's going on, at least as much as I can figure out."

"Did you understand what that claim said?" Monica asks, unsealing her cup and blowing at the steaming surface. "I didn't get all the jargon when we were looking at it yesterday."

"No, I didn't understand much," Jenna says. "I was hoping Mike could help." She hands the pages to him and he scans it. "It sounds like some kind of drug treatment," she says. "Something that produces an effect like brain surgery. It also says they were treating me for PTSD—that's another part I don't understand." She looks at Monica, who is sipping at her hot cup. "I don't remember any PTSD."

Monica's gaze darts from Jenna to Mike and back again. "I still can't believe you have no memory of this," Monica says.

"I wouldn't say *no* memory." Jenna hesitates, remembering the flashing police car lights, the crime scene tape, the extremely vivid images she "saw" the day before at the park. She reaches in her bag for her notebook where she'd scribbled some notes about it. "Yesterday, it seemed like I was remembering pieces of something. Something to do with the police. And something that happened at the park—"

Mike looks up sharply. "The park? What about the park?" He's frowning.

"You know—that kite I told you about. Well, I saw it again and it seemed to trigger a memory." She shakes her head. "I guess it was a memory. It seemed so real, though, like it was happening right then and there. I don't understand what I'm remembering." She glances at her notes. "Something about a dog, a Frisbee. And that little girl in the blue coat was there—I've seen her and her mother at the park several times."

He looks at her for a moment. "You're sure it's the same little girl?"

"Well, no, but she was wearing the same blue coat and—"

Mike places the claim printout on the table and buries his face in his hands. Monica gives Jenna a puzzled look. Jenna shrugs and reaches a hand to his sleeve. "Mike? What is it?"

He shakes his head and removes his hands, revealing an exceedingly sad expression. "I'd hoped I wouldn't have to tell you this, but—" He reaches into his inner coat pocket, pulls out a folded sheaf of papers and flips through the pages. He refolds all but one sheet and tucks the remainder back into his pocket, then hands Jenna the single page. "I found this online the other day. It's a newspaper article from about eighteen months ago."

She takes the paper from him. At the top is a grainy black-and-white photo of police cars parked near what looks for all the world like the trees at the park. Crime scene tape encircles the trees. This is a photo of the very thing she "saw" just yesterday. The words on the page blur, refusing to form themselves into sentences. Fragments leap from the page and the little bit she can make sense of causes her to tremble. *Unidentified child, strangled, blue coat.* Jenna squeezes her eyes shut. BLUE COAT. She tries to read more, but only a few words seem to make sense: *Police have no suspects.* "What is this?" she whispers. Her hand shakes so hard the paper rattles.

Mike takes the paper from her and encloses her hands in his own. His large hands are soft and warm and exude comfort. It suppresses her shaking, at least a little bit. "I'm sorry, Jenna," he says. "I didn't mean to throw it at you, but it seemed like it was related to what you've been telling me."

She nods, unable to speak.

Monica frowns and gestures at the page. It lies atop the printout from Jenna's claim form, the grainy black-and-white photo clearly visible. "What's this about?"

Mike sweeps the news article from the top of the stack, folds it and tucks it into his pocket. He shakes his head and picks up the pages Jenna had given him earlier. "I've been looking at this information Jenna gave me. It sounds very much like she's undergone a treatment to—to block a fear-based PTSD trigger. I—I've actually heard about this treatment method." Bright pink patches have appeared on his cheeks and he won't look at either of them.

Jenna and Monica both stare, and Monica says, "Where would *you* have heard about something like that?"

His cheeks flush an even brighter shade of pink. "I was pre-med before I went to seminary." He gives Jenna an apologetic look. "Neuroscience was my concentration, actually." He clears his throat and waves the pages at them. "Anyhow, I still remember a couple things—not much, but I—I actually know about this work from Hopkins they refer to in the claim." He shakes his head. "Who would've guessed my senior thesis project would come in handy later? Anyhow, the method was supposed to be a way to stop fear-induced PTSD. They were going to try it on veterans, at least eventually." He looks away for a long moment. "I thought it sounded rather dangerous when I heard about it, but they'd only tried it in mice—" His voice trails off.

Monica leans forward and places her hand on his. "Mike, what are you saying? You think they tried this on Jenna?" He stares straight ahead, and she looks at Jenna again, then back at Mike. "*Why* would they do something like that?"

He pulls the newspaper article from his pocket. "I guess you deserve to know this, too. I'm pretty sure it's related to what's happened to Jenna."

Monica yanks the paper from his hand. Her eyes flit from side to side as she reads. "A child—murdered. And it happened right here, in that park across the street." She looks up at Jenna, alarmed. "Do you know anything about this?"

A trembling starts up in Jenna's belly. "I don't know *what* I know anymore." Her eyes fill with tears. "I'm sorry—I know I should know, but all I have is a feeling. And, yes, I'd say maybe I know something about this. Or *knew* it, anyway."

Monica glances at the clock on the wall and stands up fast, her chair screeching backward across the linoleum. "Look at the time." She grabs her coat and pulls it on. "I'm so sorry. This is not a good time to leave, but I have a meeting—"

Jenna stands up, swaying slightly. "I'll go with you," she says, still trembling.

Mike stands up and grabs her elbow. "Are you sure you're okay?"

She shakes her head, reaching for her coat. "I haven't been okay for a while, but I do have to get to work."

"Okay. How about if I check in on you later?" He laughs. "Of course, I don't know how to find you. And I don't even know your last name, Jenna."

Monica watches her closely as she wraps her scarf around her neck.

Jenna fishes in her bag for a business card. "Here's my number—and it's Wright. Jenna Wright."

"Thanks." He gives her a rather sad-looking smile.

Monica picks up the brown grocery bag from the floor beneath their table. Jenna nods toward it. "What's in the bag?"

Monica grins. "I found it at the grocery store this morning—on sale. I thought it might brighten up the office, seeing as how it's decided to become winter overnight. Seventy percent off." She reaches into the bag and pulls out a potted plant. Glossy green foliage surrounds a large salmon-colored daisy.

Jenna looks at the potted flower and, as its strong floral scent reaches her nose, something like a tsunami bashes her forehead, entering through her eyes and flooding her brain with images. Pictures wash over and through her like a surging wall of raging water:

A baby in a crib.
A doll with a broken-off arm.
A pacifier.

Pain smacks her forehead and she sinks to her knees on the cold floor. The floral scent that started all of this is gone, replaced by the sour smell of dirty linoleum. She clasps her head, moaning. Monica drops down beside her. "Jenna, what is it?"

Howard smiles up at her.
His dark eyes and dark hair frame an oval face.
She can see his perpetual five o'clock shadow.
A dark-haired little girl shrieks with laughter.
The shrieking becomes a scream.
Now Howard is screaming, his face twisted in anger.
The dark-haired little girl cries.
A baldheaded priest pats her on the shoulder.

"Jenna."

She can hear a voice, swimming toward her through the flood of images. It's Monica's voice she hears. It's Monica's arms around her shoulders. She pulls Jenna into a tight hug, but Jenna senses herself slipping away. She slides beneath the tidal wave of memory and looks over Monica's shoulder. She catches sight of it again—a beautiful salmon-colored daisy that is, somehow, sending waves of pain her way.

After another tsunami whacks into Jenna, her world goes completely black.

THEY'RE ALL HUDDLED AROUND JENNA who is out cold on the floor of the deli. Mike is squatting down beside her, and Monica is at her head, slapping gently at Jenna's cheeks, begging her to wake up.

Mike has hold of Jenna's wrist. "I'm getting a pulse. And she's breathing, at least."

"I can't get her to wake up," Monica says, her voice breaking. "What's wrong?"

Mike shakes his head and looks up. A crowd has started to gather, among them the aproned deli owner. "Maybe we should call an ambulance," Mike says to Monica. She nods, and he lifts his voice, shouting to the owner, "Can somebody call an ambulance?"

The owner's eyes widen, and he reaches in his pocket for a phone.

A pale-faced man with carrot-red hair opens the door and the smell of bus exhaust wafts into the shop. He steps inside and rushes to where they are crouched. "Monica," he says.

She looks up. "Pete." She reaches up and clasps him around the neck, her eyes filled with tears. "I'm so glad you're here. We've just called for an ambulance—something's happened to Jenna."

"I—I can see that." He blushes, looking first at Jenna, then Mike. "Can I help?"

"Yes, in fact you can," Monica says. She grabs the red-haired guy's hand and he blushes an even deeper shade of red. "Could you please let my boss know what happened, and that I won't be in for a while? I need to stay with Jenna. And, if they take her to the hospital, I think I need to go with her—make sure she's okay."

Mike places a hand on the man's sleeve—Pete, as Monica called him. "Are you one of Jenna's coworkers?"

Pete nods. "I am. And I just came in for coffee. What—what happened?"

"Pete," Monica says, "this is Father Mike. He and Jenna are friends. He's the priest at the church next door to Columbia."

"St. Rita's. Yes, I've been there." A puzzled expression flits across his face and is then gone as he looks at Mike. "Lucky you were right here when this happened."

Mike wonders for a moment about Pete's expression, but dismisses it. Can't let extraneous things distract him now. "I wonder if you can help us notify Jenna's family," he says to Pete. "She told me her parents, well her mother at least, are in New Jersey. And she has a brother, although I don't know how to reach him."

"Sam," Pete says.

"You know Jenna's brother?"

Pete shrugs. "Well, I've met him. It wasn't the best of circumstances—"

"Do you know how to reach him?" Mike asks. "Or perhaps her parents?"

Pete puffs out his chest and glances at Monica. "I can find the info in her personnel file. It's only supposed to be accessible to HR, but I can get it."

"Or," Monica says, glaring at him, "we could just ask HR for the information. Why sneak around like this?"

Pete blushes again. "Just seems easier to go in and take what you need. I do it all the time." He looks at Mike. "Oh—sorry, Father. I didn't mean I steal things. It's just that some information shouldn't be locked up. You know?"

The door opens, bringing with it a blast of frigid air and two blue-uniformed medical technicians. They hurry toward where Jenna lies on her back, still out cold.

They push their way in, a medicinal scent wafting in with them. Mike stands up, grabs Pete's sleeve and tugs him away from the huddled technicians. "We need to notify Jenna's family," Mike says, his voice low. "However you get the information is up to you, but I think we better get word to them soon, right?"

Pete nods. "I can do it." He jerks his chin toward the door. "Want to come with me? We can call them from my office—assuming the info is in her file."

The EMTs hoist Jenna's limp body onto a wheeled stretcher. They've placed a plastic mask over her mouth and nose—oxygen, he assumes—which is tethered by a long tube to a canister down near the stretcher's wheels.

Mike watches, a heavy sense of doom spreading through him. He steps close to Monica, who looks totally stricken, and presses his business card into her hand. "I'll go with your friend here—Pete." Tears spill from her eyes. He wants to hug her, but he's barely met the woman, so instead he says, his voice low, "Don't worry. We'll notify her family and then I'll try to join you at the hospital. Okay?" She agrees, and he squeezes her arm. "Call me if there's any news, but I'll see you as soon as I can."

9

IT'S SATURDAY, HIS DAY OFF, and Pete is on his way to the Laundromat, a heavy duffel bag of clothes looped over a shoulder. He and Mike were able to find Jenna's emergency contact info yesterday but couldn't reach any of them. Pete volunteered to keep trying while Mike went back to work, but so far, he's only located one of her emergency contacts. He still needs to reach the other one, a guy listed as Samuel Wright—must be Jenna's brother—but is starting to realize it's not going to be easy.

Pete lives in the same neighborhood where he works, which is convenient, but it's like living, eating and breathing work, to be honest. Once he gets his promotion, assuming it actually comes through, maybe he can afford to move out of the shared apartment where he's currently staying and get his own place. Maybe then he would ask Monica out. He doesn't dare do so yet. What would she think of a guy who doesn't even have his own place?

It's sunny but cold, November after all, and as he makes his way past St. Rita's, he has a sudden memory of the day a couple of years before when he'd first met the guy he is now trying to get hold of. It had been spring and the dogwood tree in the little garden next to St. Rita's had been in full bloom. Pete had been out for a stroll that day too, uncharacteristically—usually he has no time for something so pointless, but the weather was beautiful, and he'd just gone for a walk.

That day, he reached the steps of the church just as the massive front doors swung open. A strong incense smell wafted out the door and there was an ominous-looking black car parked at the curb—a hearse. The priest, who at that time was this tall, balding man with striking blue eyes, not Mike, who's there now, stepped outside the door. Pete was struck by the sight, how the warm spring breeze billowed the priest's robes around his legs like he was some sort of celestial being. Behind him came a group of people, most of them dressed in black, many dabbing tissues to their swollen eyes, and there among them was a face he recognized—one of his co-workers at Columbia: Jenna.

He knew her by her first name at that time, and that she was a relatively new Columbia employee, but didn't know much else. She was one of dozens of data-input technicians who worked on the tenth floor and he'd helped her with a few computer glitches from time to time. That day, she stood at the top of the steps, talking to the priest, her hand threaded through the arm of a dark-haired slightly chubby fellow Pete didn't know. Both Jenna and the man she was with had red-rimmed eyes.

It was clearly a funeral he'd stumbled upon, and although he didn't want to intrude, Jenna caught sight of him just as she and the man whose arm she was clutching came down the steps toward the hearse. She nodded his way. "Hello," she said, as they reached the bottom of the steps. "It's Pete, right?"

He remembered how his face grew hot, embarrassed, as usual. He hated this about himself. He'd never been able to speak to a woman without it happening. He'd nodded at her and tried to apologize. "I'm sorry," he said, "I didn't mean to intrude—I was just passing by and saw you step out of the church."

That was when another man, tall, lanky and with features a lot like Jenna's walked down the stairs and came to stand next to her. She smiled at him and leaned into his arm as he approached. "This is my brother, Sam," she said. "Sam, this is Pete. We work together at Columbia Health."

Sam offered a hand and a sad smile. "Nice to meet you, Pete," he said. "I wish the circumstances were a little happier, though."

"Uh—I'm sorry." Pete shifted his gaze from Jenna to her brother and then to the dark-haired man who was avoiding all eye contact. "As I said to Jenna, I was just passing by—I didn't mean to intrude."

"It's not a problem," Sam said, his smile kind and rather comforting. "You didn't know, I take it."

Pete shook his head. "I'm sorry for your loss, though—was it a friend? Family member?"

Sam and Jenna exchanged a long gaze, a look that still bothers Pete, all these months later. Sam finally looked back at him. "Family," he said and shrugged.

Pete backed up and away. "I—I'm sorry to hear that," he'd said, unsure what else he could say, wanting to get out of there. "I—I'd better be going, actually."

Sam was nice about it, at least. He nodded at Pete. "Good to meet you," he said, then looked at Jenna. "Ready?" She nodded, and he reached for the back door of the hearse. He opened it and Jenna climbed inside as Pete turned and hurried away, wishing he'd waited just a bit longer to leave his apartment, so he could have avoided the awkward encounter.

That had been his one meeting with Jenna's family. She never talked about them, so he'd assumed, ever since, that the funeral was for one of her parents. Whether it was her mom or dad, he didn't know at the time, and didn't think he should pry, so he'd never asked. When he and Mike had found her personnel file with two "emergency contact" numbers, one for Howard Bernstein and a second for Samuel Wright, he decided that his assumption was right—it must have been one of her parents they were burying that day.

He and Mike had called the Bernstein guy first but found out soon enough that the hospital had already reached him. After Mike left, Pete tried Samuel Wright's number—he figured it was the same Sam he'd met at the funeral, Jenna's brother. All he got was voicemail, though, so left a message and hoped for the best.

Something is going on, however. Pete is sure of it, even though he is unsure exactly *what* is going on. He never said anything to Jenna about that day he'd seen her at the funeral—didn't want to invade her privacy and didn't think it was any of his business—but he did notice she'd been fragile and was often in tears when he'd come upon her in the elevator or the hallway. And then she disappeared, on that mysterious medical leave, and came back acting like a different person.

And now Jenna is in the hospital, and the circumstances are beyond mysterious. Monica is beside herself with worry. Pete knows he can help, and he wants to do it for her—for Monica. Pete remembers how Jenna looked, stretched out on the floor of the deli, unconscious, and wonders if what's happened to her now is related to her earlier absence. He doesn't know, but he cannot believe that it isn't. The two things must be related, and he knows how to find out. He just needs to dig a little deeper.

He reaches the Laundromat and hauls his heavy bag of laundry inside. When he's done here, he'll go back to his cubicle. It's Saturday and no one will be in. A perfect time to hack into Jenna's medical files.

MIKE RUSHES INTO THE CHURCH and heads down the darkened hallway toward his apartment. The day before, after he and Pete had looked for Jenna's contact info, he'd gone to the hospital where he met Monica. They'd taken Jenna away for some sort of procedures by then, and he still hadn't seen her. He'd stayed most of the night and spent as much time at the hospital today as he could, but it's Saturday and Mass is at five and there are, as usual, more services tomorrow.

He's sweating by the time he makes it to his apartment. He closes the door and leans back against it, trying to breathe, trying not to shake, although none of this seems to help. He buries his face in his hands. "Oh God," he moans. "What have I done?" He slides down the door until he's sitting on the floor, breathing the musty air that permeates his tiny place. His head is in his hands, agony permeating all his cells.

It's over there, across the room, in a box buried deep inside his closet. He kept the reprints of his paper with Allan Scott as a sort of keepsake, a memento of his days as a student, the one piece of concrete evidence that his time as a pre-med student had not been completely wasted or in vain.

He moans again, laboriously hauls himself up to a standing position, and heads to the closet. A few minutes later, he's pulled out his battered suitcase which is atop a box filled with old clothes and keepsakes: his baseball mitt from grade school, smelling like well-oiled leather; the trophy he'd won in the all-state wrestling match; a photo album filled with snapshots of his nieces and nephews; and, at the bottom of all of this, the thick folder with copies of the one journal article he'd published as an undergraduate.

His hands are shaking as he opens the folder and pulls out the article. It has the smell of old paper that's been closed up in an airless place for too many years. There at the top is his name, typeset next to that of his undergraduate research advisor: *Michael J. Albertino and Allan M. Scott, Department of Medicine, Johns Hopkins University, Annals of Neuroscience Techniques, Vol. 23, pp. 437-450.*

He slumps down the closet door, gripping the incriminating piece of paper in his hands, until he's sitting on the floor. He reads the title, *"Development and Testing of an Innovative Fear Amelioration Technique Utilizing a Superconducting Quantum Interference Device and Magnetic Drug-Delivery Beads."*

Tears well into his eyes when he remembers how proud and impressed his parents were when he showed them the results of his senior project. He flips to the back page and there it is, in small print near the end, the detail that led to so much soul-searching and a complete change of life trajectory: *Funded by the Department of Defense, Office of the Army.*

Hands shaking, he tears the paper in half. He continues, ripping up each copy of the paper until the folder is empty, even though he knows the evidence of his involvement in this work is available to anyone and everyone online, if they know where to look. His only hope is that no one knows where to look.

JENNA REALIZES SHE'S AWAKE, but where is she? It's dark, but she can make out metal and glass all around, and a constant annoying beeping sound. Throbs of pain course through her head with each beep.

Something is stuck to the inside of her left arm and when she tries to turn her head to see what it is, finds she can't move. Red and orange lights flash around her, and there's a strong scent of antiseptic. She's surprised she can smell it at all since there's a plastic insert in her nostrils, attached to some sort of tube. It's one of those oxygen things. She's in a bed—with metal rails along each side. She must be in a hospital and raises her head to check, but immediately regrets it when throbbing pain smashes her forehead and squeezes her skull. She sinks back into the pillow, trying to stay still since movement brings on excruciating pain.

It's dark in the room but her eyes have started to adjust. She can make out two figures, two people who both seem to be dozing, in chairs next to a darkened window. Through the window she can see orange street lights, like those in a parking lot or on a highway.

One of the two figures by the window sits up, a topknot on her head clearly visible in silhouette. Monica. Jenna tries to call to her but all that comes out is "Maaah—"

Monica crosses the room and leans down toward her. "Jenna?"

"Maaah—"

"Shhh, don't try to talk."

Tears sting Jenna's eyes. What happened? They were in the deli. Monica had come by. They'd talked. But what happened then? Monica had a bag. A brown grocery bag. And in it was—pain slams into her forehead and she cries out again.

"Jenna." Monica grabs her hand. "What's happening?"

"Oh my God," Jenna moans. "My head. It feels—aaah." She tries to grab her head between her hands but the tube that's attached to the inside of her arm tangles and pins her down.

The other figure stirs and stands up. As he approaches, she can see it's Mike. She can barely make out his face, but the orange glow from a machine above her head casts a dim light across his features. He leans down looking concerned. "How do you feel?"

"Hi," she says to him trying to smile, glad to be able to form words again. "Not too good, to tell you the truth." Her voice comes out raspy and her throat is exceedingly sore. She looks at Monica, then back to Mike. "What happened?"

Light shoots into the room as the door near the foot of her bed swings open. Mike glances at the door. "Maybe we should wait for the doctor to explain."

She tries to sit up again to see who has come in, but the light is blinding. It's a man, she can see that much, but it's only when he gets close to her bed and the orange glow from the machines illuminates his face—those familiar dark features and a crooked smile she'd know anywhere—that she sees who it is. Howard.

"What are you doing here?" Her voice gives out on the last word, rasping into a hoarse croak.

"How are you feeling?" Howard asks, grasping her hand.

She yanks her hand away. "Why are you here?"

He shakes his head, and even in the dark she can see the look of consternation flit across his face. "Dr. Andrews called me after you were brought into the ER. I got here as soon as I could."

Andrews. The doctor who'd done the procedure on her brain. She should've known Howard would be behind all of this.

The door swings open and someone else walks in—a thin, balding man in a white coat. "How's our patient doing?" he asks cheerfully, grabbing the clipboard at the foot of her bed and shining a pen light on it.

It's the man she'd seen on the website. Andrews Neurological Associates. "Dr. Andrews?" Jenna asks. She realizes she's shaking.

"Yes, Jenna." He drops the clipboard. As it rattles back into position on the foot of her bed, he walks briskly around to the side, his penlight still in his hand, lifts her chin and shines the penlight directly into one eye.

Searing pain shoots through her head and she cries out, trying to push his hand away. He grabs her wrist and shines the light in her other eye.

Pain. Pain so intense she can barely stand it. Mike pushes himself between the doctor and Jenna. "Are you all right?"

"No!" Fury rises into her chest. She glares at the doctor. "Why did you do that? What's going on here?"

Howard grabs Mike's arm and pulls him away from the bed. "It's okay, Jenna," Howard says. "Dr. Andrews just needs to do an exam."

She clenches her fists, shaking uncontrollably. "Not with that light."

Mike turns to Howard and extends his hand. "Mike Albertino," he says. "And you are?"

The doctor looks sharply at Mike, his brow furrowed. He opens his mouth as if to speak, then turns away.

Howard, though, ignores Mike's hand. So like him to be rude. "A little early to be performing last rites, don't you think?" Howard says, sneering.

Mike clenches his teeth so tightly that even in the dim light Jenna can see a muscle flex in his jaw. "I'm sorry, Mike. Howard has been known to be an ass, but not usually within seconds of meeting a person." She looks around for Monica, who has retreated to the chairs by the window. "What happened anyway? The last I remember was being in the deli with you and Monica."

"You fainted," Mike says. "And when we couldn't rouse you, we called 911."

She looks down at the tubes coming from her arm and nose. "What did they do to me?"

"I'm not sure." Mike turns to the doctor. "They said they were taking you off to get an EEG, but it seemed to take hours. What happened?"

"I'm sorry," Dr. Andrews says. He replaces his penlight in his front breast pocket and clasps his hands behind his back. "I can only discuss this with you if you're immediate family. Are you?" Mike doesn't answer. The doctor frowns again, saying, "You look familiar to me somehow." He shakes his head.

"Well, I'm the chaplain here, so I suppose we've met."

He looks shaken. Does Mike know something about this doctor? A chill grabs hold of Jenna's chest. She remembers what the claim form said: SEALED BY ORDER OF THE DEPARTMENT OF DEFENSE. Could this Dr. Andrews be involved with the military?

She looks at Howard. "What did you do to me?" Her breathing is labored. It's difficult to get words out.

Howard averts his gaze from hers and stares at the doctor.

"Howard? What's going on here?" Her voice rises in pitch and nearly gives out before she squeezes out the last word.

Dr. Andrews steps to the side, reaches for the IV stand next to her bed and turns a knob. "Jenna, I'm sorry," he says, "but you're getting too excited."

The dim room fades to dark. The orange light from the machine above her head turns to maroon. She feels like she's floating in a pool of warm water. She can barely keep her eyes open. If she wasn't suddenly so sleepy, she would panic.

Mike shoves Howard aside and leans close. He grabs both her hands. "Jenna—listen to me." His face is so close to hers she can feel the heat of his breath on her cheeks and smell the faint scent of incense clinging to his jacket. She finds his gaze and locks tight to it as the room begins to rotate around them. "Don't worry—I'll be right here with you." She must keep her gaze on his. He seems the only stable entity in the room, but his voice has become faint. "I'll be right here," he repeats, his voice coming to her as if over a vast distance. The orange light fades from maroon to gray and then to black.

Something's bumping the bed and when she takes a peek, she sees the bed moving. She rolls past doors and large pieces of silver-colored equipment. People shout and rush nearby. It's so bright it hurts. She can't bear to keep her eyes open, so squeezes them shut.

Voices float over her. A woman shouts. "We need to get to the squid—stat!"

Another voice, this one belonging to a man.

"Coming through."

She's surrounded by sound. Crashes, beeping noises, whirring equipment. She's bumped and jostled from side to side in the bed, but she's so weak she can't stop herself from hitting the bed rails. The movement stops, then, and someone grabs her hand and leans close. "Jenna, can you hear me?"

It's a man's voice. Is it Mike? It doesn't sound like Mike.

The voice again: "Jenna?"

She still doesn't recognize the person behind the voice, but tries to answer, tries to say yes. All that comes out when she opens her mouth is "Ahhh—"

Whoever has hold of her hand leans close to her. "Jenna, listen to me. The procedure is beginning to reverse itself. We need to administer another dose. Shouldn't take long." Whoever it is squeezes her hand. Is it Dr. Andrews? She tries to pry her eyes open to see, but the pain from the light is too intense. "I'll see you on the other side," the voice says. "Go ahead, nurse. Administer it now."

A sudden fatigue sweeps through her body. It's as if someone has thrown an electrical switch inside her to the off position. She cannot move her head or arms or legs. For yet another time, the world fades to black.

10

MIKE STANDS IN THE HOSPITAL LOBBY next to Monica. They've just been banished from Jenna's room by the doctor and hustled to the elevator by two gruff orderlies who tell them "visiting hours are over," even though Mike knows for a fact this hospital does not even have specific visiting hours.

"Are they going to let us back in?" Monica asks.

"I doubt that very much." Mike glances toward the coffee kiosk nearby. The scent of brewing coffee and the bubbling and swooshing sound of the coffeemaker is enticing. The scrapes on his back from the bomb-blast have scabbed over and his back is itching again—as usual. He'd love to get home and take a shower, but that scent—he turns to Monica. "Want some coffee?"

She stifles a yawn. "That sounds great. I'd love some."

He buys two cups and as they move toward the exit, both holding the hot paper cups in gloved hands, two people, a graying woman clutching the arm of a lanky younger man, come in through the revolving door.

The man approaches the information desk. "We're looking for Jenna Wright—she was admitted a few days ago, I think."

Monica grabs Mike's arm. "Mike," she whispers. "Who are those people?"

He shrugs and makes a quick decision, striding swiftly to the man's side. "Excuse me. I heard you asking about Jenna?"

The man looks up, concerned. His gaze slides to Mike's collar and back again. "Father?"

Before the fellow can draw inaccurate conclusions about the presence of a priest, Mike extends his hand. "Mike Albertino—I'm a friend of Jenna's."

The man shakes his hand, relief obvious in his expression. "Sam. Sam Wright." He pumps Mike's hand, smiling weakly. "I'm Jenna's brother."

"Of course. She's told me a lot about you." Mike places a hand on Monica's shoulder. "This is Jenna's friend—Monica."

Sam nods at Monica and turns to the older woman. "And this is my mother. *Our* mother. Eunice Wright."

Jenna's mother pulls into herself, nodding after only brief eye contact. "Samuel." Her voice quavers. "Is she here? Is my Jenna here?"

Mike steps a little closer. He puts on his best priest-voice. "Mrs. Wright, your daughter is here and is doing well—Monica and I were just upstairs visiting her."

Jenna's mother lets her breath out with a heavy sigh. "What a relief." She turns a concerned look to her son. "Do you think we can see her now?"

"Of course, Mom." He smiles weakly and nods at Mike and Monica. "I'm sorry we can't stay and talk—we've driven up from Cherry Hill today, as soon as I could pick up my mother. I just flew in from overseas a couple nights ago."

"Did Pete reach you?" Monica asks.

Sam looks puzzled. "Pete? I didn't hear from a Pete." He looks at his mother. "I had a message from Howard, though. Howard called you as well, right, Mom?"

She nods and Mike notices how tightly she clenches her teeth before answering, "That's right."

"I should be getting back to the church," Mike says. Jenna clearly needs some time with her family. "I'll try to check back in again with Jenna when I come in to do my chaplain shift."

"Thank you, Father." Sam shakes his hand again and nods at Monica. "It was nice to meet you."

He and Monica watch them head for the elevator. She pops the plastic lid off her cup and blows on the steaming liquid. "I wonder why he hadn't heard from Pete? Didn't you two find Jenna's family information?"

He nods. "Sort of. We found Howard's name and number right away. Pete called him, but as you just saw, the doctors had already been in contact, and Howard was already on his way to the hospital. Pete said that Howard assured him he'd contact Jenna's parents."

Monica frowns. "I don't understand. Why would this guy, Howard, be in her file but not one of her parents?"

Mike shakes his head. "It's not terribly unusual for an adult to have someone other than parents as their emergency contact." He stares out the glass door toward the parking lot. Something tells him that Jenna has never mentioned Howard to her friend Monica.

They push through the front glass doors and out into the crisp morning. Monica sips at her cup, lost in thought for several long moments. She glances at Mike. "I'm sorry I'm not much of a conversationalist today. I didn't sleep much."

"You were here all night again?"

She nods, yawning. "Two nights in a row. After you went back to the church, they took her off for a long time for tests. I just curled up in a chair and waited to see what would happen. They eventually brought her back, but I guess I must have fallen asleep, so I never got to ask what the tests were about. Not that they would have told me anyway." She pauses, staring blankly across the parking lot. "Mike, I still don't understand something. Who is this guy Howard? And why was he in Jenna's personnel file? She doesn't seem to like him very much."

Mike shakes his head. Apparently, Monica doesn't know about that part of Jenna's history, and he's not about to be the one to reveal any secrets she wants to keep to herself.

Monica frowns at him then looks toward the parking lot. "I guess I better be going. *If* I can find my car." She squints into the morning sun. "I'm sure it's out there somewhere."

"Should I wait until you locate it?"

She waves her hand, then pulls out a key fob. "No, no. I'll just use this and hope it will beep at me." She presses a button and a car in the second row flashes its lights. "See? There it is."

She smiles and lifts a hand in a wave as she steps toward the parking lot, but immediately stops, leans over and peers into a newspaper vending box. "Oh my God," she whispers. She looks up at him, frowning. "They found another body in our park."

Mike's hands shake as he fumbles for coins to put in the machine. Even before he squeaks the rusty door open and retrieves the paper, he knows what it will say. Monica looks over his shoulder as he scans the front page. There, in lurid color, is a photo very much like the one in the older article he'd shown Jenna: police cars, crime scene tape, tangled colorful ribbons in the bare tree branches. "Badly Decomposed Body Found in Park Pond," reads the headline. Below that is a subheading: "Similarity to Other Recent Murder Guides Police Investigation."

"Do they say who it is?" Monica asks, trying to get a closer look.

Mike shakes his head, trembling. "A child. A girl. Still unidentified, though, according to this article." *Sophie McPherson.* It must be her.

A wave of nausea rises into his throat as he remembers the angel-child's warning. *He will kill again.* Mike had been warned but he's still done nothing. But really—what exactly *can* he do?

"So sad. And scary," Monica says, interrupting his thoughts. "I thought the neighborhood was safe, but between these murders and that bombing the other night—" Her voice trails off.

Yes, Mike thinks—we all thought our town was safe. But we were wrong.

He and Monica say goodbye, and a half-hour later he's pulling into the parking lot at the back of St. Rita's. He comes around to the front only to find two police cars parked at the meters out front of the deli.

The sight brings him up short. They're probably inside getting coffee, but a cold fear creeps over him. He stares at the cop cars for a long moment, clutching the now lukewarm paper cup in one hand, the newspaper folded under his arm.

He sighs, wishing he could pray. He *needs* to pray. He needs *help*, God damn it! Children have been killed, two of them, at least, and he's pretty sure one is related to Jenna somehow. He doesn't know how, but it must have something to do with her memory loss. He thinks of the doctor, then, and shivers. That work he'd done back at Hopkins looms large. He wants to push away the memory of his involvement, but he can't change the fact that he was there when the fear-amelioration method was first developed.

One thing he doesn't understand, though, is Jenna's memory loss. It might be possible to remove fear, although he doubts the science has advanced this far already—but it really doesn't seem possible to deliberately take away memories. He can't shake the idea that this is exactly what's happened, though.

As he makes his way toward the church door, he wonders if maybe he's had it all wrong—it may very well be that the man who came to confession is not the killer of these children at all, not the one who took the life of young Sophie McPherson and one other. In Mike's pocket is a folded-up printout from a second article he'd found online just two days before—the first murdered child, a four-year-old girl, had been identified as Katie Bernstein, daughter of "Mr. and Mrs. Howard Bernstein," as the newspaper said. And the man—the unpleasant man who Jenna had not seemed at all happy to see at the hospital—was apparently the dead girl's father.

Mike scuffs up the front steps of the church. The snow that had coated them just two days before has already melted, leaving no trace it was ever there. He glances up at the rose window—the silhouette he'd seen weeks before is also no longer there. Of course. What does it all mean?

He pulls open the heavy front door and there stands Sister Mary Katherine. Her eyes are rimmed with red and she's got her arms wrapped around her own shoulders, as if she's trying to hug herself.

Her face crumples when she sees him. "Father Mike," she sobs as the door slams shut behind him. "I'm so glad to see you."

"What's wrong?"

"I think you should come with me." She reaches for his arm and pulls him toward the hallway. As they enter the dim passageway, he spots them: a half-dozen or so police officers making their way toward the door he'd just come through, each one carrying a box piled high with notebooks and pads—his notebooks. He says a silent prayer of thanks, relieved that he'd gotten rid of the incriminating journal article reprints when he did.

He steps in front of the first officer, a woman. "What's going on?" he asks. She elbows past him, ignoring his question. Another officer, this one a man, follows closely behind, cradling Mike's computer in his arms.

His heart sinks. The journal article may be shredded, but anyone who looks at his computer search history will find plenty of other reasons to suspect his involvement.

A man calls to him from somewhere down the darkened hallway. "Father!" The sound bounces off the stone walls, echoing rather ominously, but Mike can't make out the man's face until he steps from the shadows.

Detective Sloan.

This is not good. Mike draws himself up tall. "Why are you taking my things?" Sister Mary Katherine huddles behind him sobbing quietly. "And why are you frightening the sisters?" he asks, gesturing toward her, trying to act like he's in charge. It's his own church, after all.

"Father, please." Sloan lets his breath out heavily. "I need you to come down to the station. We have a few questions we'd like to ask you."

"Are you arresting me?" he asks, clenching his paper coffee cup so hard the plastic lid pops off and bounces to the floor.

Sloan jumps back as the now-cold coffee splatters the stone floor. He sighs heavily. "No, we're not arresting you. We have some questions, that's all."

"But—why have you taken my computer?" Mike gestures helplessly at the row of police who are hauling his things out of the building. "And my notebooks? All I have in there are my notes for sermons, and—"

Sloan reaches into his inside breast pocket, pulls out a sheaf of papers and waves them at him. "We have a subpoena," he says, glowering. "Your things will be returned to you once we've inspected them."

Mike clenches his fist and realizes he's trembling. He can't seem to stop the shaking that has begun somewhere in his gut. "And how long will that be?"

"Please, Father." Sloan reaches for his elbow and guides him toward the door. He holds him so close, Mike can smell the man's aftershave. "I can answer all your questions once we get to the station."

Sister Mary Katherine lunges after them. "Stop. Why are you taking the Father away? What has he done?"

Sloan ignores her and pulls Mike toward the door, sloshing more coffee to the floor. The sister's sobs follow him out onto the boulevard as he allows the detective to lead him down the stone steps and toward a fate that he knows has been coming on for some time. He may not be a suspect now, but that will probably change once his computer is inspected. He knows what they will find—evidence of multiple searches using key words such as "child killing" and "strangulation," and several documents saved to his desktop about the murder of a girl who very much appears to be related, somehow, to Jenna—a woman he's been seen in public with multiple times in the last few weeks. A woman he really has no legitimate reason to be spending time with. A woman who lies, right now, in the hospital having who knows what done to her brain, under the control of a man who might have killed his own daughter—one Howard Bernstein.

11

JENNA OPENS HER EYES. The bright light has blessedly gone away. But what about all those people shouting about squids? What happened to all of them? It seems only seconds before she was being jostled along in a bed while someone told her the procedure was "reversing itself." Whatever *that* means.

And where is she, anyway? Wherever it is, it's dark. Her eyelids feel sticky, like they're stuck to her eyeballs. She tries to turn her head. Across the room is a large red fiery ball—the sun coming up outside.

Something is stuck to the inside of her arm—plastic tubes snake away from her arm and her nose. Despite the tube in her nose, she can smell a strong scent of antiseptic. She feels as if she should know what all of this means but is totally confused. She must be in a hospital, but why?

Vague images float through her mind. A man in a white coat reaching for a knob on an IV stand. Another man nearby—no, it was *two* other men. And a woman. Someone familiar, someone she knows. The woman had a dark topknot of hair. All these people, whoever they were, had hovered over her. And one of the men—he'd leaned close and it comforted her. His eyes crinkled when he smiled. He smelled vaguely like incense.

She *knows* him, but how? Who is he? She remembers another detail: He'd had a collar. A priest's collar. He'd said, "I'll be right here," as he leaned close to her. She remembers him saying this but sees no one in the room with her. Who is he?

Despair floods through her like cold water. She knows her name at least. She's Jenna. Jenna Wright. But who are these other people she's remembering? And why is she in a hospital? She sinks back into the pillow, and that's when she notices that someone actually is there, sitting by the window in a chair.

It's a nurse, wearing blue scrubs with a matching blue cap covering her hair. She stands and comes to the foot of Jenna's bed, peering at the chart that hangs from the railing at the bottom of the bed. She flips through a few pages. Jenna wants to ask her why she's here, what's going on, but she can't seem to get any words out. The woman drops the chart and leaves, the door clicking shut behind her.

No more than a minute later, in come two orderlies, both dressed in blue scrubs with matching masks across their faces and the same blue cloth caps on their heads as the nurse had. They lean together at the side of the room, whispering, their heads bent close. One of them has a large plastic bag filled with something lumpy.

Jenna thinks again about the man with the collar. She needs—desperately—to see him, although she doesn't understand her compulsion. She wants to ask the blue-garbed orderlies to find him, but her throat is so parched and raw, all that comes out is a strangled-sounding croak and a sob.

The two orderlies look toward her. One hurries back to the door and turns the deadbolt lock with a clunk. The other, a woman, rushes to her side and pulls the mask away from her face. She smells like oranges or, maybe, lemons. It's the woman with the topknot of dark hair. Jenna recognizes those eyes, rimmed as they always are in thick black eyeliner. The only problem is, she doesn't remember the woman's name.

"Jenna," the woman whispers. "Mike and I are going to get you out of here."

"Who—who are you?" Jenna's voice is barely more than a croak.

The other orderly comes to the bedside and removes his mask. A vague scent of incense lifts off of him. It's him, the man with the collar she so wanted to see—only now his collar is gone. Jenna reaches for him, a sob catching in her throat.

He grabs both her hands and looks at the woman with the topknot. "How is she?" he whispers.

"I don't know," the woman replies, "but we have to hurry. I saw the nurses changing shifts, so there will be some confusion. We need to move now."

She carefully peels tape from the inside of Jenna's elbow and extracts a needle attached to an IV tube. Blood oozes from Jenna's arm and the man presses a gauze pad to it, then wraps tape around her arm.

"Wait," Jenna croaks, grabbing at his arm. "I know you, but—?"

His eyes grow wide. "Of course you know me. Why do you say that, Jenna?"

"No, no," Jenna says. She can barely squeeze the words out. "I mean I remember your face, but you were wearing something different." She gestures toward his neck. "A collar. What's your—I mean, how do I know you?" It's *so* confusing. She knows him, and yet she doesn't.

"Oh, boy." He frowns and shakes his head. "This is worse than I expected." He looks at the top-knotted woman. "Should we really take her out of the hospital?"

"Do you want them to do more of what they've been doing? I mean—look at her." The woman grabs the plastic bag she'd carried in earlier and plunks it on the bed by Jenna's legs. "Just imagine," she says, yanking clothes from the bag, "what could happen if we leave her here any longer." She pulls more items from the bag, jeans and a sweater. Jenna recognizes them both. They're her own clothes. The woman reaches for her arm. "We've got to get you dressed. I'll help."

The man backs away. "Uh—" he says, then heads for the door. "Maybe I should go stand guard?"

"Sure, but put that mask back on your face," the top-knotted woman hisses as he steps into the hall.

After Jenna is dressed, she moves with the woman toward the door, so weak her legs feel like limp spaghetti. Has she been in some sort of accident? A car wreck? She has no idea but is convinced something terrible has happened.

They move toward the door in the dimly lit room and there on the table beneath the light switch sits a potted plant with glossy green leaves and a strongly scented salmon-colored daisy. The image rolls toward her with the scent, bringing with it an alarming wave of recognition.

Pain smashes into her forehead. She crumples at the knees.

The top-knotted woman catches her around the waist just as Jenna's knees hit the floor.

A deli. The man with the collar stumbling toward her.

The top-knotted woman holding a brown grocery bag.

A priest with a bald head. A church filled with daisies just like this.

A top-knotted woman, this same woman, grabbing her arm as they walk into a tall office building.

Monica. The top-knotted woman is her friend.

Jenna looks up into the woman's face. "Monica?" she whispers, blinking and rubbing at her throbbing forehead.

"Whew." Monica helps her to her feet. "You really had me worried there for a minute. I don't suppose you remember Mike?"

He's holding the door open and peering intently into the hallway as she and Monica walk through.

The realization rushes in. Of course: Mike Albertino. How could she forget him? How could she forget *them*? What in the world has happened to her memory?

Mike gestures down a dark hallway toward a stairwell. "We can get out this way," he whispers. They hurry down the gloomy corridor and descend a musty-smelling metal staircase, lit at each landing by dim yellow lights.

"Mike." Jenna's voice echoes from the metallic surfaces. She feels shaky and struggles to keep from stumbling. "What happened to me? I'm trying to remember—there was a doctor, something about a squid? Oh. And Howard. He was here, right?"

They walk round a landing and she catches a glimpse of Mike's face. He looks angry. "Yes. He was here." He clomps down another round of steps. "Let's wait until we're in a safe place to talk more, okay?"

Jenna frowns. What's not safe about a hospital?

They reach the bottom of the stairs and step out into the cold dark. Deep piles of snow line the edges of a plowed parking lot. Snow is falling, swirling, pelting her eyelids. "When did it snow so much?" she asks. "There was nowhere this much snow yesterday." She starts to shiver, clad only in a light sweater and pants, and hugs herself with both arms.

Monica wraps an arm around her waist. "Your coat is in the car," she says. "Let's go."

"My coat? Why do you have my—?"

"We'll talk about that later." Monica guides her toward a beat-up old Toyota and leans to open the door. "I promise. For now, just get in and keep your head down. If anyone sees your face, we're up shit creek."

Jenna struggles into her coat and slumps low in the seat, overcome with fatigue just from the brief walk to the car. Mike slides in behind the wheel and Monica gets into the front passenger seat. They drive through back alleyways, twisting and turning down service roads, through a snow-covered gravel lot and, finally, out onto a partly plowed street. Jenna catches glimpses of dark buildings flashing past and large sparkling snowflakes swirling around the car. Sleep threatens to pull her under.

They drive for about fifteen minutes and Jenna is about to fall asleep when Monica's voice wakes her. "Make a left at the next street," she says. "It's just past the entrance to the cemetery."

"Oh right. I remember that street," Mike says. "A lot of St. Rita's burials take place here." He takes the turn, travels a couple blocks, and pulls to a stop.

Jenna looks out at a row of cars parked at the curb in front of a brick apartment building. None of it looks familiar. "Where are we?" she croaks, her voice threatening to give out again.

"You're staying at my place for a while." Monica says, as Mike switches off the engine. She reaches over the seat to grab her bag from the floor. "Mike thought you wouldn't be safe at your place."

Why are they so worried about being safe? Something must have happened, but all she remembers is a great deal of anxiety, a sense of emergency and dread. She can barely understand what's going on. She feels humiliated, like she's failed as a human being. "Thank you," she says, her voice cracking. "I really appreciate what you're both doing for me, but what I don't understand is *why*."

Neither of them answers her. Mike helps her out of the car and holds her tightly around the waist as they silently pick their way around piles of snow and over ice slicks on the sidewalk leading to Monica's door. Jenna likes the firm competence he exudes. Her legs feel like jelly and like they're about to buckle at any moment, but he holds on firmly.

Monica jiggles her key in the lock and kicks at the door. It swings inward. She walks in ahead of Mike and Jenna, shedding her coat as she goes, then bustles around the apartment, turning on lights and putting things away.

Jenna doesn't know what to do, or even where to sit. She feels shaky inside, like all her muscles have turned to liquid. She wants to trust them, but do Mike and Monica know what they're doing? Maybe leaving the hospital was not the best idea.

Monica calls from the kitchen. "I'll make some tea, okay?"

"Great idea," Mike calls back, then leads Jenna to the sofa. They sit side by side, and she wants to lean into him, bury her face in his sleeve, disappear into him, but holds herself back. Not that long ago she didn't even remember his name. What else has she forgotten about him? Mike notices her looking at him. "How are you feeling?" he asks. "You look a little 'green around the gills,' as my mother would say."

She wonders what his mother is like, if her eyes crinkle too when she smiles. "I imagine I don't look so great," she says, her voice still hoarse. She can hear Monica running water in the kitchen, opening and closing cabinet doors, rattling dishes and silverware. "A cup of tea will probably help." Her stomach aches. "I have no idea when I last ate." She looks around the room, searching for a clock. "What time is it, anyway?"

"About midnight, I think." He stands up. "How about I get you something to eat?"

"Sure—thanks." She leans back against the sofa as he heads for the kitchen.

A few minutes later he's back holding a small plate and a slightly dried-up pastry. "This is all Monica could find—I hope it's okay."

She takes a small bite of the pastry, which smells a little like baked apples, and then another bite. She's ravenous. It feels like she hasn't eaten in days. "Maybe," she says between chews, "I should have asked about more than just the time— what day is it, anyway?" He's sucking in on his lips, as if he's trying to hold words inside his mouth. She sits up straighter. "How long *was* I in that hospital?" She dares not ask, not yet anyway, *why* she was in the hospital. They'll tell her soon enough. At least she hopes they will.

He plops onto the couch. "Several days." He's still sucking his lips in.

Several *days*? "What day *is* it, Mike?"

He glances at the clock. "Well, it's just after midnight, so Sunday now."

Sunday! It was Friday when she'd met Mike and Monica at the deli, and that seems like only a couple hours ago. She's completely lost two days. Somehow. "What happened to me?" she asks him.

He averts his eyes. "We don't really know, but Monica and I agreed that whatever it was they were doing to you in the hospital was not helping." He stands up and begins to pace.

"In fact, it seemed to be making things worse. Every time you would come out of the drug-induced coma they kept putting you in, you would remember less and less."

She flinches at the word. *Coma.* "Why in the world would they do that?"

"Well, that's not such a surprise." He crosses his arms and leans back against a bookcase. "I've seen it before—many times, actually, although usually to deal with some sort of issue that requires the brain to be completely at rest."

"I don't understand—when would you have seen something like that?"

"In my duties as hospital chaplain—I told you about that."

"Well, no you didn't." She pauses, then laughs. "Although— maybe you did, and I just forgot."

Monica walks in with a tray holding three steaming mugs. She places the tray on the coffee table, grabs one of the mugs, and sinks back into a soft chair opposite the sofa. "Mmmm," Monica says, sipping on the tea. "I am soooooo tired."

"You should get some sleep," Mike says as he takes one of the mugs and returns to his seat on the sofa.

"At least I don't have to work in the morning," Monica says. "But you do, right?"

"Indeed. Early Mass, then two more services before noon—I basically work all weekend."

"Oh wow." Jenna looks around for her bag. Is her phone here somewhere? "I completely forgot about work. I have to call—"

Monica holds up a hand. "Don't worry, I took care of it."

"You did? How?"

Monica shrugs and sips again. "Signed you out on medical leave. Once I produced the ambulance report and the hospital admission form, the request went right through. Oh!" She sits upright and places the mug on the table. "Almost forgot." She shuffles through a pile of papers on the table before pulling out a white envelope, which she hands to Jenna. "The guys from work got you this."

"What is it?"

Monica smiles, grabs her mug, and blows a stream of air across the steaming surface. "Just open it."

Her hands are shaking but she manages to get the envelope open and pulls out a card covered with goofy-looking cartoon characters and glitter. "Get Well Soon!" it reads in sparkly letters. The empty spaces on the card are filled with scrawled names, most of which she doesn't recognize, along with handwritten wishes to "Get better soon!" and "We miss you!"

Tears sting her eyes. People are so kind, even people she doesn't remember. "I can't believe you guys got this card together for me so quickly. And I also can't believe I didn't remember you, Monica." She swipes at an escaping tear. "And you, too, Mike. How could I forget you guys?"

Monica widens her eyes at Mike, then shakes her head. "It's not your fault. They've been messing with your brain, for God's sake."

"I just don't understand this," Jenna says as tears streak down her cheeks. "Why would they want to take my memory away?" Mike gives a sharp look to Monica, shaking his head and frowning. Jenna sits up straight. "You know something. Tell me."

"Okay. I don't know how this can be true, but the doctors—and Howard, too—keep insisting that *you* were the one who requested this procedure."

She frowns. "What procedure? Besides, why would anyone want something that feels like this—it's so confusing."

She shakes her head. "I refuse to believe I asked for *this*. I don't remember that at all."

Mike grasps her hand. He squeezes it. "Actually, I think you should stop trying to remember."

"Why?"

He looks for a long moment at Monica as she quietly sips her tea. "Something is wrong with the way your memory is working, Jenna," he says, "or not working, I guess. The doctor *did* say the initial procedure they'd done was starting to reverse itself."

She sits up straight. "Yes—I remember that." There were voices, people shouting. Something about a squid? And they moved her, on a hospital bed, through brightly lit corridors. It was all so murky now, like it happened to someone else.

Monica plunks her mug to the tray and stands up, stretching and stifling a yawn. "I really need some sleep." She pats the arm of the sofa. "This opens into a bed, so I'll get some blankets for you, Jenna. You can borrow a pair of my PJs."

Mike helps Monica open the sofa out into a bed, then carries the mugs into the kitchen. Jenna watches, feeling like a helpless invalid, as Monica opens a sheet onto the sofa-bed mattress and spreads a couple of blankets over it. When Monica goes back to her bedroom to look for a spare pair of pajamas, Mike walks back into the living room from the kitchen and plucks his coat from a hook by the door. "I need to get going. Mass at seven a.m." He smiles weakly.

Jenna hugs the pillow to her chest and buries her face in it. It smells fresh, like clean laundry. "Thank you so much for your help." Tears threaten again, and she blinks rapidly. "I don't know how to repay you for all the help you're giving me."

"There's no need, Jenna. It's what I want to do." He walks over, removes the pillow from her arms and tosses it to the sofa, then pulls her into a hug. She doesn't resist and isn't sure she would have the strength to do so if she'd wanted to. His arms are so warm. And comforting. She wonders for a brief moment if there is something else about Mike and her that she's forgotten.

He pulls out of the hug and looks at her. He leans in, and for a moment she thinks he's going to kiss her, but he just squeezes her shoulders and smiles. "I hope I can get over here later to see you, but Sundays are always really busy for me." He flushes a slight pink and averts his eyes. "But I said that before, didn't I?"

"Of course—I understand." She tries to smile, not wanting to know that what she's feeling is deep disappointment—that he's leaving, but also that she might not see him for a few days. He reaches for the doorknob, and she lifts her hand in a wave.

After he leaves, Monica locks the deadbolt, brings her a pair of light pink pajamas, says goodnight and heads back down the hall to her bedroom. Jenna changes in the dark, crawls under the freshly scented sheet on the sofa bed and pulls the blanket up to her chin. She's exhausted and is sure she'll be asleep in seconds, but several minutes later is staring at the dark ceiling. She can still feel the impression of his arms around her, the warmth of his body between her own arms as she hugged him back. As if he were still there.

The sensation of hugging someone, someone dear—feels like an invisible touch memory. She'd held someone close, but who? Was it Mike? Her arms remembered hugging him, or somebody at least. One thing seemed wrong: His body was too large. For the second time that night, she wonders: Is there something about the two of them, something about Jenna and Mike, that she has forgotten?

She would like there to be. She would like it very much.

12

JENNA AWAKES TO SOUNDS of dishes clattering in the kitchen. At first, she doesn't remember where she is, but as she rubs at her eyes and catches a glimpse of a strange pair of pajamas, it all comes flooding back: She's at Monica's.

She pulls the blanket tight around her neck, remembering something about a treacherous descent down a metal staircase, a hospital corridor smelling of antiseptic, snow swirling as she ducked into a car. Hot tea in mugs. A dried-up pastry. It's all so vague, as if it happened to someone else. As if it was all a dream.

Monica dashes into the living room, opens the closet door and pulls out a heavy coat. Jenna sits up on the sofa bed and swings her bare feet to the floor. "Good morning." Her voice sounds more like a frog's than a human's.

Monica looks over her shoulder, grinning. "You're awake." She moves to the arm of the couch and sits, clutching the coat to her chest. "I thought for sure you'd sleep all day."

"I could definitely do that," she croaks.

"You should. It'll be quiet here today, since I have to go into work."

"Wait—isn't it Sunday?"

She nods. "I've missed so much work this week, though, what with visiting the hospital and all, that I need to get caught up." She stands up and pulls on the coat. "Mike said he'll try to come by in the afternoon to see how you are. Are you going to be alright until then?"

They'd both put their lives on hold for her—why? Tears fill her eyes. "Thank you so much for what you're doing for me." She pushes her hair back from her face, which has gotten scrambled around her head. "Mind if I use your shower?"

"Feel free." Monica dashes down the hallway and returns with a large tote bag. "Also, if you're hungry, I have some stuff in the kitchen, so help yourself." She pauses at the door, her hand on the knob. "Are you sure you'll be okay?"

"I'll be fine," Jenna says, not at all sure she will. She grabs a pillow and hugs it, forcing a smile.

Monica chews at her lip, hesitating some more. She glances at her watch. "Okay, then. I really have to run." She pulls the door open. "Call if you need me, though, okay?"

"Sure thing." Jenna hugs the pillow to her stomach. After Monica finally leaves, she shuffles down the hallway to the bathroom, but comes back to the sofa without taking the shower she'd asked about and falls promptly to sleep again. When she wakes the second time, sunlight is streaming through the sheer curtains. Dust motes dance and sparkle in the shaft of light.

She sits up, and her stomach growls loudly. She stands up, which brings on a coughing fit. And her throat—it's so sore. Is she sick? She walks slowly to the kitchen and peers into the refrigerator. A pizza box, a couple of apples, a half-filled jug of orange juice and a partial stick of butter.

She pulls a slice of cold pizza from the box, places it on a paper towel, and pops it in the microwave for a half minute. A scent of garlic and melted cheese fills the tiny kitchen. She's about halfway done eating the pizza when she hears her phone's muffled ringtone coming from somewhere near the sofa. Her tote bag is sitting there in a crumpled heap, and she grabs the phone just before it goes to voicemail.

The call is from Mike. "Hi," she croaks, holding the phone to her ear and sinking onto the couch.

"Jenna, is that you?"

"Sorry," she squeaks. "I seem to have lost my voice somewhere between the hospital and here."

"Not surprising. They had a tube down your throat much of the time."

A tube? She brings a hand to her throat again. Vague, soupy images float through her mind—nurses and orderlies in blue scrubs, beeping machines, lots of chrome and glass and flashing lights.

"How are you feeling?"

"On a scale of one to ten, about a four, I guess. Better than last night, at least."

"Considering what you've been through, four sounds good." He pauses. "Is there anything you need? I can come by."

She looks down at the strange pair of pajamas. "Well, yes—I'd love to go to my apartment. Get some things, you know. Could you give me a ride?"

There's a long silence from the other end of the line and she thinks she's lost the connection until he says, "Sure. If you can get in and out quickly, it should be safe to do that."

Why are they so worried? "I don't understand. Safe from what?"

"Until we find out what's going on, what they did to you in the hospital—not to mention what happened before that caused all this—I don't think we can assume any place you're known is safe."

Her mind feels fuzzy, like her head is packed with cotton, and she suddenly has no energy to argue with him. "Okay. But I would like to get some of my own clothes. I can be fast."

"Great. I have another round of confessions to hear, but I can come by in about an hour and pick you up. How's that?"

"That sounds good—thank you. But are you sure you have time? Didn't you say you had a really busy weekend?"

"No such thing as weekends in my life. I'll see you soon."

After eating another slice of pizza, Jenna takes a shower, puts on the same clothes she'd worn the night before in the ride home from the hospital, then settles onto the sofa to wait for him. She pulls out her phone and notices that she's had five recent calls—all from Howard—but only one voicemail.

She punches some buttons and listens to his message. "Jenna? Howard here. I—well, I'm concerned. Where *are* you?" A long pause and some scuffling noises, then his voice again. "Call me. Okay?"

A few minutes later, a knock sounds on the door. She goes to the curtain, pulls it back, and peers outside. Mike, bundled in his long dark coat and heavy scarf, is on the porch, a large grocery bag clutched in his arms. She opens the door. "Hi," she says, and steps aside so he can come in. "What's in the bag?"

He stamps his feet and snow falls away onto the doormat. "Just a few groceries. I noticed Monica didn't have much food and I knew she was busy today, so I picked up some simple things—you know, bread, fruit, stuff like that."

"You think of everything, don't you?" She takes the bag from him and walks to the kitchen.

He follows her, unwinding the scarf, and shucks out of his coat. "My mother trained me well." He smiles. "Speaking of food, would you like some? I got peanut butter." He reaches into the bag and pulls out a jar. "Jelly too."

"You know, I am a little hungry still. I had pizza, but maybe it wasn't enough?"

"Well, who knows how long it's been since you ate—" A darkness crosses over his face and he looks into the bag, pulls out a loaf of bread and a jar of strawberry jam, then turns toward the counter behind him. She remembers the rundown of his weekend schedule he'd described last night and wonders again why he's here. He glances over his shoulder. "Would you like milk? I always love that with my PB&J."

"Of course." She smiles. "Who doesn't?"

As he works, she pulls out her phone again and starts flipping through emails. There are two from Sam. She clicks the first one and reads:

> Hey, Sis. Finally found an internet cafe, but now what I lack is time to write. Mom called and said you'd landed back in the hospital. Is everything okay??? I tried to call but couldn't even get to your voicemail—and then we had to leave the capital city again, and I had even more trouble. We've been working our tails off distributing cartons of cellphones. The villagers are always so appreciative, and we know it changes lives for the better, but it's really hard work. And cold here! Got sick the first night we arrived (of course) but otherwise am good. I'll try to call again when we get back to Astana. I hope you're out of the hospital by now!! xoxo Sam

She clicks the second email dated November 20. It's just a few lines:

> Arrived Astana to find another message, this one from Howard. Am on my way to US now. Not sure if you'll get this but sending anyway. xoxo S.

There's something about Sam's message. Is it the date? She's not sure, and she can't quite put her finger on what's odd about the email. She puzzles over it for a minute, but when she looks up, Mike is standing next to the table holding two plates and wearing an odd expression. "What?" she says, taking one of the plates from him.

He sits down across from her. "Sorry—I shouldn't have been staring at you." His cheeks flush. "It's just that you had such a contented look on your face and I wondered what you were reading."

"It's a couple messages from my brother—you know, the one that should have been a priest?"

"Aha." He grins, picks up one sandwich and takes a bite. "Your favorite brother, then."

"I only have one brother—but, yes, my favorite. And it's good news—he's on his way home." She smiles at Mike, eating quietly for a few seconds, wondering when Sam's flight might get in, whether she should try to call now. After washing the sandwich down with a gulp of milk, she looks up to see Mike giving her a curious look. "I don't know what that look means," she says, "but it does make me wonder what my face looked like when I was listening to the message from Howard."

"Sorry I missed seeing that expression." He takes another bite and chews silently for a moment, his brow furrowed. "So, Jenna. I was thinking."

"Uh oh," she says, grinning.

"You *are* feeling better, aren't you?"

She snorts. "I guess. Maybe I just had a good night's sleep—which I did. Anyway, you were saying?"

"Remember that claim form you and Monica found on your case—the one with all the medical jargon in it?" She nods, and he goes on. "I remember the original work from my undergrad days. It made a big splash back then, you know. And, well—actually I know the guy from Hopkins who did the work. I looked him up online. He's still there." He pauses, looking at her intently. "We could call him."

She sits back in her chair. The odd look on Mike's face is now even odder. "Wait—you know him?"

"Yes. And I think he would be the person to see if we want to figure out exactly what happened to you."

"How do you know him?"

"I told you—from my undergrad days."

She can't read his expression, but she can tell when someone is hiding something, and Mike definitely is hiding something. "Hopkins is in Baltimore, right? Are you suggesting I go there?"

He shrugs. "It's just a couple hours from Philly—we could go up and back in the same day."

We. So, he wants to go with her. Why is he suggesting a trip like this? She shakes her head. "I don't know—this is all so sudden."

He looks away, but after a long moment, looks back, and says, "Of course, we'd want to make sure you're strong enough to travel first."

There's something else, something he's not telling her, but she decides to drop it. She's not sure she wants to know. They finish their sandwiches and he takes the plates and glasses to the sink to wash them. A dish soap scent fills the room. As he's drying the glasses and putting them back on Monica's shelf, he says, "I need to swing by my office for a minute, but I can take you to your apartment after that."

She frowns at him, but heads for the coat hook by the door. "Where's your office?"

"I have a little cubby hole up behind the organ at St. Rita's." He colors a little and reaches for the doorknob.

A few minutes later, they're pulling into the parking lot behind the church. He switches off the engine and they get out and walk around the large stone building, coming out onto the street. She can smell the garlic from the deli, and there, walking down the sidewalk toward them, is the little girl in a blue coat, skipping along next to her mother who is pushing the same stroller Jenna had seen before.

The little girl stops and points at Jenna. "Mommy," she shouts. "There's Katie's mother!"

Jenna and Mike approach, and Jenna smiles and nods at the woman. "I guess I must look like somebody she knows."

The woman gives her a puzzled look, then reaches a hand to the little girl's head. "I'm sorry she's so blunt—Annie tends to blurt things out sometimes." She laughs a little. "But then I don't have to tell you how four-year-olds are."

"Sorry?" Jenna says just as Mike grabs her arm. He pulls her toward the church, but she yanks back. "What are you doing?" she asks.

He leans close and whispers to her. "I'm worried about the direction this conversation is going—it may cause a relapse or something."

"What are you talking about?" She wrenches her arm free and walks back to the woman. "I'm sorry—I didn't understand what you meant when you said that."

The woman's face flushes red up into her cheeks. "It's okay. No one should make you talk until you're ready." She reaches for the little girl's hand. "Come along, Annie," she says, dragging the little girl away. The child keeps her wide eyes fixed on Jenna as she stumbles down the sidewalk next to her mother.

Jenna jams her hands into her coat pockets and turns to face Mike. "What did you do that for?" She's shaking, angry. "And what was that woman talking about?"

The front door of the church creaks open and a nun sticks her head out. "Father!" she shouts, waving toward them.

Mike turns toward her. "Sister?"

"They brought it back, Father—they returned your computer. Just now." She beams at him, holding the door open with one hand.

"Oh good." His shoulders seem to release, and he sags forward a little. "Did they, you know, *say anything*?"

The sister shakes her head and gives Jenna a somewhat hostile look. "Nothing." She steps to the side, still holding the door open. "Are you coming in?"

They climb the steps, and the sister, still frowning, follows them in through the front door. Mike heads toward a set of dark stairs branching off from the hallway. "My office is up here—follow me."

They climb to the "office" which turns out to be a sort of living room with a large desk in the middle. A computer, unplugged with its cord hanging over the top, is balanced atop a pile of papers and notebooks. "Oh well," Mike says. "Looks like I need to hook it up." He gestures toward the rumpled sofa pushed up against a side wall. "Have a seat—this'll only take a couple minutes."

She flops onto the sofa and loosens the top few buttons of her coat, looking around at the messy clutter—the bookcase crammed with books, the dark crucifix on the wall next to a tall, narrow window, a darkened doorway on the side that apparently leads to another room. "What's back there?" she asks, nodding toward it.

He blushes. "My apartment." He pauses, getting even redder. "That's where I live."

"You *live* in the church?"

He laughs, although she can tell he doesn't find it funny. "I know—married to the church, right?" He grabs the power cord dangling from the computer and ducks under the desk. "Sorry—the outlet is down here." His voice is muffled.

He looks more like a computer nerd—or maybe a scientist or doctor—than a priest. The collar is always there, of course, but Jenna can't shake the thought that it doesn't quite fit him anymore. "Say, Mike, was there anything online about this procedure they did on me?"

"Yes," he says, from under the desk. "A little. The guy at Hopkins I mentioned has a short description of it on his website. I could show you once I get my computer hooked up. If you want to see it, I mean."

She pulls out her phone and opens the browser. "What's his name? You said he's at Hopkins?"

"Right." He pokes his head above the desk. "Oh wait. I think I printed that page." He reaches into his inside jacket pocket and pulls out a folded paper. "Here it is—totally forgot I'd printed the thing before."

"I guess I'm not the only one with memory problems," she teases.

He grins and sits on the sofa next to her. "Like I said before, somebody is feeling better."

He's right. She feels hopeful, maybe even a little giddy at the prospect of working with Mike to figure out what's going on. She rummages in her bag for her small notebook and flips it open to the end of her notes. She'd gone over it last night, trying to review what she'd figured out before the ill-fated hospital stay. It was a good thing she'd written the clues down, or she might never have remembered them. She still can't believe Mike and Monica sprang her from the hospital like that—is that even legal? Even if it wasn't, she didn't see that the hospital had any right to do what they were doing to her—why didn't they explain it, at least?

"So, is the phone number for the fellow at Hopkins on there?" she asks, leaning to look at the papers, her pen poised over her notebook.

He points at a box near the bottom of the page. "This must be it," he says, watching her intently. Why's Mike acting so weird? Puzzled, she scans the sheet, but before she can focus on the number he's pointing at, a photo of a smiling man with thinning blond hair catches her attention and brings her gaze to a sudden halt.

She's seen this man before. She's sure of it. She points at the photo. "Who is this?"

Mike gazes at her for a long moment before he answers. "It's the guy I was telling you about—Dr. Scott—the one I knew from when I was a student. He—he's the man who invented the fear amelioration technique."

Her eyes seem to be riveted to his photo. There's a lot of other text on the page, but she can't even look at it—she's completely drawn to that face. "I know him, Mike."

He looks intently at her. "Are you sure?"

She shrugs. "I think so—I know his face, anyway. Maybe even better than I know yours," she says, as her own face grows warm. She shakes her head. "I still can't believe I didn't know who you were when we were in the hospital. How can that be?"

"I wonder if it's such a good idea for us to go seek out Dr. Scott. I mean, maybe, uh—maybe he and your doctor are working together. That would explain why you know the face." He looks at her, intent again.

She nods, puzzled by Mike's behavior. He's hiding something. She's sure of it. "That's logical. Not that relying on my shaky memory is the best idea."

"Well, it's all we have, and I'd rather be too cautious than risk making things worse." He leans his head back against the sofa, staring at the ceiling. He sits like this for a good minute or two then closes his eyes.

He must be praying. She wonders if priests always do this, launch into a private prayer at any random moment. She wonders if he's onto something—maybe praying is a good idea. She thinks of the little doll with the broken-off arm, appearing in her dream before she saw it. Maybe it really was a message from God. Mike had never said it wasn't, after all, and—

"Jenna, let me ask you something," Mike says, suddenly lifting his head and opening his eyes. "It might seem far-fetched, but I need to ask you."

"What?"

He turns a serious face toward her. "Remember what that little girl said to you on the street outside?"

"Oh. I thought you were praying and had gotten some sort of answer."

He turns a little pink. "Maybe I should have been, but no—I want you to think. Remember what she said? That you looked like her friend's mother?"

Jenna is suddenly furious. "So what? So I look like the mother of her friend? What does that mean? It means she's just a four-year-old—she's confused." She's shaking now, extremely agitated. She leaps to her feet. "What are you getting at anyway?"

He stands and moves toward her, placing both his hands on her arms. "I can see you're upset. And I don't want to upset you, but what if that little girl isn't confused? What if you *are* Katie's mother?"

"Who the hell is Katie?" She jerks her arms out of his grasp and turns away.

A Frisbee hits her in the head.

A man runs for it. Something about him—

Pain whacks into Jenna's forehead, and she sinks to her knees on the floor. The notebook tumbles from her hand. She grasps her head, moaning.

Mike kneels down in front of her and grabs her arms again. "Jenna, I'm so sorry—I was afraid this might happen, but we really need you to remember. Just this one thing."

"What are you talking about? Remember *what*?" She tries to wrench away from him as another shot of pain slugs her between the eyes. She claps both hands over her face. "No," she moans.

A dark-haired little girl in a blue coat. She's running behind a small boy. He's holding a string, attached to a kite.

The girl turns, laughing and pointing at the kite. "Look, Mommy! A kite!"

It's Katie shouting at her.

It's Katie.

Her own little Katie.

Jenna's eyes fill with tears. She's shaking uncontrollably. "Oh my God, Oh my God, Oh my God—" she repeats, over and over, unable to find any other words.

Mike is right. My God, she thinks, he's right—she doesn't just *look* like Katie's mother. She *is* Katie's mother.

Part Three

13

IT'S TAKEN PETE SEVERAL WEEKS to hack into the personnel files at the law firm, but he's finally penetrated their defenses. "Aha, got you, sucker," he shouts to the empty machine room. It's three p.m. on a Saturday, and Columbia is closed, but he's used the stolen passkey he keeps just for these kinds of occasions. He's fired up one of the sysop terminals in the room where the hard disks and processing units are stored on racks and has several searches going at once: one at Jenna's former employer, the law firm, another at Columbia and a couple more.

The room he's in has its usual electronic smell, filled as it is with rack upon rack of servers. He could've done this work from his own laptop or even from home, but there's a possibility his tracks could be traced—hence the untraceable passkey. He doesn't want to take any chances, especially if he happens upon something juicy.

He's already located one interesting item—an article he found online when he was following a hunch. He doesn't quite understand its significance, but he's sure it's related to what's going on.

He returns his attention to the documents in Jenna's personnel file at Columbia. Most of it is boring stuff—letters of recommendation, transcripts, job performance reports. He scans them. Looks like she's been a model employee. All her marks are either "outstanding" or "superior." He keeps looking and, soon, comes upon something interesting: a family leave application, filed by Jenna herself. He clicks it open. It might be related to the funeral he'd stumbled upon that day about two years ago. Perhaps the funeral was for someone in Jenna's family—however, a box labeled "Maternity Leave" is checked at the top of the file.

He sits upright in his chair, stunned. Jenna had kids? He never knew that.

He scans through the lines of the document. It's dated over seven years ago and contains little more than Jenna's name, the date and a few signatures, so he goes back to the list of files—and that's when he comes upon the complaint.

He clicks it open and reads; it was filed with the EEOC office, by Jenna herself, against one Joshua Reynolds. He scans down the pages, trying to get the gist of what appears to be a harassment claim. Apparently the guy, Reynolds, whoever he was, said inappropriate things and even grabbed her arm once and wouldn't let her pass.

Pete pops out of the space where Jenna's files are stored and, on a hunch, carries out a search on the name stated in her complaint. One Joshua Reynolds comes up immediately in an archived version of the law firm's staff directory. Aha—he and Jenna worked at the same place then, before she was at Columbia. It takes only a few moments to determine that this guy, Reynolds, had been a low-level records clerk at the firm.

These places should really be more attentive to their online security. At least the firm seemed to be aware of physical dangers. After all, they'd terminated Reynolds shortly after Jenna's complaint against him was filed, so it was reasonable to assume the two things were related. Pete is certain harassment charges would have been enough to get the guy fired—it's happened more than once at Columbia—so he doesn't even bother to explore that theory any further. Instead, he closes the law firm database and swoops over to another hacking job he'd started for a completely unrelated reason. That was a different client—someone in New York who was willing to pay big money for Pete to fix some files in the police database.

All that is irrelevant to today's quest, though. He lets out another hoot when he finds his quarry. Took him less than two minutes this time. He scans the document, a restraining order, issued by a judge in this very county, against one Joshua Reynolds. He scans through the legal jargon, not totally understanding it except for the name in the box labeled "plaintiff": *Jenna Wright*. She'd filed for a restraining order against this guy, the same one who'd harassed her at the law firm. The judge had granted it less than two years ago.

Well, this is all very interesting. Someone had been stalking her, which might explain at least some of Jenna's weird behavior. Pete still can't fully see the connection, though. She acted like *nothing* scared her. Was that normal for someone who was being stalked? It seemed backwards, actually.

His fingers trembling, Pete clicks a few links and makes his way to the public-facing FBI records. He searches for Joshua Reynolds. Anyone can do this—it doesn't require a hacker to look up a known criminal, and in seconds the man's photo fills the screen of Pete's computer. Dark hair and a slightly crooked nose, as if it had been broken once and healed incorrectly. The face is very familiar, though. It looks just like the guy he'd followed that night when he'd stumbled upon Jenna and Father Mike having pizza together. The guy he's remembering had white-blond hair, though, not dark, and it was worn in a spiky style with lots of hair goop.

Of course it's easy to change hair color from dark to light with a little bleach.

Pete closes down the databases he's hacked into and sends himself a text message with the passwords, so he can get back in later if he needs to, grabs his jacket and heads for the elevator. He needs to find a good hiding spot, somewhere behind St. Rita's, a place where he can keep an eye on the door that leads from the church kitchen into the alley.

Pete does most of his hacking in the early morning hours, usually using someone else's computer at Columbia. It's more secure that way, but it means he's spent a lot of time grabbing a smoke on the loading dock at strange times of the night. One thing he's seen, more than once, is this same guy—white spiky hair, crooked nose—sneaking in through the back door of that church at all hours. If his hunch is correct, the same guy will be there again today.

MIKE HELPS JENNA to the couch in his tiny office and pulls his phone from his pocket. He punches at it a few times and speaks into it. "I think you'd better get over here—I told her." He nods, says uh-huh a few times, then, "The front door is open, so come on up."

Her head is still throbbing and even the small amount of light from the grimy window pierces the veil of pain surrounding her head. She peers up at him as he tucks the phone away. "Who did you call?"

"Monica. She'll be right here."

"Mike, I don't understand. How did you know?" More importantly, why didn't Jenna know? How could she have had a daughter and not know it?

He shakes his head and sinks into his desk chair, one hand over his mouth as he rocks the chair side to side with his foot. A few moments later, Monica steps in, already unbuttoning her coat. She tosses it onto the sofa next to Jenna, then sits down and gathers her into a hug. "I can't even imagine how you feel right now," she whispers.

Jenna struggles away from her. "How is it that both of you know this about me and I don't?" She's shaking, angry. "What's going on here?"

"A lot happened while you were in the hospital," Monica says. "I'm sorry you're finding out like this, but you need to know."

Tears sting her eyes and she crosses her arms across her chest, hugging herself tight. "Okay." She blinks to keep the tears in. "I do need to know."

Monica pulls her hands toward her and squeezes them between both of hers. "Weeks ago," she says, "Mike found some information—online, in an old newspaper article—that said a young girl had been found dead." She pauses, watching Jenna closely. "I'm guessing, from your expression, that you don't remember when he showed you that article. Well, to make a long story short, we found out the girl's parents were 'Jenna and Howard Bernstein.'"

"Bernstein?" Jenna asks. "What are you saying? Howard and I were—?"

Monica takes a quick look in Mike's direction. He nods and swivels his chair away, gazing out the window at the brick wall outside. "We did a little more digging, Mike and Pete and I," Monica says. "And we found that *you* were the Jenna involved. The girl in that article, the one they'd found killed—she was your daughter. Yours and Howard's, and her name was Katie."

Hearing Monica say *Katie* loosens the tears Jenna has been blinking back. They escape and roll down her cheeks. "But—why didn't you tell me?"

Monica says, "We only found out ourselves after you landed in the hospital. We were waiting for the right time to—"

"But how in the world," Jenna says, sitting up straight, "can it be that I don't remember this? How can I have had a daughter and not even know it? And I was married? Really?"

Mike and Monica both lean forward and gaze at her. "We think your memory loss is related to the fear amelioration procedure," Mike says, "although the memory loss itself was probably an unintended side-effect. As I told you before, the fear-removal procedure was apparently something you requested yourself."

Monica snorts. "According to Howard, but how can we be sure?"

Mike nods at Monica. "I'm hoping we'll know more once we talk to—"

Jenna pulls her hands out of Monica's grasp. "Wait. *Why* would I ask for something like this?" She swipes at the tears. "I'm sorry. I'm just having a hard time taking all this in."

A nun pokes her head through the doorway and raps her knuckles on the doorjamb. "Father? The altar guild is here to begin putting up the Christmas decorations."

He walks to her side. "Okay, thank you, Sister. Tell them I'll be there in a minute."

The nun finally notices that Mike isn't alone. She looks from Jenna to Monica and back again. "Very good, Father. I'll tell them." She backs out of the doorway and disappears.

Jenna shakes her head. "Christmas decorations already? Wow—I thought it was just the stores that pushed us into the Christmas season too early."

Monica stands and reaches for her coat. "Well, it *is* December," she says, pulling it on. "I really need to start my shopping."

Jenna stares. "Wait," she says. "You said *December*? The last I knew it was mid-November. What day was it when you bought that daisy, Monica?"

She laughs nervously. "I'm not sure—time flies lately, doesn't it?" She steps toward the door. "I really have to get back to work—see you two later." She and Mike exchange a puzzling look and then she's gone.

Jenna stands as Monica leaves and frowns at Mike. "Where is she off to so fast? Also—I wasn't just making small talk. I'm serious—the last thing I remember it was November."

He sighs. "I know—you came around a few times when you were in the hospital, but I was certain you weren't aware of the passage of time."

"Well, how long was I in there, anyway?" She's started to shake again.

He glances at the calendar on his wall. "Almost four weeks," he says. "Yes, that's right. Almost exactly four weeks."

SHE'D HAD A DAUGHTER. A *daughter*. And she was a married woman. How can a person forget things like that? Even if there was a way to forget, why would anyone want to forget she had a child? And, furthermore, why was her daughter killed? Does anyone know? And if they do, why are they not telling her about it?

She has so many questions. A less disturbing question, but still puzzling one was: How can it be December? What happened to Thanksgiving, anyway? Wasn't she supposed to go to Mom's? And what about Sam? Did he make it home?

She remembers Sam's email, the one dated November 20, and now understands why the message had puzzled her. The last she knew, it was early November, so a message with such a late date didn't make much sense at the time. One mystery cleared up, but a bunch of others have now appeared to take its place.

One thing *is* clear: They aren't telling her everything. Mike is definitely hiding something. Maybe Monica is too.

The thing she wanted more than anything in the world was a child—it's been this way her whole adult life. Of this much she is certain. She's not sure of much else, but this she is sure of. She refuses to believe she *chose* to forget she'd had a child.

Mike tells Jenna he'll accompany her to her apartment to grab her mail and retrieve some more clothes. "The sisters will want my help soon with the decorations, but I can wait a few minutes."

"Okay—I can hurry." She hops out of his car.

He opens his door and slides out. "Wait—I should come with you."

She shrugs, and he follows. They swing the iron gate open and make their way up the brick walk, about to go around the corner to Jenna's apartment, when Mrs. Freund's door opens, and she steps out with her cat on his leash, a whiff of lilac-scented perfume coming along with her.

Mrs. Freund's eyebrows arch nearly to her hairline. "Well, hello," she warbles, when she catches sight of Mike. "What a surprise to see you here, Father." She gives Jenna a puzzled look.

"Hello, Mrs. Freund," Mike says, stopping and nodding at her. "I didn't realize you and Jenna were neighbors."

She nods tersely. Her shoulders hunch forward as she clutches the cat's leash in her gloved hands. The enormous creature tugs at the lead, trying to get away, but Mrs. Freund tugs back. "And I didn't realize you and Jenna were—well, *friends*."

Jenna steps between her and Mike. "How are you today, Mrs. Freund?"

"Fine, fine." She gives Jenna that same look she always gives her: pity, pure and simple.

Mrs. Freund knows! She knows all about Katie, yet she's not said one word to Jenna about it in over a year. Jenna clasps her hands together, holding them tight. "I've got a question. It's a bit tough to ask—but it's important." She pauses, glancing over at Mike. "I'm sorry—I know you said you were in a hurry."

"No, no—it's okay." He takes a step back. "I can wait."

She looks at Mrs. Freund, not sure how to start. Everything she can think of sounds accusatory, but there seems no way around it. "Mrs. Freund," she says, "I've seen you nearly every day for months now, and you haven't mentioned Katie once in all that time. Why?" It feels so strange to say it. *Katie.* As if this is a person she knows. As if she says the little girl's name all the time—which she doesn't, of course.

Mrs. Freund's cheeks have developed splotches of red. She glances at the ground, then at Mike, then back to Jenna. "I'm sorry, dear." She sighs heavily. "I didn't mean to be rude or thoughtless, but I thought you wouldn't want to talk about it." She blinks and there's a glint of something in her eyes. "It was so horrible what happened to your little girl." She claps a gloved hand over her mouth and murmurs, "So horrible," shaking her head.

Jenna lets her breath out slowly. Would she have been any different? If she knew someone whose child had been killed, would she have been any quicker to say something? Blinking back tears, she looks away. Mike edges past her and puts a hand on Mrs. Freund's shoulder. "It's okay," he says quietly.

"I'm sorry," Jenna says to Mrs. Freund. "You're right, of course. It *was* horrible, and I'm sorry if I sounded like I was accusing you of something." She takes a deep shuddering breath. "It would be nice to talk about her, though. With people who actually knew her."

Mrs. Freund is wiping away tears. She nods. "I know how you feel." She glances at Mike. "When my husband died, people did the same to me. Nobody would talk about him. Some acted like he hadn't even existed, even those who admired his work. He was such a talented groundskeeper." She wipes her cheeks again. "Others felt it necessary to tell me to 'move on' with my life. Such nonsense." She shakes her head. "As you know, Father, Harvey and I were married for nearly sixty years. You can't just 'move on' from something like that."

Mike squeezes Mrs. Freund's hand. "Of course," he whispers. "It *is* hard." He looks at Jenna. "It's hard even if it's been only four or five years."

After Mrs. Freund and her cat turn and leave, Jenna rummages in her bag for her key and is about to put it in the lock when the door of her apartment swings open—and there stands Sam. He opens his arms.

"Oh my God." Jenna throws herself into his embrace. "I am so glad to see you."

He hugs her tight, then pulls back and says to Mike, "Thanks for walking her over."

"Of course, of course," Mike says, smiling. "We agreed, right?"

"Right." Sam swoops a hand toward Jenna's living room. "Welcome home."

"What are you doing here?" she asks, looking from Sam to Mike and back again. "I mean, I'm happy to see you—but when did you get here? Last I heard you were in—well, whatever the name of that country is. Kazak-something?"

"Kazakhstan. It's a long story." He guides her in through the door and looks back. "Thanks, Mike. I'll let you know how it goes."

And then he's closing the door and leading Jenna to her own sofa. A cup of tea sitting on the coffee table sends mint-scented steam into the room.

She settles into the cushions and looks around at her place that is neat as a pin. Next to the steaming teacup is a stack of magazines and envelopes. "How long have you been here?" She flips through the envelopes—all of them addressed to her. She slips the entire stack into her tote bag. No time to look at them now.

He plops into the easy chair. "Just got here today—Mike and Monica told me they'd bring you here so we could talk." He leans forward on his forearms and clasps his hands together. "How do you feel?"

Tears well into her eyes and she blinks rapidly. "I—I really don't know how to feel, Sam." Her voice is barely a whisper. She looks up, searching his face. "Did I really have *a daughter*? How—?"

He moves to the sofa and sits beside her, taking both of her hands in his own. "I'm so sorry that the procedure went all wrong, Jenna. This wasn't supposed to happen."

The tears finally escape and stream down her face. He pulls her close and she sinks into her brother's chest. He smells of sandalwood. This, at least, she remembers—how it feels to be held by Sam when things are scary and wrong. It's an old feeling, one she can remember from her earliest years. Her big brother is here. She pulls out of his arms and looks at him. "*What* wasn't supposed to happen? I don't understand what's going on."

He flops back into the couch. "Maybe I should just start at the beginning. It's not clear to me what you've forgotten."

"Everything, apparently."

"Well, not everything. You know me, right?" He gives her a weak smile.

"Of course. But—when Mike and Monica showed up in the hospital, I didn't know who they were for a while. Why—?"

"We don't understand that. It seems as if the procedure went too far. They never intended to remove actual memories. I didn't think that was even possible. The only thing that was supposed to be removed was the fear response."

"I didn't think *that* was possible, but it seems to be. For months now, I haven't been able to feel fear at all. Howard claimed I asked for this—but did I?"

"You did. You don't remember that either?"

She shakes her head. "*When* did I ask for it? And why?"

"Okay, let's go back to the beginning. I might repeat some things you know, but hey—it'll all be out there this way and we can go from there. Okay?" She nods, and he takes a deep breath. "After Katie was killed—"

Jenna claps a hand to her mouth, her stomach cramping. "This is harder than I thought. Okay, tell me. How did it happen?"

He lets his breath out with a heavy sigh. "It was in the park. Down the street. You were there for a picnic, you said, and she ran off chasing after a boy with a kite."

She sits up straight. "A kite. I remember that."

"Good. That's good, Jenna." He leans forward on his forearms, clasping his hands together again. "She disappeared into the crowd, or that's what you told the police anyway. They—they found her body in the pond the next day."

She hears his words but feels nothing. No sadness, no fear, nothing. "I don't remember that part." She shakes her head. "And I don't remember *her*."

Sam blinks back tears. "I can't believe it went this far. On the other hand, I warned them this was way too experimental. Anything could happen, I said—"

"Them?"

"Dad. And Mom, too. They were both eager to pay for the procedure, but I told them the whole thing could backfire. The technique hasn't been approved for general use." He bolts from the sofa and paces around her living room. When he stops moving, his face is like stone. "It's really my fault, you know."

"How can it be *your* fault?"

"I—I found the doctor. I'm the one who heard about the procedure." He presses both hands into his hair and looks up at the ceiling. "I'm the one who brought that *Dr. Scott* into our lives."

"The one in Baltimore?"

He nods. "I heard about Scott's technique, at a conference on 'New Uses of Technology to Improve Life'—some title like that, anyway. I'd gone to this conference trying to get backers for our cellphone distribution project. It was really just a fluke that I happened to hear Scott's talk. Anyway, he'd developed a thing he called a Fear Amelioration Technique. They were planning to use it to treat PTSD in veterans. It sounded like a good idea, but—well, I'm not so sure now. And then I made the mistake of mentioning it to Dad at Thanksgiving that year."

"I remember that phrase—fear amelioration was written up in my insurance record." She rummages through her bag, searching for her notebook. When she finds it and flips through the pages of seemingly disconnected phrases, she looks up, puzzled yet again. "Sam, do you know about something called a 'squid'? I saw that in the document, too. And I *heard* them talk about it—at the hospital."

"Yes. It stands for superconducting quantum—oh geez, I don't remember exactly now. Dr. Scott explained it in our first consultation. They use this squid thing to direct the injected magnetic particles, the ones that carry the chemical agent, to the right place in the brain. I think it's called the amygdala. Anyhow, the chemical agent the particles deliver blocks the fear response—somehow. Mike, your priest friend, actually read the papers and tried to explain it to me, but at a certain point, he lost me, just like the doctor did back then."

"Mike explained it? Really?"

"Yes. He said he'd been pre-med before going to seminary."

"Oh right—I remember him saying that now." Her memories all have the consistency of dreams. "I *think* I remember it, anyway."

"Anyhow, Mike said this whole process somehow blocks the fear response. I think that's what the amygdala is all about, but don't quote me."

"Yes. Yes—I remember that word in my insurance claim record." She leans her head back on the couch, trying to think. It's a lot to take in. "So, Sam—why did I ask for this again? I still don't get that part."

"You just kept saying, 'I refuse to live in fear. I refuse it.' And when I, offhandedly, as a joke, mentioned this technique, Dad immediately jumped on it and by the next day he'd gotten you an appointment with Dr. Scott."

"In Baltimore."

"Yes. In Baltimore."

"Did you go with me to see Dr. Scott?"

"We all did. Me, Mom, Dad. Even Howard." There's a pause and he looks at her for a long moment. "Jenna—Dr. Scott never said a thing about removing memories. This wasn't supposed to happen."

She's hugging herself tightly with both arms. It's all so unbelievable, and she doesn't remember any of it. She looks up at Sam. "You know, I don't even remember her. I don't— you know, even remember what she *looked* like."

He frowns, then stands up and fishes in his back pocket for his wallet. He pulls out a small rectangle and holds it out to her. "Here's her school picture."

She reaches for it, her hand trembling, and gazes on the face of a little dark-haired girl. She's dressed in a blue top with a rounded collar, her hair pulled back with two barrettes. She smiles for the camera, a cute little girl that could be anybody. Jenna does not recognize her.

She flips the picture over and there it is, in blue ink: "Katie, age 4." She recognizes only one thing about the tiny photo: her own handwriting on the back.

14

SAM WAITS WHILE JENNA GATHERS some clothes and items from the bathroom, then they lock up her place, head outside and walk the short distance to St. Rita's. Sam says that Mike will give her a ride back to Monica's.

They come around the corner, and Jenna spots Mike. He's standing behind the church near his car, waiting. "Wait, Sam. I have one more thing I want to ask you." Jenna stops, reaches into her bag, and pulls out the little battered doll. She holds it out to him. "Do you know what this is?"

His eyes fill with tears as he reaches for it. "Where did you find this?"

"It was in my apartment. In the kitchen. It—it was Katie's, wasn't it?"

He nods. "It was. I gave it to her myself." The tears escape down his cheeks and he swipes at them. "For Christmas." He hands it back to her. "You should keep this. It was hers, after all."

"Sam—I wonder. Do you think the dead can be in touch with us?"

He frowns. "What do you mean?"

"It's just that this doll appeared so insistently, right there in my kitchen, just as I was trying to figure out what was happening to me. It—it seems, now, like Katie herself was trying to get in touch with me."

He smiles at her through his tears and hugs her. "Maybe," he says. "That may very well be what happened." He excuses himself once he's handed her off to Mike. He tells them both he's headed to Cherry Hill, to Mom's, and promises to catch up with her later.

She's just tossed her bag in the trunk of Mike's car when his cell rings. He presses it to his ear, saying, "Yes," then "Who?" and then "Okay—I'll be there." He checks his watch and turns to her. "I thought I could take you back to Monica's, but that was the hospital. One of our parishioners, a man who was in for yet more cancer surgery, has taken a turn for the worse. They're requesting last rites."

"Oh, I'm so sorry. This is someone you know?"

"Not well. He's been in and out of the hospital most of the time I've been at St. Rita's. My predecessor, Father Ted Mahoney—that was him on the phone—knows him well but is at the airport waiting to board a flight and can't get there." He looks at his watch again. "I can make it back in time for Mass if I go now. Do you think maybe you could get a ride back to Monica's place with her?"

She's still thinking about what he said, something about a Father Ted—the name sounds so familiar, but why? Another tendril that may fall into place someday. But then he said something about going to Monica's. "What? I mean—well, maybe I should just go back to my place." She points back down the sidewalk to her apartment.

"That's not a good idea," he says.

"Why not?"

"Monica and I—and Sam, too—are just not sure it's safe for you to be there alone. I mean, we did spring you from the hospital without permission, so somebody might come after you."

She's confused. Why are they so worried? Maybe this is yet another time when she should be afraid but isn't. "Monica is right upstairs," she says, "in her office. I could just walk around to the building and go find her there—"

"Excellent idea." Mike reaches for the car door handle. "But you're not walking. Hop in and I'll drop you at the front door of your building." As she slides into the passenger seat, he turns to her, his face serious. "But you must promise me you won't go anywhere except Monica's office. She'd kill me if I let you wander off."

"Really? She'd kill you?" These two sound like they're on much better terms than Jenna had known. But, of course, she's been out of things for a month. A *month*.

She still can't believe it.

DESPITE WHAT SHE PROMISED MIKE, Jenna heads for the third floor where she finds Pete. He's in his cubicle in the chilly machine room, tucked into a corner and tapping at his keyboard. The room smells, as usual, of electronics and plastic.

He looks up sharply, his hands hovering. "I thought you were in the hospital."

"I was, until last night anyway. Mike and Monica—uh, they picked me up."

He swivels to face her. "So the hospital released you? How do you feel?"

She ignores his question and pulls up a chair. "Pete, I don't know who else to ask, but I think you might be able to help me."

"Me?"

He blushes, and his voice squeaks a little, but Jenna can tell he's pleased to be asked. "Yes, you." She pulls out her pen and notebook and flips to the last page of her notes. It's filled with scribbles about squids, little blue-coated girls, a doll with a broken-off arm, and several dozen more clues that don't seem to be fitting together into a whole.

She writes *Katie Bernstein, daughter??* below the last line and stares at it. "I'm trying to piece together what's happened." Her voice shakes. She had a daughter? How could she have not known such an important thing? "The thing is, Pete, I'm still missing a big portion of important information. I'm hoping you might be able to help me find out more."

He crosses his arms over his chest and leans back in the chair. "Like what?"

She lets her breath out heavily. "Okay. You know Mike, right? Father Mike?" He nods, his eyes grown wide. "This is the thing. He's hiding something. He's been helping me, but I can't shake the thought that he knows more than he's letting on."

Pete looks away for a long moment, as if he's thinking. "Okay," he says, jumping up from his chair and striding across the cubicle. He reaches behind a large filing cabinet, pulls a folded sheaf of papers from a battered manila envelope, and thrusts the papers toward her. "Take a look at this."

Her hands shake as she opens the papers. It's a printed article from some place called "Annals of Neuroscience Techniques," dated nearly twenty years earlier. In the title are familiar phrases: "fear amelioration" and "superconducting quantum interference device" among them. The rest is highly technical jargon.

"I don't understand," she says. "What is—?" As her eyes scan downward, the words seem to leap from the page: *Authors: Michael J. Albertino and Allan M. Scott, Department of Medicine, Johns Hopkins University.* "Oh my God," she whispers. She looks up at Pete who is standing very still watching her. "What is this, Pete? Where did you get it?"

He shrugs. "It's easily accessible online. I had a hunch and did some searching—it didn't take too long to find it once I had the name of the technique they used on you."

"But how did you know even that?"

"It was in your claim, remember?"

She looks at the page again, shaken. "Mike said he knew about Dr. Scott and his work. He said it made a big splash. He said—"

Pete shakes his head. "Not just knew *about* him, Mike actually worked with the guy. On the very technique they used to remove your memories."

She leans back heavily in her chair. "I don't think removing memories was their intent, though," she says. "It sounds like it was the fear response they were trying to eliminate."

"But why would they do that?" Pete asks. "I mean—everyone wants to be free of fear, but why you? Why not anyone? Why not everyone?"

She shakes her head. "My brother says it was experimental. And I volunteered."

"Don't you think it a little odd that the very guy who worked on the first study that proved that this approach might work is right next door? And that he seems compelled to be involved with you?"

"It *all* seems odd, to tell you the truth. Does Monica know about this paper?"

"You're the only one I've shown it to."

"And Mike doesn't know you have this information either?"

He shakes his head, and she looks back at the paper, trying to read it, but understanding nothing. She flips through the pages and there, at the very end, is a paragraph set off in a box. As she reads it, the hairs on her neck stand on end: *Funded by the Department of Defense.*

"Pete." She holds her finger to the boxed-in words. "Did you see—?"

He's standing stock-still, watching her. "Yep, sure did. And it sure seems like the military is behind all this, doesn't it?"

"I wonder what that means?"

He shrugs and looks away, his face grown dark. "I don't know. I have a hunch, but I need to do some more digging." He gives her a weak smile. "I'll let you know if I find anything more."

A FEW MINUTES LATER, she's in Monica's cubicle, her shoes kicked off and her feet tucked up under her in the chair. "I just don't understand this," Jenna says. "How can a person forget something like this. I had a child!"

"You didn't forget, exactly." Monica is sorting papers into several piles on her desk. "They took the memories from you."

She watches Monica work for a few moments. How much does Monica know about Mike's involvement? She wants to ask but decides she should keep it just between her and Pete—for now. "Do you really think I gave my permission for this, Monica? That I requested it, as Howard said?"

Monica shrugs. "I'm not sure I'd believe it just because Howard says it." She gives Jenna a quick look. "No offense—I realize this is your husband we're talking about."

"Was." She shakes her head, now not sure. "At least I assume we're no longer married—we're not living together, after all."

Monica looks at the cubicle doorway for a long moment. "You know, the thing I don't really understand—even though your record was 'sealed,' for some mysterious reason, why didn't your family say something?"

Jenna nods, but says nothing.

"It just seems odd to me," Monica says, "that your brother or your parents would not have said anything to you about your daughter. I mean, surely that would have come up at some point?"

Jenna leans back in her chair. "Sam just told me all about it—but for all I know, we've talked multiple times about it and I just don't remember." She sighs. "If I talked to my parents more, it might have had a chance to come up. I haven't had a conversation with my dad in—oh, I don't know—four months?"

"Well, what about your mom?"

Jenna stares at the floor for a long moment. "It's never like that with my mom. She never talks to me about *anything* in my life—every phone conversation I've ever had with her has been all about *her*. The last one—she went on and on about this flower show she'd entered and got third place in. I couldn't get a word in at all. And the time before that it was all about some topic her book group had discussed."

"But this was her granddaughter."

Jenna clenches her teeth. "Well, she never showed much interest in her daughter, so why should she care about a granddaughter? Seems very consistent to me." Jenna swallows, trying to stuff the rage that's bubbled into her throat back into her belly where it lives most of the time. She's forgotten many things about her life, but unfortunately, she's not forgotten this.

Monica finishes up, shuts down her computer and they head to the parking garage beneath the building. It's dark and damp and smells of stale car exhaust. After they find Monica's car, they drop by the grocery store on the way to her place and fill a couple of plastic containers at the salad bar. Several minutes later they're both curled up in Monica's living room, eating their salads with plastic forks. Jenna's smells tangy and tastes delicious, full of herbs, balsamic vinegar and lemon.

"I guess I'd better do it. You know, call my mom." Jenna sighs. "I'm not sure how to start a conversation like this, though." She pauses, thinking. "And the other thing I'm wondering about is what happened for Thanksgiving. I mean, I was supposed to go to Mom's. I never got a chance to ask Sam about that earlier."

"Well, I *do* know the answer to that. Howard told us that your Mom called him *on* Thanksgiving. To check on you. Howard told her you were recovering but couldn't see anyone."

"Really? Why would he tell her that?" Was Howard in on this too? So many secrets, and so many people involved—Jenna's head is starting to swim.

Monica shrugs. "It was just one of the many odd things Howard did that finally convinced us, Mike and me, that we had to spring you from that place."

Could Howard have had something to do with Katie's death? She shakes her head, uneasy about the direction her thoughts are veering. The very idea should scare her to death, *if* she were a normal person. But, of course, she isn't. "Anyhow—my mom," Jenna says. "I have to call her. But how do I even start?"

Monica nods. "I see what you mean. Maybe something like: 'Hi Mom. Say, I just discovered I had a daughter. Know anything about that?'" She laughs, shaking her head. "Maybe not the best approach."

Jenna stabs a piece of dressing-drenched lettuce with her fork and takes another bite. "How about this?" she says, waving the fork in the air and staring into space. "Hi, Mom. I've been having some problems with my memory and I keep seeing this little dark-haired girl. Know anything about that?"

Monica shrugs. "You mean pretend you don't know yet? Let her volunteer the information."

"Right. Wouldn't that be better?"

"Why?"

"Well, as you pointed out, the records were sealed—maybe my family didn't want me to know about Katie."

"I would ask why in the world your family would want to hide something like that from you, but it's not stranger than anything else that's happened."

"Exactly."

Monica finishes off her salad and plunks the plastic container to the coffee table. "You gonna call her now?"

"I don't want to—but I should."

"Well, how about your dad then? Would that be easier?"

She shakes her head. "No—definitely harder. As I said, I haven't talked to him for months."

"I know that's what you said—but why is that?"

"My parents are divorced. It was a pretty nasty breakup."

"So? What does that have to do with you and your dad?"

Jenna places her nearly empty salad container on the table next to Monica's. "Yes, I know what you're thinking—it was their marriage that failed, and I shouldn't be taking sides. But I did. He was always demeaning to her. Had been for decades. The yelling. The put-downs." She pauses, biting her lip. "Even the occasional beating."

Monica's eyes widen. "Oh wow. He hit her?"

She nods. "We—Sam and I—weren't supposed to know. But we could hear him knocking her around at night while we were in bed upstairs pretending to sleep. My mother lived in constant fear."

Jenna's own words ring in her mind: *My mother lived in constant fear*. It means something. Something important—but what?

"Did he hit you and Sam too?" Monica asks.

Jenna shakes her head. "No. He yelled a lot, though. Called me stupid and all sorts of other terrible things, but he never touched me. Same with Sam. Lots of verbal put-downs." She pauses, thinking of Sam, barely sixteen, running downstairs one night to force himself between their parents. Dad had pulled his fist back, as if he was going to hit Sam, but stopped, turned away, and stormed out of the house. That night was the beginning of the end of their parents' marriage since Dad did not come home—that night, or any night after.

"I can see why you don't enjoy talking to your father. But he might have information you need."

Jenna puts her face in her hands and leans her head back on the sofa. "You're right—I guess I'd better get this over with." She reaches for her bag and rummages for her phone. When she pulls it out, she sees three missed calls—all from Howard. And three voicemails, also from Howard. She grins at Monica. "Well, there's an idea."

"What?"

"Howard keeps calling and leaving messages. Maybe I should just call *him*—it sure sounds like he knows what's going on."

Monica frowns. "No—that's a bad idea. He was definitely in on what they were doing to you at the hospital."

"Well, maybe he was, but since he was my husband—I still can't believe that part—he *would* be in on it. Besides, Sam says it was all an accident, that the memory loss was never supposed to happen."

"I'm not sure I believe all this stuff about an accident." Monica frowns, seeming to think for a moment. "What's in Howard's messages?"

Jenna shrugs. "I'll check." The first two messages are the same: Howard pleading, *Call me when you get this*. In the third message, though, dated the previous night, he sounds downright panicked. *Where are you, Jenna? I'm at your apartment and it's well past midnight and nobody's home! And the hospital says they can't find you! Call me as soon as you get this message. Please.* His voice cracks on the last word.

Tears sting Jenna's eyes and she presses a hand to her heart trying to quell the ache that has appeared there. He sounds so concerned, so unlike the Howard she remembers. Had she and Howard really been *married*? How could that have happened and she not know it?

The tears she's been trying to hold back spill out, and Monica comes to her side and wraps an arm around her shoulder. "This has got to be so hard," she says, hugging Jenna close. "I don't know how you can even stand it."

After Jenna cries for a while, she sits back. "I know I should call someone—my parents, my brother, maybe Howard—but I can't do it."

"Then don't. There's no reason you have to call right away, that's for sure. I mean, as far as you're concerned, you found out about this only a matter of hours ago, right? You should give yourself some time—let it sink in."

"You're right. I feel like a fire hose of information has hit me today. I'm exhausted, actually."

Monica pops up and heads for the kitchen. "How about some tea? I have chamomile, I think."

"That sounds nice." Monica brings a fluffy afghan and wraps it around Jenna's feet and knees, then carries two large mugs into the living room. Jenna settles into the soft armchair and sips at her tea. Fragrant steam curls around her face. "You'd make a good mom, Monica. I feel positively doted over."

Monica snorts. "Can't be a mom without a willing guy."

"I suppose."

Monica turns sideways on the sofa, pulling her knees up and wrapping her arms around her legs. "It amazes me you don't remember being a mom, not to mention married."

Jenna sips at the hot tea. "I know what you mean. And here I'd been thinking, for months really, that I was always going to be an old, unmarried woman with no chance of ever having kids. Now I'm finding out I had everything I dreamed of." Jenna stares at the steam twirling up from her cup.

Monica is watching her quietly. "It doesn't seem fair," she finally says, then looks away for a moment and reaches for her own mug that sits on the coffee table. "Although—and maybe I shouldn't say this—but I'm not sure being married to someone like Howard would be my idea of 'everything I'd dreamed of.'"

"Well, he must've had a few positive qualities." She smiles. "He does, actually."

"I know you probably can't remember, but what do you think possessed you to marry him?"

She shakes her head. "That's just it. The last I remember, he was married to a woman named Deirdre—not me. Of course, I remember nothing about Katie, either, so maybe our marriage had something to do with her?"

"I'd wondered that, too. It makes him seem a little more admirable, though, don't you think?"

"In what way?"

"Well—that he would marry you if you got pregnant."

"Sure, but he was already married—so that means he'd have to divorce another woman first. That part is easier to believe, though."

"How do you mean?"

"Let's just say he never had much of anything positive to say about his wife."

"They never do, do they?"

Jenna watches Monica sip at her cup. It seems rude to ask, but she really wants to know. "So, have you ever done it?"

"Done what?"

"You know—had an affair."

Monica gives her a quick look. "What, me? Little ol' me?" She shakes her head vigorously, grinning. "Never."

Jenna laughs. "I guess that means yes."

"I guess your guessing is spot-on." Monica takes another sip of tea. "I'm not proud of it, mind you. But it is what it is." A smile crosses her lips. "I was young. And stupid. I have no other excuse. But enough about me. What I want to know more about is Mike."

"Mike?" Monica just smiles, so Jenna asks again. "Mike Albertino?"

"What other Mike do we know?"

"What about him?" Jenna's face has grown hot.

"Come on, Jenna. I've seen how you two look at each other. And you have to admit he's taken an inordinate interest in this whole thing for someone you didn't even know a few weeks ago."

Jenna gazes at her tote bag. The paper Pete handed her that afternoon is in there. She can't show it to Monica, though. Not yet. "He's a priest, Monica. I can't—"

"Priest, shmiest. Just because you can't, doesn't mean you won't. I mean, we know you had an affair with a married man, right? Someone who should be unavailable. Just like a priest. Just because Mike is unavailable doesn't mean you aren't interested."

"I see your point." Jenna looks away. "The only problem is, you're wrong."

"About what?"

"There's nothing going on. Nothing between us."

"Maybe not yet."

"No. It can't happen. I won't let it." She glares at Monica. "I've apparently been responsible for breaking up one marriage. I'm not about to—"

"Wait just a minute. Who says it was your fault Howard's first marriage failed? You don't know that. He might very well have left her of his own accord."

"Maybe." She shrugs, an emptiness opening up in her chest and spreading wide. "I wish I could remember how that happened—all of it. Even the bad parts."

JENNA GOES TO SLEEP for the third night in a row on Monica's couch. When she wakes, sun is streaming through the window and the clock shows it to be well after ten a.m. She takes a shower, breathing deeply of the soap-scented steam, then has a little breakfast. Afterward, she sits on the couch, staring out the window, or trying to. Her notebook is open in her lap and she's made a few scribbles in it, trying to connect the dots, but failing. She's still missing something crucial. But what?

Despite nearly twelve hours of sleep, she still feels exhausted. She wonders if it has something to do with what happened in the hospital. Is this normal? She has no idea, but it feels like someone's pulled the plug on her internal energy supply.

The sheer curtains block most of her view, and all she can make out is brightness outside. She walks to the window and pulls back the curtain. It's gorgeous out—bright blue sky, not a single cloud. The snow she'd seen when they left the hospital has mostly melted, although small white drifts are still visible in shady spots beneath bushes and next to the apartment buildings that line the street. She'd love to get outside, go for a walk. She knows Monica and Mike would not approve, but she bundles up in coat, hat, scarf and gloves and steps outside, locking the door behind her with the key Monica lent her. The air is crisp and smells of pine.

She glances up and down the street. Which way? Monica's apartment is near the end of the row and beyond that are small homes with tiny yards. She heads toward them, feeling better as she walks. The trees are nearly devoid of leaves—not at all the way it had been the last time she'd been out.

A shrub with a few flaming red leaves still attached draws her attention. It makes her think of the park, the red and gold leaves swirling from the trees, the colorful ribbons tangled in the branches. A dull throb begins in her forehead and she pushes the thoughts away. Remembering causes pain and she just doesn't need that today.

She rounds the corner at the end of the block. A large grassy expanse of rolling hills spreads away on the other side of the street and is bordered by an expensive-looking wrought-iron and brick fence. She crosses the street and walks along the fence. After a few minutes of the same featureless grassy landscape, she sees the headstones, arranged in neat rows and spreading away from the fence, off over the hill.

It's a cemetery. She remembers, now, how Mike told Monica the night they sprung her from the hospital that St. Rita's does a lot of burials at a cemetery nearby—this must be the one he meant. Could Katie be in there? She must be buried somewhere, after all, so why not here? It's not that far from Jenna's apartment, and would be a logical place for a grave—somewhere she could visit easily. She gazes at the rows of headstones outlining the topography of the grassy hills.

None of it looks at all familiar but she can't shake the thought that something, some invisible force, is pulling her toward it. She does want to investigate, but it seems stronger than mere curiosity. In fact, it seems as if Katie herself is luring Jenna toward her. She thinks of the doll with the broken arm that almost presented itself to her, as if a clue was being thrown at her. Maybe this is another clue.

She keeps walking. At the corner, the fence ends in a gate and beyond it stands a small stone building, smoke curling from a tiny chimney. A driveway leads to the small house and connects to a gravel-covered road that curves away over the grassy hill.

On the brick pillar of the gate is a speaker box beneath which is a sign: *Caretaker Hours (See Below) – Press Button to Summon Attendant*. She punches the button and leans toward the box. "Hello? Anybody in?"

The speaker crackles and a warbly voice answers. "Yes! May I help you?"

"Do you have records of those—well, you know, the people buried here?"

"Yes, ma'am. Sure do. Who ya lookin' for?"

Jenna draws back, surprised. She didn't expect it to be so easy. She leans toward the speaker again. "I'm looking for a Katie—uh, well, Bernstein, I guess. The last name is Bernstein."

"The name rings a bell," the warbly voice says. "Might take me a few minutes to look it up. Would you like to step in from the cold?"

"Sure. Thank you." The gate clicks and swings slowly inward, as if powered by hidden electronics. After she steps through, it swings closed behind her, latching with another loud click.

"Miss? Over here." The door of the tiny stone house is open a crack and an old man is poking his head out. When he sees her look, he beckons.

She crunches down the gravel path toward him. The wood smoke from the chimney smells homey. He swings the door open and steps out onto a stone slab. He's thin, bent over and dressed in overalls atop which he wears a faded red sweatshirt peeking out from under a bulky dark jacket. His long gray hair is pulled back into a curly ponytail and he smiles and waves a bony hand toward her.

"Hello," she says, approaching the stoop. "Thank you for your help. I didn't actually expect anyone to be here today."

"I'm here every day." He grins, revealing a missing tooth. "Well, except Christmas and New Year's, o'course. I always take them two days off. Every year."

There's something about the old fellow that seems familiar, but she can't quite place who he is. "Only two days off a year? That's pretty dedicated."

"Nothing to do with dedication. It's what I love. Sittin' with the dead, you know—nothin' better." He steps to the side and sweeps his hand toward the open door. "Would you like to come in and set a spell while I look up the records of your loved one?"

"Sure." She steps in through the door as a blast of sweet-smelling warm air hits her, carrying with it a scent of cinnamon. "Smells great in here," she says as he follows her in and closes the door.

"Been makin' some cinnamon spice tea." He waves a hand toward a cast-iron stove in the corner. A battered and blackened teakettle sits atop it pouring steam from its curving spout. At the other end of the small room is a desk piled high with paper and file folders, several banged-up metal file cabinets and a round wooden table surrounded by four rickety chairs. He gestures to the table. "Have a seat—would you like a cup?"

"That sounds great." She sits at the round table, choosing a chair that looks a little less rickety than the others. "It's a bit brisk out today, isn't it?"

"Indeed. A nip in the air, for sure. But sunny, so we can't complain, right?" He busies himself with the teakettle and pulls a couple of cracked mugs from a battered wooden cabinet next to the stove.

Jenna loosens her coat and removes her gloves and hat, watching the old man shuffle slowly across the room with two hot mugs. He carefully places them on the table and, just as slowly as he walked across the room, moves toward the desk. He does everything in slow motion—sliding open a drawer, rummaging through it for an interminable period before finally returning to the table with a small pad of paper and a stub of pencil.

He sips noisily at his cup several times, then picks up the pencil and holds it, poised, over the pad. "Now. Tell me the name of your loved one again. Gotta get the spelling right, you know—so many people have such similar names."

She suppresses a smile. He probably doesn't get many visitors. "It's Katie, but I don't know for sure if it's K-a-t-i-e or, perhaps, K-a-t-y."

He taps the pencil on his tooth, avoiding the gap where one is missing. "Hm. Maybe the name is actually Katherine?"

"Yes—I suppose that could be it."

He slurps noisily at his cup and says, "Let's start with K-a-t-i-e and see what we find. Last name?"

She flinches a little. "Bernstein. Although it might, actually, be Wright."

"Uh huh." He regards her for a long moment then scribbles something on the pad. "I take it this was not a particularly *close* loved one."

She flinches again. "Sorry?"

"You know—since you don't know the name, she couldn't have been too close a relative. Right?"

Stung, she looks away, then turns back to him. He's frowning at her over his steaming cup. "That would be a logical assumption. Actually," Jenna says, her voice quavering a little, "I don't even know if she's buried here—so, as you say, not a close relative."

He stands up, the pad of paper clutched in one bony hand. "Let's start with Bernstein, then, and if she ain't in the B's we'll look at the other name—what was it?" He peers at the pad. "Ah, right—Wright." He chuckles, turning toward her and grinning. "Right Wright. Right Wright—get it?"

She smiles weakly as he shuffles toward the file cabinet. She sips at her tea for several long minutes until, finally, he yanks a folder out of the drawer and holds it aloft. "Here we go!" he says triumphantly. "Found it on the first try." He shuffles back and sinks into his chair, spreading the folder open on the table. "Now then—let's see what we can find."

She watches him run a bony finger beneath the rows of words. His lips move, and he mutters, flips to the next page, mutters some more, does this several more times. She can't make out what the paper says, since everything is upside down.

"Here we go!" he crows again. "Row sixteen, plot H." He grabs the stubby pencil and writes "16-H" on the pad. He peers at her, the pencil gripped in his bony fingers. "Would you like me to run you out there?"

"Sorry?"

"The gravesite is around the hill, on the backside. It's a bit of a walk. Most folks who visit that part of the cemetery come in a car and drive over."

"How far is it?"

He shrugs. "About a mile. I'd be happy to run you over. My truck's out back."

She nods. "Thank you—a ride would be nice."

"Okey-dokey." He pushes his chair back with a screech. "Shouldn't take but a minute or two to get round the hill."

"I do appreciate your help. By the way, I'm Jenna." She extends her hand.

"Harvey," he says, shaking her hand and grinning. "Pleased to make your acquaintance."

Harvey's "truck" turns out to be more of a golf cart than a truck. It smells like a garage and has a homemade wooden cab attached to the back end. It's small and barely wide enough for two to sit side-by-side on the cracked vinyl seat. He leans to open the door for her. "Watch yer step now."

After he gets in, they bump across the grass dotted with patches of snow where the shade hits it to the gravel road, then they veer around a long curve that runs alongside the bottom of the hill behind Harvey's stone cottage. As they come around the bend Jenna catches sight of a huge tree, completely leafless, surrounded by a carpet of bright yellow leaves. The hillside is dotted with headstones. It's breathtaking, with the wide sweep of blue sky beyond. As they draw closer, she sees that some of the headstones are decorated with plastic flowers or sad-looking potted plants that have all gone to brown.

They bounce to a stop below the leafless tree. Harvey leans forward on the steering wheel and points at the hillside. "It's below that tree, a newer grave, o'course—but I guess you knew that. You can recognize the newness by the way the sod is— hasn't filled in around the edges yet."

She looks toward where he's pointing, trying to quell a trembling that's started in her belly and is moving toward her throat. "Over there?" she asks quietly.

"Yes, ma'am," Harvey says. He looks at her gently. "I can wait here for you if you'd like a few moments with your loved one."

The shaking in her belly increases. Is this fear? It's been so long, she's no longer sure. She can't walk away from this, though, now that Harvey's gone to so much trouble for her. It takes all the effort she can muster to say, "Thanks, Harvey. I'll just be a minute."

She walks across the golden carpet of leaves. It smells pungent, like fresh damp earth. Light flickers through the bare branches that arch overhead. Beyond them is that flawless blue sky. She focuses on it, and it seems to give her strength. She reaches the first headstone and squats down to read it. "Johnson." This isn't the one, so she keeps walking, scanning the headstones until she finds it near the crown of the hill.

It's a simple rectangular granite stone into which has been carved an image of a sitting lamb. The lamb's little legs are tucked beneath it, and it looks off into the distance. "Katie Wright Bernstein" is carved across the top of the stone. Two dates are beneath the name, separated by a dash. The latter one is almost two years earlier—March of the previous year.

She sinks to her knees. When she glances over her shoulder, she sees that Harvey has gotten out and is standing by his truck, leaning back and looking at the endless blue sky. The tombstone has been polished to a high sheen. She rubs her fingers over its glossy surface. Her own face reflects back to her. The sun, brilliant and high overhead, glints off the stone, setting the golden carpet of leaves afire. It's like she's kneeling at the edge of heaven, a place guarded by a very unlikely angel named Harvey.

She keeps expecting something to hit her, some sort of revelation or memory, but she senses nothing. Absolutely nothing. If this is really her daughter, her own daughter in the grave, shouldn't she feel something? Shouldn't she remember her?

She stares at the name, her own last name there in the middle, Howard's at the end. The trembling she'd noticed in Harvey's truck has disappeared. She feels utterly empty. She pulls the little doll from her purse and holds it in her hands, stroking the matted hair, rubbing a finger over the cool plastic. Still nothing.

She stays for what she hopes is a respectable length of time, then tucks the doll away and goes back to the truck. As she slides in, Harvey asks, "Was it her?"

"I believe so. Thank you, Harvey." She glances at him. "I do appreciate your assistance today."

"No problem. It's my job." A chirping sound fills the cab of the truck. "Oops—sorry." Harvey reaches to the inside pocket of his jacket and pulls out a large brand-new phone. "Uh huh. Yes, certainly," he says into it. "Since you know where the plot is, I'll just open the gate and you can come on in." He punches a couple of buttons on the phone, then talks into it again. "Okay, then—I've opened it. Take your time and stay as long as you like. All righty then—good-bye."

He tucks it back in his pocket then looks at her with a grin. "I do love my new phone. My grandkids got it for me, you know. Lets me open the front gate for visitors from anywhere on the property."

Jenna raises her eyebrows. "You don't look like the sort of fellow who'd have a phone like that—you're full of surprises, Harvey."

He guffaws. "I know. Grandkids say that, too. Anyhow, the speaker box on the gate out there gets routed to the phone somehow or other. I can be out doin' whatever I have to do and don't have to be at the lodge to hear em. Makes it easier on them *and* me, you know?"

He shifts into gear, and just as he pulls back onto the gravel road, a black car comes around the side of the hill. Harvey pulls off onto the grass to let them pass, raising a hand in a small wave as the car rolls by. "Yep, these new smartphones are really something. Grandkids were sure right about that."

Jenna stares at the black car as it passes, sending a blast of strong-smelling exhaust in through the open window. The man in the front seat doesn't seem to see her—but she sees him.

It's Howard, headed in the direction of Katie's grave.

15

MIKE IS OUT ON THE FRONT STEPS OF THE CHURCH, shoveling the inch or so of light snow that fell during the night. The storm had been threatening all week, an incessant wind that rattled the windows and didn't let up for days, but now it's calm, sunny and cold.

He's gotten into a rhythm, and the chore is going fast, which is good since he's got a lot of paperwork to do today. He scrapes across half of each step, starting in the middle and sliding the shovel outward, alternating sides and working his way down the four steps that lead from the landing in front of the church's double doors to the sidewalk below. It's very quiet, and the air is fresh, cleared of the usual bus fumes and car exhaust on the boulevard. The snow muffles the city sounds, strangely subdued today, as if the entire metro area has been evacuated.

He loves it, the quiet, but the solitude he craves is broken by a hesitant voice from the sidewalk below. "Father?"

He stops and leans on the handle of the shovel. He's started to sweat, and his forehead is beaded, so he wipes at it and peers down to see who's there. It's one of his parishioners—at least, he thinks it is. It's an older fellow, in his seventies or so, dressed in a tan jacket with a knitted brown hat pulled so low over his ears and forehead that his face is obscured. His hands hang loosely at his sides and are stuffed into a pair of puffy gloves, and on his feet are black rubber galoshes, like the kind Dad used to wear with metal clasps that fold over the front seam and snap into place.

The man is now wringing his gloved hands together. "Father Mike? Gotta minute?"

He really doesn't have a minute, but he knows need when he sees it, and the man is clearly distraught. "Yes, certainly," Mike says, propping the shovel against the handrail. "Let me come down to you." He notices that the man is trembling. "On second thought, it's a little cold out—how about we go into the church?" He waves a hand toward the front doors and the man nods as he picks his way up the partially-cleared steps.

He stamps his galoshes on the landing when he reaches it and pulls off his hat. It's McPherson. "I appreciate you taking the time, Father," he says. "I normally wouldn't interrupt you. I know how busy you are." McPherson looks away for a long moment, then turns back. "It's my wife, and I don't know—" And then there are tears welling in his eyes and he's blinking rapidly, trying to hold them in but failing.

Sophie McPherson, his granddaughter, had been on the prayer list for months, but so had Mrs. McPherson, his wife, as she battled the cancer that had invaded her body at a most inopportune time. So much grief in one family.

Mike reaches for the door and swings it open. "Let's go to the small front room," Mike says, waving Mr. McPherson into the darkened interior. "We can sit and chat there." He leads the man down the narrow corridor and into the small sitting room. A tiny sofa and two stuffed chairs are placed around a low coffee table on which is a large Bible. "Would you like some coffee?" he asks. "Or tea?"

"No, no, thank you, Father." McPherson pulls off his gloves and stuffs both them and the hat in his pockets. His thinning hair, damp with sweat, is askew and he smells of Ivory soap. He runs a shaky hand through his hair, clasping his hands in front of his coat. "It's my wife, Father. She died. In the night." The tears that have threatened to overtake the man finally do, and they streak down his cheeks. His voice is pinched and high. "I don't know what I'm going to do now."

Mike pulls him into his arms. The man sobs as Mike holds him. There's nothing more he should do right now. He knows that. No words will be as helpful as this simple gesture—so he holds Mr. McPherson, and soon they are crying together.

BY THE TIME JENNA RETURNS from the cemetery to Monica's place, she's ready for lunch and a nap. After a bite to eat, she pulls the blanket and pillows from under the coffee table and is asleep in seconds.

She awakes to late afternoon sun slanting through the curtains. Strange images from an unsettling dream drift up: a funny old man in a rickety blue truck, a tiny coffin and a bald-headed priest in a dark church scented with cinnamon.

She's had a dream like this before—she's sure of it, but now wonders if some of it's a memory, not a dream. That must be Katie's coffin, but who's the bald-headed priest? Certainly not Mike who has a full head of dark hair.

Her phone rings, and when she picks it up, she sees it's Mike—as if he's reading her mind. "I was just thinking of you."

"Well, I was thinking of you, too, which is why I called. How are you feeling?"

"A little tired. I slept hours more than I would have thought possible the last couple of days and just had another nap."

"I'm sure you need the sleep. You've been at Monica's all day?"

"Mostly. I went for a walk, though, and found something interesting."

"What?"

"A cemetery. In fact, *the* cemetery. The one where Katie is buried." She pauses. "I saw her grave."

"Wow. How did you find it?"

"There was a nice old man there—the caretaker, I guess. He looked it up and took me out to it."

"Did it upset you to see it?"

"That's just it, Mike. I didn't feel a thing. Nothing. It's odd, since I thought it was only fear I couldn't feel, but I felt nothing at all. No sadness. Certainly nothing even slightly resembling grief." She sighs. "I was hoping that seeing concrete evidence she'd been real—you know, a tombstone with her name on it—would convince me *she* had been real. Do you think that's normal? That I felt nothing?"

"I have no idea what would be normal in a situation like yours. All I can say is it's a lot for a person to take in all at once." He pauses a moment. "Say, are you and Monica planning to stay in tonight?"

"You know, I haven't seen her since early this morning. She had a meeting, I guess. Maybe she had to work late? What's today?"

"Monday."

"Well, she might be at yoga—we usually went to a class on Wednesdays, but I know she was going on Mondays sometimes as well. I'm sorry to say I've missed most of the classes I paid for."

"Maybe you should go tonight," he says.

It sounds appealing. "I would like to, but I'm stuck here without a car."

"I can pick you up. I just left the hospital and I pass Monica's street on my way back to the church."

"Well, sure—if you're coming by anyway—"

"I am. Well, actually—" There's a long pause. "I'm here."

She jumps up and goes to the window, pulls back the curtain, and there's his car at the curb. She can see him through the windshield, waving. Seconds later, he's bounding up the steps.

She opens the door, smiling. "Did you plan that whole thing?"

He grins. "I don't know what you're talking about." He steps through the door, smiling, and she remembers Monica's words: *I've seen how you two look at each other*.

He shrugs out of his coat, and she catches a whiff of incense, a scent of the church he seems to carry everywhere with him. The crinkly eyed smile is gone, replaced by a tiny furrow between his eyebrows.

"Have a seat." Jenna gestures toward the sofa. "It'll take me a minute to get ready." She pauses. He's still frowning. "Is something wrong?"

"What do you mean?"

"You look a little—I don't know. Worried, maybe. Did something happen?"

He stares at the floor for a long moment. When he looks up he says, "Something *did* happen. The hospital yanked my chaplaincy credentials."

She sits down heavily. "Why would they do that?"

He shrugs. "The reason I was given was vague. I know they got wind of our little escapade, springing you from the hospital." He looks away. "Of course, it could've been something else."

"Like what?" Her belly has started to tremble. She doesn't like his tone and she can't stop thinking about that paper with his name on it, still tucked inside her bag on the floor next to the sofa near her feet.

He looks at her for a long time and something dark crosses his face. He shrugs again and looks away.

"I'm so sorry, Mike. I don't want to get you in trouble—would it help if I talked to the hospital? Told them I went with you willingly?"

He shakes his head. "It isn't that simple."

"I shouldn't have mixed you up in this."

"You didn't mix me up in anything, Jenna. I was already involved."

It's about time—maybe he'll finally explain what that paper is all about. "What do you mean?" she asks. "Exactly how were you already involved?"

He scoots forward on the couch and grabs both her hands in his. Intense desire swells up inside her and there's a throbbing, deep down inside. He'd said it, straight out: *I was already involved.* She lets her breath out carefully. "Mike." She remembers Monica's words: *I've seen how you two look at each other.*

He springs to his feet. "I'm sorry," he says stepping away. "I just can't."

She flinches. It feels like he's hit her. Has she misunderstood? She must've misunderstood. He's a priest, for God's sake. "I'm sorry." She presses a hand to her mouth. She doesn't know whether to want him or be wary. What about that paper in her bag? It's all so confusing.

He shakes his head so hard a lock of hair falls across his forehead. He swipes at it, angry. "No, I'm the one who should be sorry. This isn't at all fair to you. I shouldn't be feeling what I'm feeling."

"How can you not—? But wait. What *are* you feeling?"

He sinks back into the sofa. "Of course you don't understand. I'm sorry to be so obtuse." He looks at her. "I'm thinking of leaving the priesthood."

Both hands fly to her mouth. "Oh no. But why?"

"See?" He stands up and begins to pace. "I told you I shouldn't be feeling what I'm feeling."

She watches him walk back and forth. "I'm sorry I reacted that way, Mike. I mean, you told me weeks ago, that night when we had pizza, that you had doubts."

"Yes, but it's different now. This time I'm really thinking of doing it."

"Is—is it about me?" Her face grows warm even before she finishes stammering out the question.

He looks at her, his mouth gaping. "Oh my." He looks away and then back at her. "It isn't about you, Jenna, if that's what you're thinking."

"It isn't?" She can barely squeak the words out.

He goes to the window, pulls the curtain back and stares outside for a while. "You know," he says, letting the curtain drop back. "Maybe it is about you. I'm not really sure now."

She reaches for her tote bag and pulls out the folded paper Pete gave her. She holds it out to him. "Does this have anything to do with what you're *not* telling me?"

The blood seems to drain out of his face as he takes the paper from her. He sinks into the chair opposite her, lets his breath out heavily and leans back to stare at the ceiling for a long moment. When he returns his gaze to her face, he asks: "How did you find this?"

"It was Pete's doing—he can find anything, or so it seems." She pauses, watching him, and when he doesn't respond, she says, "Tell me what's going on."

He leans back in the chair. "Okay. I'll tell you everything. You deserve to know, after all. I told you before that I was an undergrad pre-med major, right?"

"Yes."

"I went to Johns Hopkins. My senior thesis project was with Allan Scott, a neuroscientist." He nods at the paper in his hand and places it carefully on the coffee table. "This was the paper he and I wrote on my work. My mom and dad were so proud." His voice catches, and she sees a glint of tears in his eyes.

"Mike, there's something else. Tell me. And tell me the part about the funding."

He looks up sharply, a flare of anger crossing his face. "That was the part I knew nothing about as a student," he says. "We were working with rats, and my job was to administer the drug regimen to the animals and help carry out tests on them. We would present them with situations that ought to scare a rat—loud banging noises, bright lights, even a cat we brought in to the lab—and I would record their reactions."

"That's it?"

He sighs. "Yes, that was it for a while, and then we went to a conference. I was really nervous. It was my first talk, and the crowd was huge—four hundred people at least. But I got through it, and afterward, my advisor introduced me to the man who'd funded our work. He gave me his card. 'Department of the Army.'"

"So—the Defense Department, right? Is that what you're saying? The military was involved."

"It made no impression on me at first, but then I was pulled into a conversation in the hallway with some of Scott's collaborators." He looks at her evenly. "One of them was named Peter Andrews."

"My doctor! You knew him?"

"Yes, but this was twenty years ago. I doubt he remembers me. He certainly didn't recognize me in the hospital that day."

"But, Mike, why keep this a secret from me? Why didn't you tell me that you'd worked on this project?"

He shakes his head. "I should have said more. I told you I knew about the project, but what I didn't tell you was why the Army wanted the work done."

"And why is that?"

He looks away. A small muscle in his jaw flexes a few times, then he looks back at her. "The initial intent was to develop a technique to treat soldiers suffering from PTSD—veterans, you know. It didn't take long for someone to realize that soldiers who don't feel fear could be very valuable."

A wave of gooseflesh crawls up her back. *Soldiers that don't feel fear.* "But—did they try it? I mean, did they try it on people? Soldiers?"

He nods. "They did, and it showed some promise. It was Andrews who proposed expanding the study from rats to humans."

She shakes her head. "Didn't he understand how awful that would be for people, though? I mean—look how miserable my life has become. When you can't feel fear, you lose so much of yourself." She had a daughter. And a husband. They *took* those memories from her.

He moves to the sofa next to her. The faint scent of incense on his clothes brings a small measure of comfort. "I wasn't sure they ever pursued the idea—until I met you." He looks away, his face dark. "I was opposed to Andrews' idea and I said so to my advisor. Of course, I was just a student and Scott didn't really care what I thought. 'You're free to leave the project, if that's how you feel,' he said. So I did."

"And that's when you went to Europe."

He nods. "That's when I went and rode the trains in Europe. And the whole trajectory of my life changed." He clasps her hand between both his own. "And then I met you, Jenna. And my whole life changed again."

"Mike. I—I don't want to be responsible for something like that. You should never have gotten involved with me."

He shakes his head. "It's not *your* fault." He averts his gaze. "I need to get going. That radiator is broken again, and I have to get it fixed."

"Duty calls." She smiles at him, tears in her eyes.

"Yes. Duty calls." He reaches for his coat. "Can I give you a ride?"

A few minutes later, they pull up in front of the yoga studio. "I'm glad we talked." She reaches for the door handle. He gives her a weak smile, so she says: "Really. It's better to talk about it than not. Believe me—I understand."

"Thanks."

She opens the door and steps out, when Monica walks up, smelling of lemons and dressed in yoga pants. She has her mat in a holder slung over one shoulder.

"Jenna! What are you doing here?" She leans down and peers into Mike's car. "Hey slugger—how ya doin'?" He shrugs and gives her that same weak smile. "That good, huh?" She looks again at Jenna. "What happened?"

"For one thing, Mike got banned from the hospital." She looks at him as if to say, *that's all I'm saying.* He smiles gratefully.

Monica flings her hands in the air. "Oh geez." She slides into the passenger seat of Mike's car and turns to face him. "What happened? Do you think it had anything to do with us taking Jenna out of there?"

He shrugs again. "I'm sure it did—but it might be more than that."

Monica leans her head back against the seat and rubs at her forehead. "Oh God. I'm so sorry." She suddenly turns back to him. "Oops—sorry, Mikester. Oughta watch my language more around you. I keep forgetting you're a priest."

The frown on his face dissolves. "I am so glad to hear you say that."

She gives Jenna a puzzled look, then turns back to him. "What do you mean?"

"It's complicated." He shifts the gear shift into drive. "Don't you girls have a yoga class to go to?"

"All right already." Monica jumps out of the car, grinning. "I can take a hint." She closes the door and leans down, propping her arms on the open window. "Cheer up, Mike. We'll get your hospital pass back for you—I promise."

"I'll believe that when I see it." After Monica steps back and lifts a hand in a wave, he pulls away.

Jenna turns toward the studio, and Monica grabs her elbow. "I want a full report, but it has to be fast. Class starts in five minutes." They hurry inside and head for the dressing room.

Monica sits on the bench, untying her shoes. "So what's going on with Mike?"

Jenna hangs her coat on a peg. "I'm worried about him."

"Because of the hospital thing?"

"It's something else. He seems to be having a crisis of faith."

"Why do you say that?"

Jenna shakes her head. "It's causing him a lot of distress, I know that much." She grabs a yoga mat from the shelf and follows Monica into the studio.

The teacher greets her, then lowers her voice to a whisper. "Monica said you were in the hospital. Is everything okay?"

Jenna forces a smile and nods, then finds a spot for her mat. Soon she is lost in the rhythm of the flow, grateful she has nothing to think about except following directions. For over an hour, she moves from pose to pose, stretching and reaching, feeling more and more relaxed, enjoying the sensation of having a body, of not being controlled by a brain that isn't working right.

"Okay, now. Let's move toward our final relaxation pose," the instructor says, as she dims the lights. "Stretch out on your back and use any props you like. Make sure you're warm enough. We'll be here a while."

Jenna reaches for her socks and pulls a sweatshirt over her head, then lays back on her mat. A recording plays—some soft droning and occasional sounds of bells. She closes her eyes. Exhaustion sweeps through her body and it feels like she's sinking into the floor, descending into the recesses of her mind. Images flash before her mind's eye, as if she's flipping through a photo album.

Sam beside her on the sofa, his shoulders hunched, hands clasped, a look of pain on his face.

A golden carpet of leaves beneath a wide, spreading tree. A polished granite headstone, carved with the image of a lamb. An endless blue sky.

Two hospital orderlies dressed in blue scrubs hovering by her bedside.

Stepping out of a stairwell into the dark, snow swirling around Mike's old beat-up car, his arm, firmly around her waist.

It's all real, all memories she knows to be true—so unlike the images that hit her just before she fainted and landed in the hospital: a boy with a kite; a little girl, she knows now is Katie, chasing the boy; a dog and a Frisbee that hits her in the head; a man, leaping for the Frisbee, colliding with her—who was the man? And what does it all mean? How does any of this fit into a whole?

And how could she have had a daughter and *not know it*?

Katie, she reminds herself. My little girl's name is Katie, but it's like Katie has been erased. Completely erased.

The instructor speaks from the front of the room. "At times, thoughts may enter your mind," she says. Jenna suppresses a laugh. "When this happens, just let those thoughts go. Let them float away like clouds in a blue sky, soaring past you."

She thinks again of that blue sky beyond the hilltop gravesite, imagining a little dark-haired girl, floating away like a cloud. People try so hard to empty their minds of thought, she thinks, when all that Jenna wants, all she dreams for, is to bring those thoughts back—thoughts of a little girl who deserves to be remembered.

LATER, SHE AND MONICA CHANGE BACK into street clothes, pull on their coats and step out of the studio just as two guys, smelling of cigarettes and bundled in jackets and scarves, hurry past. Both of them, oddly enough, have spiky blond hairstyles. One guy turns to Monica. "Hi," he says. "Steve, remember?"

"Steve! How are you?" Monica seems rattled as she gestures toward her. "Do you remember Jenna? Jenna, this is Steve—we met at happy hour one night a couple months back."

Jenna notices that Monica doesn't even bother to ask, "Do you remember?" Even Monica knows her memories have all but evaporated.

The other fellow has a crooked nose that looks like it might once have been broken and healed wrong. He steps forward. "Hey, Jenna. It's Josh—I think I ran into you at that pizza place one night. Remember?"

She nods, although she really doesn't remember.

"We're just heading to McGinty's." Steve points down the block toward the bar. "They've started having happy hour every night of the week. Want to join us?"

Monica glances at Jenna. "Do you feel up to it?"

"Sure—I'm game, if you are."

Monica takes her arm. "We don't have to go—if you're not feeling well."

Josh frowns. "Is everything okay?" he asks.

"Yes, everything's fine," Jenna says, her voice a little louder than she intended. She turns toward the bar. "Let's go."

It takes a moment for her eyes to adjust to the dark. Clumps of people, maybe two dozen in all, cluster near the bar and along a buffet table that holds a half-dozen trays of food. The place is full of food smells—some kind of meatballs, something cheesy maybe. Music pumps from a stage at the back. There are microphone stands and other equipment strewn around, but no musicians—the music is coming from a sound system with glowing red and green lights.

"They're supposed to have live music," Steve shouts. "But I guess the band isn't here yet." He points to a table near the back. "How about that spot?"

Monica nods, and the four of them make their way through the crowd. The bar is decorated with a strange mix of orange pumpkin lights, little paper turkeys and a miniature Christmas tree. They reach the table and Jenna shucks out of her coat. Monica leans close. "This place seems confused about which holiday season we're in."

"I share their confusion," Jenna says, smiling.

"Are you sure you're okay?" Monica asks. "I don't want to push you if you're not ready for something like this yet."

"It's okay." She waves a hand toward Monica. A waitress carrying an empty tray thinks Jenna's motioning to her, so moves to their table and takes their orders.

Jenna orders a glass of red wine and then another. She's halfway through the second glass when Monica grabs her wrist. "You need to slow down. At least eat something first."

Josh hops up. "I'll get something from the buffet. What would you like?"

Steve says, "See if they have those little meatballs like last time."

A few minutes later, Josh returns with a large plate of meatballs smothered in a sour cream sauce and a pile of toothpicks. Monica pushes the tangy-scented plate toward Jenna. "Eat," she orders.

Jenna eats one meatball then reaches for her wine glass and downs the rest in two swallows. "Where's the waitress?" she asks. "I need another drink."

Monica raises her eyebrows. "I don't think so." She points at the plate of meatballs. "Eat some more of those first."

Josh grins. "You sound like her mom."

"She does *not* sound like my mom." Jenna laughs. "My mom would never order me to stop drinking." She giggles, and they all stare at her. "My mother doesn't know the meaning of 'too much to drink.'"

Monica reaches for a toothpick, spears another meatball and hands it to Jenna. "Yeah, well, your mom isn't here but I am—so watch yourself." She nods at the meatball in Jenna's hand. "Eat that."

"Okay, already." Jenna puts the entire meatball in her mouth.

"I just think you need to slow down with the alcohol," Monica says.

"I know one way to slow her down." Josh pushes his chair back and extends a hand. "How about a dance?"

She glances toward the wooden dance floor. One other couple is there, moving slowly. The band has arrived and is setting up their equipment while the canned music continues to thump from the sound system. She looks up at Josh. There's something about him—but she can't place it. "Sure." She takes his hand.

They dance to two songs from the sound system, take a rest, and go back for another round of dancing once the band sets up. She loves the sense of being moved by the music, loves the way Josh looks at her, loves the way the sound penetrates her body and mind, saturating her tissues with music and washing away the strange sense of dullness she's felt ever since she woke up in that hospital.

The band switches to a slower piece. Josh holds out his arms. "One more?"

He's a nice guy. Really he is, but she's not sure she wants to dance in his arms—he takes her hesitation as a "yes," though, and gathers her close. He smells like stale cigarettes and beer, but it feels good to be held and she lets herself sink into his chest. She ignores the memory that springs immediately to mind—Mike taking the pillow from her that first night at Monica's, pulling her into a hug, holding her close.

She's with Josh. Not Mike. She should think of Josh. A nice guy. Really.

Just not the guy she wants right now.

Later, as they're leaving, Monica threads her arm through Jenna's and they head off down the sidewalk toward the parking garage beneath the Columbia Health building. When they reach the garage entrance, Josh puts his arm around Jenna's shoulder and pulls her away from Monica. "How about a nightcap?" he whispers. "My place?"

He leans closer and she thinks he's going to kiss her when a dark figure, a man, walks briskly toward them on the sidewalk. Even though he has his head down, even though it's dark, she knows it's Howard. She's sure of it. How did Howard find her? He must've come to return her to the hospital.

She tries to get free from Josh's arms but he won't release her. He's gripping her arm. Panic rises in her chest. She should be excited by this symptom of fear but she's more confused than anything. Is it Howard she's afraid of? Or this guy Josh?

Josh. There's something about that name. And about *him*, but she just can't place it. She pulls back trying to free herself and ends up pressed into the building behind her. Josh grips her wrists so hard it hurts. He whispers, suddenly furious, suddenly threatening. "Stop it!" he hisses, just as the dark figure—Howard—walks by, a familiar scent, a faint whiff of incense, sweeping past with him. The dark figure looks up then and his gaze meets Jenna's, but it isn't Howard.

It's Mike.

Mike stares at her, his eyes moving between her face and Josh's. "Jenna," he says, his voice barely a whisper.

Josh lets her wrists drop and steps away. She's suddenly dizzy and reaches for the wall to steady herself. Josh smiles broadly at Mike. His smile looks completely fake. "Hey, Father." He claps Mike's shoulder. "Nice to see you again."

"What?" Mike says. He looks terribly confused, as confused as Jenna feels. What happened to Howard? Wasn't Howard just here? She was sure she'd seen him walking down the sidewalk. She looks up and down the street, panic rising, and sees Monica a hundred feet away with Steve who is gripping her elbow tightly.

"Oh, sorry," Josh says, laughing a bit too loudly. "Remember? We met at the pizza place one night. You were counseling Jenna here—remember?"

"Counseling—?" Mike shakes his head. "Sorry—I don't remember."

"Well, maybe you weren't *counseling*," Josh says. "To tell you the truth, I don't really know what priests do."

"Oh wait—I do remember now. Jenna and I were talking. You came in to get a pizza for a game on TV, right?" When Mike looks at Jenna, his eyes grow wide. "What's wrong?"

She tries to speak, but no words come out. She's afraid. She's afraid. She's actually afraid—the problem is, she doesn't want to be afraid. Not now. Not ever.

"Jenna?" Mike grabs her by the shoulders. "You look like you've seen a ghost. Are you okay?"

She shakes her head and the words finally come. "I—I—it wasn't a *ghost*. I—I thought you were Howard. Just for a second."

Mike lets his breath out in a heavy sigh. "Okay. I'm not, of course, but I can see why that might spook you."

Josh jams his shoulder between them, separating Mike from Jenna. "Who's Howard?"

Mike pushes him aside and steps closer to her. "Why did you think I was Howard?"

"Maybe because I saw him earlier? I hadn't really been thinking about it, but I *did* see him."

Mike leans closer. "Where?"

"At the cemetery—I told you about it."

"Yes, but you didn't say you'd seen Howard there."

"What cemetery?" Josh asks, trying to nudge his way between them again as Monica runs up.

"Hi, Mike," Monica says. She looks rattled and keeps glancing back over her shoulder. "Burning the midnight oil?" A ways down the sidewalk, Steve is standing in the shadows, both hands jammed into his pockets. She frowns at him and steps closer to Mike.

Mike smiles weakly at her. "I suppose." He pauses. "Although it's only barely eleven p.m."

"Is it that late?" Monica reaches for Jenna's arm. "Better be going—some of us do have to work tomorrow." She nods at Josh, then Steve, her face expressionless. "Thanks for a fun evening," she says all business-like, then pulls at Jenna's arm. "We need to head home now."

And then she's tugging Jenna down the street. Mike follows closely behind and the three of them hurry to the parking garage entrance. When they reach it, Monica and Mike stop and look back toward the place they'd left Steve and Josh—but they're both now gone.

"Whew. *That* was close," Monica says, sagging.

"I'll say," Mike agrees.

"We should never have gone with them," Monica says. "I could tell right away when we got to the bar that something just wasn't right with those guys."

"What are you two talking about?" Jenna asks, dizzy and discombobulated.

"I'm just not sure about that guy, Josh." Mike gazes at the now-empty sidewalk. "I told you that before," he says to Jenna. "I'd steer clear of both him *and* his friend."

Jenna stares at him. "When did you tell me something like that? And what do you mean you're not sure about him?"

He shrugs, but there's a flash of anger in his eyes. "Just a feeling." He turns and stares down the street one more time. "You know—intuition."

Monica tugs on her arm. "Come on, let's get you home."

PETE JAMS HIS HANDS in his jacket pockets and turns the collar up around his exposed neck. He takes one more drag on his cigarette, crushes it under his heel, then hurries from Columbia's loading dock toward the alley that runs behind their building and the church next door. It smells sour, like rotting garbage. He'd been keeping an eye on the place, and from his vantage point on the loading dock, hidden partly by a dumpster, he'd just caught sight of his quarry: two guys, both with spiky blond locks that stick straight up on their heads. They'd come out of the bar with Jenna and Monica.

What was Monica doing out with a creep like that? He'd lost sight of the girls for a couple minutes, then spotted the two white-haired guys they'd been with dashing into the alley. They seem to be heading for the back door of the church, the one that Pete has discovered opens into the church's kitchen.

He reaches the corner of the crumbling yellow brick school building and crouches down, peering into the darkness. He can see the two men hurrying toward the door. A sliver of light shows through a crack along its length—a sure sign they've jammed something into the opening to keep the door propped open. Again.

Sure enough, once the men reach the door, they open it, as if it wasn't even latched shut much less locked and disappear inside. Pete can hear the latch click into place from where he's crouched. The sliver of light disappears. He waits a few seconds, until he's sure they've moved away from the kitchen door, then sprints around to the front of the building. He stops by the front steps, the ones that lead up to the massive front doors and looks up. There's a round stained-glass window above them, darkened at night as it usually is. As Pete watches, a dim light comes on inside, and then he sees them—one silhouette, then another, passing in front of the rose window as two men in the loft area above the door make their way into what Pete is sure must be the bell tower at the top of the church.

JENNA WAKES EARLY THE NEXT DAY. Monica is already in the kitchen getting coffee when Jenna shuffles in, blinking in the bright overhead light and inhaling the morning scents, brewing coffee and toast. Monica glances over her shoulder. "Look who's up. I didn't expect to see you so early."

"What time is it?" Jenna asks, her voice raspy.

"About six. Want some coffee?"

"Sounds great." Jenna yawns, and then it all comes back to her: the sidewalk, Howard who wasn't Howard but was actually Mike. Those two creepy blond guys. And fear. *Actual fear*. She should be happy about feeling it, but she's mostly puzzled.

Monica pours a second cup and slides it to her, watching her carefully. Jenna stirs sugar and milk into her coffee and sips at the mug for a few minutes, drawing the heady scent in through her nostrils as Monica bustles about the kitchen. A radio plays somewhere down the hall, probably in Monica's bedroom, and she can hear the clock ticking on the wall. A stack of papers—catalogs and what appear to be bills—are lying on the table. She flips absently through them. "Maybe I should go into work today."

Monica's eyes widen. "Are you sure?"

She shrugs. "I don't see any reason to hang around here if I'm not actually sick. And besides, I need to check on some things." She waves her hand at Monica's mail. "Like my mail—I picked up a pile of stuff when I was at my place, and I'm sure I've got bills to pay." She thinks for a minute. "What's the date? I probably need to pay my rent."

Monica pulls out a chair and sits down with a mug of her own. "It's the fifteenth—do they give you a grace period?"

Jenna nods. "Only five days, so I'm late. I have to pay it today—at the office."

"Is that in your building?"

"No, actually, it's in the Columbia building. Right next to the bank, in the lobby. You've probably seen their sign—Patriot Properties?"

Monica nods. "I have seen it. You could go by on the way to the office."

"Yes. And who knows what has piled up for me there—I really ought to go take a look."

Monica frowns and looks away for a long moment. When she looks back, her expression is serious. "Okay, but only if you promise to stay in the building. The whole reason you're here with me is so we make sure they don't take you back to the hospital."

Jenna shakes her head. "I doubt that would happen. I saw Howard yesterday, and it sure didn't look like he was searching for me."

Monica stares. "You did? Where did you see him?"

"At the cemetery." She points toward the street. "The one down at the end of your block. Howard was coming in just as I was leaving."

"What were you doing there?"

She shrugs. "I just wandered by and decided, on a whim, to look for Katie's grave." She pauses, staring out the window.

"Did you find it?"

She nods. "I did." She pauses again. "And I can only assume that's why Howard was there—he was heading right for the gravesite, after all."

Monica shakes her head. "Well, if you're out walking around the neighborhood during the day and nobody's tried to pick you up and return you to the hospital, why shouldn't you go back to work?" She pauses, looking closely at Jenna. "Assuming you really feel okay."

"I feel fine."

Monica is quiet for a long moment and then asks, "Are you sure?"

A flare of irritation makes her spit the words out. "What are you getting at?"

Monica stares silently for a moment. "Okay," she finally says. "It's just that you weren't at all yourself last night. I've never known you to drink like that."

Jenna wants to say, *Well, maybe you don't really know me*, but instead she says, "I know. I was upset I think." She shrugs. "It's been pretty hard."

Monica nods, glancing at the clock. "I'll hop in the shower, but then we'd better go. I have yet another meeting at eight o'clock."

They enter the Columbia Health building an hour later. As they walk across the lobby, filled with Christmas decorations and smelling of pine, Jenna points to a storefront near the back of the lobby. The place looks closed and dark. "That's where I pay my rent—but they don't appear to be open."

Monica looks at her watch. "It's not even eight yet." She pushes the elevator button.

The elevator arrives, and Jenna follows Monica in. "I guess I'll have to come back down later." She punches the button for her floor.

Monica gives her a sharp look. "That would be okay—as long as you *stay in the building*."

"All right already." Her earlier irritation is starting to feel more like full-blown anger. "I'm not sure we need to be all this cautious."

Monica glares at her. "Are you sure this is just not 'Jenna who feels no fear' talking?"

She shrugs and keeps her gaze fixed on the numbers flashing to higher and higher values as the elevator climbs. Finally they reach their floor and step out. She turns to Monica. "I might not be as fearful as some people, but there's got to be a middle ground, right? I mean, who would want to live in constant fear?"

"Of course. But there is such a thing as common-sense caution. I mean really, Jenna—we still have no idea who is behind this."

"Okay. I'll be careful." She gives Monica a weak smile. "I'm sorry I got angry."

Monica nods. "Fair enough." She glances at her watch. "I've got to get to my meeting." She starts to walk away, then turns, dashes back and hugs her. "It's going to be all right. Let me know when you're ready to go home—I've got a jam-packed day, so text me or something and I'll check back with you later." She pulls away, smiling. "And now I really have to run."

After Monica hurries away, Jenna starts pawing through the multitude of folders and inter-office memos and unprocessed claim forms stacked on her desk. She sorts things into piles and begins to tackle some of the easier tasks. She works for over an hour and it feels good to be productive again. To not be thinking about problems she really doesn't even understand. People start dropping by, asking how she's feeling, saying they're glad to see her back.

She's beginning to feel like a normal person again, simply Jenna who works at Columbia Health, nothing more, when she finally notices the time: nine-thirty. Surely the rental office is open now. She'll pop down to the lobby and pay her rent. She yawns, standing up, reaching for her purse. She could really use more coffee.

Monica would be furious with her, though, if she leaves the building. She grabs her coat anyway and hurries to the elevator.

After she writes a check and hands it to the clerk at Patriot, she pulls on her coat and heads out the front glass doors. The deli is only a half block away. What could possibly happen in so short a distance?

People hurry past, bundled in winter coats, scarves, hats. No one pays her any more mind than usual. It seems totally safe out here. No less safe than inside the building.

She approaches the deli and reaches for the handle. A strong aroma of fresh coffee greets her as the door swings open. The line is blessedly short and most of the tables are empty. Only one man is at a table by the window, his face hidden by a newspaper. She gets in line, waits to give her order, and is standing at the condiment table stirring sugar and milk into her cup with a wooden stick when somebody steps close. "Jenna?"

She turns and looks into Howard's face, the stick clattering to the floor. She steps back. Her heart is actually pounding. She's feeling fear again, the second day in a row, the emotion she'd thought she'd never ever feel again. "What are you doing here?"

16

HOWARD'S FACE IS CREASED WITH WORRY. A deep furrow forms between his brows. "I've been calling you for days," he says. "Weeks. I've left all sorts of messages, not sure if you were okay—and yet here you are, acting like nothing at all has happened. Jenna, what is going on?"

She replaces the lid on her cup, her hands shaking, now with rage, rather than fear. "Unless you've forgotten, the last time I saw you was at the hospital where you were instructing that doctor to do who knows what to my brain."

His mouth falls open. "I wasn't *instructing* him! We were only doing what you wanted, Jenna."

She shakes her head, furious. "That's not true. I know that's what you kept saying, but how could I possibly want something like that?"

He grabs her arm. "Jenna, please." She wrenches it away. He motions toward the table where he'd left his coffee and folded-up newspaper. "Can we just talk for a minute?"

She looks around. There are about a dozen people scattered at the tables and in line, including two police officers who've just rushed in. It doesn't seem like Howard's about to kidnap her. If she has to talk to him, this has got to be the safest place around. She turns back to him, clutching her coffee cup and leaning against the counter. "I don't see what there is to talk about."

"Well, for starters, we can discuss why it is you don't seem to recall your instructions to the doctors. I was right there when you told both of them, Dr. Andrews and Dr. Scott, not six months ago, that you wanted this."

Andrews and Scott. So, the two were still working together. Is she part of some sort of military experiment? It all seems too incredible. She shakes her head to clear it. "Sam said that, too, that I wanted this, but I'm still not sure I believe it. Why would I ask for such a thing?"

"You didn't just ask—you begged. Pleaded." He looks away, and she catches a glimpse of tears in his eyes. When he looks back at her, he grabs her hand. "After the way I treated you, and after what happened to Katie, how could I say no?"

She has so many questions. Maybe Howard has answers. "I saw you at the cemetery," she says quietly. "Yesterday."

"You were there?"

She nods. "I was just leaving when you drove in."

He shakes his head. "I didn't see you, I guess." He looks at the table. "I miss her too," he whispers.

The shaking starts in her gut and travels up to her throat. "I wish I missed her. But how can I? I—I don't even know who she was."

He stares, his eyes wide. "What? You don't even know—?"

She turns toward the table, still hesitant, but needing to know what Howard knows. "Let's sit. I guess we do need to talk."

They move to the table, and she shrugs out of her coat, pops the top off her cup and wraps both hands around it, inhaling the strong coffee scent, not sure which of her million questions to ask first. He looks sad. "What happened to us, Howard?"

"You and me?" He sags forward. "I'm not sure I can explain it either. I had it pretty good."

She stares at the steam billowing up from her cup. "That's not what I was asking. Apparently, we were married? And had a daughter?"

The color drains from his face. "Of course—why are you asking something like that?" His voice catches in his throat.

"I don't remember, Howard. Any of it. The last I knew you were married to Deirdre."

He stares. "Are you kidding me?" He leans forward, his hands clasped on the table. "You don't remember our wedding? The reception where your relatives and mine tried to mingle and failed miserably?" She shakes her head, and he sits back heavily in his chair. "You don't remember Katie?"

Tears sting her eyes and she blinks furiously. "I want to remember, but I didn't even know she existed until just the other day."

He lets his breath out in a burst. "Well, no wonder you don't remember giving the doctors those instructions. If you don't remember anything that happened five years ago, how could you remember six months back?"

"I want to remember, though."

He shakes his head. "I don't even know where to start."

"Well, how about just start with Katie. I don't remember her. I don't remember her being born, much less—well, you know." The tears she's been blinking back spill over her lashes. "I don't remember being pregnant." She swipes at her cheeks. "Was I pregnant before we got married?"

He nods. "Yes, but that wasn't the reason we got married. When Deirdre found out about us, she left and filed for divorce. We'd already set a wedding date when we learned you were expecting." Tears appear in his eyes again. "Katie was a sweet little surprise who happened to enter the picture a couple months earlier than anyone expected."

"So, she was born before we got married."

He shakes his head. "We got married soon after my divorce was final. Katie arrived about six months later. You were, shall we say, a little on the pudgy side in your wedding dress." He laughed. "Still pretty, though. Of course. I'm sorry, Jenna. I really didn't know how good I had it with you."

"So, how did it end, Howard? I assume it did, since I haven't seen you for months—not until you showed up at the hospital."

"I often wished I could forget that part. Let's just say I was an idiot. As usual." He's grinning, staring at his hands clasped on the table. He looks up. "You really don't remember?" She shakes her head and he laughs. "I've wished so many times that you'd never found out—but I'll tell you." He takes a deep breath. "She was also an intern at the firm. Like you had been."

She jerks back, stung. "You had another affair?"

He sighs. "I told you I was no good. Anyhow, when you found out about her, you took Katie and moved out. I understand the Columbia Health job was your top choice so you could be close to Katie's school."

"Which school?"

"You know—preschool. At St. Rita's."

She stares. "Katie went to St. Rita's?"

"She started in the three-year-olds and would have gone to kinder—" He stops, breathing slowly, then looks up at her. "They called the four-year-olds the 'bluebird' class. The threes were the 'robins.' We never got to find out what bird she'd be in kindergarten." He wipes the tears from his face, then gazes at her, his eyes shining. "You were a good mother, Jenna. A doting mother, really. I could totally understand why you would want to get away from the fear and the pain after she was—well, you know."

"Murdered."

He flinches and looks away. "You say that so matter-of-factly." He shakes his head. "Maybe the procedure worked well after all."

"It worked too well. Surely they didn't intend to remove the memories I had of her? Of us?"

He searches her face. "You really don't remember we had a daughter?"

"I still can't believe I asked for this."

"*Begged.*"

She stares at him for a long moment. "You were there? When they did the procedure?"

He nods. "You asked your dad to help you find this doctor you'd heard about, from Sam, I think. The doctor could perform a 'fear amelioration technique.' Sam had learned about it somehow, I'm not sure how, but I checked it out—found Andrews, who was located here in Philly, through this guy Dr. Scott. He was the one who'd invented the method." He pauses, frowning. "You don't remember any of this?"

She shakes her head. "No, none of it. It's like you're talking about something that happened to another person. I still don't understand why I would even want to have this done."

"You were adamant. You kept saying, 'No more fear,' and 'I refuse to live in fear.'" He grabs her hand. "How could I say no, Jenna? You loved her so much."

SHE GOES BACK TO WORK and buries herself in an endless supply of claim forms. She's grateful for the work, grateful for the distraction. Whenever she stops for a moment and allows herself to think, she simply cannot take it in.

She'd been a married woman. A mother and a wife. She'd had a mother-in-law and a father-in-law and a daughter. And

Howard had been her husband. She'd lived with him, loved him, married him, even divorced him. How could anyone forget all that?

No surprise that Howard had had another affair. Certain things about people just never change. But if Howard was right about all that had happened, if he was telling the truth, she'd somehow, maybe unwittingly, brought the memory loss, not to mention the strange fearlessness she's suffered, upon herself.

Around four-thirty, Monica rushes into her cubicle. "I have some great news."

Jenna swivels in her chair. Monica hugs a pile of file folders to her chest and stands tall, beaming. "What is it?" Jenna asks.

Monica smiles broadly. "I got a promotion."

"Wow." Jenna shakes her head. "I didn't even know you were up for one."

"I wasn't. It was a complete surprise. The division head called me into her office after staff meeting this morning and told me they were promoting me to section leader."

"That's great, Monica." People's lives were moving forward, things were happening that she knew nothing about, while Jenna remained stuck in a past she didn't even remember. Monica is still beaming. "So, you hadn't applied for the position?" Jenna asks.

"Nope. But I wondered why my boss kept sending me to substitute for her at meetings. That's why I've been so busy this week—I was filling in for her." She sits in the chair and crosses her legs at the ankle, sighing contentedly. "The best part is, I get a big raise. I might be able to pay off my student loan now—finally."

"We should celebrate," Jenna says. "Go out to dinner or something."

"I don't know. Do you think it's a good idea to be out on the town again?"

"I'll just have one drink. That's it—I promise." Jenna grins. "But it will be champagne. My treat."

Monica snorts. "I wasn't talking about the drinking. I meant, aren't you worried that you might be spotted? Somebody might see us if we go to a restaurant."

Jenna waves a hand at her. "It doesn't matter. There's no danger anymore."

"Jenna, I told you before that your lack of fear is clouding your judgment."

"It's not that. I saw Howard today. He explained the whole thing to me."

Monica springs upright in her chair. "You saw Howard? Where?"

"At the deli."

"What were you doing at the deli?" she shrieks. "I *told* you—"

"I know, I know. But it doesn't matter anymore, like I said. Howard is not looking for me."

"He's not?"

"Well, he *was* looking for me—but not to take me back to the hospital. He just wanted to talk."

"About what?"

"Well, he wanted to see if I was okay, basically."

"That's all?" Monica shakes her head. "I don't know if I trust him—"

"Monica, he's okay. Really." She pauses, staring at the floor. "I was the one who chose to have that procedure."

"That's what Howard kept saying, but if you don't remember deciding it, how do you know it's true?"

She shakes her head. "I don't *know*, not in any way I can prove, but I have to trust somebody, Monica. Sam said the same thing, and neither he nor Howard have any reason to lie about this. Besides, Howard could have grabbed me while we were at the deli and taken me back to the hospital, if that's what his plan was."

"That's true." Monica frowns. "I still don't know if I trust him."

"I must have trusted him at one time—a lot. I married him, after all."

"So did you guys talk about that? I mean, did you find out how the marriage ended?"

"Yes. Not that I remember any of this, but he apparently had another affair and I left him."

"Hm," Monica says. "And this is the guy you say we should trust?"

17

THEY GATHER SOME COWORKERS together and walk to a nice restaurant a few blocks from the building. Monica chatters on all evening, accepting hugs and high-fives from everyone, and enjoying being the center of attention. Jenna tries to join in the conversation, not wanting to be a drag on Monica's moment, but her thoughts keep wandering away.

She thinks about Howard, and how tearful he had been as he talked about Katie. She thinks about what he said about their breakup, another affair with a woman he'd not named. She thinks about his questions: *You don't remember our wedding?* and *You don't remember bringing Katie home from the hospital?*

She thinks and thinks and the more she does, the less energy she has. At one point, it occurs to her that she might be depressed. Is it possible to be depressed about something you don't remember? She doesn't know how the brain works, and she's finding now that she needs to know. She does have a lot to be depressed about, though. Not only Katie's murder, but apparently a divorce.

Divorce. She'd never thought the word would apply to her. After her parents' divorce, she'd vowed that if she was lucky enough to marry, she would never end the marriage.

She looks around the table at the crowd of people she knows from work, watching Monica laughing and chatting with the others. She surveys the diners around the room: couples, larger groups of friends, even some families, with children sitting on booster seats. Everybody is with somebody else, all with people they know, and know well, but Jenna, looking around the table at the people she's with, does not feel like everybody else—she feels like a freak. A divorced woman with a dead child she can't even remember.

A sudden question occurs to her: Is she really a *divorced* woman? She can't recall Howard saying when their divorce took place. She concentrates. He'd said she'd moved out when that second affair was discovered, said she'd gotten the job at the insurance company, but he really hadn't used the word. *Divorce*.

AS THE GROUP WALKS BACK to the parking garage after dinner, Monica hurries to her side and falls in beside her on the sidewalk. "Thanks, Jenna, for the celebration dinner. I really had a good time."

"Oh, good. I'm glad." Jenna squeezes Monica around the shoulders. "You should be proud of yourself—you're going to be a great section leader."

"Thanks," Monica says proudly. "Maybe we'll have to have another celebration dinner when they promote you."

"I don't think that's going to happen."

"Why not? You could go for it, put your name in. If you could get through law school, you ought to be able to be a section leader at Columbia."

"Well, that sounds logical, but my brain seems to have changed considerably since the days I apparently was in law school. But, thanks for the vote of confidence—maybe when things settle down I'll consider it."

The group enters the parking garage under the Columbia Health building and, one by one, the others walk away, waving, headed for their cars. Jenna and Monica find their way through the damp, musty place to Monica's car on the second level below ground.

After they've pulled out into traffic, Jenna says, "You know what occurred to me a while ago?"

"What?"

"Howard never actually said we were divorced."

"What?" Monica shoots a quick look her way, then returns her eyes to the road. "You mean you're still married to him?"

"I don't know. I was thinking, though, and realized that he said I'd moved out, gotten this job and the new apartment, but he really didn't say we'd gotten divorced."

"Wow," Monica says. "You might have a *husband*?" She stops at a red light and turns to Jenna. "I guess you could just ask him. Right?"

"I had the same thought." She pulls out her phone. "I hope it's not too late."

Monica peers at the clock on her dashboard. "It's only eight thirty. He's not an early-to-bed kind of guy, is he?"

"Not that I remember." Jenna punches his number, laughing. "Not that *that* means anything." He answers on the third ring. "Howard," she says, "I'm sorry to bother you, but something occurred to me after we'd talked. It's important."

"Sure. Anything."

"This might sound strange, but did we get divorced?"

He sighs, and she imagines him running his hand back through his hair in that way he does when he's tired. "We're still married, Jenna, although if you're saying you want a divorce, I can certainly understand it. I told you that before."

She lets her breath out, unaware until that moment she'd been holding it. It's worse than she thought: Not only had she once been a married woman, she still is.

"Jenna? You still there?"

"I'm sorry. I didn't think anything could shock me anymore."

"What do you want to do?"

She presses a hand to her forehead. "I don't know. Day before yesterday I didn't even know we were married, didn't know we had a daughter. It's all pretty hard to take in."

"I'm sure it is. But think how I feel."

She clenches her teeth. She remembers this much, at least. It's so like Howard to turn the spotlight back on himself. "I'm sorry, Howard. I'm sure it's hard for you, too."

"Don't get me wrong. I know that you're suffering, that it was difficult for you when Katie died. But it was difficult for me, too. The timing was not good, either."

"What timing?"

"It happened only a few months after you moved out."

"Oh." She pauses. "So, when *did* I move out?"

"November. Two years ago."

"So, we'd been separated for—what, four months?"

"Yes, something like that." After a pause, Howard goes on. "Jenna, I know I have you at a disadvantage here, but as I said, we talked about this before. A lot."

"We did?"

"Yes. You said you were planning to file for divorce. As far as I know, though, you never did."

"Oh." She pauses, her mind a whirl of thoughts, so confused she can't sort them out. "So, I wonder why I didn't file?"

"I don't know, Jenna," he says, sighing. "I really don't know."

SHE STAYS AT MONICA'S that evening, but the next morning while they're having coffee in Monica's kitchen, she says, "Thank you so much for taking me in, Monica, but I think

I can go back to my apartment now." Howard has proven himself to be harmless, so what is there to fear? Besides, she needs to do some checking—about this Dr. Andrews and his connections to the military. Her conversation with Mike and his early involvement has given her a lot more leads than she had before.

Monica nods. "I can understand that you'd want to get back to your routine. And, yes, I don't see any reason for you to stay 'in hiding' anymore."

"I do appreciate all you've done for me, though. Really."

Jenna does as much as she can at work that day but has fallen way behind. She finally gives up trying to be productive, comes down the elevator and walks through the pine-scented lobby. It's deserted, nearly seven p.m. on a Friday, and everyone seems to have left already. She turns right when she leaves the building. As she walks past St. Rita's, her heels clicking on the pavement and echoing off the church's stone walls, a wave of intense loneliness sweeps through her. She stops and looks at the church, dim lights shining through its upstairs windows and through the round stained-glass rose window above the main door. A shadow, and then another, pass by the window, as if something is moving inside the church.

He's in there, she knows. Perhaps in the church itself, maybe upstairs in the apartment he says he lives in, the one above the pipe organ. She stands for several minutes, looking at the light in the windows, wondering if she's just caught a glimpse of him and someone else up behind the stained-glass window. Who is he with? She wants to go in and find him but knows she can't do that.

It can't be a sin to feel what you honestly feel, she had said to him. And yet, here she is, feeling the same, as if she should somehow eliminate the feelings she has for him, because they're inappropriate, inconvenient and way too complicated.

Just like she'd tried to eliminate the feelings she'd had after Katie died. And not just tried—succeeded.

She wants to walk up those stone steps and into the church, go down that darkened hallway, and find him, but how would that accomplish anything? It would only make a complicated situation worse, so she keeps walking, all the way to her apartment. She spends the first part of the evening sorting through a pile of mail, clearing spoiled food out of the refrigerator and watering her dried-out and nearly dead plants. She falls into bed hours before her usual bedtime and sleeps for well over ten hours. The sleep helps a little, but after going to the grocery store to replenish the spoiled food, runs completely out of energy again.

She must be depressed. Fatigue is a sign of depression, isn't it? Of course, she has every reason to be depressed—multiple reasons, in fact—but it still doesn't make sense she'd be depressed about things she's forgotten. Wouldn't someone facing a depressing reality want to forget, and wouldn't that make the memories and the feelings go away? After lunch and a nap, she still doesn't really know what to do with herself. Maybe she needs to see somebody. A therapist?

That seems like a really bad idea. She can't talk to a therapist about this, any of it. What if there is some sort of government involvement? What if she has somehow, unwittingly, got caught up in some sort of weird experiment?

She looks for her phone in her bag but comes up with the battered little doll. She holds it, stroking the matted hair, wondering why she still doesn't feel anything, and decides to call Sam. He answers on the first ring but is breathing hard. "Did I catch you at a bad time?" she asks.

"No, no. I was just moving some furniture for Mom. Want to come help?"

"Uh—"

"Just kidding. I've moved this dresser to its new spot, which she decided she hated, so moved it back again. You really don't want to get involved with this."

"I'm sorry she's being difficult. Did you talk to her about the retirement community we discussed?"

He sighs. "I tried. She said she'd think about it, but you know Mom. She really doesn't want to leave her home."

She can hear a scraping sound, like a heavy dresser being dragged across a wooden floor. "It sounds like I *did* catch you at a bad time."

"It's okay. What's up?"

"Nothing, actually. I just wanted to talk. You know."

"It's okay, Jenna, like I said. Anytime." He pauses for a moment. "Do you want me to come over?"

"No! I mean—well, you're busy. Mom needs you more than I do."

"Jenna. Tell me."

The tears she's been trying to hold in escape and roll down her cheeks. "I—I don't really know. It's just so hard. I had a daughter! A daughter I don't even remember."

"How about I come over when I finish helping Mom? We can have some dinner and talk about it. Sound good?"

She swallows her tears. "It does sound good. Thanks, Sam. It—it's so good to have you home."

After she hangs up, she makes a cup of cinnamon tea and sits on the sofa with it, sipping and staring at the brilliantly sunny day, thinking about another day not that long before when she'd gone for a walk and ended up at the cemetery. The cinnamon-scented steam from her cup reminds her of that funny old man, Harvey, who had given her tea and driven her out to Katie's grave. He'd exuded such comfort, and she wonders if he's there, at the cemetery, working—and knows that, of course, he is. *I'm here every day—except Christmas and New Year's,* he had said.

It's barely past noon, hours before Sam will be free for dinner, so she grabs her coat and heads for her car. It hasn't been started in over a month, and the starter motor whines a little, threatening to give up before turning over. It finally catches and the engine roars to life. Another thing that's been neglected—she really needs to get back to her life. *And* herself, whoever that is.

After she pulls up outside the gate, she reaches to push the "talk" button on the intercom box. Harvey's warbly voice crackles out of the speaker. "Yes? How can I help you today?"

"Harvey, it's Jenna. Remember me? I was here the other day—looking for Katie Bernstein's grave."

"Course I remember," he shouts. "Just a second—I'll open the gate for ya." He's on the stoop, waving, and hobbles to her car as she rolls to a stop. "I see ya got yer car today."

"I thought it might be easier to drive out to Katie's grave."

He smiles when she says, "Katie," and pauses for a moment before answering. "Yep, it's a bit of a hike out to them plots. But you remember the way, right?"

"I remember." She sits, engine idling, both hands on the steering wheel, then turns to look at him. "Harvey—do you believe those who have died can communicate with us?"

He pulls back from the car, his eyebrows hiked high. "Why do ya ask?"

She shrugs. "I—well, it's just that I can't seem to shake the idea that Katie is trying to reach me. To contact me somehow, even though she's dead."

He clasps his hands together and stares over the top of her car toward the hill. Katie's grave is around that bend. He looks back through the window at her. "In my business, I hear a lot of tales like that—and, to tell ya the truth, I really don't know if any of them are true." He smiles. "Seems to me anything's possible, though."

She puts the car into gear. "Thanks, Harvey—nice to see you again." He waves as she drives off and up around the hill. Within a couple of minutes, she's pulling up under the wide spreading tree. The golden carpet of leaves that had been there before has blown away, leaving only a few yellow leaves scattered over the grass.

She switches off the engine and reaches into her pocket, pulling out the photo Sam had given her. She'd tucked it in her pocket that day and it's still there—along with a business card. She turns over the card and sees that it's Mike's—also tucked into her pocket on a day not that long ago.

She doesn't know this little girl, but she wants to. She runs her finger over the image, tracing the outlines of the little girl's face, the glossy dark hair and big eyes, the smile that reminds her of Howard's crooked grin. So, Katie looked somewhat like her father, but did she look like her mother—like Jenna? Well, there's the dark hair, but other than that, Jenna can see no resemblance, no evidence that this cute little girl was, indeed, her child.

She tucks the photo and card back into her pocket, gets out of the car and makes her way to the grave, set at the crown of the hill. As she comes around to the front of the tombstone, she reaches into her bag and pulls out the little doll. Maybe she'll leave it on the grave as an offering of sorts. As she's placing the doll beside the carved stone, she sees it: a potted flower, its leaves glossy and green beneath a large salmon-colored daisy.

She looks away, but before she can think it through, try to figure out how it is that a potted plant can still look fresh on such a frigid day, a wall of pain rolls into her head. She falls to her knees, groaning, the little doll tumbling to the ground. The daisy's strong floral scent wafts toward her like a great wave. She squeezes her eyes shut, which helps, but when she opens them again, catching sight of that flower, the same type of flower that Monica had brought into the deli that day she landed in the hospital, the pain comes coursing back like a giant wave of agony threatening to split her head open. She groans, images pouring into her mind:

Howard, his face twisted in anger, screaming as a little dark-haired girl cries in Jenna's arms;

A priest with a bald head standing behind a tiny coffin, bathed in colored light streaming through stained-glass windows;

A lace canopy draped above a man in a prayer shawl and yarmulke; Howard stomping on a glass goblet wrapped in white linen;

A tiny baby's hands, her fingernails perfectly formed, lying in Jenna's arms, asleep.

Jenna moans, her head clutched between her hands, wanting to see all of this but unable to bear the pain the images bring with them. A hand grabs her shoulder and a voice sounds in her ear: "Jenna, are ya okay?"

She cracks her eyes open and looks up at Harvey, pain stabbing her in the eyes. "No," she moans. "No, I am not all right."

"Is it yer head?" He kneels in front of her.

She nods, squeezing her eyes shut to block out the image of the flower. It seems to be the source of the intense stabbing pain. "Yes. It's my head."

"What should I do?" His voice trembles. "Do you have some medicine in the car I can get for ya?"

"No, no medicine for this," she says weakly. She opens her eyes to a mere slit and squints at him. "Harvey, I need to get to the hospital. Can you take me?"

"Of course." He jumps up. "I've got me truck down yonder, next to your car."

"Good. Thank you, Harvey. Oh—but before we go, grab that plant that's over on the grave, okay?"

"That plant?"

"The daisy. It's over there on Katie's grave."

"Well, sure, okay." He scrambles to the headstone and plucks the potted plant from the ground, returns to her side and helps her to stand by grabbing her elbow. "But why do I need to get the plant?"

"I don't know, but it has something to do with this enormous headache I have. I want the doctor to see it, so—ah!" Pain smacks again into her forehead as she accidentally glances at the flower. Her knees buckle, and she falls to the ground next to the little doll. She grabs it and stuffs it in her pocket.

Harvey grips her elbow, lifts her up and guides her to his blue truck, urging her into the front seat, muttering all the while, "Mercy, mercy." He tosses the plant onto the floor of the cab, fires up the engine and takes off in a cloud of blue smoke that smells like burning oil. They bounce down the gravel road, and she opens her eyes, just a crack, when he stops at the gate, but makes the mistake of looking at the flower again.

A flood of pain rushes into her head, and she tries to push it away with her mind, to no avail. As the pain intensifies, she feels herself slipping away, and then the world goes black.

18

SHE COMES TO as some hospital workers are lifting her out of Harvey's truck and onto a gurney. Harvey stands on the sidewalk under the emergency entrance awning, clutching the potted daisy and her coat. He looks completely miserable. "Harvey," she croaks, reaching toward him.

"Be still, miss," one of the nurses says. She leans close and peers into Jenna's eyes. "We need to get you inside and out of the cold."

"But I need to talk to Harvey," she insists, trying to sit up.

"Sir!" the nurse yells, waving toward him. "Could you step inside with us, please? We gotta get her out of this cold air." They push the gurney in through the wide doors, bumping it up over the curb and into a brightly lit hallway smelling of antiseptic. As they trundle down the hallway, she tries to look around, tries to find Harvey, but all she can see are nurses and orderlies, all dressed in scrubs of various colors.

They push her into a cubicle and rotate the gurney around, so her head is up against the wall. She finally spots him, outside in the hall, holding back the cotton sheet that had been pulled aside as they brought her into the tiny room. "Harvey!" She reaches for him.

He shuffles to her side, still clutching the flower and her coat. "I'm here," he says, his voice quavering. "Are you all right?"

She shakes her head, closing her eyes, trying to avoid the sight of that plant. The light is so bright in here. "I don't know,

Harvey." She holds her forehead. "Listen: Look in my coat pocket. There's a business card in there, for Father Mike Albertino. Would you mind calling him and telling him where I am?"

"Yes, miss. Certainly." Harvey trembles, which sets the glossy green leaves of the daisy trembling as well. He rummages in her coat pocket, pulls out the card and stares at it. Eyes wide, he asks, "Is he your priest?"

"Something like that. And Harvey? Leave that plant here, would you? I want to talk to the doctor about it, like I said."

The nurse pushes her way past Harvey as he reaches to place the potted daisy on the side table. "I need to check her vitals." She wraps a blood pressure cuff around Jenna's arm, clamps a plastic device over the end of Jenna's index finger and jams a thermometer into her mouth.

"Harvey," Jenna mumbles, trying to talk around it.

"Please don't talk, miss." The nurse scowls at her. "We won't get a good reading if your mouth is open."

Jenna nods and waits impatiently until the nurse pulls out the thermometer and peers at it. "Harvey. I know this sounds weird, but who put that flower on Katie's grave?"

His face darkens as he shrugs. He grows darker and the room murky.

"Her pressure's dropping!" the nurse yells. It's the last sound she hears before everything, yet again, goes black.

THE NEXT TIME SHE WAKES UP, she's in a darkened room. Through the window, she can see orange streetlights and a dark sky. It must be night, but what day is it? Has she lost time again? How many days this time?

Nobody is in the room with her. She squeezes her eyes shut, trying to remember. She *must* remember it this time. She thinks: Harvey brought her to the hospital. She remembers him standing by her bedside clutching a potted daisy.

The daisy. Is it here? She opens her eyes and looks around the dark room. Something that appears leafy, like it could be a plant, sits on the table along the wall near the foot of her bed, and she can detect a faint floral scent.

She closes her eyes again. When somebody comes by to check on her, she'll ask for Dr. Andrews. She has to figure out a way to ask him about what Mike said, about the military-funded project that seems to have led to all that's happened to her. But first, she'll show Dr. Andrews the plant, ask him why it is this wall of pain and these odd images rush in with such force whenever she catches a glimpse of a flower like the one that someone must have left on the grave—but who?

She looks around for her bag, the one that contains her notebook with all its clues but sees nothing. Where did they put her things? How can she figure this out if she doesn't have her notes?

Howard. It must've been Howard who left the plant on the grave. She should have had Harvey call him, too. Instead, she'd asked him to call Mike—but Mike isn't here, apparently. Had he gotten her message and not come? Had they banned him completely from the hospital? That would explain it, but why would they do that?

Tears squeeze out from behind her eyelashes and she turns heavily on her side, exhausted again. She has no idea what time it is. Or what day. It could be the middle of the night, a time when she should be asleep. Maybe that's why Mike isn't there. Or Monica. Maybe they'll come in the morning.

She dozes off, and when she opens her eyes it's lighter in the room. A man dressed in a dark suit is standing by her bed.

She looks up and is relieved to see a white band around his neck—a priest's collar.

She starts to say Mike's name, but before she can get any sound out, she sees it isn't Mike. This man is older and balding. There's something familiar about him, something she thinks she should know. She reaches a hand toward him, grabbing his sleeve. "I know you," she whispers. "But I don't know who you are."

He smiles and places a warm hand over hers. "I'm Father Ted Mahoney, Jenna. We've known each other for a long time—but I understand you've been having some memory problems?"

Ted Mahoney. Where has she heard that name? He said she knows him, and he's probably right. She really needs her notebook. Maybe she wrote it down.

"Father," she says, her voice hoarse. "You must know Mike Albertino."

"Of course." He pats her hand. "He took over for me at St. Rita's."

"So, you were the priest there before Mike?"

"Yes, Jenna." He pauses. "As I said, we—you and I—have known each other a long time."

"I'm so sorry—it seems rude, I'm sure, but I really don't remember you."

"It's okay. I understand. Let me help—we first met when you and your husband brought your baby daughter in for baptism."

An image washes over her: *a bald-headed priest holding a baby in a long white dress, colored light streaming in through stained-glass windows.*

"I remember that. It's you I've been seeing!"

Another image: *a tiny black coffin and the same bald-headed priest.*

He's so patient, waiting for her to remember all these details. "So, I suppose it was you at her funeral, too, then?"

"Yes," he says softly.

She searches his face. "Why are you here, Father? How did you find me?"

"I was doing my shift as chaplain when they brought you into the ER. The hospital paged me, so I came down. They said the caretaker at the cemetery found you crumpled up and in pain?"

"Yes, I remember that much. It was Harvey who brought me in." Ted startles as she says this, so she pauses, thinking for a moment. "Ted, I still don't understand. Why are you here instead of Mike? I asked Harvey to call him."

He grabs her hand. "I'm sorry to have to tell you this, considering your situation—but Mike is in trouble."

"What kind of trouble?"

He looks away for a long moment, then back at her, his gaze serious. "He's in jail. He was arrested several days ago."

Part Four

19

HE KNEW IT WAS COMING, or he should have known, at least. After the police found him at the scene of the bombing with no credible explanation for why he knew it would happen, it was just a matter of time. After all, in addition to that incriminating situation, he's been seen in the company of one Jenna Wright, mother of the slain child whose killer has not yet been found. Plus, the police found troves of evidence on his computer when they seized it a few weeks after he filed his report about the man's confession: dozens of searches for information about child abductions and murders, and all on the computer of a priest.

And everyone knows priests are child molesters, right?

So, he's not surprised when they finally showed up, red and blue lights twirling on top of their squad cars. He finds it rather cruel of them to arrest him just days before Christmas, one of the busiest times of the year in a priest's life. They cuffed him on the steps of the church as Sister Mary Katherine and the others stood inside the door, hugging themselves and each other, crying. He'd been trying to repair the broken lock on the stairs that lead to the bell tower when the police got there. He tried to send "Be brave!" thoughts to the sisters who gathered to watch him be marched to the patrol car, his toolbox still on the floor by the loft stairs. Sister Mary Katherine smiled at him, but he wonders if she thinks he's guilty, too.

He, of course, knows he's not guilty—at least, not of what the police suspect. He *is* guilty of one thing, though: of not listening. Selections from scripture march through his mind: *You hypocrites! You know how to interpret the appearance of the earth and the sky. Why don't you know how to interpret the present time?* He's had ample clues, insistent and repeated, and he's chosen to not believe that any of what he's seen and heard is real.

At least he saved that woman's life. He had no earthly way of knowing the bomb was about to go off, but it was happening just like in his dream, and he reacted without thinking. So, he wouldn't have it any other way, and the woman is safe. And no major wounds from the bomb except for that small injury on her knee, but it is ironic, isn't it? After all, if God is truly trying to get him to turn back to Him (this is Mike's current working theory, the one he's finally settled on after months of agonizing worry) it seems funny that He would do that by sending the authorities to arrest him and put him in chains.

Rather like the way you treated your own Son, Mike thinks. The police sergeant holds his head and guides him gently into the back seat of the cruiser. He takes one last look at the church, the nuns cowering in a clump on the steps at the door, and wonders as the police car takes off if he'll ever see the place again.

JOSH IS IN THE TINY BATHROOM near the nave of St. Rita's, putting bleach on his roots, his eyes watering from the sharp scent of ammonia that now encircles his head. The dark hair has started to show, and he needs to keep his disguise current. He bought the bleach at the local drugstore with money he stole from the collection plates. The priest at this place is such an idiot—he thinks the take from the offering is low every week because people are just not giving and never imagines that what's happening is one of the volunteer ushers, Josh himself, is taking the collection before it ever makes it to the office to be counted. All Josh has to do is put on his suit, stand at the side door as the plates are brought out, and offer to take them to the office. There's never more than a hundred bucks in each plate, so he slips a couple twenties in his pocket on the way down the hallway, and no one is ever the wiser.

The church has become his hideout. He's amazed how open it is. They leave the front doors unlocked all the time so people can walk in—to pray, supposedly. They never imagine that someone like him might have made a home in the belfry, the area at the top of the stairs condemned by the fire marshal, the place no one has gone into for over a year. It's the perfect hiding spot, and he's able to get hot soup for lunch every day *and* be close to Jenna, which is the whole point of being here.

Something has happened to her, though. She doesn't seem to know who he is anymore, which makes it a lot easier to get close to her. Maybe his disguise is better than he realized.

He'd originally tried the old persuasion route, back when they were both at the law firm, jumping through the hoops that women want you to go through—asking her out, being rebuffed, asking again, rejected again—and when she wouldn't give it willingly, he decided to take it by force. And that's when this guy, Howard-what's-his-name, came into the picture. Howard was a jerk, but he did have a mean left hook, which he used that one day when he came upon Josh and Jenna in the mailroom. Josh was just trying to talk to her, and, yeah, he might have grabbed her arm, but it didn't hurt her. No reason for that jerk, Howard, to break his nose. It healed but has never been the same, and then that same Jew, the jerk, got him fired, which left Josh unable to get any other job. It's people like him who run the country and they've got to be stopped. Josh is convinced of this.

When he met Steve shortly after getting canned, he felt like God had answered his prayers. Josh wonders if living in the church, a holy place, has rendered him especially blessed somehow.

Steve is inspiring. It was Steve who first gave Josh the idea of a disguise. He learned that white-blond hair done up in a spiky style is, apparently, a secret signal to others who share their philosophy. What they want is a return to a majority-white nation, one devoid of scum like the Jews who have taken over most businesses, including that Howard dude, the one who got him fired.

It is now December, close to Christmas, a holy season for sure, and Josh and Steve think it would be fitting to mark the occasion by bringing a bomb into the church. They plan to set it off in the middle of the Christmas Eve service. Silent Night my ass, thinks Josh—it'll be the opposite of silent. No one will be able to ignore him then, not even Jenna. His presence will be obvious to everyone, and he and Steve will ignite a religious war since everyone will blame the Jews or maybe the Muslims for bombing a Christian event. It's the perfect cover and it will get their country back on the right track. People will thank them. Eventually.

MIKE IS IN A JAIL CELL, nothing much but concrete, a hard sleeping shelf jutting out from the wall, a metal toilet bowl in the corner, gray pockmarked cement walls. The place smells of stale urine and damp concrete. No windows, not much light other than the dim yellowish glow from the corridor that runs between the row of cells on his side and the row on the other. Directly across from his cell is another, occupied by a disheveled man with stringy dark hair and a face shrouded in shadow. Despite the fact that Mike can't see the man's face, he can't shake the sense that this is the guy who came to confession that day, the one who said he'd killed a young girl. If it was Katie or Sophie he'd killed, and Mike worries it is, it would be the height of coincidence—so, Mike does not want to believe it. But—what if it's *not* a coincidence that the killer is right here with him? How amazing would *that* be?

He listens to the man muttering. The guy talks constantly to himself, as if responding to a voice only he can hear. It's sad, Mike thinks, how many of the mentally ill have ended up on the streets. The man keeps mumbling, and although Mike can't make out the words he's saying, it's clear from his tone that he's involved in a bitter argument with a figment of his imagination.

Mike walks to the bars of his cell and grasps them with both hands. "Hey buddy," he says, as gently as he can. "Is something wrong?"

The man looks up at him, his eyes dark. And his hair is dark, too. Didn't the guy from his confessional have spiky white hair? This one is dressed in a threadbare cloth coat, frayed at the elbows, dusty dark gray pants, tan work boots, one of which has a hole in the toe. "Nah, nothing wrong," the man says, shaking his head. "It's just this guy here. He's such a pain in the ass. Won't leave me alone."

"What guy is that?" Mike asks.

The man tips his head sharply to the side. "*This* one," he says, waving his hand dismissively. "This one right *here*." He turns and glares at the empty cell. "I told you to shut up," he snarls. "I don't want any more of your lip."

There's no one in the cell with him, of course, but Mike just watches, and then the man goes back to mumbling, his chin resting on his chest, rambling away in some long diatribe only he and the imaginary soul he's talking to can hear.

20

JENNA GAZES AT THE PRIEST who's appeared beside her hospital bed. Father Ted, he calls himself, and says he knows her. "Why would they put Mike in jail?" she asks.

He shrugs. "I don't know the charges. I do know there's a doctor here who *wants* to press charges, but the real problem is some incriminating evidence they found on Mike's computer."

"Evidence about what?"

"I haven't been told. The bishop has been in touch with a lawyer, and we're hoping to get to the bottom of this—but it doesn't help that he's so involved with you."

She flinches. "Involved? We're not in—"

He waves a hand in the air. "I don't mean it that way. It's just that he's spent an inordinate amount of time with you lately. People in the parish have noticed. And then when the doctor filed that complaint—"

"What doctor?"

"Your doctor, Jenna. Dr. Peter Andrews."

She looks away, a flare of anger rising inside her. She knew Andrews was up to something—she knew it before, but then when Mike told her about the military funding his project, it became even clearer that Andrews is up to something. She believes this Father Ted knows her, but she remembers so little. "Father, I have a lot of questions," she says, turning to him. "You say we've known each other for years—but how well do you know me? I mean, was I a member of your church?" She really wishes she could get her hands on her notebook—she needs to write this down.

"No, you weren't actually a member, but you did enroll your daughter in St. Rita's preschool. After the baptism, though, I didn't see either you or your husband at Mass very often."

"Well, I can understand that. Howard is Jewish, after all."

He nods. "Interfaith marriages carry their own set of complications. Anyhow, to answer your original question: No, you weren't a member of the parish, but I saw you frequently, since you worked next door and often came to visit your daughter."

"I wish I remembered that."

"We talked occasionally, but I didn't really get to know you until the day you came to me asking for some pastoral counseling." He watches her. "So, you don't remember that either?"

"I don't, but I'm wondering if it has anything to do with Howard."

"Yes. You had some concerns—"

"Well, I don't remember any of this, but I have learned in the last few days that Howard and I had serious marital problems." She pauses, thinking. "Father, during this counseling you said I sought from you—did I talk about divorce?"

"Apparently, your husband had had an affair. I advised you to see a marriage counselor before taking such a drastic step. Since I was due to retire a few months after you sought me out—this was about two years ago, I guess—I referred you to a colleague of mine."

"Did we see him?"

"Her. She's an excellent couples' counselor, but my understanding is that you and Howard only went a couple of times."

"I wonder why we stopped."

"I assume it wasn't helping—you told me several months later that you'd decided to file for divorce."

"Howard tells me that we are not divorced, though—maybe I didn't actually file?"

He shakes his head. "I doubt very much if it would have been a priority—you see, Katie was killed the day after you told me about your decision to divorce."

"I see." Her gaze is drawn to the window, which has grown considerably lighter as they've talked. "Father, let me ask you something else: Do you know anything about the procedure that the doctors carried out on me? After Katie was killed, you know."

"Only a little. You told me it was an experimental program, that they'd found a way to 'erase fear,' as you put it. I advised you against it, but you insisted."

"Why did you advise against it?"

"It seemed wrong to me, even if it was medically possible, to intercept the normal grieving process. I was concerned you were running away from your feelings." He steps closer and reaches to squeeze her hand. "It's understandable, of course—the pain you were in at the time was immense."

Two men in white coats come in through the door. She recognizes the first one right away: Andrews, and he's with someone else, another doctor, judging from the white coat. "Good morning," Andrews says. He glares at the Father. "I see we got here just in time before the clergy take our patient away again."

"Good morning, doctor," Father Ted says. "I just stopped by to visit—nothing more."

Andrews looks at him. "Ah. You're not the same guy."

Father Ted extends a hand toward him. "Ted Mahoney. But, actually, I believe we've met."

Dr. Andrews ignores the Father's hand. He nods at the other doctor. "This is my colleague, Dr. Scott, from Hopkins.

When I heard Jenna had been readmitted, I asked him to come in for a consult."

"Dr. Scott?" Jenna says, trying to prop herself up on an elbow. She's tangled in tubes again, though. "You're the one who developed this procedure."

Dr. Scott steps around the foot of the bed and comes close to her side. He leans down, and she catches a whiff of soap and something antiseptic. His face is kind and he has a nice smile. "Yes, Jenna. So, I take it you don't remember me?"

She wants to trust him, but all those things Mike said are eating at her. "No, but I'm starting to get used to this. I don't remember much."

He frowns and pulls out a penlight, leans close to her face and flips the light on, aiming it into one of her eyes. Searing pain blasts through her head. "Ow!" she shouts, pushing him away. "What are you doing?"

"Hm." He flicks the light off and returns it to his pocket. "Light sensitivity," he says, nodding at Doctor Andrews. "It's consistent with reversal."

"Reversal?" Jenna asks, rubbing her throbbing forehead.

"We think the fear amelioration procedure is reversing itself again, Jenna," Dr. Andrews says. "Despite the fact we gave you a second treatment the last time you were in."

"So, this is not expected then?" Father Ted asks.

"I'm done discussing this with you, Father," Dr. Andrews says. "You know the rules. Only family from now on."

"It's okay." Jenna is beginning to get irritated with this doctor. "You can tell him anything you would tell my so-called 'family.'"

"Mrs. Bernstein," Dr. Andrews says, "the last time I allowed one of these *parasites* in your room, he took it upon himself to interfere and remove you from the premises."

She flinches. "What do you mean parasites?"

"Just what I said." Andrews glares at Father Ted. "They prey on patients who are desperate for hope, who will cling to any sort of meaningless drivel, when what they *really* need is competent medical care."

Dr. Scott walks to Andrews's side and places a hand on his arm. "Peter, please. This isn't helping."

"It's true." Andrews clenches his fists. "You know as well as I that it's religion at the root of everything going on these days. Most terrorists are motivated by fanaticism, after all."

Scott shrugs. "I don't know that it's always religious fanaticism, though. I heard that the authorities suspect a homegrown separatist group for this latest round—apparently they arrested some people with white nationalist leanings."

Andrews shakes his head. "Doesn't matter, really." He jams his hands in his white coat pockets. "Thanks to you and your group's discovery, Doctor, we now have a better way to deal with all those terrorists. A way to fight back that will really work. It's a great advance you made all those years ago."

Father Ted has stepped away from the bed and stands near the window, his back turned to them.

"Doctors," Jenna says. "Tell me more about your project. I understand it was funded by the military? The Army?"

The Father turns from the window and looks at her sharply.

Andrews glances at Scott, then gestures toward Father Ted. "I told you—I can't discuss this with anyone but your family."

"As I said before, Father Ted isn't the same guy who helped me leave the hospital the last time."

"I see that!" Dr. Andrews explodes. "But they're all the same. I mean, seriously—why do you trust these people?"

"Peter, please," Dr. Scott says. "This is a Catholic hospital, after all. The chaplains have as much right to be here as you do."

"Not when they violate hospital procedures, *steal* patients and hide them so we can't take care of them."

"Mike didn't *steal* me," Jenna says. "He might have helped me get out of here, but I wanted to leave."

"That doesn't make sense," Dr. Andrews says. "If it were true, why did you come back here? That old guy who brought you into the ER said *you* were the one who requested he bring you to the hospital."

"Harvey? Well, sure, I asked him to bring me here—but I was in pain. It felt like my head was about to split in half." She remembers how he'd looked standing there on the sidewalk by the ER entrance, clutching her coat and—"Wait. Where's that potted flower?"

She props herself up on an elbow and peers around the darkened room. Sitting atop the table is what appears to be a potted plant, shrouded in semi-darkness. "There it is." She points at the plant. "Doctor, take a look at that flower. It has something to do with what happened to me."

She averts her eyes, afraid to look directly at it again. Andrews turns and gazes at the daisy. "I have no idea. It's just a potted plant. A daisy, from the looks of it." He turns back to Jenna. "What do you mean it has something to do with what happened to you? When?"

Father Ted walks to the table where the plant is sitting and looks at it for a long moment. He turns to Jenna. "I know what happened."

The doctors stare at him.

He lifts the potted daisy and as he brings it closer she can smell the strong floral scent. She inadvertently glances toward it. Pain slams into her forehead and she averts her gaze. An image flashes in her mind:

A little dark-haired girl sits next to her on a sofa, pressed into her side.

A book is open across both their laps.

The girl is Katie. It's Katie!

Jenna, shaking, rubs her forehead. She can almost remember this. Almost.

Katie points at the page, beams up at her, starts to say something.

The Father replaces the plant on the table and steps in front of it, blocking it from her view. "Flowers just like these were all over the church during Katie's funeral. You chose them yourself, Jenna."
"I did?"
He nods. "They're called Gerbera daisies—I'd never heard of them, but you said they were Katie's favorite flower." He chuckles, a bit sadly, she thinks. "You said she had a favorite picture book with drawings of flowers that looked just like these."
"I remember that," she whispers. "I remember it!"
Father Ted steps closer to the bed. "What do you remember?"
Andrews tries to push himself between the Father and Jenna's bedrail. "Now just wait one minute."
"Please, Doctor," Jenna says. "Before the Father said that I saw something—in my mind's eye, I mean. It was a little girl—I'm sure it was Katie—and I was reading a book to her."

Andrews flings his hands in the hair and huffs. "Just as I suspected. It's a trigger." He turns to Scott. "You predicted this could happen—I think it was in that first paper from your group, the one by Albertino and Scott, right?"

"*Albertino*?" Father Ted turns to the doctors. "What does *Mike* have to do—?"

"Wait," Jenna says. "What's a trigger?"

"Just what it sounds like," Andrews says. "The flower is triggering bits and pieces of memory and your brain is trying to reconstruct full memories around the time of the traumatic event. It's very dangerous." He waves a hand toward Scott. "Dr. Scott and his first student, the one who figured out the initial steps in the fear amelioration procedure, also predicted this complication. We've seen it happen, just like they predicted, in other patients." He glares at Father Ted. "This is what I was trying to warn you about."

The Father's eyes have grown wide and he steps closer to Jenna, as if he's about to say something. She's having a hard time thinking straight. A surge of excitement into her chest keeps bringing her back to this idea of a trigger. "Doctor," she says, trembling now, "are you saying that if I see certain objects—like this flower, say, or a doll—I might be able to recover some memories of Katie?"

Andrews frowns. "Wait. You don't remember her?"

"That's what I've been trying to tell you! It's like the last five years of my life have been completely erased."

"Oh my." He pushes a shaky hand back through his hair. "It sounds like the procedure went much further than we intended."

Father Ted steps close to the bed, his teeth clenched. "Yes, doctor," he says, seething. "It certainly seems that way. Rather like Pandora's box, don't you think?"

"I don't need *you* lecturing *me* about medicine," Andrews explodes.

"Peter, please." Scott pulls him away from the Father, then turns to Jenna. "Let me get this straight, Jenna: you don't remember anything of the last five years?"

"Very little. I didn't remember I was married, for example."

"Oh wow." Scott shakes his head. "It was never supposed to go that far. We were just trying to remove the fear response to one particular—well, you know. *The murder.*"

Jenna nods. "I understand. But, doctor, please—I need to know more. You say that the procedure is reversing itself, and these triggers are causing that. I've been having these terrible headaches, not to mention nightmares. Is all that related to the reversal?"

"It could be. I'm afraid we have no experience with this."

"What do you mean?"

"Well, simply that: It's never happened before. None of our other patients have ever wanted to have the procedure reversed."

"So, this is something you have no experience with at all, then?" Father Ted asks.

Scott shakes his head. "I'm afraid not."

"But wait." Jenna looks around the room for her bag. Where in the world is it? And where's her notebook? She really needs to write all this down. She's going to black out again and lose everything she's figured out. She turns to the doctors. "Tell me this: Why am I having such terrible headaches? And the light—it's very painful to look at light," she says, looking away from the window, which has become much brighter as they've talked.

"It sounds like a migraine," Scott says. He turns to Andrews. "Has she had migraines before?"

She starts to say no, but Andrews answers, saying, "A migraine would indicate an increased blood flow into certain regions of the brain."

"But, what does that mean?" Jenna is getting more and more agitated as they stand there talking about her like she's not even in the room. "Does the increased blood flow mean my memories are coming back?"

Andrews shakes his head and finally looks at her. "We have no idea, Mrs. Bernstein. We are in uncharted waters here."

"But wait." She's desperate now. "If seeing a trigger, like that flower, can give me a migraine, can't we just try it again—I mean, find some other trigger and see if it will bring back more memories?"

"I don't know what it would do. Your brain might not be able to handle it."

"But why? These are my own memories. How dangerous can they be?"

"A person's own memories *are* dangerous, if they've experienced trauma. That's why our work is so important. Besides, look what happened to you before—seeing the trigger knocked you unconscious."

"Yes, but only for a little while. I came out of it."

"I don't know, Jenna." Andrews shakes his head. "It's very dangerous."

"Any more dangerous than the original procedure?" Father Ted steps closer, his arms crossed over his chest. "You didn't seem to show that much concern before."

"We were following established guidelines." Andrews turns his back on the Father again. "And, as I said before, this is important work—it will help people overcome debilitating fear. That's what we *all* want, isn't it? To live, free of fear?"

Father Ted shakes his head but doesn't answer. He looks at Jenna.

"I want to try," she says. "If it means I will get Katie back—well, memories of her, anyway—I want to try. I don't care how dangerous it is."

Father Ted unfolds his arms, walks to her bedside, reaches out and grabs both her hands. "Jenna. Listen. I agree that if you can get your memories of Katie back, that would be best—but it doesn't mean you will get *her* back." He pauses, biting his lip. "Katie is dead, Jenna."

She nods, tears welling in her eyes. "I know that. I do understand what you're saying, Father. But I want her back—" She pulls one of her hands out of his grasp and presses it to her chest, tears rolling down her cheeks.

"Ah, I see." He squeezes her hand. "You want her back in your heart."

She nods, blinking back tears. "Yes," she whispers.

"Jenna," he says, smiling. "Something tells me that she's *always* been in your heart—and always will be."

21

MIKE MAKES HIS WAY to the hard shelf in his cell. It serves as a bed, an uncomfortable one, but he stretches out on it, not sure how long he'll be here or what's going to happen next. He lies on his back for a while, then rolls to his side, drawing his knees up and curling an arm under his head. His thoughts roll from topic to topic, from memories to imaginings, and soon he is caught up in a sexual fantasy.

It's a familiar sequence, one he's visited in his imagination more than a few times in his own bed in his tiny apartment, and it involves Jenna. Her long auburn hair keeps switching to blond in Mike's thoughts as she gets mixed up with an old girlfriend from college, someone who looked nothing like Jenna, but who excited the same sort of swelling and pressure in his trousers as Jenna now does.

The mumbling from across the way has stopped, and the man has started to snore. Mike figures he should try it too, but sleep eludes him. The fantasy slips away as well, and as he stares into the dark, a light appears in his cell and then there he is again, the boy with the tight yellow curls. A frisson of excitement jitters through Mike's body. The angel-boy is dressed, as always, in the tattered gray loincloth, his arms smeared with something like dried blood or mud.

Mike sits up and swings his legs around, letting them dangle toward the floor. There's an odd scent, something strongly floral, like roses, completely covering over the previous smell of urine. He's hyper-aware of the angel-child and a little annoyed that the guy in the other cell has chosen this moment to be asleep—he'd like to have another witness for a change. Not that the man is a reliable witness. He'd just been talking to an imaginary being, after all.

Mike is well aware of the inconsistency of his thoughts. If the disheveled man across the hall is caught in a delusion, talking to someone who isn't really there, then what is this that Mike sees in front of him? It's the child, the same one he's seen in the church three times before, but now he's not in the church. There's no way he could have gotten into this cell without going through the walls, plus the bars of the cell are only inches apart.

Mike lets his breath out heavily. "Why are you here?" he whispers.

"You don't need to whisper," the boy says, his voice piercing and clear. It sounds, inexplicably, like a bell. "No one can hear you." He nods toward the cell across the corridor. "He's asleep now."

Mike laughs. "Just my luck. I was hoping someone else would be here to see you—one of these times."

"That's not going to happen, and you know it." The angel-boy looks at Mike for a long moment. "You think he's the one," he says, nodding toward the disheveled man. "You think he's the one you're looking for."

A bile-like bitterness rises into Mike's throat. "Why should that matter? There's nothing I can do about it. The police aren't going to believe *me*. Not now." He shakes his head. "Besides, I'm not looking for *anyone*."

"They'll let him go," the boy says, "He'll kill again." He turns and gazes at the man who is curled into a dark lumpy ball, his breathing heavy. "There's nothing you can do about this one. It's a compulsion he has, you see?" The angel takes a step closer to Mike. The light from the dim bulb outside the cell falls across his young face. The angel-child used to look young, anyway, but now he seems old. Ancient. "It's a *compulsion*," the child repeats, his voice ringing. "It means he listens to the voices in his head and they tell him to kill. He simply obeys." He glances at the snoring man, then returns his gaze to Mike who realizes he's started to tremble.

Yet another scripture pops into Mike's mind: *The fear of the Lord is the beginning of wisdom.* The trembling continues, starting somewhere in his gut, shaking him uncontrollably. He does not like the direction this conversation is going and wishes he could close his ears to it but knows there's no escape. "And then there's you, Mike Albertino," the angel-child says. "You hear the voice of God and choose *not* to obey. There was a time when you were obedient. A time when you were young, working with a great doctor who promised that, together, you would unlock the secrets of the mind—you saw the error of your ways then and turned away. You knew the work would be your undoing, would harm others, and yet you refuse to own your part in the tragedy unfolding before your very eyes. Why?"

Mike jerks backward. *You hypocrites! You know how to interpret the appearance of the earth and the sky. Why don't you know how to interpret the present time?* The angel, if that's what it is, is still there, gazing at him calmly. "Wh—what do you want me to do?" Mike asks, the trembling now so intense his voice shakes.

The angel-child nods toward the man in the cell across the hall. "There's nothing you can do about the one across the way. He's a lost soul—lost to you, anyway." He turns back to Mike, his gaze piercing him like a knife. "But there is another you can stop—and you can atone for the wrong that led to your friend's current pain. You know how to help her. Find the man with hair white as snow. You know where he is. He appears as the angel of death—in the rose window, in the highest reaches of the sanctuary." He pauses and the light in the cell dims. "You know what you must do, Mike Albertino, and yet you choose not to obey. I ask you again: Why?"

Mike tips his head back and stares in frustration at the darkening ceiling. *I did listen*, he wants to say. *I saved that woman from the bomb, and I've tried to help Jenna, for months now, but look where it's got me. In jail!*

He tips his head back down, wanting now to answer the boy—the angel, the messenger—but the boy has disappeared. Of course.

As Mike knew all along he would.

PETE ARRIVES AT ST. RITA'S early in the morning, before eight a.m., as he and Sister Mary Katherine have arranged. He'd suggested she call the police, get the authorities involved, but she's wary of the cops and doesn't understand why they've taken Mike away. Pete can understand this, so he's agreed to help. The sister cracks open the heavy front door as he hurries up the steps, taking them two at a time. "He's here," she whispers loudly enough that he can hear her as he approaches.

"Did you see him?" Pete whispers back, breathing hard from the sprint he just did down the street.

She nods. "Mrs. Freund arrived to open up for the altar guild, and she saw him in the bathroom by the front door—putting some sort of goop on his hair."

An older woman with graying hair and dimpled hands peers around the sister's shoulder at him. This must be Mrs. Freund.

Pete steps inside the door and pushes it closed with one hand. The hallway smells of wax with a faint whiff of incense. "We should lock this door, if possible, so he'll be trapped." He reaches into his pocket for his phone. "I'll call the police, but one of you needs to run back to the kitchen and lock the door that leads to the alley."

The old woman frowns and looks over her shoulder toward the hallway. "The kitchen? Is that how he got in?"

Pete nods. "I think it is. I saw him come in that way earlier this morning."

"Earlier? It's barely eight o'clock as it is."

Pete feels his face grow a little hot. "Let's just say I'm an early riser." He punches the button for the stored number of the police. "I saw him come in that way, so we really ought to lock it up—just in case, you know."

Mrs. Freund hurries toward the kitchen to lock the door leading to the alley.

22

THE DOCTORS LEAVE shortly after Ted does. Jenna's thoughts are swirling, and she's agitated by all she's heard. First thing she needs to do is find what they called a "trigger," something like the potted daisy, something that can bring back even more memories—and second thing she needs to do is find out what's happened to Mike. But she can't do either—she's stuck here, tied down by tubes that snake into her nose and a vein on her arm.

She tries to nap and eat some lunch and is waiting for somebody to remove her food tray when Monica hurries in through the door. She rushes to her bed and flings her arms around Jenna's neck. "I *knew* I shouldn't have let you go back to your place alone." She hugs her tight and rocks her side to side.

"Nice to see you, too. But I'm okay." She pushes Monica back so she can see her face. "And it might have happened even if I'd stayed at your place."

"You had another episode like the one at the deli?"

"Yes—and induced by the same thing." She nods toward the potted daisy, which she can now tolerate short glimpses of.

Monica stares at it. "Wow. It looks just like that one I got for my office."

"Yes. Apparently, it was Katie's favorite flower."

"Really?" Monica turns back to Jenna. "And you remembered that?"

"Not consciously. But some part of me did remember and every time I saw a flower like that, I would be thrown back to her funeral. Apparently, the church was filled with them."

"That's amazing." She perches on the edge of the bed and grabs Jenna's hand. "So, how are you feeling?"

"I'm okay. A little tired, but basically okay. Monica, listen: Did you hear what happened to Mike?"

Monica frowns. "What are you talking about?"

"He's in jail, Monica."

"What?"

"In jail. Ted Mahoney told me." She shrugged. "I actually don't know much more than that—it may have something to do with you and Mike springing me from the hospital."

"Oh no." She sighs heavily. "It's all my fault. I've got to get him out of there."

Jenna shakes her head. "No, no—it's not your fault. Something else is going on. Mike was involved somehow in everything that happened to me. I don't know how exactly, but that doctor, the one from Baltimore, worked with Mike back when they were developing this very technique."

"Are you kidding me? Mike was involved? How is that even possible?"

"Remember he told us he was familiar with the work from his days as a neuroscience student? Well, that's when it started. I don't know the rest of the details, and I also don't know why he's in jail. Anyhow, when Ted left, he said he was on the way to pick Mike up. I'm still not sure, but it may be the bishop that posted bail."

Monica frowns. "I'm sorry. Who's Ted again?"

"Ted Mahoney. He was the priest at St. Rita's before Mike. He came to see me this morning. Apparently, we're old friends."

Monica snickers. "You seem to have a thing for priests."

"Not *that* kind of friend." Jenna swats at her. She looks down, rubbing the back of Monica's hand. "He baptized Katie. He knew a lot about me. And he knew a lot about *us*—Howard and me."

"Like what?"

"He said that I'd come to see him when I found out that Howard was cheating on me. He said I was planning on filing for divorce when—well, you know. When it happened."

"But you didn't."

"I guess not." She pauses. "Monica, I'm thinking I need to see Howard again."

"Why?"

"Well, I think he might have some things that would help me recover more of what I've forgotten about Katie."

"What kind of things?"

"You know, toys, clothes maybe. That doll I found seemed to spark all sorts of feelings. Sam said it was hers. And I wouldn't have guessed that a potted daisy would be relevant, but it turns out it is."

When Dr. Andrews comes back to check on her, she convinces him that there's no reason for her to stay another night in the hospital. "I'm fine," she says. "Nothing more wrong with me than a migraine—they have medication for that, don't they?"

He refuses to write her a prescription for migraine medication. "We can't risk it," he says. "There's no telling how the medication might interact with the fear amelioration drug," but he agrees she's well enough to be discharged. Monica waits through all of this, sitting on a chair in the corner, checking her messages on her phone every once in a while, never complaining about how long it's taking to get Jenna out of the hospital.

When they finally release her at around three o'clock in the afternoon, the nurse wheels her to the lobby in a wheelchair while Monica pulls her car to the door.

"Monica, what would I do without you?" Jenna says, as they pull out of the hospital driveway and head back toward Jenna's apartment. "I'm sure you had plenty of ways you could have spent your time this weekend other than waiting around for me to get out of the hospital."

"It's no problem. Really." Monica glances in the rearview mirror. "I just want to make sure you get home safely this time."

"Are you sure?"

Monica sighs. "Jenna, I don't know if this idea of yours—to get Howard to bring things that might jog your memory—is such a good one."

"But why?" Jenna feels the tears threatening. She's afraid Monica is right.

"Well, because it could send you into a tailspin—the way that potted daisy did." Monica grips the steering wheel and stares straight ahead. Jenna can see a little muscle flexing in Monica's jaw. She pulls up to a red light, stops and turns to Jenna. "Promise me you won't look at anything he brings unless somebody else is around who can take you to the ER if things get bad."

She agrees, shaken by the memory of the pain in her head in the cemetery. "Oh wait!" She grabs Monica's arm. "My car is still at the cemetery. Can you drop me there instead? I really ought to pick up my car. You know where the cemetery is, right?"

"Yep. Right near my place," Monica says, changing lanes. "The front gate is down this way, I think."

They pull up to the cemetery gate and it swings inward as Monica's car approaches. Jenna thinks of Harvey's delight at his smartphone and its ability to open the gate regardless of where he might be. They roll past his small stone house, dark and empty. Jenna stares at it. "I wonder if Harvey's here."

"Who?"

"Harvey. He's the caretaker."

"So, where's your car?"

Jenna directs her around the hill, and there sits her car, pulled off to the side, just where she left it. Monica hugs her before she gets out. "Call me when you get home, okay?"

Jenna stops by Harvey's house on her way out, parks and walks to his door. She knocks, but there's no answer. She goes to the window and placing a hand against the glass, peers inside. Nothing but darkness. She steps away and looks around. No sign of Harvey and no sign of his blue truck. Somehow, she's not sure how, she knew this is what she'd find. Perhaps it should concern her, maybe even scare her, but instead it brings comfort. Harvey is here somewhere. She's sure of it.

A half-hour later, she's just settled into her own comfortable easy chair, glad to be back in her own place again, when her phone rings. She doesn't recognize the number. When she answers, a robotic voice informs her she has a call from the county jail. She accepts the call and a familiar voice comes on the line: Mike.

"It's so good to hear from you," she says.

"It's good to hear your voice, too. Ted said you were in the hospital?"

"Was. I'm actually at my apartment now. I had to be a little pushy, but I finally convinced the doctor to let me go."

She can hear a commotion on the other end of the line, something like a metal door clanging shut, then his voice comes back on the line. "So you're okay, then?"

"Well, my headache is gone, so that's good. Actually, I'm more than okay."

"What do you mean?"

"Well, it seems that I've been starting to recover bits and pieces of my memories whenever I encounter an object that reminds me of Katie. The doctor called them triggers."

"Aha—like that doll with the broken arm."

"Right. And then there was the potted daisy that Monica had—there was another just like it at the cemetery, which is what sent me into this latest tailspin." She wants to tell him about Harvey and the boarded-up house, but he interrupts.

"Jenna, listen—I want to tell you something to make sure you don't hear it from someone else." After a short pause he says, "I'm calling you from—from jail."

"Father Ted told me this morning. What happened, Mike?"

"It's a long story. The police brought me in two days ago. They had their reasons, not least of which involved someone springing you from the hospital."

"I don't want you to be in trouble because of me. I need to get down there, explain to them—which jail are you at?"

"No, Jenna. Don't come. Ted is on his way to pick me up, and we've got to get back to the church. I—I just wanted to let you know what was going on, like I said. I'll fill you in on the rest later."

"Okay. I'll come by and check on you." She pauses. "And Mike? Don't worry. It's going to be alright. I'm sure of it."

23

MIKE FOLLOWS THE GUARD down the long dim hallway to a harshly lit reception area, and there stands Ted, clutching the back of a chair over which Mike's coat is slung. On the table next to the chair, a large plastic bag sits in a lump. The room smells like stale cigarettes, despite the "No Smoking" sign on the wall.

Mike walks over. "Thank you for coming to pick me up," he says, looking into the bag. Inside it are his wallet, keys and the small pocket knife he's had since he was a kid. He reaches in, retrieves the items and begins putting them in his pockets. "They told me someone tried to post bail—was it you?"

"The bishop was all prepared to do that," Ted says, "when the police told him they were releasing you for lack of evidence. Seems they got the DNA results back for the little girl's murder, and the second child as well, and yours didn't match." He holds Mike's coat out to him. "Where's your collar, Father?"

"Oh right." Mike reaches into his pocket. "I took it off last night." He doesn't want to tell Ted the real reason he removed it—he feels completely unworthy to wear such a thing anymore.

Ted nods toward the door, which the guard has just opened and is standing next to. "Shall we go then?"

Mike nods, and they make their way outside into the bright day. A blast of cold hits him as he blinks in the sunshine, trying to see. He's been in the dark so long that his eyes seem unable to take in the light.

Ted heads for a car parked at a meter a short distance away, walks around to the driver's side and opens it with a key. "I'll give you a ride back to St. Rita's."

After they get in, Ted sits in the driver's seat, both hands on the steering wheel, sagging a little, but not starting the car.

Mike looks at him from the side, wanting to ask his question, but unsure how to start. Finally, he blurts it out. "Why didn't you tell me what was going on?" His friend shoots him a quick look, his eyes sad. Mike shakes his head. "You *knew*."

"Knew what, Father?" Ted's voice is so quiet Mike can barely hear him.

"You knew about Jenna. Knew her daughter had been murdered. You didn't tell me, even when you knew I'd met her and was trying to figure out what had happened."

Ted stares at his gloved hands, gripping and releasing the steering wheel. He turns slowly and looks at Mike. "Yes, I knew, I admit it, but I couldn't reveal that to you. Sure, part of it was sanctity of the confessional—but the main thing was that those doctors had me convinced I shouldn't. They said any reminders, anything at all, of Jenna's past could be dangerous to her." He grips the wheel and shakes his head. "I was afraid that when you were talking to her, you'd spill something that would hurt her. I shouldn't have listened to them, though." He looks at Mike, his face clouded with an inexplicable darkness. "Father—why didn't you tell me you were involved with the development of the very technique the doctors used on Jenna?"

Mike feels all the air rush out of his body. He sags forward and turns to look at Ted who looks back calmly, waiting patiently for Mike to confess all his sins in this whole disastrous episode. Tears stab at Mike's eyes, and he buries his face in his hand, unable to hold the tears in.

Ted's hand comes to Mike's shoulder. He squeezes it gently. "It's okay, Mike. You know where the true power lies. Just say it."

Mike shakes his head and brings his hands to his lap. "I can't. I don't believe any of this anymore—"

"No, no. That's not what I'm getting at. The power is in confession, Mike. You know that, Father. You know it."

Mike's tears escape, streaming down his face. He leans his head back against the seat back, exhausted. "It was my fault," he whispers. "All of it."

"I'm not sure it was. But go on. *What* was your fault?"

Mike swipes at his cheeks. "If I had not done that work with Scott, all those years ago, not been seduced by all his promises of fame—my misguided thoughts about how I, too, could be a brilliant doctor!" A sob catches him off guard, and he takes a deep breath, sensing a great weight lifting off his chest. "When I heard they believed, truly believed, that they could eliminate all fear, it was exhilarating to contemplate. But if I'd known what could happen, what *did* happen, to Jenna I mean—I would never have done it."

"Whether you or the other investigators did that work or not would make no difference in what happened to Katie, though."

"That's true, but at least Jenna wouldn't have forgotten her own child. I was the cause of all that despair."

"Maybe. Or maybe not. I never told you that Jenna came to me for marriage counseling, not to mention her fears about a guy who was stalking her."

Mike stares at his friend, who still refuses to meet his gaze. "What are you talking about? *Who* was stalking her?"

Ted shrugs. "I don't know the fellow's name. He was someone she'd worked with at her previous job. A law firm, I think. She'd gotten involved with a married man, as you know, and this other fellow, the stalker, had reacted with jealousy. I think it was more than mere jealousy, though, to tell you the truth. The fellow was obsessed with Jenna." He starts the car. "One other thing. Sister Mary Katherine and a couple of parishioners surprised and cornered an intruder in the church early this morning."

"Who was it?"

"The police haven't identified the guy, although they took him into custody."

"Is everyone okay? The sisters?"

"Yes, they're all fine." Ted pulls the car out into traffic. He smiles at Mike briefly, then returns his gaze to the road. "Everyone is anxious to see you again. They will be so glad to get you back."

JENNA HAS JUST FINISHED PAYING the last of her overdue bills when Howard returns her call. "I got your message. I have some of Katie's things here at the house. I could bring them by this evening if you'd like."

"What kind of things?"

"Some toys, a few other items. There's actually a whole box of stuff. I'm not totally sure what's in it."

"I'd love to take a look."

"I could be there around seven."

"That sounds great. Oh, and Howard? Monica made me promise that I wouldn't look at anything unless somebody was here with me."

"Oh. Well, I'm not sure I can *stay*. I had plans for dinner. Plus, it's a pretty big box of stuff." There's a long pause on his end. "I—well, to tell you the truth, I'm not sure I can face looking at her things again."

"It's okay. Monica might be able to come by."

"Okay, good. Whatever works for you." He sounds distracted. She can hear voices in the background on his end. "Look, Jenna, I gotta run—I had only a couple of minutes before depositions begin, and the judge is calling us back now."

He does come that evening, like he said he would, but arrives nearly an hour early. Monica had said she could come over but hasn't yet arrived.

"Here it is." Howard lugs a bulky cardboard box into her living room and plunks it down. A puff of musty dust wafts up as the box hits the floor. "Hm." He peers at her furnishings. "I never pictured your place looking like this."

"So, I guess you've never been here."

"Nope. First time for everything." He reaches toward the end table by the sofa and holds up the battered little doll. "I haven't seen this for a while." He turns it over in his hands. "Where did it come from?"

She shrugs. "It was in my kitchen. I have no idea how it got there."

"Katie must have lost it in there," he says, handing it back to her.

She puts it back on the table. "Sam said he gave it to her as a gift."

Howard nods. "She loved it. One of her favorite toys." He gives her a sad look. "I'm sorry I can't stay. Will somebody be here when you look in the box?"

"I hope so." She grabs her coat and follows him around to the front of the building. His car is parked at the curb. A blond woman sits in the passenger seat staring straight ahead, not looking at them. "Is that your date?"

"You don't know her," Howard says, jamming his hands in his coat pockets.

"Well, even if I did, I probably wouldn't remember," she laughs. "Howard, listen: This may not be the time or place to talk about this, but maybe it's time we went ahead with the divorce proceedings."

He frowns. "Divorce?"

"It appears you've moved on." She nods toward the car. "And, after talking to Father Ted, I've learned I was probably ready to move on months ago."

"Hm." He rocks back on his heels. "Well, okay. I guess we could talk about it." He glances at the car. The blond woman has turned and is looking at both of them. Jenna can't see her face clearly, but she imagines that the woman is plenty annoyed at the scene in front of her.

Jenna steps between Howard and the car. "I don't think there's much to talk about." She nods her head toward the woman. "It's clear you've moved on—and, as I said, I'm ready to move on, too."

"Move on? So, there's somebody else?"

"There might be."

"It's that priest, isn't it?"

"Oh, come on. How could it be a priest?" She's well aware she's lying, but Howard doesn't need to know that. "After all," she says, "they're married to the church, right?"

He snorts. "So I hear." He leans forward, grabs her by the arms, and kisses her on the cheek. "Nice seeing you, sweetheart. Gotta run."

She goes back inside and stands looking at the box, pushing at it with her foot, trying to judge the weight. It's heavier than one might expect if it was filled with teddy bears and stuffed animals. Maybe it's full of blocks or wooden toys?

Jenna is itching to get into it, but Monica would kill her if she opens it while she's alone. She runs to her purse, rummages for her phone and punches in a number. Sam answers on the first ring.

"Hey," she says. "What are you doing tonight?"

"Helping Mom clean out the attic. Why? Want to help?"

"Could you come over?"

"So I guess that's a no."

"I have a box of Katie's things here. I—I'm thinking they might help me remember more. Howard just dropped them off, but Monica made me promise I wouldn't look at any of it alone—and she's not here yet."

"What kind of things did Howard bring?"

"I don't know for sure. Toys, probably. But I haven't opened the box, so I don't really know. Can you come over?"

"I'd love to take a break, but I promised Mom I'd help her. Let me see if I can wiggle out of this for a while."

"Why is she cleaning out the attic?"

He sighs. "It's been coming for some time, as you know. She says she's ready to consider going into that retirement community we talked about. I figured helping her downsize might move the decision along."

Everyone's life but hers, even Mom's, is moving forward. She's certain the key to breaking her mental logjam is in that box, but she really ought to wait for Monica. "You know, I'm just being impatient. Monica will be here soon. Thanks anyway." She leans back on the sofa and tries to read a magazine she finds on the coffee table, but the words blur together. She checks the clock—Monica should be there by now. Maybe she got held up at work. She waits, patiently at first, then impatiently, getting up for a glass of water, then to check her email, water the plants—whatever she can find to pass the time. A full hour passes, and she's gotten out the feather duster and has started to clean when a knock sounds on the door.

She runs to open it, and there stand Monica and Sam, side by side, on the steps. Sam has a thick manila envelope tucked under his arm. "Hey," Monica says as she walks in, unbuttoning her coat. "I'm so sorry. I was going to drive over, but the police had the street blocked off near the church for some reason and I had to walk a few extra blocks—and then I ran into Sam in front of your building."

She moves aside so they can come in. "Sam, I thought you had to help Mom."

"I thought so, too, but she got weepy looking at old things and decided she needed a nap. So—here I am!"

Jenna smiles. "Well, this is great—you're both here." She pulls Monica toward the box. "This is what Howard brought over."

"Maybe you should go ahead and open it." Monica grins at Sam. "It looks like you're well-protected now."

Jenna settles onto the sofa, Monica next to her while Sam sits in the easy chair. He places the thick envelope on the floor at his feet, face down.

Jenna takes a big breath. "Here goes nothing." She opens the box, revealing a pink and blue quilt, spread over something lumpy. It looks familiar but doesn't trigger any memories. She buries her nose in the quilt, expecting something to hit her. It smells like laundry detergent, nothing more. No waves of pain, no tsunami of images. "Well, that was easy. It *does* look vaguely familiar, though." She glances at Sam. "Was it Katie's?" He shrugs, so she folds the quilt and places it next to her on the sofa.

Beneath the quilt is a stack of flat plastic boxes. They look like old-fashioned CD cases. Monica pulls one out. "What's this?"

"I don't know." She takes it from Monica and looks it over. It's labeled in her own handwriting, with dates, several years earlier.

"Maybe they're photos," Monica suggests.

"Actually, I think they're videos," Sam says. He takes the case from Jenna and looks at the writing on it. "It looks like one of the DVDs I made for you." He holds the case out to her. "I think you ought to watch it. Judging from the date, I bet this will have what you're looking for."

Jenna sees a glint of tears in his eyes as she reaches for it. "Okay." She takes it from him. "I assume I have a DVD player somewhere in here. Wait—here it is." She opens the DVD box and slides the disc into an opening beneath the TV. Static fills the screen. She grabs the remote, looks at it closely, then hands it to Sam. "I can't figure it out—you do it."

He inspects the remote, then punches a couple of buttons and there on the screen is a little dark-haired girl. She's wearing a party hat and blowing out candles near a sunny window. You can see green trees outside, tossing in a breeze, and a table piled with wrapped gifts.

Jenna's own voice comes from somewhere off-screen. "Katie," the Jenna on the video says. "What are you wishing for?"

"Mommy," the dark-haired girl says, turning toward the off-camera voice.

"I'm wishing we'll always be together," Jenna says, staring at the screen. Monica grabs her hand and squeezes it.

The little girl looks into the camera. "I'm wishing we'll always be together."

Monica stares at her. "How did you know she was going to say that?"

Tears well in Jenna's eyes, and suddenly she's laughing and crying at the same time. Sam moves to the sofa and slides an arm around Jenna's shoulders. She leans into his side, breathing in the sandalwood scent.

"Jenna, how did you know?" Monica asks, squeezing her hand again.

Jenna blinks back tears. "Because I remember it. Like it happened yesterday. I actually remember it."

As she sits there in Sam's embrace holding Monica's hand, it all rushes back.

After they'd finished opening Katie's presents and eating birthday cake, both Howard and Sam had left. "I'll see you next weekend," Howard said, giving Katie a big hug and following Sam out the door.

She'd bundled Katie in her favorite blue coat and the two of them headed for the park. It had been a beautiful day—blue sky, bright green grass, the first flush of spring. When they arrived at the park, a kite-flying contest was in full swing. Katie was excited by the colorful kites and wouldn't sit still on the blanket Jenna spread on the grass, so she'd let her run and play. She kept a close eye on her, though, as always.

And then it happened. She was watching Katie run, chasing a little boy with a kite that dangled colorful streamers for a tail. A large dog dashing after a tossed Frisbee collided with Jenna at the same moment something heavy hit her back. She'd turned to see what it was, and there was Josh Reynolds. He grabbed her, wrapped his arms tight around her shoulders, and hissed in her ear: "Shut up! Now you'll pay." She could smell the alcohol on his breath and a strong scent of old cigarette smoke on his clothes.

She'd struggled, trying to keep Katie in sight, but Josh had wrestled her to the ground. A man—no one she knew—ran over. "What are you doing? Get off of her!" he'd shouted, pulling at

Josh, who stood up, one foot on Jenna's wrist, and slugged the guy. "Hey!" the man had yelled as he hit the ground.

Jenna grew more and more frantic, unable to free her arm, searing with pain beneath Josh's boot. The ground smelled damp and earthy beneath her. "Katie!" she'd yelled, simultaneously panicked and furious. Despite the court order, Josh had followed her to the park, probably from her apartment where he'd been caught lurking multiple times. The restraining order forbade him from getting within twenty feet of her, but here he was, his foot pinning her forearm to the ground. The pain in her wrist was excruciating, but the big problem was Katie—Jenna had lost sight of her.

The second man finally got up and yanked at Josh's arm again. As Josh stumbled back, she was freed from her pinned position, scrambled to her feet and headed in the direction she'd last seen Katie. She'd run, shouting, "Katie! Katie!" She'd run for what seemed hours screaming for her daughter, the child she never saw again.

"What is that?" Monica is pointing at the manila envelope Sam brought in.

Jenna shakes her head to clear away the horror of what she's longed for months to remember. "What did you say?" she asks.

"That envelope," Monica says. "I was just asking Sam what the envelope was."

Sam has gotten up from the sofa and leans to pick it up. Tears glint in his eyes again as he hands it to Jenna. It smells musty and is heavy, filled with at least a half ream of paper. The front is addressed to Jenna at her previous apartment. The return address reads: *Department of Homeland Security*, and there's a street address in Washington, D.C. "Oh my." Jenna glances at Sam. "Look where this is from. Where did you find this?"

"It was in Mom's attic. In a box of items that included your high school yearbooks, some stuff from law school, and some other things." He sits back down on the sofa. "I found it right after you called and decided I should bring it with me. I didn't open it, but I think I know what it might be."

Hands trembling, she opens the envelope and pulls out a thick stack of paper. On the top is a stapled document, entitled "Waiver," and there is her name, printed, and below it her signature. Below that are two familiar names: Dr. Allan M. Scott and Dr. Peter Andrews. She flips through the pages, and the documents in front of her turn to a blur. She holds the paper out to Monica. "You look for me. I can't seem to focus on this right now."

Monica turns the pages one by one, her gaze scanning the text. Her brow is furrowed and she's quiet for a long moment. "It's a waiver for participation in a clinical study. And it's got your signature, Jenna—so, like Howard said before, it looks like you agreed to this." She shakes her head. "I had no idea *what* you'd agreed to, though."

Jenna reaches for the papers. "What does it say about the study? I still don't fully understand."

Sam sighs and sits back into the sofa. "Okay. It looks like I'm going to have to explain this. I know you knew this before, Jenna, and I understand that the procedure itself has interfered with your memory, but as you can see, you did agree to participate. You agreed, and so did Howard, despite the fact that the rest of us—Mom and Dad and I—thought it was way too risky. As you can see from the letterhead, it was sponsored by the Department of Homeland Security."

"I thought it was Defense that funded this."

"They did, initially, but then the project was expanded. Someone suggested that if soldiers could be rendered fearless, why not the general population? So—"

"Aha," Monica says. "Like that phrase: 'the war on terror,' right?"

Sam nods. "The whole idea was to render terrorism ineffective. If the country could shield their population from the fears being spread by terrorists—well, that would eliminate the terrorists' main weapon. You can't spread terror if nobody is afraid."

Jenna stands and begins to pace. This whole thing was so perplexing. She was part of some kind of experiment? Why can't she remember any of this? "There is some logic to that, I guess," she says. "If people can't feel fear, terrorism might cease to exist." She wouldn't wish her fearless state on anyone, though. She turns back to Sam. "You're sure I volunteered?"

"You did. You were strongly motivated to never be afraid again, after all, so it seemed a natural fit. Howard was the one who suggested you volunteer for the project. They needed ordinary citizens—civilians—and were looking for people who'd suffered trauma."

"I knew Howard had something to do with it." She stops and looks at Sam. "Why didn't anyone tell me?"

"We thought you remembered. It was all your idea, Jenna, after all. We really thought you knew."

Another knock sounds on the door. "Good grief. It's like Grand Central Station here today." Jenna opens the door and there stands Pete. She laughs. "You might as well come on in—looks like everyone else is here anyway."

"I should ask why I wasn't invited to the party. But first I need to know this: Where's your remote?"

"My what?"

He picks up throw pillows and tosses them back to the sofa. He just misses hitting Monica with one of them. "Hey, Monica—you're here too? I didn't see you 'til now." He grabs another pillow and looks under it. "Your remote, Jenna. You know, for the TV. I wanna show you something."

"It's right here," Sam says. Pete turns, and after Sam hands him the remote, he extends his hand. "Hi—I'm Sam. Jenna's brother."

"Oh hey! I think we actually met. A couple years ago?"

Sam frowns. "We did? I'm not sure I remember."

"It's not important. And, actually, I need to show Jenna something now—while it's still on." He punches a few buttons on the remote until he finds the local news. A woman in a navy-blue coat stands outside a familiar-looking stone building, clutching a large microphone.

"Oh my God—it's St. Rita's!" Jenna says. The newswoman gestures toward the crowd gathered on the church steps behind her. There, among them, is Pete.

"Wait—is that you?" Monica asks.

"Sure is." He beams.

They listen and watch as the reporter interviews Pete, then recaps the story of how a nun and two other unlikely heroes, one of them Pete, had surprised an intruder in St. Rita's. Video footage of a man with spiky white hair, hands cuffed behind his back, being marched to a police van, flashes on the screen.

Jenna's hand comes to her mouth and a cold sensation grips her chest. Something is terribly wrong. "Is that Steve?"

Pete nods. "Yep. It's him."

"Monica," Jenna says. "That's the guy you and I were with at McGinty's."

"I think you're right. It sure looks like him. Although, all I could really see from the back is white hair, so it *could* be Josh."

Sam scoots forward in his chair. "Josh? *Josh Reynolds?*"

Jenna stares at Sam, trembling, as it all comes together in her mind. The Josh at McGinty's, the one Monica is thinking of, the one Jenna danced with and who is Steve's friend—has white hair, spiky, not like Josh Reynolds, who has dark hair. Bleach can easily take care of that discrepancy, though. She sees it now. Of course. "It *is* Josh Reynolds," she says.

Pete shakes his head. "No, the guy they arrested was Steve, but you're right. His friend, the one you and Monica have been hanging with, *is* Josh Reynolds. I've been tracking both of them for some time, and I'm pretty sure this is the same guy you knew at the law firm."

Jenna stares at him. "How did you know about Josh and the law firm?"

Pete ignores her question. "Funny the guy would go to all the trouble of changing his hair color but keep the same first name."

Monica frowns. "Wait. I'm confused. Are you talking about the guys Jenna and I met at McGinty's? They were hiding in Mike's church?"

"Yep. Same guys. Apparently, the two of them had been camped out there for months. That place is full of little rooms and closets that people never look in. This lady, Mrs. Freund, was convinced they were stealing the offering."

"Mrs. Freund?" Jenna asks. "She was there too?"

"You know her?" Pete asks.

"She's my neighbor."

The newscaster recaps the story again as video of a white-haired Steve being marched toward a police van plays multiple times.

Monica is staring at Jenna, her eyes wide. "I always thought those two were a little weird and creepy. How did you know they were hiding out in the church, Pete?"

"Just been keeping my eye on them," he says.

Sam stands up quickly and steps between the group and the television. "Something has me concerned." He looks at Pete. "You only found one guy today, yet there were two hiding there. Where's the other guy? You know—Josh."

Pete shrugs. "Never saw him. I guess he wasn't there."

Jenna leaps to her feet. "I'm not so sure about that." She's at the door, reaching for her coat, yelling back at the others as she opens the door. "I'm going to St. Rita's. You can come with me if you want, but I have to warn Mike!"

MIKE HAS BEEN BACK at St. Rita's for all of a half-hour, but is already buried in work. He's in his office, trying to sort through a stack of papers, looking for his handwritten edits on the final draft of the Christmas Eve service bulletin. He'd been nearly done with it when the police arrived to haul him off to jail, and he must get it finished—it's December 21st and he's got to get the thing to the printer today or it will be late for the service.

Just as he finds the document and begins to fill in the missing hymn numbers, Sister Mary Katherine bolts in, patches of red on her cheeks and a wisp of hair escaping near her temple. "Father, could you come downstairs for a minute? The police are still here and won't let the children into the nave for our final rehearsal."

He looks up, his fingers hovering over the keyboard. "Sister, I don't know if there's anything I can do—"

"Please, Father. They say they need your authorization before they'll let anyone into the worship space."

He runs both hands back through his hair. "Okay. I'll follow you down."

The front hall is swarming with a half-dozen police officers. Two dozen or so children are crammed into the small meeting room off the hallway. They're chattering and laughing and pushing at one another. Some are jumping up and down in place. Crime scene tape blocks the door to the front restroom as well as the arched opening that is the entrance to the sanctuary.

Mike pokes his head into the meeting room. Two small shepherds, their heads topped with towels tied with rope around their foreheads, hover near a young Mary dressed in a long robe with a pillow tucked beneath to create a pregnant belly. Several angels with wings made of cotton balls glued to wire frames, are grinning and jumping up and down, which makes their wings "flap." Christmas is always exciting to the youngsters of St. Rita's, and this year is apparently no exception. One of the shepherds waves shyly. "Hi, Father," the young boy chirps.

Mike smiles and lifts a hand to the boy. Sister Mary Katherine hurries into the room, trying to herd the kids away from the door. "Children, the Father is going to talk to the nice police officers. We should be able to start your rehearsal soon."

He smiles weakly and heads back out in the hallway. A blue-uniformed officer wearing latex gloves walks by with a crushed box of what appears to be hair dye that exudes a strong ammonia-like scent. "Excuse me, officer," Mike says. "The sisters are asking when they might be allowed into the sanctuary." He points at the yellow tape stretched across the entrance into the worship space. "They're concerned about being ready for Christmas Eve services, you see."

"I'm sorry, Father. I understand, and I hope we'll be done gathering evidence soon. If you could tell them to just hold tight a little longer?"

The front door creaks open and someone walks in. Mike can't see who it is, at first, since the light is to the person's back. When he gets closer, Mike's stomach twists. It's the detective, holding a clipboard.

"Father," Detective Sloan says. "We meet again."

He looks around and sees Sister Mary Katherine watching the two of them warily. "Detective," he says, trying to sound polite. "Nice to see you again."

"Our paths keep crossing, don't they?" Sloan even looks a bit apologetic. He holds the clipboard out. "Actually, what I need from you now is your signature so we can release the scene back into your care."

Mike scribbles his name across a line at the bottom while Sloan glances down the hall toward a group of a dozen or so children, all clad in Christmas pageant costumes. The sisters are trying to get them to line up, a seemingly hopeless task. He looks back at Mike. "Father," Sloan says, "I just want to say I'm sorry for what happened. Blame it on a neighborhood full of jittery people and a serious case of profiling."

"What kind of profiling?"

Sloan shakes his head. "You know as well as I that we've been working two murder cases, both young girls. Neither showed evidence of sexual assault, but I guess it's natural to suspect the local priest these days." When Mike says nothing, he goes on. "Besides, springing the mother of one of the girls from the hospital didn't make you look exactly innocent." He clears his throat. "The thing is, though, we know you didn't do it."

Relief washes through him. "Did you find who it was? Do you know who killed Katie? And little Sophie?"

Sloan shakes his head. "I'm sorry, we still don't know the answer in either of those cases. What we do know, from DNA evidence, is that it wasn't you." Mike flinches as he says it, even though it should be good news. Sloan waves his hand toward the sanctuary where a uniformed officer is pulling down the yellow crime scene tape. "You're free to use the space again."

"Thanks." Mike shakes his hand. As Sloan walks away, Mike turns to Sister Mary Katherine who is trying to keep control of a hoard of children who are clustered at the door. "Sister," he says. "The police say we can use the sanctuary again, so if you want to start your rehearsal now—"

Before he can finish the sentence, the kids burst forth, shouting and running and pushing as they pour into the sanctuary. The pageantry scenery is already set up. The nave smells like dried grass and there's a large cardboard "stable" balanced at the top of the stairs. In front of it is a cardboard "manger" holding a plastic baby doll, several bales of hay, a stuffed cow and another large stuffed animal that could possibly be a camel, although it's anybody's guess.

Light shoots into the hallway as the front door creaks open again. When Mike turns, there's Jenna. The sight of her fills him with complete joy. He hadn't realized how much he wanted to see her. She smiles as she watches the children running and jumping into the nave. He hurries over. "I'm so glad you're here, but why *are* you here?" He wants so much to hug her, to envelope her and never let her go.

Jenna pulls him to the door and they step outside as a police officer pushes past to exit the front of the building. He's got several large Ziploc bags in his arms. Monica, Pete and Sam are all standing on the landing just outside the door. "Oh my—you're all here." Mike looks at Jenna. "What's up?"

"Pete came to my apartment a little while ago," she says, "and told us—me and Monica and Sam—that he and Mrs. Freund encountered an intruder here today? It's all over the news, Mike."

"Yes, it's true. I'm still not sure what happened. Ted and I saw the news cameras as we drove up, and it's been total chaos since then. We were coming from—from, well, you know. The jail." His cheeks flush pink as he says it. He turns to Pete. "I didn't know it was *you* who discovered him, though—Ted and I arrived after the news vans left. The police told us they think the guy was stealing the offering?"

Pete nods. "That's what Mrs. Freund said."

"She was here too?" Mike looks from Pete to Jenna and back.

Jenna lets her breath out. "There's more to it than that, Mike. The guy they arrested was a friend of Josh's—you remember him, right? We met him at the pizza place that first night we talked, then again on the sidewalk outside. You kept warning me away from him. Telling me he was dangerous." She looks at Mike, her gaze intense. "He *is* dangerous. Very."

Mike nods. "Yes, sure, I remember the guy." He frowns. "*That's* who they arrested? Here at the church?"

"Not Josh—not the guy you met," Jenna says. "They arrested his friend Steve. They're up to something, I tell you. Something really bad. But listen, Mike: I've remembered a lot more since I talked to you earlier. Howard brought a box of Katie's things over and they triggered all sorts of old memories. And Sam brought even more things." She reaches for Sam, and he grabs her hand. "All those things have really helped me to remember. One thing I now know for sure is that Josh was there that day."

"What day?" Mike asks.

"That day in the park. He was there the day Katie was murdered." She stops and looks at Sam for a long moment, "In fact, Josh had a lot to do with what happened that day."

"Are you saying he killed Katie?" Mike asks.

"No. I don't see how that could be, since he was with me the whole time."

Mike frowns. "I'm still not following this."

"It's kind of a long story, but there was a dog and a Frisbee and then I felt someone grab me from behind. It was Josh. Mike, he knocked me to the ground, stepped on my arm. He wouldn't let me go after Katie. He threatened me, but all I could do was watch helplessly as she ran away." She blinks back tears and puts a hand over her mouth. Sam steps closer and wraps an arm around her shoulders. "He wouldn't let me go—" Tears roll down her cheeks.

"I don't understand," Mike says, but as he says it, he realizes he does, in fact, understand. It all starts to make sense. He remembers, first, what the angel-child said to him in jail: *There is another you can stop. A man with hair white as snow.*

"Wait, Jenna. You mean this guy Josh, the one we met at the pizza place, had assaulted you before?"

"Yes, and not only that, I'd apparently gotten a restraining order from a judge against him. But Mike, listen—the main point is that he and the guy they arrested here this morning, this Steve character, are working together. I'm not sure what they're up to, but it can't be good." She looks at the church door. "Josh might even still be here."

Mike stumbles back. It takes him what is certainly only a second or two to put the rest of it together. *Hair as white as snow*...that fellow in the soup line, the man in the confessional, the bomber—they all had white-blond hair. *Hair as white as...* And then there was this: the dark silhouette in the rose window last fall, a sense that what Mike was seeing was an omen, a portending of death. *He appears as the angel of death*, the angel-child said. *He appears in the rose window, in the highest reaches of the sanctuary.*

Pete steps forward, grabs Mike's elbow, and pulls him aside. "Mike. Listen. This may sound crazy, but I think they've been hiding in the belfry. Up there."

Mike hears what Pete has said, but the fear ballooning up inside him threatens to overwhelm him. He tries to keep his voice calm. "You know what—I think you're right about that. Thanks, Pete."

He goes inside, but everything seems to move in slow motion. He can barely convince his legs to move as he makes his way to the loft stairs. He checks the padlock and finds it opens easily, just as he suspected. After all, he'd never gotten around to getting it fixed.

Mike tries to stay calm, to not let on about what he knows. After all, he really has no good explanation, beyond Pete's astute observation about why he *knows* that guy is upstairs. He goes back outside and gestures to the others. They all crowd into the hallway where Mike stands with the detective.

"The fire marshal condemned those steps a year ago," Mike says to everyone. Jenna frowns, but he goes on. "You—well, something tells me you might want to check up there before you leave."

After Sloan inspects the latch and finds that, just as Mike said, it's broken and has been open all along, he directs two officers to ascend to the loft. Jenna tugs on Mike's sleeve. "What's up there?" He pulls her away from a group of police who are hurrying toward the loft stairs. "I don't know for sure, but I think these two guys, Josh and Steve, are involved with all the bombings that have been going on. I—I can't really explain how I know."

"The bombings?"

"I never told you, but I saw the guy who set off the bomb a few months ago, the one that went off in the garbage can just outside on the boulevard. You remember it."

"I do remember. You think this has something to do with Josh and Steve?"

"As I said, I saw him, the bomber. He had spiky white hair just like these two guys. The man dropped a backpack in the garbage can, and I saw him do it. It apparently had one of those pressure cooker bombs in it—you know the type."

It's been less than a minute, but the first two officers are back from the loft. They huddle with Sloan who listens for a minute, then walks over. Mike tries to stay focused but he's trembling and can't seem to control the shaking, although Jenna's presence at his side is comforting.

"I'm sorry, Father," Sloan says, "but we're going to have to evacuate the church." He lowers his voice to a whisper. "I don't want to alarm the children, so maybe you can help us do this in an orderly fashion."

Mike leans close. "What did you find?" He can smell the detective's aftershave, a scent that makes his stomach twist as it reminds him of being cuffed at the detective's orders and placed in the back of the patrol car.

Sloan gives him a worried smile. "I can't say for certain, but it looks like the place is wired. We seem to have a bomb situation on our hands."

Mike looks at Jenna whose eyes have grown round. "Just as I was saying," he whispers. "I had a feeling those bombings were involved. Jenna, I need to go talk to the sisters now, but I think you'd better wait outside with the others. Maybe best for *all* of you to leave, find a safe place, you know? I—I'll try to find you later, okay?"

He can see her trembling, but she lifts her chin and nods. She reaches up, giving him a quick firm hug, as if he's the one who needs to be comforted. "I'll wait for you. It'll be okay, Mike. I'm sure of it."

24

JENNA IS PRESSED INTO A CORNER of the hallway at St. Rita's, trying to stay out of the way as Mike and the sisters herd a couple dozen children back toward the school. The corner has a strange odor—something sharp and ammonia-like. Police have been swarming in and out of the church ever since Sloan got on his radio and called for back-up.

Monica, Pete and Sam have gone to the Columbia building and are in Monica's office. They tried to convince Jenna to go with them, said it was too dangerous to stay. Mike agreed and wanted her to go as well, but once the group stepped outside, Jenna told them to go on without her. "I'm not going to leave Mike here to deal with this alone," she said. "After all, it's totally my fault he and his church are involved."

Sam objected, but she insisted she was staying, and once the other three left, she stepped back into the hallway, so she could keep an eye on things. Keep an eye *on him*. Mike seems so rattled. She still hasn't been able to ask him what happened in jail, or even why he was there. There hasn't been time, and now she's lost track of him. She's trying to spot him in the crowd of blue uniforms, angel wings and shepherd robes when the front door opens and *Josh* saunters in. He has a large backpack slung over one shoulder.

Jenna starts shaking almost immediately, panic rising in her chest. His white hair is still arranged in that spiky style, and he passes so close to her she can see the darker roots and smell the stale cigarette smoke on his jacket. She can't believe she didn't recognize him before, even with the different hair color, but it must be one more bit of her memory that had been suppressed.

A shiver runs through her. She'd gotten the shaking under control for a moment, but it's back again. Fear, real and true, the kind she's been wanting to feel for months now. Josh strides right past, not seeing her. She's hidden pretty well, pressed back into the shadowy corner. It's just like Mike predicted—Josh has a backpack filled with something bulky. It's very large, not a normal-looking backpack at all. Maybe big enough to hold a pressure cooker?

She watches him walk nonchalantly down the hallway. There are children swarming everywhere, in and out of the sanctuary. The nuns are doing their best to round the kids up and send them toward the school section, but there are still a couple dozen kids in the church, some walking on the pews, then jumping off, their cotton-ball wings fluttering. They laugh and shout, acting like they're out for recess, not in a place where someone has a bomb.

Josh steps through the arched opening and into the sanctuary. He has a strange smile on his face. His gaze passes over the kids and the lopsided Christmas pageant scenery as he moves toward one of the pews. He slides the backpack off his shoulder and drops it to the wooden bench. As he turns away from it, he pulls a cellphone from his breast pocket, then exits the sanctuary.

Jenna's trembling becomes full-blown shaking. This is real fear, the emotion she so longed for—full-blown, gut-wrenching fear, and although she's amazed to realize it's back, it makes it difficult to think clearly. There's something about his phone—she's heard about this. They use cellphones to detonate bombs from a distance. Don't they?

Josh walks swiftly down the hall, heading back to the front door, still oblivious to her presence in the shadows.

Her legs are shaking so hard she can barely move them. He sweeps past her, pushes the door open, the cellphone still in his hand, and steps out. She orders her legs to run toward the arched opening. She smells the hay bales up front in the manger scene, before she spots the backpack, lumpy and dark, slumped onto the end of a pew.

She's terrified and she knows it, but she keeps thinking of Josh with that cellphone, his finger hovered over a button. He could press it at any time. The bomb in the dark backpack could go off at any moment. She looks around at the swarm of children, oblivious to the danger. She must get that backpack out of there.

She remembers all the other times she should have been afraid and wasn't—standing on the rooftop of the Columbia building, stepping in front of cars, walking down dark alleys at night—all these moments come rushing back, and she wonders if they were a sort of rehearsal, a practice run for today.

Jenna reaches deep inside herself, remembers what it is to be fearless, and heads straight for the backpack.

Two children, chased by a nun, nearly collide with her as the nun herds the kids out of the church and toward the hallway. There are still a half-dozen children roughhousing on the floor up front. She must get the backpack as far away from them as possible. She looks around, frantic for a place to move it to, and spots a row of dark birds through a window at the side. There's a door next to the window.

The backpack could blow up in her arms, but she reaches for it anyway. Hands shaking almost more than she can control, she hugs the backpack to her chest and runs toward the side door. Through the yellowish window she can see the birds—a row of crows lined up on a stone wall, heads bobbing, wings flapping.

It seems to take an eternity to reach the door, but when she does, she flings it open and tosses the backpack through. The birds hop away. No more than a second later a loud concussion and flash of light throw her back from the open door and she lands heavily on her side on the stone floor. The birds take flight, fleeing the explosion that is ripping the backpack apart, demolishing the door, shattering the yellow glass.

She curls into herself, raising an arm to shield her head from the debris that's pelting her. She can hear the screams of children as an acrid scent, vaguely reminiscent of an electrical fire, blows over her. She's aware of a wet warmth on her arms and cheeks. When she wipes at her face, her hand comes away red, just before another loud boom brings a torrent of stone pieces raining down upon her head. She instinctively covers her head with both arms as the room fills with a muggy scent of rusty steam. A hot billowing cloud pours from the radiator that is now in pieces, exploded when the wall next to it caved in.

THE SANCTUARY HAD BEEN FULL OF COPS, but now there are just two doing the last bit of evidence collecting. The bomb squad got straight to work, sending robotic devices into the loft armed with cameras and mechanical manipulators. So far, it's taken them the better part of the evening to disconnect all the explosive devices the police found up there. Detective Sloan tells them they were arranged around and above the sanctuary, set to go off in the middle of the first Christmas Eve service.

Mike and Jenna sit on the cold stone bench in the courtyard just outside the side chapel. She's got bandages up and down one arm and on her face. Her clothing is covered with stone dust from the wall that exploded toward her. It's a nicely sheltered spot, still warm from the afternoon sun, which has melted much of the snow on the stone slabs that cover the tombs.

A large tarp has been stretched over the opening in the wall that the bomb blew out. Inside, a group of volunteers who descended on the church when Mrs. Freund started working the phones are still sweeping up debris.

Mike watches Jenna run the toe of her shoe over the carvings in one slab. "I never knew these tombs were here," she says. She looks up as a crow flies in and lands on the stone wall behind the rose bush. "In fact, I don't think I knew this courtyard was here. Every time I came over to have lunch with Katie or pick her up from school, I somehow missed this spot."

Mike watches the crow bob its head up and down at the two of them. He looks back at Jenna. "What made you think to throw the bomb out this door? I mean, if you didn't know this space was here?"

She shrugs. "I looked up and spotted the birds through the window. I remember thinking that I'd never noticed this spot, but after that it was just instinctual. 'Get the backpack outside.' That's all I was thinking. Just get it out, away from those kids."

"I guess it was a blessing, then—your inability to feel fear, I mean."

"But that's the thing, Mike. I *did* feel fear. A lot of it. I don't know why or how the fear came back, but maybe it had to do with that box of Katie's stuff. Or, maybe, like the doctors kept saying, the procedure finally reversed itself. Whatever the reason, I was feeling fear just like I used to feel it, and that's when I realized: I had been in danger many times this past year, and I had faced it fearlessly, since I didn't know better. The only difference this time was what was inside my own head."

He reaches for her un-bandaged hand and encloses it in his own hands. "You were very brave, Jenna. You saved a lot of lives today."

She smiles. "As did you, Father Mike."

"*Father* Mike." He shakes his head, then lets his breath out heavily, smiling. "I guess that's who I am."

"Who else would you be?"

He shrugs. "Just Mike. Mike Albertino, an ordinary guy from Jersey." He looks through the door at the pieces of the broken radiator now stacked in a neat pile near the rubble from the wall. "Probably not a plumber, though." He smiles. "At least I won't have to try to fix that radiator anymore." His phone buzzes in his jacket pocket and he reaches for it. "Aha—Monica just texted me. They arrested Josh. It was on the evening news just now."

"Thank God." She looks up. "I wonder why Josh brought the backpack in? I mean, if they'd wired the place to go off on Christmas Eve, why would he do that?"

Mike shrugs. "Maybe it was their 'Plan B.' After all, once Steve had been hauled in by the police, it was just a matter of time before they discovered the wiring in the loft. I'd say those two were pretty determined to make a statement with their bomb this time." He scoots closer and wraps both arms around her, pulling her to him. She threads one arm behind him, the other across his chest, and they hold each other. He rocks her side to side. "You did good, Jenna."

After a moment, he tries to pull away, but she's holding on tight, so he stays put, holding her for a long moment—long enough that he starts to worry about what might happen when she finally lets go. He wants her so much it hurts.

She finally pulls back. "Mike," she says, clearing her throat. "You know we never talked about—"

He holds a finger to her lips. "Sh. Don't say it."

"But Mike—"

He leans in, and without thinking about it a moment longer, he kisses her. Full, on the lips, the way he's been wanting to for months. She kisses back, wrapping her arms around his neck. She pulls away and gazes at him. He says, "I love you, Jen—"

She holds a quick finger to his lips. "Don't say it." She shakes her head and scoots away. "We can't have this, you know."

Tears are stinging his eyes, and he knows she's right. He nods, unable to get any words out.

"I mean, I'm actually married, right?" She laughs, bitter now. "Who would've guessed *I'd* be the one that had made vows that shouldn't be broken."

Vows that shouldn't be broken. She was right. He'd made vows, too. He'd made a mockery of them, for months, but he could start anew, think this through. Plus, if he really cared about her, he would start thinking about what she's endured, and how hard it must have been for her, all these long months.

"Jenna," he says, "I wanted to ask you: Was there something in particular in the box Howard brought to you that triggered the rest of your memory?"

"A disc with some home movies." She hugs herself, and Mike notices she's trembling a little. He wants to scoot closer, put his arms around her again, hug her tight one more time, but he can't. She looks at him. "How did you know Josh had been in the loft?"

"Pete suggested it, actually, but to be honest, I think I already knew."

"But how? And what about the bomb? How did you figure all that out?"

He shakes his head. "You wouldn't believe me if I told you."

"Try me." She slides closer, grabs his hand and squeezes it. He can feel her body pressed into his side, the warmth of her flesh contrasting with the cold stone of the bench beneath him. "Jenna," he says, shaking his head. "We can't. You said that, and you were right."

She smiles, sadly he thinks. Or maybe it's his own wish, projected on her. "I know," she says. "It's just—I want you to know I'm here for you. If you need to talk."

He can feel the tears, then, not just stinging his eyes, but spilling over his lashes. He blinks fast, looks away, not wanting to feel what he's feeling. "Let me put it this way. I paid attention, finally, to what a little child was trying to tell me."

She smiles. "We have something in common, then."

"How do you mean?"

"I did the same thing—finally listened to what a little child was trying to get me to remember." She turns, watching a crow as it hops from the wall to the ground and struts across the carved stone slabs.

"You mean Katie."

"Yes. Katie. I'm sure it was Katie herself who threw all those 'triggers,' as the doctors called them, at me. Well, I *believe* it was her, anyway. I guess I don't really know, but what else could it be? The doll with the broken arm, the flower that Monica just happened to find at the store that day—I mean, it all seems calculated to get me to remember her. I even think it might have been Katie who led me to the cemetery."

He squeezes her hand. "Maybe it was her, as you say—and maybe it really was an angel who told me the bomber was hiding in my own church." He wants to be as sure as Jenna seems to be, but the truth is he's still plagued by doubt.

She nods, smiling, and lets her head drop to his shoulder, then sits up straight and points at the stone slabs near her feet. "Oh wow—look at this." She's pointing at the name carved in the closest of the tombstones.

Mike knows which one she's seen. It's the one that often sports a pot of daisies. "It's Mrs. Freund's husband," he says. "Harvey. He died a few years ago."

"It can't be the same Harvey." She looks again at the tombstone. "Can it?"

He shrugs. "I'm not sure who you mean. Harvey and Mrs. Freund were lifelong members of St. Rita's. Even though he worked his whole life as caretaker of the cemetery, the one out near Monica's place, she wanted him buried here."

"But—I saw him at the cemetery. He brought me to the hospital. He—"

"Excuse me, Father," a police officer says, pushing the blue tarp aside and stepping out into the courtyard. "We're about done here. Can I get you to sign some papers?"

Mike stands up and holds out a hand to help Jenna to her feet. She's staring at him, her eyes wide with wonder. "Duty calls," he says. "As usual."

IT'S CHRISTMAS EVE. Mike steps outside the church to the front steps, robed and ready for the first service of the evening, the bulletin miraculously finished on time and the sanctuary returned to normal. They've evaded a major disaster and that very service, the one that had been targeted, the one featuring the children's Christmas pageant, is set to start soon. The kids never did get to rehearse, so the pageant may end up being a little chaotic—everyone will love it, though, of that much he is certain.

It's not yet six o'clock but has been dark for a couple of hours already. Soft snow is falling, and the air is cold and dry. He turns and looks back at his church. The altar guild has decorated the front doors with two large wreaths that fill the air with a strong scent of pine. Light spills through the rose window and out into the street. It's beautiful, and he's overcome with a sudden sense of gratitude and a sweep of assurance that all will be well. Somehow.

"Mike!"

He turns to see who's calling him, and there's Monica, dressed in a dark overcoat, walking toward the church arm-in-arm with Pete. He waves to them and sees that following them up the stairs is Jenna. She's still got one bandage on her forehead and down across her right temple. She's with Sam, and an older woman who clings to Sam's arm. She must be their mother.

Mike walks over and leans to kiss Monica's cheek. "Merry Christmas." When he turns to Jenna, she already has her arms open, so he clasps her in a quick hug.

She pulls back and puts a hand on her mother's arm. "Mom, you've met Father Mike, right?"

Jenna's mother nods and smiles weakly, her eyes slightly glazed. She's clutching Sam's arm tightly. Sam pats his mother's hand and says, "We're looking forward to the service. Mom was just reminding me that the last time we were here was to say good-bye to Katie."

Mike gazes at Jenna. He hasn't seen her for about a day, but is reminded, again, of her words. After the bomb squad had finished clearing the space and he'd signed the papers, he told her everything—how he'd seen the little yellow-haired angel-child in the side chapel, the kitchen, even the jail. "Who's to say there aren't angels?" she'd said, then told him about an old fellow she'd met at the cemetery. "He seemed like an angel to me. Right there when I needed him, every time."

As Mike walks toward the heavy front doors of the church with Jenna's family and friends, the doors open and out steps Ted. He's got a potted plant with a bright orange daisy in it. "Father, you're needed inside," he says. Ted sees Jenna and the others and smiles broadly. "Merry Christmas," he says to the group. A strong floral scent trails behind him as he carries the daisy toward the burial courtyard. It is, Mike is sure, from Mrs. Freund herself. She brings them every Christmas to place on her husband's grave.

Mike walks with Jenna's family as they enter the sanctuary, lit all around by a multitude of candles and smelling strongly of burning wax. Jenna and the others find a couple of seats near the back—the rest of the pews are already occupied with an assortment of people, regular parishioners and many others, like Jenna's family, who come only once a year.

Ted returns from the burial courtyard, without the potted plant, and Mike follows him into the hallway. As they round the corner, they come upon Sister Mary Katherine and a group of youngsters, mostly second- or third-graders from the looks of them, dressed in their pageant outfits.

"Break a leg, Sister," Ted whispers, nodding and smiling at her as she steps back to let the children pass. They walk down the semi-darkened hallway toward the sanctuary, holding hands in pairs and glancing up and grinning at the two priests. Occasionally one of the children raises a tiny hand in greeting when they catch sight of Ted. "Merry Christmas, children," Ted says.

"It's good to see you again, Father Ted," Sister Mary Katherine whispers as she comes to stand next to them. "The children were excited when they heard you would be here tonight." She smiles at the kids as the final pairs march toward them.

There he is, at the back of the line, holding another kid's hand. There's the same tight yellow curls, the same cherubic face, but no loincloth—the angel-child is dressed in one of those costumes, the ones with cotton-ball wings.

As he and his partner walk past, Mike catches a strong floral scent—roses. The yellow-haired angel turns and gazes at Ted, who leans toward the sister, whispering. "Isn't that young Sophie McPherson's twin brother?"

She nods. "Yes, that's him."

"Sophie McPherson had a twin brother?" Mike asks, trembling.

Ted nods and looks at Mike. "Have the police charged anyone in Katie Bernstein's murder yet?"

Mike shakes his head. "Not that I've heard. They've charged those two guys we caught in the church with the bombing—one of them was, as we suspected, the same fellow who was stalking Jenna—but neither his DNA nor that of his partner matched evidence from either murder. Apparently, the murderer is still at large."

"Such a shame." Ted turns to Sister Mary Katherine. "And how is the young McPherson boy doing?" he whispers. "I mean, it's been almost a year since his sister disappeared, and I know children are resilient, but still—"

She sighs. "He's doing better than before. At least he's stopped taking off all his clothes at random moments and running out of the classroom." Her eyes dart to Mike's face and she says, "Maybe now that—well, you know, now that her body has been found…"

Her voice trails off and she turns to watch the children marching away, two by two. Just as the line of kids disappears around the corner, the yellow-haired child turns back. His eyes meet Mike's, and the angel holds him in his gaze for a long moment. Again, in a way that hasn't happened since that summer long ago in Europe, Mike senses a vast Presence watching him.

And again, like so many years before, Mike Albertino knows he has been seen. He also knows, in some inexplicable way, a way that is far from rational, that the Presence had been there all along.

And then, as the sense of being seen spreads through Mike's body, the angel-child becomes a boy again—an ordinary child with wings made of cotton balls.

Ted threads a hand through Mike's elbow. "Time to go take our seats for the show—right, Father?" They make their way through the softly lit space to pews near the side chapel. The blue tarp is still there, augmented by a large sheet of plywood, and the area still smells a bit like rusty water. The door is open to the burial courtyard, for some reason. Cold air swirls into the side chapel space, now permanently frigid after the final spectacular demise of the decrepit radiator.

"Excuse me a moment," Mike says to Ted, who is settling into a pew, grinning and waving at the children clustered up front—towel-clad shepherds, Mary with her pillow-belly, and two of what should be three angels.

Mike heads for the open door, steps through it to grab the handle, and there stands an old man, his bent back turned to

Mike. The usual rose scent in the courtyard seems stronger than normal. "Yes, indeed," the old man is saying, his voice wavering. "Nothin' better than sittin' with the dead. Nothin' better."

"Excuse me," Mike says. "The pageant is about to start. Would you like to come in and find a seat?"

The old man turns and grins at Mike. He looks vaguely familiar and is clutching the potted daisy that Ted brought out just moments before. One of the old man's front teeth is missing. "Don't mind if I do, don't mind if I do," the old guy says.

Only then does Mike see who the man had been talking to—it's the child with tight yellow curls, dressed in an angel costume, cotton-ball wings and all.

Acknowledgments

BEFORE I STARTED WRITING, I thought it was something one did while utterly alone. As every writer knows, though, this is simply not true. Without the feedback and help of many people, the simple spark of an idea I had years ago would never have become the finished book you hold in your hands. Therefore, I have lots of people to thank.

First, I must thank the members of my critique groups who are always generous with their time and expert advice. I am fortunate to have many friends and colleagues, all willing to help with almost any request, and I'm reluctant to try to list them all, lest I miss someone. I must, though, give special thanks to Margaret Rodenberg, Lorie Brush, and Stephanie Joyce, who gave crucial and very helpful feedback on several drafts of this book.

I must also thank my writing teachers, who provided not only encouragement but also big doses of crucial feedback. The late Grace Kimbro was the first teacher to tell me that I should write, so thank you, Mrs. Kimbro. Thank you also to Margaret Meyers, Ed Perelman, and the other faculty and students in the writing program at Johns Hopkins University. The excellent workshop experiences I had at Hopkins showed me how to turn a vague idea into a full-blown book. Huge thanks also to Jim Mathews, Hildie Block, and the other instructors at the Bethesda Writers Center who encouraged my early work.

Finally, thank you to my family—to my sons for your unwavering support and to my husband, Ken, who understood before I did that I need to write to be happy.

RAIMA LARTER is a writer from Arlington, Virginia. Her short fiction has appeared in *Gargoyle, Writers' Journal, Mulberry Fork Review, Chantwood Magazine* and others. This is her first novel. Her second novel, *Belle o' the Waters,* is due to be published by Mascot Books in 2019. Prior to devoting herself to full-time writing, Larter was a college chemistry professor and government scientist and is now a freelance science writer. Read more about her work at her website, raimalarter.com.

Made in the USA
Middletown, DE
04 March 2019